C000112067

ONCE IS NEVER ENOUGH

A JAMES FLYNN ESCAPADE

HARIS ORKIN

Black Rose Writing | Texas

©2022 by Haris Orkin

All rights reserved. No part of this book may be reproduced, stored in a retrieval system or transmitted in any form or by any means without the prior written permission of the publishers, except by a reviewer who may quote brief passages in a review to be printed in a newspaper, magazine or journal.

The author grants the final approval for this literary material.

First printing

This is a work of fiction. Names, characters, businesses, places, events, and incidents are either the products of the author's imagination or used in a fictitious manner. Any resemblance to actual persons, living or dead, or actual events is purely coincidental.

ISBN: 978-1-68433-963-1
PUBLISHED BY BLACK ROSE WRITING
www.blackrosewriting.com

Printed in the United States of America
Suggested Retail Price (SRP) $22.95

Once is Never Enough is printed in Book Antiqua

*As a planet-friendly publisher, Black Rose Writing does its best to eliminate unnecessary waste to reduce paper usage and energy costs, while never compromising the reading experience. As a result, the final word count vs. page count may not meet common expectations.

Author Photo Credit: Laura Burke
Cover Art Credit: Juan Padron

Praise for
ONCE IS NEVER ENOUGH

"Delusional Double-0 wannabe James Flynn is back, crushing evil and stealing hearts. Fast-paced fun and dynamic plotting make *Once Is Never Enough* a choice read for spy enthusiasts and anyone who loves a good story with a lot of laughs."

—Catherine Pelonero,
New York Times **bestselling author of** *Kitty Genovese*

"Haris Orkin's sequel to *You Only Live Once* thrusts his dashing, reality-challenged hero into a smart, funny, action-packed adventure that tackles the greatest dangers of today's high-tech world. *Once Is Never Enough* kept me turning pages from start to finish."

—Dan Jolley,
USA Today **bestselling author of the** *Gray Widow Trilogy*

"A pure comic delight. Ian Fleming on laughing gas. I laughed out loud on every page. More please!"

—R. Lee Procter,
award-winning author of *Atomic Bombshell*

"Hilarious and hallucinatory. Haris Orkin channels Ian Fleming and Ken Kesey in this highly original, high-speed romp that not even a Dr. No or Nurse Ratched could slow down. Fasten your straitjacket and enjoy the ride."

—Dwight Holing,
bestselling author of the *Nick Drake Mysteries*

"Orkin can be hilariously inventive, and James is a memorable protagonist—simultaneously sane and bonkers, diffident and brave... A comically free-wheeling espionage tale."

—Kirkus

"An outstanding blend of action and fun designed to keep readers engaged and guessing to the end."

—Midwest Book Review

I dedicate this one to my late friend, Michael "Feeve" LeFevre, who we lost in 2017. Writer, artist, composer, actor; he was a true renaissance man and one of the funniest people ever.

ACKNOWLEDGEMENTS

First off, I want to thank Cheryl Kaye Tardif for all her encouragement and wisdom. Once is Never Enough wouldn't exist without her help and support. I also want to thank my patient and brilliant editor, M.J. Moores, who helps create the illusion I actually know what I'm doing.

Much appreciation to all my early readers who gave me their insights, critiques, ideas and reassurance. Dwight Holing, Richard Procter, Dan Jolley, Lisa Orkin, Terry Evans, Jeff Fisher, Greg Moore, Michael Niemann, Alison McMahon, and Catherine Pelonero.

My mom loved to read and laugh and loved physical comedy, whether it was Lucille Ball or one of her kids taking a header. She was always my biggest fan and her unflagging belief in me actually made me believe in myself.

My father, a master of comedy, taught me everything I know; from how to write a joke to how to be a father.

My siblings and my Uncle Sandy are steadfast supporters and cheerleaders.

My wife, Kim and my son, Jakob, patiently read much of what I write, including this book in all its many forms. They are my sounding boards and my proofreaders and I greatly appreciate their love and patience.

Finally, I want to thank Penny, our fuzzy little rescue mutt who sits with me as I write, making sure I'm never lonely, and scaring the pants off me by barking randomly at passing strangers.

ONCE IS NEVER ENOUGH

CHAPTER ONE

Flynn was outnumbered and unarmed and he knew they'd show no mercy. His footfalls echoed off the high cinderblock walls as he raced down the wide corridor. Sweat drenched his face and burned his eyes, causing his glasses to slip down his nose. He tried metal door after metal door, but none would open. Cold fear squeezed his heart as his pursuers closed the distance between them. Their shoes echoed louder as Flynn moved slower, his legs now rubbery, heavy and numb.

He rounded a corner, slid on the slippery linoleum, bumped into the wall, and tripped over a box. The floor flew up and smashed him in the face. On his hands and knees, fighting to catch his breath, Flynn forced himself to stand. He had nothing left. No strength. No fight. They would capture him and do who knows what to him and there was nothing he could do to stop it. He rolled over on his back, a dog offering his belly.

Submitting.

Surrendering.

And that's when he saw a way out.

An air vent high on the wall had a tiny gap at the top, two screws loose. He pushed himself to his feet, reached up and worked his fingers under the curled edge. He pulled down hard and bent it with the full force of his two hundred and forty-seven pounds.

His enemies drew closer, their footfalls echoing louder. The air vent rested shoulder high. Flynn backed up to take a short running start. He sprinted and leaped headfirst into the hole, kicking his feet to propel himself forward. His sweaty hands scrabbled for purchase as he fought to pull himself deeper into the vent. Just a little farther and he'd be out of reach. They might not even see him. They might run right past him. All he had to do was wriggle forward, but it was a tight fit. No room for a grown man to stand or crouch or even crawl.

Flynn undulated like a dolphin to inch himself in, but he was not a petite man. Before he made it very far, he squeaked to a painful stop. At one time, Flynn was lean and wiry and tightly muscled, but those muscles now hid beneath fifty pounds of fat. Most of that weight collected in his belly and butt and it was his ample ass that couldn't squeeze past the aluminum ductwork. The friction pulled his shorts down, exposing the pale flesh of his buttocks. The sound produced by his scraping skin was like a squeegee on glass.

"There! There he is!" shouted one of Flynn's pursuers. He sounded no older than seventeen.

His partner in crime laughed with glee. "What the hell's he doing in *there?*"

The third kid clapped his hands with excitement. "Fat ass on a stick is stuck! Grab 'em by his ankles!"

Hands locked onto both his ankles. He tried to kick free as they laughed and tugged, the hair on his derriere pulled tight, trapped between flesh and metal.

"Stop it! Stop it!" Flynn shouted, his voice echoing in the duct work.

"Pants 'em!" the second kid screamed as the others laughed.

A breeze blasted his butt as they yanked his shorts down to his ankles. His neck and face burned with embarrassment. Tears filled his eyes.

"Please... Please."

His tormentors just laughed harder. That laughter brought up memories of ancient junior high school humiliations. The wedgies. The Indian burns. The noogies. On the school bus. In the locker room. On the playground at recess. Back then every day was a nightmare. The only peace he found was in the classroom. And even there he suffered daily embarrassment and shame.

Of all his tormentors, one in particular never stopped taunting him. Never stopped riding him. Never stopped belittling him. This voice was impossible to escape, because this voice resided in Flynn's own head. *You're worthless. Useless. Fat. Stupid. Ugly. Unlovable.* All his other tormentors only confirmed what that voice already knew.

Flynn was hopelessly wedged in the vent. They pulled off his shoes and socks and tickled his feet and slapped him on the ass.

Finally, a fourth voice shouted over all the mocking laughter. This one was older and deeper and had an Armenian accent. "What do you boys think you're doing?"

The three adolescents tormenting Flynn sprinted away, their laughter and footsteps fading off as they fled. Flynn's rescuer didn't pursue them.

"Jimmy! You okay in there?"

"Mr. Papazian?" came Flynn's hollow response, plaintive and ashamed.

"Those boys are a menace. I can't even remember how many times I kicked them out of the galleria."

"Can you get me out of here?"

"Of course." Warm hands grasped his ankles and Mr. Papazian pulled. "Boy, you're really stuck in there."

"I know."

"You push and I'll pull." Papazian pulled. Flynn didn't budge. "Are you pushing?"

"I'm pushing."

Papazian grunted and pulled again, but Flynn remained stuck. "Shit!" Papazian was already out of breath. "Try to stay calm while I go get some help."

"Please don't leave me," Flynn's sad voice echoed in the ductwork.

"I'll be right back, Jimmy. I promise."

"No, wait! My shorts! Can you please pull them up?"

"Of course. Yeah, let me just…pardon my reach."

"Ow."

"Sorry."

"It pinches."

"Yeah, that's as far as they go."

Another voice joined the conversation. "Papazian? Who the hell is that?" The higher pitched voice belonged to a middle-aged Hispanic man.

"It's Jimmy. Can you give me a hand?"

"What's he doing in the vent?"

"He was trying to get away from those young hooligans. Don't just stand there, Rodriguez! Help me pull him out!"

Two sets of hands grabbed Flynn's ankles and pulled. At first Flynn didn't move, but then the two men put their backs into it. Flynn's flesh squeaked as his buttocks squished back through the ductwork and finally, he was free.

Flynn quickly pulled up his bright red shorts and pulled his tight, striped polyester shirt (red, white, blue, and yellow) down over his generous gut. He wiped the sweat off his face with a sleeve and smiled at his rescuers.

"Thank you." Flynn's voice was gentle and tentative with the generic accent of a native Angelino.

Balding with bushy eyebrows and a pencil-thin mustache, Papazian wore the ill-fitting uniform of a mall security guard. Rodriguez stood a half a foot shorter and fifty pounds chubbier and wore the disheveled brown outfit of a maintenance man.

Flynn smoothed back his hair. "My hat!" he spun around, looking at the ground in a panic. He peered in the open vent, but his hat wasn't there either. "I lost my Hot Dog on a Stick hat!"

"Can't you get another hat?" Papazian asked.

"Mrs. McKinney will dock me for that!"

"Over there," Rodriguez said. It lay a few feet away, next to a pile of empty boxes.

Mr. Papazian picked it up and handed it to Flynn. Bent and misshapen, someone had obviously stepped on it. "Jimmy, you're a grown man. You need to stand up for yourself."

Flynn blinked away tears and tried to fluff up his hat before putting it on his head. "I don't know why they keep bothering me. I've never done anything to them."

"Pendejos like that feed on fear. Papazian is right. You can't run from them," Rodriguez said.

"Maybe it's time to find a new job. Something more dignified than Hot Dog on a Stick. I'm not sure it's appropriate for a man your age."

"He's right, my friend." Rodriguez agreed. "It's hard to get respect when you're wearing tiny red shorts and a stupid poofy hat."

"Where am I going to find another job?" Flynn sounded like he might start crying again. "No one wants to hire someone like me. Someone who was…who is…"

"You don't seem all that crazy to me, ese. You *do* look like you put on a few pounds recently," Rodriguez said.

"I eat when I'm anxious."

Papazian nodded. "Look, I get it. But you're still a relatively young man. Barely middle-aged. If you lost some weight maybe you'd feel better about yourself. You might even find someone who wants to go out with you."

"Don't be getting his hopes up, man," Rodriguez warned.

"I'm just saying."

"And I'm just saying don't get his hopes up."

CHAPTER TWO

During the depths of the Great Depression, a massive earthquake rocked Southern California. Schools were hit hardest and city officials decided to build a park on the beach; a place for all the displaced kids to play. The site chosen was just south of Santa Monica Pier. Known by locals as Mussel Beach, out of work vaudeville jugglers and acrobats often practiced in the new park and before long Mussel Beach became known as Muscle Beach.

After World War II, thousands of veterans flooded Southern California, buying up little bungalows with G.I. Bill benefits. By 1946 as many as ten thousand sun worshipers crowded Muscle Beach each day. Some of those lifting and flexing included Jack LaLanne, Joe Gold, and Steve Reeves, who later played Hercules in the movies.

It seemed a perfect place to sell hot dogs, and that's just what Dave Barham decided to do. Using his mom's secret cornbread recipe, Dave created the very first Hot Dog on a Stick. He took his new culinary innovation to county fairs and then later expanded into another new concept called the shopping mall. Eventually, Hot Dog on a Stick was ubiquitous in food courts from Rancho Cucamonga to Seoul, Korea.

In 1998, when Jenny McKinney was fifteen, she took a job with Hot Dog on a Stick. She started as a counter girl and worked her way through high school and community college deep-frying dogs and hand stomping lemonade. Eventually, she became a cashier and then an assistant manager and then the general manager of the Glendale Galleria location.

Hot Dog on a Stick gave Jenny a future and she wanted to use her position and hard-earned wisdom to help others lift themselves up; not just feckless high schoolers, but anyone left behind by society. She contacted the city and told them she wanted to help those less fortunate. So, they connected her with various social welfare agencies, and she hired whoever she could. Some were intellectually and developmentally challenged, some were on parole, some were recovering from catastrophic injuries or alcoholism or drug addiction, and some, like James Flynn, were trying to overcome mental illness and make a new life for themselves.

Mrs. McKinney sat at her cluttered desk in the tiny back office and glowered at a teary-eyed Flynn. His Hot Dog on a Stick hat sat crooked on his head, bent and misshapen and decorated with a dirty footprint.

"You know the rule," she said.

"Your hat is never allowed to leave the store," Flynn replied.

"Do you know why?"

Flynn wiped a tear away and shook his head. "Not really."

"Because they are coveted. They are special. Just like this place is. That's why we want to share it with people like you, Jimmy. People having difficulties. People who have lost their way. There are rules to follow and if you follow them, you will find success. I did and I'm no one special. I was a "C" student with a bad attitude and no self-esteem. But Hot Dog on a Stick taught me discipline and the benefit of hard work. It taught me how to deal with the public and to be empathetic, because you never know what kind of day someone else is having. They may have lost their job. May have lost a loved one."

"I know what that's like."

"I know you do and that's why I want you to learn the lessons this place can teach you."

"I really appreciate you bringing me in, Mrs. McKinney."

"You are part of the Hot Dog on a Stick family now and we take care of our own. Do you know the names of the boys who were harassing you?"

"I don't."

"I know you're afraid, but you don't have to be. If you see those boys again, you tell me, okay?"

Flynn nodded.

"No one deserves to be treated like they treated you. Everyone deserves respect and that means you also need to respect yourself.

Take responsibility to be who you want to be. Do you know who you want to be, Jimmy?"

"Not really."

"Someday you will, but it's a journey. And part of taking responsibility is taking good care of yourself. Being smart. Healthy. Which means you need to start watching what you eat. A Hot Dog on a Stick is a delicious treat, but too much of a good thing can often be a bad thing. I know there's a lot of temptation here, but we mustn't succumb to our base appetites. Do you know what the good book says about that?"

"Not really."

"Lead us not into temptation and deliver us from evil."

"Okay."

Mrs. McKinney looked Flynn over from head to toe. He self-consciously tugged his top down over his gut. "Let's get you a new uniform that fits you properly and a brand-new hat."

"Thank you, Mrs. McKinney."

"Don't thank me. You'll be paying for it out of your next paycheck. How's life at the group home?"

"Good."

"Wonderful. That's why we do this, so people like you can become self-reliant, self-sufficient, tax-paying citizens. When you can take care of yourself, then you can take care of others. That's what we do. We pay it forward. And expand the circle of kindness." Mrs. McKinney scraped back her chair and stood. "Punch in and get to work. That lemonade isn't going to hand stomp itself."

•   •   •

Flynn cut lemons as Ashley, Becky, and Emma worked the front counter. Ashley was a petite Filipino with long dark hair and glasses. Becky was blonde, perky, pretty, and sarcastic. Emma had a tattoo of Pikachu on her ankle, a tiny gold stud in her nose, and purple highlights in her dirty-blond hair.

When Flynn first met them, they all put on happy smiles, but it was obvious they wanted nothing to do with him. Flynn struggled to make small talk, and they did their best to ignore him. He could tell they didn't understand why a man his age would want to work at Hot Dog on a Stick. He wondered if they knew he was living in a halfway house for the mentally ill.

His shyness around them pained him. His left eye would sometimes twitch, and his constant discomfort made it difficult to breathe. He often had to use an asthma inhaler. All three girls seemed so sophisticated. So much smarter than him. Quicker. Faster. Funnier. They would talk amongst themselves and laugh and Flynn would want to join the conversation, but he never knew what to say. He would stutter and mumble and when he did get the occasional word in, they would stare him like he was a talking dog. He vaguely remembered a version of himself that was so much more confident and comfortable in his own skin. But that self-assured part of his personality had disappeared, leaving him to fend for himself in a cold and unforgiving world.

Ashley trained Flynn. She showed him how to properly cut lemons and stomp lemonade. It was his least favorite part of the job. He often nervously gnawed on his nails, so his cuticles were cracked and often bled. The lemon juice irritated the broken skin and would squirt in his eyes and burn.

When he had fifty lemons cut into quarters, he'd put them in a large plastic bucket and plunge a metal masher into the mix to hand stomp them. Ashley told Flynn to move the masher through the lemons with a thrusting, circular motion, up and over and up and down until the bucket made a sound like a heartbeat. Flynn would mash and mash and mash for what seemed like forever. The sharp citrus smell would get up his nose and he'd struggle not to sneeze, because one time he did and had to throw out all fifty lemons and start again.

This was Flynn's seventh week at Hot Dog on a Stick, but he still didn't feel like he belonged. The shifts would change and so would the girls, but Flynn always got stuck cutting lemons. He much preferred putting wieners on sticks, dipping them in the corn bread batter, and plunging them into the hot oil. He found the ritual oddly satisfying, but he rarely had the opportunity as he was always relegated to lemonade stomping duty.

While Ashley and Emma mostly ignored Flynn, Becky taunted him.

"Jimmy!" Becky held up one of the wieners on a stick. "Look at the size of this wiener!"

Heat rose on his neck as Ashley giggled. Becky stuck out her tongue and pretended to lick the flaccid wiener. Ashley cackled with laughter.

"You are so bad," Emma said.

Becky approached Jimmy with the wiener on a stick. "Jimmy knows I'm just teasing." She offered it to Flynn. "Do you want to hold it?

"No, thank you."

"Why don't you put it in? I know you want to."

"Becky!" Emma admonished.

"Just put it in and pull it out."

She dipped the hot dog on a stick into the vat of cornbread batter and pulled it out, twirling it as the batter dripped off the end.

"It's easy!" She put it in the hot fryer and smiled at him. "In and out. In and out. That's all there is to it, Jimmy." Becky moved closer and held the hot dog up in front of his face. "I see how you look at these big old wieners. You want a bite?"

Ashley laughed so hard, she started to hiccup. That made Becky laugh and that set off Emma. Soon all three were laughing their asses off.

·   ·   ·

Dulcinea Delgadillo sat at a red plastic table in the Glendale Galleria food court. She watched Flynn's humiliation at the hands of a trio of snotty teenagers. His once handsome face now puffy and pasty and blotchy with pimples. His hair appeared to be thinning and his ugly plastic glasses didn't disguise the fact that his left eye twitched uncontrollably. His gut strained the buttons on his Hot-Dog-on-a-Stick outfit and his red shorts sported a prominent muffin top.

Dulcie was surprised when Flynn voluntarily went back to City of Roses Psychiatric Institute after saving the world. He was still delusional then; still believed he was a Double-0 working for Her Majesty's Secret Service. She could barely believe that everything that happened actually did, but the fading scar on her forehead was a daily reminder. A daily reminder that she was lucky to be alive. A daily reminder of how Flynn changed her life.

He was a patient when he escaped and carjacked a young orderly named Sancho. Together they saved Dulcie from her abusive boyfriend and set off on a series of dangerous and terrifying adventures, culminating in the rescue of the ten richest men in the world. Flynn's derring-do was the top story on cable news for three weeks. He didn't just save those billionaires, but the entire world economy.

Unfortunately, all the attention was too much for him with constant visits and messages and phone calls from journalists and TV producers. They all wanted to talk to him and interview him and uncover the real James Flynn, but even Flynn didn't know who the real Flynn was.

The strong confident man she knew began to question everything. That caused anxiety and paranoia and severe mood swings that dropped him into a deep depression. His psychiatrist, Dr. Nickelson, was finally forced to drug him. He put Flynn on all kinds of antipsychotics and antidepressants, but Flynn only sank deeper into darkness. Sometimes he'd sit for hours, frozen in place, staring into space. Sancho told her that Nickelson even tried shock treatment and something called transcranial magnetic stimulation.

No longer a patient at City of Roses, Dulcie had visited Flynn every other day. Sancho would often be there as well and together they'd talk to him. It wasn't always clear Flynn knew who they were, but they didn't lose hope. They didn't give up on him. Just like he never gave up on them when their lives were hanging by a thread. Little by little, Flynn began to remember them and eventually found his way back to reality.

But he was Jimmy Flynn from Van Nuys, California, an orphan who lost his parents at age ten in a tragic car accident. Not the sexy, self-assured James Flynn she had fallen in love with. As a child he had lived in nine foster homes over a period of seven years and was emotionally abused. He loved spy movies from the 1960s and developed an imaginary personality to protect himself. He became the most capable and powerful person he could imagine; a secret agent with a license to kill.

As Flynn worked with Dr. Nickelson to come to terms with his new reality, Dulcie continued to visit him, though it was hard for her to reconcile Jimmy Flynn with James.

As Jimmy, Flynn no longer had that sexy English accent. He sounded like your typical nerdy white guy. Now shy and socially awkward, he even carried himself differently. He slouched and walked with a clumsy, ungainly gait, a symptom of how insecure he was. While James exuded confidence, Jimmy lived in a perpetual state of embarrassment. Dulcie constantly reassured him the way he used to constantly reassure her. She wanted to be there for him, but she missed the old Flynn. Ached for him. Spending time with Jimmy made her sad and she visited him less and less frequently. Until finally, she only saw him once a week and then once a month and then not at all.

During the time she visited Flynn, Dulcie managed to turn her life around. She attended Narcotics Anonymous meetings at a shuttered mini-mall in Panorama City. In her purse she kept fourteen coins. They were all different colors and commemorated the number of months she had managed to maintain sobriety.

It was Sancho who told Dulcie that Flynn now worked at Hot Dog on a Stick. Dr. Nickelson decided Flynn should leave the hospital and take some tentative steps into the real world. To help him make the transition, Nickelson found a job for him at the Glendale Galleria and arranged for him to live in a supervised group home in Eagle Rock. Dulcie hadn't seen Flynn for over a year when she finally worked up the nerve to visit him at the mall.

As she watched him behind the counter at Hot Dog on a Stick, she came to a sad realization. The Flynn she fell in love with never existed at all. He was only a figment of Jimmy Flynn's imagination. He was a beautiful fantasy and she loved him and missed him, but he was gone for good.

Glendale Galleria was a thirty-minute bus ride from her beauty school. Dulcie had fully intended to visit with Flynn over lunch. Talk to him. Connect with him. But that was before she saw him. Before she felt such embarrassment for him. She knew Flynn would see the pity in her eyes and she couldn't do that to him. At least, that's what she told herself.

Dulcie stood up to leave and looked back one last time, accidentally catching his eye. While in the midst of cutting lemons, he looked across the food court and saw her. Dulcie offered Flynn a half-hearted wave. Recognition dawned just as she turned her back on him. She quickened her pace past Panda Express and Dunkin' Donuts and hurried off. She blinked away tears, overwhelmed by guilt and the knowledge that she would never see Flynn again.

CHAPTER THREE

The Federal Social Readaption Center No. 1 was considered escape proof. Known informally as Altiplano (Plateau), the high concrete walls were ten feet thick to discourage ramming or high explosives. Air space around the facility was designated as a no-fly zone to prevent an aerial escape. Armed personnel carriers surrounded the prison in case of a ground assault.

Yet even with all those security precautions, Mexico's most infamous drug lord, El Chapo (Shorty), found a way to escape. One evening he squeezed through an opening in the floor of his private shower, climbed down a thirty-two-foot-long ladder, and kick-started a waiting motorcycle on a rail. He roared through a well-lighted tunnel and emerged to find himself a mile from the prison. A getaway car waited and El Chapo found freedom. At least temporarily. Eventually, he was caught and this time extradited to the U.S. for trial.

When Mendoza found out he was headed for Altiplano to serve out his 140-year sentence, he believed he'd spend the rest of his life there. After El Chapo's legendary escape, the Mexican government put new security protocols into place. Mendoza knew that the new government would never want to suffer the international embarrassment of another high-profile escape. Especially after what his boss, Francisco Goolardo, had attempted to do.

Goolardo kidnapped the ten richest men in the world. He hoped to make billions. Instead, he lost everything he'd accumulated over twenty years of ruthless criminal activity. Including his freedom. The most galling aspect of that entire debacle was the cause of that failure. Francisco wasn't foiled by the DEA or CIA or FBI or Interpol or MI5 or any other international law enforcement organization. He was foiled by a mad man. A mental patient. An idiot.

Mendoza knew something wasn't right with Flynn the first time they'd met him. How his boss, a brilliant and ruthless criminal mastermind, fell for Flynn's act still remained a mystery. Goolardo acted as if Flynn was an equal and showed him the kind of respect he never showed Mendoza. He always treated Mendoza like a dimwit. Like muscle. His suggestions were ignored. His every idea criticized.

Goolardo didn't lose his admiration for Flynn until Mendoza finally exposed him for who he was; an escaped mental patient from Pasadena. Goolardo ordered Flynn's death. Yet still the pendejo wouldn't die. It wasn't because he was highly trained or the best of the best, because he wasn't. Flynn survived because he was stupid-lucky and would do things no one in their right mind would. Professional boxers don't like fighting drunks in bars for much the same reason. It's hard to counter someone who doesn't attack you in a way that makes any logical sense. Instead of countering with a right cross, they stab you in the balls with a broken beer bottle.

As Mexico's most secure prison, Altiplano held the worst of the worst; including most of the rival drug lords and enforcers that Goolardo battled and defeated. Mendoza and Goolardo needed to prove their place in the pecking order if they hoped to stay alive. Goolardo spent much of his life in prison, so he understood what it took to survive. At age nineteen he was sent to Candido Mendes, a high-security prison on the Ilha Grand, an isolated island that once housed Brazil's most dangerous prisoners. That was where he spent his formative years and those instincts had returned quickly.

By their tenth month at Altiplano, dozens had died and he and Mendoza sat at the top of the pecking order. With no one left to challenge them, they took control of many existing criminal enterprises. They smuggled drugs and weapons, cigarettes and booze, pornography and even prostitutes. As prisoners were released, Goolardo's reach extended beyond the prison walls. Mendoza assumed that eventually Goolardo would put out a contract out on Flynn. Someone would find the idiota and kill him. Mendoza would have preferred to murder Flynn himself, but he knew that wasn't possible.

Eventually, Goolardo acquired enough pull to get himself and Mendoza moved into the palatial cell block previously occupied by El Chapo. They had everything they desired. Everything but their freedom. Then one evening, as they dined on langostas from Puerto Nuevo, Goolardo said a curious thing.

"I think it's time to go."

"Go where?" Mendoza wanted to know.

"Away from here. Away from this place."

"What do you mean?"

"I think we've been here long enough. Don't you?"

"Yes, I guess." Mendoza sighed and stared down at his langostas and rice and refried beans. He took a bite, afraid to meet his boss's eyes.

"You think I've lost my mind, don't you? You think I'm as crazy as the cabron who put us here, huh?"

"I didn't say that."

"You don't have to. I can see it on your face."

"There is no way to escape from here. You know that."

"Do I?"

"I thought you did."

"Well, did you know that I am still worth fifty million dollars?"

"How is that possible? You invested everything you had in your plan. You lost everything."

"Not everything. I had shelter corporations with accounts in banks in Cypress, Belize, Panama and the Cayman Islands."

"But I thought...you said were..."

"Broke. Yes. That's what I wanted the authorities to believe. That's what I wanted my rivals to believe. That's what I wanted everyone to believe."

"So you didn't lose everything?"

"Are you even paying attention?"

"Now you're just being hurtful."

"You seem confused."

"I am confused."

"Well, let me confuse you a little more. We aren't here at Altiplano by accident. I paid off certain people to make sure if I was ever caught, ever arrested, ever sentenced, that this is where I would be sent."

"Why?"

"Because this is where they sent El Chapo."

"I don't understand."

"I know you don't, which is why I have to get out of here. As a bodyguard, you are exceptional, but as company, you are abysmal. There is nothing going on in that melon-sized head of yours. You never have anything interesting to say. If I have to sit in this pinche prison with you as my only companion for one more day, I will have to kill myself. And I will do so gladly because I will likely go straight to Hell, and that Hell would be better than this Hell."

Mendoza pouted. "I don't know what you want from me."

"I know you don't and that's exactly the problem. I don't blame you for being dull. It's who you are and why you're good at what you do."

Mendoza moved his lips as if he wanted to say something, but thought better of it.

"I can see you have a question."

"Why would you want to be sent here?"

"Because I knew that the Mexican authorities would be too cheap to fill in El Chapo's tunnel. It's a kilometer and a half long. And if they tried to cave it in or blow it up, the whole prison would come crashing down. So I figured they'd fill in both ends to save some money and leave it at that, and I was right. That's exactly what the cheap bastards did."

"So you had someone dig out the parts they filled in?"

"Over a year ago. Before I was even convicted. It was an insurance policy."

"So there's an escape tunnel?"

"You really aren't very quick, are you?"

"You don't have to be so insulting."

"It was an honest question."

Mendoza sighed. "So where do we find this tunnel?"

"Under the floor of my private shower."

"And we'll leave the same way El Chapo did?"

"Now you're catching on."

"When did you want to do this?"

"Do what?"

"Escape."

"Now would be a good time."

"Now?"

"Yes, because someone was paid to spike the guard's water supply with a powerful, quick-acting laxative. At this very moment, every guard in this prison is worried about one thing and one thing only—getting their ass on a toilet. As preoccupied as they are with pooping, they won't notice our departure for quite some time." Goolardo scraped back his chair and stood. "You ready?"

"I guess."

"You don't sound very enthusiastic. Are you enjoying your time here? Would you rather stay?"

A part of Mendoza wanted to take Goolardo's face between his two huge hands and squeeze until his cabeza cracked like a walnut. But another part of him, a larger part of him, loved Goolardo like the big brother he never had. Big brothers know how to push your buttons and Mendoza understood that. He knew Goolardo only talked to him like that because he loved him and trusted him. So, the more patient side of Mendoza protected Goolardo from his more ferocious, feral, and savage side. And that was why he said, "No."

"Then let's go."

Goolardo headed for his private shower and Mendoza followed, excited to escape, but irritated nonetheless. Why did Goolardo always have to be so insulting?

"I was going to send killers to take Flynn out." Goolardo shook his head. "But I decided that wouldn't be good enough. He humiliated me in a very public way, so that's how he needs to die. And I need to be there. I need to be seen. People need to know it was me who put that lunatic out of his misery."

"He turned you into a laughingstock."

Goolardo stopped and glared at Mendoza. "What did you say?"

"Not me. I didn't say it. That's what other people said."

"What people?"

"Stupid people. People who don't know you."

"I want to know who those people are, because they need to die too." Goolardo started moving again and they continued on in silence as they reached his private cell.

The shower was so tiny it only accommodated Goolardo. Mendoza watched as Goolardo removed the large metal grate that covered the drain, revealing a three by three-foot plastic drainage pipe. Goolardo sat on the edge and then slid down feet first, disappearing instantly into the hole. Mendoza's bulk barely fit in the shower stall, let alone the three by three-foot drainage pipe, but since that hole was the only way out, he had no choice but to follow.

He heard Goolardo's voice from below. "Come on! Let's go!"

"It's a tight fit."

"Maybe your clothes are catching!" Goolardo said. "Take them off!"

"No, no, I can do it. I just need to push!" Mendoza struggled but didn't make any progress.

"Quickly! Clothes off or I leave without you!"

"What?"

"Take your clothes off!"

Mendoza clumsily pulled himself out of the drainage pipe and quickly stripped down. He caught a glimpse of himself in the steel mirror. Naked, he looked even larger. From the bottom of his ass to the top of his chest, he was one formless, hairless, slab of refrigerator-sized flesh. As such, he still couldn't fit through the hole.

"Soap yourself up," Goolardo shouted from below. "Quickly. Lather up!"

Mendoza grumbled and turned on the shower and soaped up his massive torso. When he was lathered up from his thighs to his neck, he gingerly eased himself down into the plastic pipe, wiggling and struggling to get himself deeper. He kicked and shimmied and started to slide. He slid gradually at first, like a rat slowly moving through a snake, and then picked up speed, faster and faster, until he popped out the other end and landed with a sound like a canoe paddle slapping a side of beef. Embarrassed, he quickly scrambled to his feet and immediately slipped and fell back down on the soapy cement.

A small motorcycle waited and Goolardo sat astride it. It took three tries to kick start it, but finally the engine roared to life. Mendoza lifted a large soapy leg to climb on the back of the banana seat and Goolardo held out a hand to stop him. "What do you think you're doing?"

"Climbing on."

"No, no, no, I don't think so."

"You want me to walk? It's over a kilometer."

"And your naked and wet."

"I have no shoes!"

Goolardo closed his eyes and sighed a sigh of annoyance. "Fine. Climb on. Just make sure nothing bumps into me from behind."

Mendoza climbed on and put his arms around Goolardo, who grimaced at the damp embrace. Goolardo twisted the throttle and the motorcycle roared. Mendoza's added weight caused the bike to pop a wheelie and Mendoza, wet and slick as he was, lost his grip and slipped right off. His wide sudsy ass hit the ground hard as the motorcycle sped away, disappearing down the tunnel.

"Chinga tu madre!" The naked enforcer scrambled to his bare feet and ran after the departing bike, the engine's whine growing more distant as he gingerly made his way forward over the rocks, dirt clods and rubble.

CHAPTER FOUR

The first residents of Eagle Rock were the Tongva. They lived in the shadow of the massive rock that sat atop the San Rafael Hills, and then the Spanish arrived and constructed the Mission San Gabriel Arcangel. The Tongva were decimated by old world diseases and forced relocation. In 1785, the Tongva's female chief, Toypurina, rallied the last of her tribe and led a violent rebellion, but the Tongva were outnumbered and outgunned and the insurrection was crushed. When Mexico gained its independence from Spain in 1821, the new government sold mission lands to ranchers and the Tongva were forced to assimilate or die.

Thirty years later, California was ceded to the United States following the Mexican-American war. The Tongva were nearly gone and largely forgotten by those who had supplanted them. In their place were citrus farms and, later, housing developments that advertised the wonders of the California climate to cold and miserable easterners looking for a little warmth. They were told that unlike San Francisco, Southern California was an earthquake-free twentieth century Garden of Eden.

From the window of Flynn's room in the Bella Vista Residential Treatment Facility, Eagle Rock's shadow fell upon the fast-food restaurants, strip malls, and gas stations that now crowded the valley floor. He shared his room with another former patient from City of Roses who also worked at the Glendale Galleria. Rodney Shoop was twenty years older than Flynn and fifty pounds heavier. He had white hair that fell to his shoulders and a large, bushy beard. As Flynn struggled to button his Hot-Dog-on-a-Stick uniform, the new one hadn't arrived yet, Rodney had a similar problem with his bright red Santa pants.

His roomie sucked in his gut and worked to push the stubborn brass buttons into the holes. He put on his big, shiny, black vinyl belt and zipped up his zipper. Next came the high black boots. Then the bright red Santa jacket with the fake fur. He watched Flynn put on his Hot-Dog-on-a-Stick hat.

"You put on any more weight and you could be a damn Santa yourself," Rodney said.

"Do you like being Santa?" Flynn asked.

"I'm not really Santa."

"I know."

"I just pretend to be Santa."

"I know, Rodney."

"My problem was opioids. Substance abuse. Got hooked after back surgery. Unlike you, I was never delusional."

"Do you like *pretending* to be Santa?" Flynn asked.

"Depends."

"On what?"

"On the kids. Some are cute and polite and when I ask them what they want, they don't have some long-ass list. They tell me the one thing they want and then they're done. But a lot of kids are assholes. They complain that I didn't bring them what they wanted last year and then reel off a list that never frickin' ends. Ungrateful little jerks. But they aren't even the worst."

"What are the worst?"

"One-year-olds. Two-year-olds. Mom hands them over and they scream like frickin' banshees. Shrieking and wriggling and grabbing my beard with those icky, sticky fingers. Meanwhile, I'm supposed to smile because we're getting our picture taken. What are those parents thinking?" After finally buttoning the last button on his jacket, Rodney carefully positioned the Santa hat on his head. "What time is it?"

Flynn glanced at the alarm clock on the rickety side table between the twin beds. "Late."

"Shit," Rodney said. "No time for breakfast. Let's go."

They hurried from the group home and down the block to where they picked up the bus to the mall. It was drizzling and chilly as they huddled in the bus shelter.

Flynn eyeballed Rodney's Santa suit. "That suit looks pretty warm."

"It's not. It's fake fur and velour. No lining. Nothing."

"Where'd you get it?"

"Santa School."

"Santa School?"

"You gotta be certified if you want to work professionally and I went to one of the best in the country. CWH, Midland, Michigan. It's not the North Pole, but about as frickin' cold."

"What do they teach you there?"

"Everything from the history of Santa and St. Nick to how to dress and trim your beard. You'd be surprised by how many Santas wear fake beards. Personally, I think that's second rate. A professional Santa needs a real beard and forget those fat suits. If you want to have a good 'ho, ho, ho' you gotta have meat on your bones. Lung capacity. Resonance. They even teach you accounting and business tips. Marketing advice. It's not cheap and I had to get a student loan, but a good Santa can make up to twenty grand a season."

"Twenty grand? That's not bad."

"Better than what you make at Hot-Dog-on-a-damn-stick."

The bus arrived and Rodney and Flynn boarded. An elderly Armenian couple, two middle-aged Hispanic women, and a young Asian woman with a four-year-old boy sat on board. The kids' eyes grew wide at the sight of Santa Claus. Two tough-looking teenagers sat two rows behind the young mom, sniggering and grinning at Flynn and Rodney.

"Hi Santa," said the little boy.

"Merry Christmas," Rodney replied.

"How come you're not riding your sleigh?"

"Umm, I only take that out on Christmas Eve," Rodney said.

"How come?"

"'Cause, um, I don't like to tire out the reindeer."

"How come?"

"'Cause if they're tired they can't, you know, help me out on Christmas Eve."

"How come?"

Rodney's voice was a little sharp. "I don't *know*." The boy's mother reacted to Rodney's tone and shot him an angry look. Catching himself, Rodney sighed and put on a phony smile. "What's your name, kid?"

"Daniel."

"Have you been a good boy?"

"Pretty good."

"Very good," his mom said as she patted him on the head. "Danny, tell Santa what you want for Christmas."

"A Wonder Chopper RC Mini Stunt Drone."

"Okay. Great. Good to know," Rodney said.

"Hey Santa," the bigger of the teens sniggered. "Can I tell you what I want?"

"How about you don't," Rodney replied.

"I've been a good boy."

"I doubt that," Rodney said.

"What's that supposed to mean?"

"It means it's time to shut your mouth."

The teenager stopped smiling and stood. The mother pulled her little son closer. The older people on the bus looked out the window as the teenager moved up the aisle towards Rodney. "Who the hell do you think you're talking to, old man?"

"Boy, you better watch your mouth."

"Hey, it's okay. He didn't mean anything by it," Flynn said.

"Who the hell asked you?" The teen raised his chin.

"I'm just saying —"

"And I'm not talking to you. I'm talking to Santa!"

Rodney's face turned pink as he lurched to his feet. The big teen stood his ground and Flynn tugged on Rodney's sleeve. "Rodney, come on, sit down."

Rodney stood toe to toe with the teen. He was twice as wide, but a foot shorter and the teen towered over him. The teen looked down at four-year-old Danny and said, "Hey, kid, you know this asshole really isn't Santa, right? He ain't real."

"Shut your mouth," Rodney growled.

"He's just some fat old dude wearing a stupid red suit."

Flynn stood up and edged his way between them. "He is real. He's real if you believe in him."

"I used to believe in Santa too." The teen poked Flynn in the chest. "But now I know Santa's a lie. To shut kids up. To keep 'em quiet. Play nice and believe in Santa and you'll get everything you want. But that's bullshit."

"Watch your mouth," Rodney said.

"Is this beard even real?" The teen reached past Flynn and tugged hard on Rodney's beard.

"Ow! What the hell!" Rodney jerked his head back, but the teen held on tight and laughed.

A tiny hand grabbed the teen's arms. "Let him go! Let Santa go!" Little Danny was furious. Tears filled his eyes.

Seeing how upset Danny was, the teen let Rodney go, smirked at his friend and returned to his seat. Rodney wanted payback, but Flynn gently prodded him back and sat down next to him.

Danny's mom hugged her boy close as he continued to cry.

One of the middle-aged Hispanic ladies, a woman in her fifties, offered them all a little advice."Todo el mundo necesita algo en que creer.

Her friend translated for Rodney and Flynn. "Everyone needs something to believe in."

• • •

The lemon juice burned. Flynn blinked and rubbed his right eye. It was already noon and the line at Hot Dog on a Stick was ten deep.

"Is that lemonade ready?" Becky asked.

"We're almost out." Emma clapped her hands. "Come on, Jimmy! You need to pick up the pace."

Flynn looked up at her with one watery eye. "Okay." Flynn hand-stomped faster, mashing the masher, mumbling, "Faster, faster, faster…"

Juice splashed in both his eyes and up his nose and he blinked and squinted and held a sneeze in. He scrunched up his face and tried to stifle it and stopped mashing to concentrate on not sneezing, but it was too late. It was loud and wet and right in the bucket and the people waiting in line watched it happen.

The line of customers uttered a collective, "Ewwwwww."

"Throw it out! Start again! Start cutting!" Becky shouted.

Three days before Christmas, the crowds at the Glendale Galleria were insane. As the holiday grew closer, the lines at Hot Dog on a Stick extended farther and farther into the food court. Each day Flynn didn't think the mall could hold any more frenzied shoppers, and each day he was wrong. Patience grew thin. Tempers flared. Pressure mounted. Flynn worked right through lunch. His back ached from being on his feet for so long as he cut and squished and squinted through stinging, watery eyes. He didn't get a break until 3:00 p.m. when his manager, Mrs. McKinney, told him to take a late lunch.

Flynn held a tray piled high with fries, a Cinnabon, and two Hot Dogs on a Stick as he searched for an open table in the food court. Every single red plastic table was occupied. Kids screamed and parents yelled and Flynn just wanted to get off his feet and eat.

"Jimmy!" It was Mr. Papazian, the elderly Armenian security guard. He and Mr. Rodriguez shared a table. "Join us!" Flynn gratefully walked over, putting his tray on the table and his ass in the seat.

"You look beat. When was the last time you ate?" Papazian said.

Flynn shrugged. "I was late for work today and missed breakfast."

"That's not good." Rodriguez lifted a forkful of broccoli beef. "This time of year, with all the craziness, you gotta take care of yourself."

Flynn nodded and bit off the top of a corn dog, closing his eyes as he chewed.

"How's your Christmas shopping going?" asked Papazian.

"I don't have anybody to buy for," Flynn said.

"You don't have any family?"

Flynn shook his head.

"So where are you spending Christmas?" Rodriguez asked.

Flynn shrugged. "At the group home, I guess."

"No, you're not." Papazian pointed his spork at him. "You'll be with me and my family. Though we celebrate Christmas on January sixth."

"The sixth?" Rodriguez wiped his mouth with a napkin. "Who celebrates Christmas on January sixth?"

"Armenians. We're Eastern Orthodox."

"That's messed up."

"That's the date Jesus was born and baptized. That's the real Christmas. The twenty-fifth was a pagan festival dedicated to the Sun God. The Catholics took it over like they take everything over."

"So, what do Armenians do for Christmas?" Rodriguez asked, intrigued.

"Same as you. We do a whole thing. My wife makes a fish dish called ishkanatsoog and for dessert, anoushabour, which is like a pudding made with berries and apricots."

"Christmas pudding?"

"Yeah, sweets to make the next year sweet."

Rodriguez raised a curious eyebrow. "So, what do you do on the twenty-fifth?"

"Nothing."

"Nothing?"

"It's not Christmas," Papazian replied.

"Then Jimmy can spend the twenty-fifth with my family." Rodriguez beamed. "My wife, Rosa, makes Christmas tamales and a roast pork leg that's so tender it falls right off the bone."

"Can I come?" Papazian asked.

"For Christmas?"

"For the tamales."

Rodriguez smirked as he stood up and picked up his tray. "Why not?"

"I better get back to it too. I can't wait for this stupid holiday season to be over." Papazian rose and grabbed his tray. "Happiest time of the year my ass. People turn into animals. There's more theft. More fights. It's fucking crazy."

Papazian and Rodriguez disappeared into the crowd and Flynn tucked into his fries.

The next time he looked up, a slightly chubby twenty-something

Hispanic man stood over his table. "Hey, Jimmy."

"Sancho..."

"Sorry I haven't been by for a bit."

"That's okay."

"No, it's not, but I've been busy." Sancho sat across from Flynn. "You've been busy too, by the looks of it." Flynn nodded and took a huge bite of his Cinnabon. "Q says hi. So, does Dr. Nickelson. Says he's going to stop by and see you soon."

Flynn nodded again and took another big bite.

"You doing okay? How's work?"

"Okay," Flynn replied with a mouthful. Flynn could tell Sancho was uncomfortable, but so was he. Sancho knew him as James, not Jimmy. He had an emotional connection to his delusional alter ego, but now that James was gone, a distance settled between them. A sadness hovered behind Sancho's eyes. A sense of loss. Pity even. Sancho kept trying to remind Flynn of who he used to be, but Flynn didn't want or need to be reminded.

"Looks like you've put on a few," Sancho pointed out.

"A few what?"

"Pounds." Sancho seemed almost embarrassed to mention it.

"I guess."

"It's because of the anti-psychotic medication you're on. One of the side effects is rapid weight gain."

Flynn nodded as he took another giant bite of Cinnabon.

"It also could be why your hair is thinning and your eye keeps twitching like that."

"My eye's twitching?"

"It's another side effect. Facial tics and spasms."

"It makes me sleepy too. I don't like it."

"I know, but at least you're not ..." Sancho hesitated.

"Delusional."

"Yeah."

Flynn stuffed the last of the Cinnabon into his mouth, his lips slick with icing, eyes involuntarily blinking. He didn't know what to say. Didn't know what Sancho wanted to hear. They sat there silently, awkwardly. Sancho abruptly blabbered to fill the silence.

"I'm still studying psychology at PCC and next Fall I'm planning to transfer to Northridge. I had a class on pharmacology last semester. That's how I know about those side effects. Anyway, I was wondering if you wanted to come by mom's place for Christmas dinner?"

"I can't."

"How come?

"I'm busy."

"Busy?"

"Yeah, I made some new friends here and they invited me over."

"Good. That's good. Glad to hear it. New friends, huh?"

"Uh-huh."

"Did you see Dulcie? Did she come by?"

"Yeah, I saw her."

"She said she wanted to see you."

"She saw me." Flynn didn't bother mentioning that she only stared at him from a distance and never came over to talk to him.

"So, there's one more thing I wanted to talk to you about. It's a little disturbing and I don't want to freak you out, but I thought you should know."

"Okay."

"It's about Goolardo."

"Is he the one who kidnapped the billionaires?"

"That's him."

"Didn't I push him out of a plane?"

"That's right."

"He was really mad at me, wasn't he?"

"Yes, he was. You remember how he went to prison for kidnapping and attempted murder?"

"Uh-huh."

"What else do you remember?"

"I remember everything. All of it. But none of it feels like it happened to me. It's like a movie I saw or a nightmare or something that happened to somebody else."

"I guess it kind of did."

"So, what did you want to tell me about him?"

"He broke out of prison last week and since he's the kind of pendejo who holds a grudge, he might try to find you. Come after you."

"To do what?"

"Nothing good. He's not a nice guy. Listen, there's probably nothing to worry about, but keep your eyes open, okay? Just be careful."

Flynn slurped the last of his lemonade and it made a gurgling sound. "I better get back to work."

"Do you understand what I'm telling you?"

Flynn stood. "You want me to be careful."

"Yes. Can you do that? Can you be careful?"

"I guess."

"Good."

Sancho rose and awkwardly embraced Flynn. "Good to see you, ese. And starting next year, me and you are going to the gym."

"I better get back before Mrs. McKinney gets mad."

"Go. Get going. I got some Christmas shopping to do. I'll see you soon, all right?"

Flynn nodded and headed off. He glanced back to see Sancho staring at him. He looked so sad.

CHAPTER FIVE

For over one hundred years, the traditional holiday shopping season always began the day after Thanksgiving. Black Friday became the moniker of that first official day of Christmas shopping because retailers hoped that all their heavily promoted sales would push them into the black for the year. They advertised like crazy to create as much foot traffic as possible and sometimes some of that crazy infected the shoppers.

In 2008, a seasonal employee opened the doors at a Long Island Walmart and two thousand people stampeded inside, knocked him to the ground and trampled him to death. Since 2006, twelve people have died and one hundred and seventeen have been shoved, poked, punched, pepper-sprayed, slapped, kicked, choked, stabbed, tased or shot on the first day of "the most wonderful time of the year."

In the weeks leading to Christmas, the Glendale Galleria played a nonstop selection of holiday music over the PA system. At first, Flynn thought it was fun, but over time the endless loop of happy and joyful Christmas carols turned into a grating and ironic counterpoint to all the stress and angst emanating off the shoppers. As Flynn slaved away, hand-stomping lemonade, Bobby Helms sang, "*Jingle Bell Rock.*"

Flynn's supervisor at Hot Dog on a Stick, Mrs. McKinney, told him that twenty years ago the Galleria used to be even crazier at Christmas. With the opening of the Americana at Brand and the ease and the popularity of shopping online, Black Friday at the Glendale Galleria didn't see the same crowds as decades past. She claimed that indoor malls were less popular in general and the Galleria was a prime example.

You could have fooled Flynn. He couldn't imagine how the mall ever held more people. At 2:00 p.m. on Black Friday, every table in the food court was occupied by shoppers carrying multiple bags. The lines at Hot Dog on a Stick were longer than ever, and Flynn's arms and shoulders ached from hand-stomping all the lemonade those thirsty shoppers needed to wet their whistles. Ashley worked the cash register, Emma made the fries, and Becky dipped and deep-fried the dogs.

"We're getting low on lemonade!" Ashley shouted.

"Come on, Jimmy. You're slowing down!" Becky barked.

Juice squirted in Jimmy's eye. "Sorry," he mumbled.

Mrs. McKinney stepped out from the back office and took charge when she saw the crush of customers. She opened the register next to Ashley. "Jimmy, take this register. Becky, you start cutting and I'll hand-stomp. Let's go, people." She clapped her hands three times and Becky just stared at her. "What are you looking at missy? Let's move!"

Flynn took over the register and people rushed over from the other line. First up was a harried thirty-something mom with panicked eyes and two wild toddlers yelling for attention, each on their own bright blue leash.

"I don't want a hot dog! I want McDonald's," the little girl screamed.

"The line's too long at McDonald's," Mom hissed.

"McDonald's! McDonald's!" the girl shouted.

Her dirty-faced brother chanted along, "McDonald's! McDonald's!"

The mom looked at Flynn beseechingly and shouted over her screeching kids. "Three hot dogs on a stick, three fries, and three lemonades!"

"McDonald's! McDonald's! McDonald's!"

Flynn had to shout over them as well. "What flavor lemonade? We have cherry, we have lime—"

"McDonald's! McDonald's! McDonald's!"

"Regular! Whatever!" The mom's voice was hoarse from too much shouting and too many cigarettes—the acrid smoke lingering on her clothes and breath. The kids tugged on their leashes and pulled her off-balance.

"McDonald's! McDonald's! McDonald's!'

The mom jerked both leashes, pulling the kids off their feet. The little boy cried and the girl joined in. Soon the crying grew louder than their chanting had been. Flynn took the mom's money and rushed to fetch their food and drinks. His hands trembled as he hurried to assemble everything. A high-pitched buzzing filled his ears. The stress overwhelmed, and he struggled to keep it together.

When Flynn returned with the tray, the mom shouted at both her kids, "I'm telling Santa how bad you've been, and you'll get nothing! *Nothing*!" The kids cried even louder as Flynn handed her the tray and she dragged away her offspring.

Next in line was a sixty-something woman carrying an incredible array of shopping bags. She stared up at the menu board, totally perplexed. Flynn posed a question, "What can I get you, ma'am?"

"How many calories are in the veggie dog?"

"Um…" Flynn consulted a plasticized sheet with ingredients and calorie counts. "Two hundred and twenty."

The woman stared at the menu board some more. "How many are in the turkey dog?"

"Um…" Flynn consulted the sheet again. "Two hundred and forty."

"Hmmm," the woman said. She stared back up at the menu board.

The hulking forty-something man in line behind her sighed loudly.

"How many calories are in the all-beef dog?"

Flynn consulted the sheet. "Three hundred and eighty."

"Okay," said the woman.

"You want the beef dog?" Flynn asked.

"Do you know how many grams of fat are in that?"

The huge man behind her sighed in exasperation and mumbled, "Jesus."

Flynn checked the sheet again. "Looks like twenty-three grams."

"That's a lot of fat. How many are in the turkey dog?"

"Lady, I gotta get back to work," said the hulking guy behind her. "I know what I want. Can I just order please?"

"Wait your turn," she said.

"There are fifteen people behind you, ma'am," said the man.

"Would you please stop interrupting me?"

"Thirteen grams of fat," Flynn offered.

"Well, that's quite a bit less. What about the veggie dog? How many grams of fat are in that?"

"Jesus Christ!" the man shouted.

"Eight," Flynn said.

"Great. I'll take the all-beef."

"Can I get you anything else?"

"How many calories are in the cherry lemonade?"

"Unfuckingbelievable!" The hulking man behind her stalked off and Flynn, for the first time, saw the man standing behind the disgruntled patron.

Francisco Goolardo.

And he was smiling.

Flynn nervously consulted the calorie sheet. "One hundred and seventy in the small cherry lemonade."

"Give me a large," the lady said. Flynn rang her up and took her money. He handed her a tray with a hot dog on a stick and a large cherry lemonade.

Goolardo now stood first in line. He rested his hands flat on the counter. He wore a charcoal gray Armani suit and a blue and gray Hermes tie.

"I almost didn't recognize you, Mr. Flynn. You put on a few pounds since we last met." Though his accent was Brazilian, his English was perfect.

Flynn smiled the same insecure smile he smiled at all the customers. "What can I get you today?"

"I'd like the last year of my life back. I'd like all the many millions of dollars you cost me. I'd like my reputation restored."

"I'm not sure what you're asking me, sir."

"Your very existence is an embarrassment to me. That I was taken down by a fat, balding, pimple-faced, mental patient who works at Hot Dog on a Stick is simply…unacceptable."

The twenty-something man behind Goolardo tapped him on the shoulder. "Are you going to order or what?"

Goolardo slowly turned his head and focused his angry eyes on the young man's employee tag before raising a furious gaze to his face. "Mr. Garza, I don't believe I was talking to you."

"If you're going to order, order. There's a lot of people waiting in line. That's all I'm saying."

Goolardo hit Garza in the throat. He stumbled back in shock, grabbing at his neck with both hands as he struggled to breathe. His face turned red as the rest of the line scattered in fifteen different directions. That's when Flynn saw Mendoza and two more dangerous-looking men behind Goolardo.

Ashley and Becky, Emma and Mrs. McKinney watched in stunned silence as Goolardo turned back to the counter and offered Flynn a charming smile. "Your bill is due, Mr. Flynn. Today you pay for all the pain and trouble you caused me. Today you die a slow and agonizing death."

Flynn backed away from the counter, tripped over a bucket, and landed on his back, spilling lemonade everywhere.

"Take off that stupid hat and come out from behind there." Goolardo leaned over the counter to look at him. "Please don't make this more difficult than it has to be. We wouldn't want anyone else to get hurt, now would we?"

Flynn saw the flash of anger on Mrs. McKinney's face. She was frightened, but the insult to the Hot Dog on a Stick hat was more than she was willing to take.

She strode up to the counter and glared at Goolardo. "Who the heck do you think you are, sir?"

Goolardo eyed her nametag before meeting her indignant gaze. "I am chaos, Mrs. McKinney. I am darkness. I am death. I am the anarchy that underlies the artifice of civilization and civility. If you ever hope to live to see another day you must run away."

Tears filled Mrs. McKinney's eyes as terror gripped her heart. Ashley, Becky, and Emma were all equally terrified and teary-eyed.

"Run, Mrs. McKinney. *Run!*" Goolardo shouted.

And she did.

Flynn tried to stand and slipped and landed on his ass in the lemonade. He tried again, and fell again and crawled on his hands and knees for the back office. The dangerous men with Mendoza leaped over the counter and pulled him to his feet, but they didn't see the lemon halves in his hands. He raised them and squeezed, squirting them both in the eyes with juice. They shouted with pain and surprise, clawing at their eyes as Flynn disappeared into the back office.

Flynn's mind emptied of anything but fear and adrenaline. It was a familiar feeling. As a ten-year-old orphan living in foster homes, he was often bullied and abused. Other kids, older kids, bigger kids stole from him, beat him and terrorized him. Fat. Afraid. Alone. Helpless. Defenseless. The fear pushed out any rational thought and completely immobilized him.

The deafening clap of a gunshot brought Flynn back into his body. Christmas shoppers ran and screamed as panic gripped the Glendale Galleria Mall. The heat of a bullet passed by Flynn's face before he even heard the gunshot. When he glanced back, he saw Mendoza and the two dangerous men not far behind.

One fired at Flynn and the rotund man next to him went down. Surprise flashed in the man's eyes as he fell. A bullet hole in his yellow shirt. The blood. The man mouthed the words "help me," but Flynn didn't stop. He just kept running.

Up on the second level, Flynn looked down on the Santa stage and all the panicked parents and kids running for cover. He ran past Baby Gap and Apple and The Lego Store and joined the terrified crowd fighting to get on the down escalator.

People shoved and punched and pushed each other. An old woman fell. Some tried to scramble over her. Others slid down the metal separator between the up and down escalator. Flynn followed one of them and dove headfirst down the slide-like separator. He tobogganed all the way down to the first level and belly-flopped on the linoleum floor.

Someone stepped on his hand.

Someone else kicked him in the head.

Flynn tried to get up, but he couldn't. People kept stepping on him and kicking him. He curled into a fetal position, the same way he used to when bullies beat his ass on the playground during recess. He tried to cover his head and squeeze into a ball as small as possible. The screaming and shouting and crying and yelling overwhelmed him. Paralyzed him.

Flynn thought he heard someone call his name. But it was distant. Faint. Then he heard it again. Louder this time. "Flynn! Flynn! *Flynn!*" Santa loomed over him, grabbed him by the arm, and pulled him to his feet. Only it wasn't really Santa. It was his roommate, Rodney Shoop.

"We gotta move! Let's go," Rodney shouted.

"They want to kill me," Flynn said.

"They want to kill everybody!"

"No, just me. They want to kill *me!*"

"It's not always all about you, you know!" Rodney scolded as he pulled Flynn through the hysterical crowd of people running every which way. "Fucking terrorists hate our way of life! They hate us for our freedom!"

"Santa! Santa!" A five-year-old boy, his face full of snot and tears, clamped his hand on Rodney's red sleeve and held on for dear life. "I can't find my mommy!"

Rodney grabbed the kid's wrist and pulled him along. Another gunshot boomed and Flynn glanced back to see Mendoza aiming at him as shoppers scattered. The muzzle flashed. The shot cracked. Rodney spun around and looked at Flynn with surprise as all two hundred and seventy-five pounds of him fell to the ground. He clutched his arm. Blood leaked between his fingers.

"I'm shot. I'm frickin' shot!"

"They shot Santa," the five-year-old cried.

Rodney watched Mendoza advance and shouted at Flynn, "Go! Go! Get out here!"

Flynn scrambled to his feet and ran as fast as his fat ass could carry him. Gunshots echoed behind. Flynn didn't know which way to go. The stampeding crowd made that decision for him. He was buffeted back and forth as he struggled to stay on his feet.

The human wave carried him through the doors of Target where he crashed into a large display of holiday wrapping paper. He fell and crawled behind a customer service counter. There he hid, helpless and alone, a high-pitched buzzing filled his ears as sheer terror overwhelmed him.

. . .

From the time he was twelve, Sancho agonized over what to buy his mother for Christmas. That was the year his father disappeared, and Sancho and his mother moved in with her parents. They never had much money, but Sancho always insisted on giving his mother something. Having been abandoned by his father, he didn't want to lose his mother too. At twelve, he felt responsible for his dad's leaving. At twenty-seven he knew that guilt wasn't logical, but as a student of psychology he also knew it was common for children to feel like they were the cause of their parents' breakup. Because of this, Sancho was extremely devoted to his mamá and that feeling was never more intense than around Christmas.

His mother claimed that just having Sancho there for Christmas dinner was enough, but Sancho always wanted to give her more. He couldn't afford much, but he would save all year to buy her something he hoped she'd love. His mother worked hard all her life cleaning other people's houses and rarely spent any money on herself. It was enough just to buy food and pay the rent. She would always gently scold her only son for spending his money on a present, but he loved the look in her eyes when she'd pull off the wrapping paper.

Since September, she'd been raving about her friend Blanca's Instapot, so this year he decided to buy his mother her own Instapot. Now Sancho just had to pick one. He was in Target, trying to choose, but it wasn't easy. The six-quart Instapot seven-in-one came with seven functionalities and fourteen smart programs. The Plus 60 had a more advanced interface with a mode indicator and a pressure gauge. He finally decided on the eight-quart Ultra because it was also a rice cooker, a yogurt maker, and a warming pot. It was more than he could afford, but if he put it in on a card he could pay it off over time.

He stood waiting in line at the cash register when the first gunshot echoed through the mall. Everyone in line looked at each other as they weren't immediately sure what the sound was. But then came another shot and another one and everyone in line left in a hurry. Even the cashier disappeared. The shoppers converged on the exit and Sancho joined them, but then he remembered Flynn. His old friend seemed so distant and depressed, confused and helpless. What if those gunshots had something to do with him?

What if they had something to do with Goolardo?

The mob pushed Sancho for the doors and Sancho tried to fight the flow and swim against the tide. He shoved his way back through the crush of panicked shoppers. People were irritated and terrified and angry, but Sancho kept saying "excuse me, excuse me" as he pushed and elbowed his way through. He was just about back to the mall when another gunshot rang out.

More terrified shoppers stampeded into Target and nearly swept Sancho away, but he stood his ground and finally made it through.

He found himself by Santa's throne on the raised platform with the gaudy red, green and gold lights, and tinsel. It was where Santa sat to have his picture taken with all the hundreds of sticky-faced kids. The line usually stretched forever, but at the moment there were no kids waiting, no elves to usher them forward, and no Santa.

Sancho headed for the escalator that led to the second-floor food court and Hot Dog on a Stick. That's when he saw Saint Nick. The big, bearded, red-suited symbol of the holiday season lay on the floor, bleeding out. A crying five-year-old boy sat next to him, sobbing and holding his hand. Sancho knelt on the ground beside them. "What the hell happened here?"

"Some asshole shot me," Santa snapped.

"Where'd you get hit?"

"Left arm." Santa kept pressure on it with his right hand even as blood leaked through his fingers.

"I'll get you some help," Sancho said.

"Get this kid out of here first. Get him somewhere safe."

"No," said the little boy. "I wanna stay with you."

"Don't be naughty! Go with the man. Go!"

The boy nodded as tears streamed down his dirty face. Sancho took the boy's hand, but he also had a question. "Which way did the shooter go?"

Santa raised a bloody finger and pointed across the mall. Fifty feet away, Sancho saw Mendoza. Fear filled his guts like ice. The last time Sancho saw the burly enforcer was the trial where Sancho testified against him.

"Shit."

Mendoza saw Sancho as well; and Sancho could tell that Mendoza knew exactly who he was. As Mendoza raised his weapon, Sancho leaped to his feet and turned to run, pulling the boy with him. That's when he bumped into Francisco Goolardo.

The drug lord seemed pleased to see him. "Well, look who it is! What a small world we live in."

Sancho tried to get around him but Goolardo grabbed him by the front of his shirt.

"Where are you going? Don't be rude." He looked at the little boy. "Is this little one yours?"

"No."

The two dangerous men with Goolardo held one of Flynn's Hot Dog on a Stick co-workers. Sancho didn't know her name, but he remembered how she talked to Flynn. How she treated him with disrespect and looked at him with contempt. Her Hot Dog on a Stick hat sat crooked atop her shoulder-length blonde hair, her pretty face messy with melted mascara and tears.

Mendoza arrived and took Sancho by the arm. His huge hand encircled Sancho's bicep easily.

"Sancho, isn't it? Isn't that your name?" Goolardo asked.

"Yeah."

"Mr. Flynn's Sancho Panza. How very fitting. I'm assuming you visited him today. Not the same man he used to be, is he? Now that he's medicated, he's not nearly as impressive. It's unfortunate really. I miss the old Flynn. He was a worthy opponent. Now he's just fat, frightened, and stupid like most Americans."

"Let the boy go. He has nothing to do with this."

"No. No one goes. Not the boy. Not the girl. Not you. Not even Santa. Not until I find Mr. Flynn. Do you know where he's hiding?"

"No."

"It's fitting is it not, that this all ends in a place like this? This palace of conspicuous consumption. I imagine it was once awe-inspiring. Sometime in the '80s perhaps. But now, like America itself, it is in decline. These stores packed with useless merda that no one needs or even wants until they are brainwashed into believing that without this or that they are worth nothing. I sold a product people did desire. One that required no advertising at all. The demand was there, and I filled it and made billions and they sent me to prison for not playing by the rules put in place by your rapacious government.

"I was punished for not lining the pockets of your politicians. Your leaders have always been greedy, but now the unwashed and ignorant have elected leaders just as ignorant as they are. The stupid leading the stupid. Poetic justice I would say. The American experiment will collapse in chaos. I tried to hasten the inevitable with the plan your friend foiled, but it will happen even without my help. And very, very soon."

Goolardo fired his gun in the air. Sancho and the girl flinched. The boy wailed. Goolardo raised his voice until it echoed throughout the cavernous mall. "Mr. Flynn! I know you're hiding here somewhere. And I know you can hear me. I have your friend, Sancho, and the pretty blonde girl who works with you. Becky." He held up her name tag. "If you don't want them to die, then I need to see you. We need to talk. We need to finish this. Do not prolong your pain. I can see how unhappy you are. They have filled your brain with chemicals and turned you into one of them. A worker bee. A fat, stupid drone, laboring to make the rich richer. Come! Let me help you. Let me put you out of your misery!"

When no one answered back, Goolardo struck Becky in the forehead with the butt of his pistol. She would have collapsed without the support of the two dangerous men. The cut he opened on her once flawless forehead bled heavily.

"Don't make me beat this beauty into something ugly. There is no escape for you. You know that. In the end, you will die for what you did to me. There's no reason to take these innocents with you."

"Let the girl go!" An elderly security guard with an Armenian accent held a trembling gun on Goolardo. Mendoza and the two dangerous men swung their weapons in the direction of the lone security guard. Yet, he kept coming. "Put the guns down!" he ordered.

Goolardo laughed. "I applaud your bravery, sir, but I believe you are outgunned." Goolardo put his pistol to Becky's head. "Continue to point that weapon at me and I promise this young woman will die. As will this young man and this innocent little boy. I might even shoot Santa just for good measure."

"Put the guns down!" The security guard repeated, his voice shaky.

Goolardo looked at the girl. "Tell that old fool to put his gun away before he gets you killed."

"Please, Mr. Papazian, do what he says. I think he really means it."

"SWAT is on the way." Papazian blinked away sweat burning his eyes. "You might as well surrender because there is no way you're getting out of here."

An angry Goolardo turned his weapon on Papazian. "There's a fine line between bravery and stupidity and I think you just crossed it."

Goolardo fired, hitting Papazian in his left shoulder, spinning him sideways. Goolardo fired again and that bullet caught the guard in the arm. Papazian fell. His gun clattered across the floor. He tried to crawl for it. Goolardo fired once more, catching him in the side. Papazian winced, yet he continued to crawl. Goolardo laughed and crossed over to the old Armenian. Papazian's breathing grew ragged and labored. Blood smeared the floor as he doggedly crept forward, straining to reach his revolver.

"It's important to be persistent, but now you're just being ridiculous." Goolardo aimed at Papazian's head.

"I believe you're looking for me!"

Sancho recognized his old friend's voice. Not the new heavily medicated version with the high-pitched, mealy-mouthed American accent, but the old Flynn, the masterful one, with the deep voice and the British accent with just a touch of Scottish burr. He was above on the second floor, looking down over the railing at the tableau below. He was dressed in black from head to toe and held the biggest orange, white, and blue Super Soaker Sancho had ever seen.

CHAPTER SIX

Mobile, Alabama didn't offer much opportunity for a young African American boy in 1949. That was the year Lonnie Johnson was born. The son of a truck driver and the grandson of a cotton farmer, he was inspired by the life of George Washington Carver. Always curious, he loved taking things apart to see what made them tick. When he was ten, he nearly burned down his family's house trying to make rocket fuel.

Fourteen years later he earned a master's degree in Nuclear Engineering from Tuskegee University. Six years after that he was a senior system engineer on the Galileo Project at NASA's Jet Propulsion Laboratory. While engineering a cooling system that would run on water instead of freon, he invented a super squirt gun he dubbed the Power Drencher. He worked with various toy companies to develop it and in 1991, the gun was renamed the Super Soaker and launched to worldwide acclaim.

Johnson filed suit in 2013 for nonpayment of royalties and in that same year was awarded seventy-three million dollars.

"Mr. Flynn!" Goolardo shouted with obvious glee. "How good of you to join us!"

"How could I refuse such an enthusiastic invitation?"

"It's a pleasure to have you back."

"It's a pleasure to be back."

"What is that you're aiming at me?"

"A high-powered, top of the line, state of the art weapon that offers four different firing modes. Jet Stream. Scattershot. Triple Shot. And Atomizer."

"Impressive."

"Indeed. It has a range of forty feet and comes complete with a detachable stock and multiple banana clips. It's quite ingenious really."

"He's loco," Mendoza mumbled. "A lunatic."

Flynn saw Becky staring up at him with a mixture of surprise, shock, and awe. Blood ran down her face and all over her Hot Dog on a Stick outfit.

"This is between you and me, Goolardo. Let the guard and Becky and the little boy go!"

"Why would I do that?"

"Because they have nothing to do with this."

"So, you don't mind if I pop a cap in Santa?"

"I would prefer you wouldn't."

Rodney winced as he shifted his position to look up at Flynn. "You do realize you don't have a real gun, right?"

"It's as real as I am," Flynn replied.

"And what exactly is your plan, Mr. Flynn?" Goolardo pointed at himself with both index fingers. "You know, I'm not the Wicked Witch of the West."

"Let them go. I won't ask you again." Flynn shouldered his weapon and drew a bead on the Brazilian drug lord.

"I'm glad to, but only if you come down here. Do that and I will release them."

"Sancho too?"

"No. Not Sancho. Like you, he needs to pay for what he did to me."

Sancho turned his terrified gaze to Flynn, who kept his weapon trained on Goolardo.

"Fine. I'm coming down. But I'm not putting down my weapon."

"I wouldn't expect you to."

Flynn crossed to the escalator and rode it down. The hostages all held their breath as Flynn slowly descended, his bright plastic weapon resting in the crook of his arm. When he reached the first floor, he once again took a bead on Goolardo.

"Now...let the girl go."

Goolardo nodded to the two dangerous men and they unhanded her.

"Becky, take that little boy and get him to safety." Becky stared at Flynn in stunned silence. "Becky! Can you do that for me?"

The teenager seemed numb, but she nodded in the affirmative.

"Good girl. Now, go. Go!"

Becky took the little boy's hand and hurried off across the mall.

Keeping his weapon trained on Goolardo, Flynn glanced sideways at Rodney in his Santa suit. "Can you move?"

"How come you're talking with that funny accent?"

"What accent?"

"The limey accent. Why are you talking like that?"

"If you can move, you need to get up and get out of here."

"I'm shot."

"I know. I can see that. And if you'd like to avoid getting shot again, I would suggest you move."

Rodney winced in agony as he rolled over on his knees and used his one good arm to pull himself to his feet. He staggered off slowly, trailing blood.

Distant sirens filled the air as Goolardo and the two dangerous men aimed their weapons at Flynn. "Time to go, Mr. Flynn," Goolardo said.

Flynn was perplexed. "Go as in go the way of all flesh or go as in go with you?"

"I could shoot you both here, but what would be the fun in that? You don't deserve a quick death. You deserve to die slowly and painfully and by the end of our time together you will be begging me to end your misery."

Flynn continued to hold his weapon on all three of them. "It appears we find ourselves in a Mexican standoff then."

"A Mexican standoff is a confrontation between multiple combatants where there is no strategy that will allow any one party to achieve victory. That is not the case here. I have a Brugger and Thomet MP 9 machine pistol. It fires nine hundred rounds per minute. My colleagues are threatening you with semi-automatic Berettas. Mr. Mendoza holds a Smith and Wesson on your friend. You, on the other hand, are threatening us with a squirt gun." The sirens wailed louder now as Goolardo barked, "Take him!"

The dangerous men moved for Flynn. He fired his pump-action Super Soaker Switch Shot Blaster, hitting them both full in the face with the jet stream mode. The two men screamed in agony and clawed at their eyes, dropping their guns as Flynn turned his Super Soaker on Mendoza, catching the big man full in the face and right in the mouth. He gagged and grunted in pain, blinded by the bleach in the banana clip. Sancho slammed his elbow back and hit Mendoza square in the nose. The big man stumbled backwards, gagging and blind.

Goolardo unloaded on Flynn, but the two no longer dangerous men provided excellent cover and their body armor caught the brunt of the fire. Flynn ran quickly, in a serpentine fashion, staying low, as Goolardo struggled to get a bead on him. Just as he got Flynn in his sights, Mendoza, blinded and staggering, stumbled into the line of fire.

"Fi de rapariga!" Goolardo screamed.

• • •

Becky hid behind a pillar and captured all the action on her iPhone. The little boy crouched beside her as she shot every insane second of it. She couldn't believe what Jimmy was doing. And what was up with that accent? He sounded like Jon Snow on Game of Thrones. Strangely, Jimmy seemed much more attractive to her with that accent. Or maybe it was the fact that he just saved her life.

The guy Jimmy called Goolardo was totally pissed off and spraying bullets everywhere. When Flynn ran by where Becky hid, some of those shots ricocheted off the pillar. She ducked down but didn't want to stop videotaping. This was crazy shit and she had to get it on YouTube.

She caught Jimmy's friend, Sancho, diving behind Santa's throne and that huge Mr. Mendoza dunking his giant head into a fountain and splashing water into his eyes. Then Jimmy ran back into the frame and Goolardo unloaded on him. Jimmy moved pretty fast for a fat guy. She couldn't believe the way Jimmy fought back. He always seemed like such a doof.

That Goolardo guy was totally pissed. He kept shooting until his gun ran out of bullets. He was running and reloading, and Jimmy popped out from behind a palm tree and sprayed him right in the face with that giant squirt gun.

Goolardo screamed, totally blind, and fired his little machine gun everywhere, randomly shooting out store windows and shredding plants and ripping the shit out of a sunglass kiosk. Jimmy dove behind a mall directory as Goolardo tripped backwards over a potted plant and kept on firing as he fell, shattering a giant skylight a hundred feet up. Glass rained down.

Becky watched as Jimmy surveyed the damage. "Sancho! You okay?"

"I'm okay." Sancho slowly peeked out from behind the down escalator.

"Becky?"

"I'm okay," Becky said even as she continued to shoot her iPhone video.

Sancho looked around with concern. "Where's Mendoza? I don't see him."

"Behind you!" Becky screamed.

Sancho turned in terror, but Mendoza wasn't there. It was Jimmy who Mendoza stood behind. The big man tackled him and Becky caught the whole thing. Mendoza's two hundred and seventy-five pounds knocked the wind out of him and the Super Soaker skittered away. Jimmy tried to wrestle his way out from under him, but Jimmy was fat and out of shape and no match for Mendoza.

The enforcer grabbed Jimmy by the throat and squeezed. Jimmy kicked at him and flailed away, but his sneakers and fists didn't do much. Mendoza was too pissed off to feel anything. Even from where she was, Becky could see Mendoza's red and bloodshot eyes bugging out of his head.

Jimmy gagged and choked as Mendoza strangled the life out of him. Becky considered putting down her iPhone and trying to help, but what could she do? She couldn't stop Mendoza. She was no match for that huge guy. At least if she got it all on her phone, she could show the police what happened to him. Poor Jimmy. He wasn't even fighting now. His eyes rolled back in his head and she wondered if he was already dead.

• • •

A foot smacked Mendoza in the face. It caught him by surprise and when he turned to see where it came from, it smacked him again. It was a bare foot. A plastic foot. A manikin foot. And Sancho was swinging it. The big toe poked Mendoza in the eye. Mendoza let Flynn go with one hand to grab for it. He missed and the foot hit him in the mouth. The attack wasn't painful or physically damaging, but it was extremely irritating. The manikin leg was like a bug buzzing around, bumping into the big man's face.

Mendoza let Flynn go to focus his attention on the plastic leg. He pushed onto his feet as Sancho shifted his grip, moving his hands to the ankle so he could swing the leg like a baseball bat. The shapely plastic thigh caught Mendoza square in the nose and staggered him back. Emboldened, Sancho swung again, but this time Mendoza caught the leg in his massive hand and ripped it out of Sancho's grip. He swung it one-handed and brought it down on the crown of Sancho's head. Sancho sank to his knees. A second blow knocked him face down on the floor.

Mendoza raised the leg again to deliver a coup de grâce, but it wouldn't budge from the apex of the swing. When he turned around to see why, he saw that Flynn held onto the plastic thigh with both hands. Flynn kicked him behind the knee and Mendoza fell backwards. His head bounced off the ground. That's when he saw the little boy loom over him. He had Flynn's Super Soaker. The bright green barrel hovered inches away from his nose.

"You hurt Santa!" screamed the kid and he sprayed Mendoza square in the face.

His eyes burning with bleach, Mendoza screamed and rolled over onto his knees. He crawled forward and staggered up, started to run, tripped over a bench and smacked into the ground, breaking his nose yet again. That's when he heard the flashbangs explode. Everything went white and a high-pitched ear-piercing whine drowned out all sound.

• • •

When Flynn's vision cleared from the flash of the M84 grenade, he saw ten heavily armed men storm the Glendale Galleria. He couldn't hear them, but he could see them as they ran in, rappelled down, and came at Flynn from four different directions. They wore green combat fatigues, helmets, masks, and military-style body armor. Each held an assault rifle. As the ringing in his ears faded, he heard orders shouted.

"Glendale PD!"

"On the ground!"

"Face down!"

"Drop your weapons!"

Flynn raised his hands as they grabbed him by either arm and hurled him to the floor. Sancho stayed where he was, nose against the ground, arms spread wide. Someone pulled Flynn's arms behind him and slapped handcuffs on his wrists. A SWAT officer scooped up the little boy and ran him to safety. From his limited vantage point on the floor, Flynn looked around but couldn't find either Mendoza or Goolardo.

"They're getting away!" Flynn shouted, but no one heard him. They were too busy securing the area and yelling things like *"area clear, suspect down"* and *"Santa's Village is secure."*

Flynn saw Becky recording the scene. A SWAT officer grabbed her phone and ushered her away, all the time asking her if she was okay.

"That's my phone! Give me my phone!" she shouted.

Flynn tried to get off the ground, but a foot kept him down. "They're getting away!" he yelled again. This time someone heard him.

"We have the perimeter secure and the situation under control, sir."

"Take these handcuffs off me!"

"Not until we understand the situation. Until then *everyone* is a suspect."

"I'm with Her Majesty's Secret Service. Listen to me. You're letting Francisco Goolardo get away!" Flynn turned his head far enough to see one SWAT officer roll his eyes at another. "You are making a serious mistake!"

Becky pulled free from the SWAT officer and pointed at Flynn. "He's not the bad guy! He saved me! He saved us all! It's all on my phone! Give me back my phone!"

The officer grabbed her by the arm and dragged her off.

"I want my damn phone!"

An emergency medical crew attended to the wounded security guard. Santa was carried away on a stretcher.

Two SWAT officers pulled Flynn to his feet as a third checked his ID. That's when Flynn saw the two dangerous men who worked for Goolardo being frog-marched across the mall, their hands cuffed behind them, their eyes squeezed shut, their dirty faces wet with tears. Flynn motioned to them with his head. "They aren't the only ones. There are other terrorists here. You need to find them before they get away."

The SWAT officer holding Flynn took off his handcuffs and handed him over to a nearby uniformed officer. "Get this one looked at. I think he might be suffering from shock."

"Would you bloody well listen to me."

"Sir, you need to calm down," the SWAT officer said. "You're safe now. Everything's okay."

"Not if Goolardo gets away!"

"Do you want me to put these handcuffs back on you. Is that what you want?"

Flynn held up his hands. "Clearly not. Sorry I bothered you, officer. Carry on."

As the SWAT officer turned to go, Flynn unsnapped the cop's holster and drew his sidearm. The uniformed officer saw the Sig Sauer in Flynn's hand and fumbled for his own gun.

"Gun!" he screamed.

Every police officer in shouting distance saw the semi-automatic in Flynn's hand and turned their weapons on him.

"I'm sorry," Flynn said. "But I cannot let that madman get away."

A taser dart hit Flynn from behind and fifty thousand volts ripped through his nervous system. He lost complete control of his body and collapsed, hitting the ground hard. The uniformed cop kicked the gun out of his hand as another taser dart hit Flynn in the shoulder and a third hit him in the leg. He bucked and flopped like a fish out of water, shuddering and shaking, grunting and spasming as wave after wave of electricity coursed through his body.

"Hey, hey! What the fuck!" Sancho shouted. "You're killing him!"

CHAPTER SEVEN

Ellis Island was opened in 1890. That same year, Wyoming was admitted as the forty-fourth state, the Dalton Gang robbed their first train, and the Pasadena Valley Hunt Club held the inaugural Rose Parade. It has been held every New Year's Day since, unless January first falls on a Sunday, then it is held the following day. The exception was instituted in 1893 as organizers didn't want to spook any horses hitched outside for Sunday Church services. The idea was to showcase and promote Southern California's mild winter weather. As Professor Charles F. Holder put it, "In New York, people are buried in snow. Here flowers are blooming, and our oranges are about to bear. Let's hold a festival to tell the world about our paradise."

The nurses, orderlies, and patients at City of Roses Psychiatric Institute surrounded the TV in the rec room and watched massive motorized floats covered in fresh flowers, seeds, bark, vegetables, and nuts trundle down Colorado Boulevard, less than half a mile from where they sat. If they could open the windows, they might hear the marching bands. If allowed to leave, a walk of a few short blocks would have put them in the middle of the gargantuan crowd lining the parade route.

Sancho sat in a chair at the rear of the recreation room and stared at the back of Flynn's head. Recently promoted from part-time to full-time, Sancho finally had regular hours. Once he received his degree, he hoped to transition from a mental health technician to a certified nursing assistant. His ultimate goal was to become a mental health nurse practitioner, but for that he'd need a degree from a nursing school.

Most of the patients wore jeans, sweatpants or pajama bottoms with slippers, sneakers or flipflops. James Flynn, however, upped the sartorial ante by wearing well-worn Ferragamo loafers and a blue single-breasted Armani suit. He sat on a threadbare couch between Ty, a rotund African American man in his early twenties, and Q, a skinny, wild-eyed seventy-eight-year-old with a scraggly white beard and a receding mop of curly white hair.

Ten days after the attempt on his life, Flynn was back at City of Roses. Because he refused to take his meds, his psychiatrist, Dr. Nickelson, had no choice but to move him out of the group home and back to the locked ward for closer monitoring. The trauma of the attack at the Glendale Galleria triggered his delusional disorder. Flynn once again believed that the hospital was the headquarters for Her Majesty's Secret Service and that he was a secret agent with a Double-0 designation.

When Flynn first moved into the group home, Nickelson told Sancho to give away all of Flynn's clothes. He wanted to remove all the old associations to the delusional behavior. Sancho had loaded up the trunk of his '92 red Mustang with Flynn's large wardrobe of vintage designer wear and drove over to Goodwill. He opened his trunk and stared at Flynn's clothing. Those suits were all that Sancho had left of the Flynn he knew. Sancho couldn't bear to abandon the last bit of James that existed, so he kept the clothes in the trunk of his car. Every time he saw them, he'd feel sad and guilty; sad that his friend was gone and guilty that he wasn't happy that Jimmy had found his sanity.

When Flynn returned to City of Roses, he wanted his old room back along with his clothes. He was convinced he had been on an undercover assignment at Hot Dog on a Stick. That was why he turned into Jimmy. Why he gained all the weight and changed his accent. His assignment was to infiltrate the Armenian mafia and he believed that Mr. Papazian, the elderly mall security guard, was his inside man. Goolardo's attack was unexpected and had blown his carefully constructed cover. Now he had to start all over. Drop the weight. Get back in shape. Turn himself into the lean, fit, lethal weapon he once was. At least, that's what he told Sancho.

All eyes focused on the TV. Sancho was surprised by how quiet everyone was. Leeza Gibbons and Mark Steines hosted the parade on KTLA and their professionally cheerful patter filled the recreation room.

"Congratulations to the City of Sierra Madre," Steines said with his resonant radio announcer voice. "They are this year's trophy winner for the most outstanding display of fantasy and imagination." Sancho saw a float with a big green dragon, a knight in shining armor, and three beautiful princesses.

"We are reminded that chivalry isn't dead," Leeza Gibbons said. "Helping others through acts of kindness takes courage!"

"The young knight is crafted from rice powder, silver leaf, and cranberry seed," Steines said.

"The dragon's made from galax leaves, pepitas, mung beans, and cornmeal grit," Leeza added. "And ñriding with them we see three beautiful princesses from the Rose Queen's Royal Court!"

The princesses shivered in their revealing outfits. Ty grinned. "Those shawties are freezing their asses off. Looks cold as hell out there."

"It's all relative," Q replied. "In northern Minnesota it's likely ten below zero right now."

"I miss the old Rose Parade hosts," Doris Frawley said. "Bob Eubanks and Stephanie Edwards had such great chemistry." At ninety-one, she was the oldest patient at City of Roses. A former beauty queen from Arkansas, she arrived in California in 1948 and worked as a bit player in two Cecil B. DeMille extravaganzas.

Doris had dated Jack Parsons, the eccentric founder of the Jet Propulsion Laboratory, and L. Ron Hubbard, the equally eccentric founder of the Church of Scientology. She participated in sex magick rituals in various locations around Pasadena, La Cañada, and San Marino and in 1952, shortly after Parson's death, gave birth to the anti-Christ. At least that was what she relayed to Sancho.

"Bob and Stephanie were the best hosts ever." Doris flashed her once-famous smile. "He is so darn handsome and Stephanie Edwards has such pretty blue eyes. It's just not the same without them. What do you think, Mr. Flynn?"

"I have to agree," Flynn said. He returned Doris' smile and she reciprocated by batting her eyes.

"Of course, he's not as handsome as you. You do know we missed you here, don't you?"

"I missed you as well, Doris."

"Did I ever tell you I once dated Kirk Douglas?"

"Indeed, you did."

"And William Holden. And Marlon Brando."

"You've lived quite the life, Doris. Turned many a head."

"I'm not the beauty I once was, but I still know how to treat a man right." She lowered her gaze and parted her lips and looked up at Flynn in a pose that mimicked her famous 1950s pinup picture.

"Nothing like a woman with experience," Flynn said.

The forty-something Filipino nurse sitting next to Doris was touched by Flynn's kindness towards the elderly starlet and offered Flynn a smile of her own. Mrs. Reyes was recently divorced, and Sancho could see she was already falling for Flynn's confidence and easy charm.

"Here we go," he whispered to no one in particular.

•   •   •

Upside down with his feet in the air and his heels against the wall, shirtless and glistening with sweat, Flynn did inverted push-up after inverted push-up. The hospital workout area was open as the yoga class was over. Sancho watched Flynn through the little window in the door and marveled at his fitness.

He'd dropped forty pounds in six months. He was tight, taut, muscular, and cut. Sancho could barely get himself to take the stairs let alone get to the gym, but here Flynn was already back in top condition.

Soon after his return, Flynn instituted a brutal exercise regimen. At first, he could barely do ten push-ups. But he kept at it, three times a day, increasing his reps to twenty then thirty then fifty then one hundred. He did wide grip, close grip, one clap, one-legged, and one-handed. Every morning began with four sets of fifty inverted pushups, followed by five hundred crunches, reverse crunches, V-Ups, and

Torso Twisters. After breakfast, he would jump rope for a full hour and then do yoga stretches and move to hell squats, frog hops, lunges, planks, pull-ups, chin-ups, and hanging straight leg raises.

He was just as careful with his diet. At City of Roses, meals were mostly carbs. Flynn ignored them and stuck with protein and vegetables. The pounds didn't melt off all at once. He would plateau for a week or two, but he stuck with it and showed no weakness.

In the afternoon, Flynn ended his daily exercise regimen with a series of complex Shotokan karate katas. He moved gracefully, yet with purpose and aggression, kicking, spinning, sweeping, and punching with precision, speed, and power, reducing his imaginary opponents to pummeled heaps of defeat. Flynn was consistent and disciplined and by July he was once again back to his fighting weight.

Sancho wasn't the only one watching Flynn pump out his inverted pushups. His afternoon exercise routines drew the attention of quite a few of the nurses, including Mrs. Reyes, who Sancho saw sneaking out of Flynn's room one morning before dawn.

Flynn grunted as he completed his last inverted push-up. With his feet back on the floor, he wiped his glistening face and torso with a towel.

"Looking good, mano," Sancho said.

"Getting there. You should join me now and then, amigo. You could stand to lose a few yourself."

"I get to the gym now and then. Not a lot of time between working here and going to school."

"And Alyssa? How much time do you have for her?"

"Not as much as I'd like."

"Is she still working at El Pollo Loco?"

"Yep and taking classes at PCC. With both of us so busy, we don't have as much time to hang out, so I was thinking maybe we should move into together."

"That's a big step."

"I know."

"I'll be honest"—Flynn threw the towel over his shoulder—"sustaining a lasting long-term relationship can be difficult for people who do what we do."

"I guess."

"Traveling the world, dealing in danger, risking death. But the most difficult part is keeping secrets from those we love as that's the only way to keep them safe. By dint of what we do, we put them in peril. Having a wife and family makes an agent vulnerable. If I can keep a distance from those I love, I can keep them out of harm's way."

"Doesn't that get kind of lonely?"

"Yes. But that's the sacrifice I make to keep this world safe. Luckily, there are others, like you, who understand what I do, and in my world, those are the only friends I can afford."

"So, you never want to have kids?"

"How can I? A man who lives like I do? They too would be put at risk. Besides, as often as I'm gone, how could I ever be a proper father? I would never be there to tuck them in at night or help with their homework." A flicker of pain passed behind Flynn's eyes and he quickly changed the subject. "Any word on Goolardo?"

Sancho shook his head. "Nope."

"Those stupid policemen wouldn't listen to me. They let him get away."

"They'll find him."

"I asked N to send me after him, but he said there's a joint taskforce already tracking them down. FBI. DEA. The Marshals service. But they don't know him like I do. They don't know how he thinks."

"I'm sure Nickelson has his reasons."

"Do you think he's using me as bait? Hoping Goolardo and Mendoza will come for me here?"

"You think they'd come for you here?" The possibility hadn't occurred to Sancho.

"N's a hard man who makes hard choices. Sending men into battle. Sending men to die. Perhaps he is simply setting a trap."

Sancho's blood pressure rose along with his anxiety. "Guess that's why that cop car is always parked outside. It's not like it's a secret you're here. You're blowing up on YouTube, dude."

"Excuse me?"

"YouTube. It's on the internet."

"I know what YouTube is."

"That video that Becky shot. The attack at the mall. It has like fifteen million views. People are putting music to it. Movie music. Heavy metal. It's crazy."

"That might explain why all those reporters are hounding me."

"Yeah, that's crazy too."

"Becky never should have posted that video. Luckily, she identified me as Jimmy from Hot Dog On a Stick. So, everyone thinks I'm a mental patient and that this facility is actually a mental hospital. So at least, for now, our cover story is holding."

"Yeah. Good thing."

Nurse Durkin opened the door to the workout room, and she was not smiling. Of course, that wasn't unusual. Nurse Durkin never smiled. At six feet tall, she tipped the scales at two hundred pounds and had a stare that could cut through steel.

"What are you doing in here, Perez?"

Sancho had no answer for her as she glared at him.

"Don't you have patients to attend to?"

"Yes, ma'am. I do."

Flynn offered Durkin a smile. "Nurse Durkin! What a wonderful surprise."

"What did I tell you about monopolizing this room, Mr. Flynn?"

"N wants me in tip-top shape. I'm just keeping myself fit and ready for whatever is necessary."

"Don't you have group therapy?"

"Not for another hour." Flynn stepped closer and turned on the charm." Perhaps you'd care to join me for a bit of exercise yourself?"

But Durkin was impervious to Flynn's charisma. "From now on this room is off limits to you. And Perez, stop spending so much time with Mr. Flynn and attend to your other patients."

"I'm sorry if I've been monopolizing Mr. Perez's attention. But I consider him a friend and colleague."

"But he's not your friend. He's an orderly and you're his patient. It's time you understood who you are and why you're here, Mr. Flynn. Put on your shirt and follow me."

"Right now?"

"Put on your shirt!"

Flynn put on his t-shirt and black warm-up jacket. He offered Sancho a surreptitious grin as he followed Nurse Durkin out the door.

. . .

Durkin led Flynn down the hallway at a brisk pace. She glanced back at him. He smiled at her and that just irritated her to no end. She didn't understand how all those other nurses were so easily taken in by him.

This was Nurse Durkin's fourteenth year as an employee of City of Roses and twenty-sixth year as a member of the California Nurses Association. As one of the most senior employees at the institute, she was both respected and feared by senior management and the hospital's board of directors. As Head Nurse for the last seven years, she knew where all the bodies were buried and was privy to every scandal and screw up.

She thought Nickelson was too lax with many of the patients, especially those who suffered from delusions. He didn't confront their delusional behavior the way she believed was necessary. Flynn was the perfect example. Nickelson relied more on therapy than on medication and she thought that method antiquated at best. He finally agreed to put Flynn on anti-depressants only after therapy failed to pull him out of the severe depression he fell into following his escape and misadventures.

Eventually, at Durkin's urging, he even prescribed an antipsychotic. The result was that Flynn's delusional thinking disappeared. He recovered to such a degree that Nickelson sent him to live in a residential treatment facility. Durkin didn't think Flynn was ready and told Nickelson as much. In the end, she was right, as it only took one traumatic incident to bring his delusions back. Now Nickelson was reluctant to continue with the antipsychotics. He was back to treating him with psychotherapy, allowing him to once again live in fantasy.

Nurse Durkin refused to indulge Flynn.

His fame had finally faded and life at City of Roses just returned to normal when that incident at the Galleria made the man more famous than ever. He was all over the news. Reporters camped outside City of Roses, hoping for an interview or an exclusive or even a passing glimpse. Durkin had no patience for those who wanted to turn Flynn into something other than what he was; a deeply disturbed and delusional mental patient. The onslaught caused the hospital to beef up security and she did everything she could to keep the reporters at bay. As far as she was concerned, the situation at the hospital was now untenable and Durkin was determined to put an end to it. She knew Flynn would screw up again and when he did, she'd be waiting for him.

Durkin stopped outside the door to the group therapy room and glared at Flynn. "Unless you'd like to see Perez fired, you need to stay away from him. Is that understood?"

Flynn nodded. "Yes, mum."

"It's not mum. I'm not your mum. Is that clear?"

"Of course, operational security requires that we stick to our covers. I understand completely."

Durkin scowled and pointed, and Flynn entered the room. She shook her head as she strode off, more determined than ever to get rid of him. Only this time, he would go to a place that wouldn't indulge his heroic delusions. This time, he would be sent somewhere like the Atascadero State Hospital for the Criminally Insane.

CHAPTER EIGHT

Nellie Bly was not only one of the first women journalists, but an investigative reporter who often put herself in danger to get the story. Writing in the 1880s, she investigated the dictatorship of Porfirio Diaz in Mexico and had to flee the country to avoid arrest. She recreated Phileas Fogg's trip in "Around the World in 80 Days" by circumnavigating the planet in seventy-two days, taking only the dress she was wearing, an overcoat, and a few changes of underwear. She stopped bathing and brushing her teeth and stayed up for days on end to feign insanity and go undercover in the Woman's Lunatic Asylum on Blackwell's Island. Once inside, she documented horrible, dangerous, and inhumane conditions and was only set free after the newspaper sent a lawyer to arrange for her release.

Bettina O'Toole-Applebaum grew up in Chicago, Illinois. Her father was the great-grandson of a slave and her mother was an Ashkenazi Jew. She was baptized as a baby, but later was bat mitzvahed at Temple Shalom on Lakeshore Drive at the urging of her mother's parents. She majored in English at Knox College and received a master's from the Medill School of Journalism at Northwestern University. After interning at Chicago Magazine, she went on to write for Mother Jones, The New Yorker, Vanity Fair, and Rolling Stone. Intrigued with the coverage on Flynn, she requested an interview. Seventeen times. And each time she was refused. So instead of asking again, she decided to get herself some facetime with Flynn, Nellie Bly-style.

Bettina didn't shower or brush her teeth for two weeks. She wore the same clothes for that entire time and didn't sleep the three days before she voluntarily committed herself to the City of Roses

Psychiatric Institute. She claimed she was having suicidal thoughts and the doctor on duty diagnosed her with depression and borderline personality disorder.

Once inside City of Roses, Bettina discovered that she didn't seem any more or less crazy than anyone else. She wasn't a stranger to depression and struggled with anxiety and OCD. She had been on anti-depressants and anti-anxiety medication for most of her twenties, so fitting in didn't require much more than being herself. And that's exactly what she did when she found herself in a group therapy session in a small conference room with five other patients.

One of them was James Flynn.

She'd watched the video of the incident at the Glendale Galleria multiple times, but Flynn looked almost nothing like that man. He was at least fifty pounds lighter and wore a black polyester warm-up suit that fit him like a glove. He was tall and lean and powerfully built. His eyes were a gunmetal blue and he was strikingly handsome. Movie star handsome. His English accent had a touch of Scottish burr and it was spot on. She spent a semester in London at King's College and knew an authentic English accent when she heard one. She could tell Flynn found her attractive as he flirted with her shamelessly. But then Flynn seemed to flirt with every female he encountered. He even flirted with Doris Frawley; a ninety-one-year-old former 1950s pin-up queen.

Bettina was used to men coming onto her, but she had no illusions about her looks. She knew she wasn't a bombshell. She was on the short side and because of that, battled her weight ever since junior high. She kept herself in shape with Pilates, yoga and morning runs around her Echo Park neighborhood. Her ex-boyfriend, a writer at Rolling Stone, told her she looked a little like an amber-eyed Rashida Jones. Others had said the same. She kept her distance from Flynn at first. She didn't want to come on too strong and raise any suspicions. Her intention was to play the long game and get Flynn to trust her. To open up to her. Which was why she finagled herself into Flynn's therapy group.

The fifty-something female psychologist who ran the session offered Bettina a big smile. "Welcome everyone. As you can see, we have someone new joining us today. Her name is Bettina and she has only been at City of Roses for a few days."

The group mumbled a greeting with not a lot of enthusiasm, but Flynn, at least, offered her a charming smile.

"I'm Dr. Judy," the psychologist said and then went around the room, introducing each patient in turn. She nodded to a thin, elderly man with a shock of curly white hair and an equally unruly beard. "This is Quentin, though he often goes by Q." Q nodded at Bettina, but quickly looked away. Next to Q sat a chubby, twenty-one-year-old African American man wearing a baggy Oakland Raider's jersey with number twenty-four. "That's Ty."

"Hey, Betty." Ty stared at Bettina intently, but didn't say anything more.

Dr. Judy motioned to a large middle-aged man with a big white beard. "This is Rodney."

"Hey," said Rodney.

"Next to Rodney is Mary Alice." Mary Alice looked furious. She was a big-boned middle-aged, freckle-faced lady in her late fifties with dyed red hair and graying roots.

"Bettina?" Mary Alice spit out the name with contempt. She had a southern accent and sounded like she smoked three packs a day. "What kind of nitwit name is that?"

"Now, now, Mary Alice."

"I'm not blaming her. It's not her fault her dumb-ass hippie parents hung that on her. What the hell happened to all the normal names like Susan or Nancy or Amy?"

"Or Mary Alice," Rodney added.

"Exactly," Mary Alice croaked, her face getting red as she revved herself up. "All these millennial names like Paisley or Destiny or Sierra? Everybody has to be a special precious snowflake nowadays. They can't just be normal!"

"Center yourself, Mary Alice. Breathe. Take a deep breath."

Mary Alice glared at Dr. Judy, but finally, she relented and inhaled deeply before letting it out and letting her anger dissipate. Until she noticed Ty staring at her. "What the hell you looking at, fatty?"

Ty immediately looked down, cowed by Mary Alice's volcanic rage.

"Jesus Christ, Mary Alice," Rodney said. "Hold it together!"

"Fuck you," Mary Alice growled. "Maybe I'm having a shitty day. Stuck in this stupid hospital with a bunch of half-wit lunatics!"

"I've known quite a few redheads with fiery tempers." Flynn raised a flirtatious eyebrow at Mary Alice. "And you're no exception. But I hope you know you're among friends here."

Bettina was surprised to see Mary Alice's whole demeanor change in an instant. She offered Flynn her version of a come-hither smile, pushing her tongue coyly between her tobacco-stained teeth. "Well, aren't you a love? At least *you* understand where I'm coming from."

"You're a passionate person," Flynn said.

"Yes, I am."

"Yes, indeed. But that's why you must direct your fury towards our real enemies, because make no mistake, Mary Alice, they are out there, and they are waiting to strike. Q knows what I'm talking about."

"What?" Q had drifted to sleep, but the mention of his name startled him awake.

"You know our enemies never rest, which is why you never do, Q. Why you're constantly creating cutting edge technology to aid in the battle against those who would do us harm."

"What kind of cutting-edge technology?" Bettina asked.

"Quentin ain't making shit," Ty said.

"It's all right, Ty, we can talk to Bettina. If she's here at headquarters I'm sure she has the proper clearances. Go ahead Q. Tell us what you've been working on."

"Well, I'm still consulting for DARPA as I was one of the minds who originally conceived of that particular agency."

"DARPA?" Bettina asked.

"The Defense Advanced Research Projects Agency," Q replied.

"Bullshit," Ty said.

"Currently I'm working on an ultrasonic weapon that can create traumatic brain injury, hearing loss, and damage to the central nervous system," said Q.

"Have you been testing it on yourself?" Mary Alice asked.

Q ignored her snarky comment. "It interferes with synaptical communication and can also affect the inner ear, causing vertigo and nausea. Some believe a similar technology was used against U.S. and Canadian diplomats living in Havana, Cuba in 2017."

"What else?" prompted Flynn.

"Self-guiding bullets. A real-time optical guidance system allows them to change direction and target in flight. So, no matter how bad a shot someone is, they can never miss."

"That's…astounding."

"Not as astounding as my Cyborg insect spies. I implant nano-computers in their little brains and control them using the neural implant inserted into mine. I direct them where to go. Who to watch. Who to sting. I can even see through their eyes. That fly on the window there? That's one of mine."

"So, make that fly over there fly over here to me," said Ty.

"Why? So, you can smash it? I don't think so."

Ty stood up, walked to the window, and smacked his hand against the glass in an attempt to squish the fly. The windowed shattered and a jagged edge severed an artery in his right wrist. Flynn was up and on his feet. He tore off his jacket and wrapped it around Ty's arm, twisting it into a tourniquet. Dr. Judy yelled down the hall for help. Orderlies rushed in, Sancho among them, and they carried Ty to the infirmary, blood leaking everywhere.

The rest of the group sat there in silence after Ty was carried out. Bettina noticed a spray of blood on the wall.

"Would anyone like to say anything?" Dr. Judy noticed a few bright red drops on her white silk blouse.

"Don't let that set." Mary Alice poked her finger toward the bloodstains. "You want to wet that with cold water before that dries. Dab it with diluted ammonia and rub with soap."

Q pointed to a fly on another window that was still intact. "My mind-controlled fly easily avoided him. Look at him. I can see the world through his compound eyes, each one consisting of thousands of individual visual receptors."

Dr. Judy stood up. She offered everyone a tight frustrated smile. "I think we can call it a day. I will see you all Thursday. Same time. Same place."

• • •

Later, at lunch, Bettina saw Flynn eating with Rodney and Q and approached their table. "Do you mind if I join you, gentlemen?"

"Please," Flynn said as he pointed to a chair. He had changed out of his black warm-up outfit and now wore a vintage light-gray Brioni suit and some well-worn Italian loafers. He was, by far, the best dressed man in the cafeteria.

Bettina put down her tray and sat next to Q, across from Flynn. "That was very quick thinking today, the way you turned your shirt into a tourniquet."

"Training. Of course, I'd rather be using that training in the field, but for now N wants me here. I believe he's using me for bait."

Rodney Shoop looked up from his Swiss Steak. "Bait?"

"Goolardo wants me dead and N is trying to draw him in."

"Here?" Rodney's normally reddish complexion turned pale.

"Speaking of Goolardo, how's your arm? Lucky for you that bullet you took went right through the meat and missed the bone."

"Yeah," Rodney said sarcastically. "Lucky me." He looked at Bettina. "Freakin' EMT's put me on morphine in the damn ambulance. The doc gave me Oxy for the pain and before you know it, I'm freakin' hooked again. That's why I'm back in here. I almost OD'd."

"You're in detox?" asked Bettina.

"Yeah. You?"

"No, I was feeling like I wanted to hurt myself so I thought maybe I should, you know…"

"Yeah, I know," Rodney said.

"Have you heard anything new on Mr. Papazian?" Flynn queried.

"They moved him to a convalescent hospital in Burbank," Rodney replied. "Got him started on physical therapy."

"That's good news."

"He's frickin' lucky he's alive. Assholes shot him three times."

Bettina watched as Q tore into his meatloaf like a ravenous wildebeest. He didn't cut it, just picked up the entire rectangular chunk and bit into it. Gravy dribbled into his beard. She looked at the sad dinner salad on her tray, speared a cherry tomato and popped it in her mouth.

"So where were you posted previously, Bettina?" Flynn queried. "I haven't seen you here at headquarters before."

Bettina pointed to her mouth to indicate she was chewing and when she finished the bite said, "I've been all around. New York. San Francisco. London. Berlin."

"And what do you do? Are you a field agent? A cyber security specialist? A counterintelligence analyst?"

Bettina hesitated as she wasn't sure if she should play along with Flynn's delusion. She obviously didn't want to let him know what she really did, but she was having second thoughts about her cover story. Flynn's eyes locked on her like heat-seeking missiles and she knew she had to say something. "Cyber security."

"I see. So, you're an expert in virtual private networks?"

"Um, yeah."

"Do you work with web application firewalls?"

"Um, sometimes."

"What about secure socket layers?"

"What about them?"

"Do you even know what they are?"

"Yeah, they are socket layers that are extra, you know, secure."

Flynn focused on Bettina with laser-like intensity. "You have no idea what I'm talking about do you?"

"Of course, I do."

"A woman as attractive as you showing up here out of the blue, ingratiating yourself with me? I can't help but wonder if you're here under false pretenses."

"What do you mean?"

"I have a sixth sense about these things, Bettina, if that's even your name. I can tell when someone's lying to me just by looking into their eyes."

Bettina couldn't disguise her surprise and looked down at her salad to hide her guilty baby blues. She speared a garbanzo bean and took a bite.

"Look at me Bettina. Be honest with me."

"I am!"

"I like the feigned outrage, but I'm not buying it. Not one bit. Who do you work for? Smersh? Spectre? The Corsican Mafia? Or is it Goolardo?"

"Goolardo?"

"Did he send in a beautiful assassin to finish the job?"

She laughed at that. "You think I'm an assassin?"

"It wouldn't be the first time a ravishing young woman was sent to do away with me. You seem fit. Strong. I'm guessing you're an expert in some sort of deadly art. Ninjutsu perhaps?"

"I'm more into Pilates."

Flynn picked up a spork. "I could take this spork and open your carotid artery, but I wouldn't want to ruin lunch for everyone. So, for now, I'll let you live." Flynn offered her one of his patented charming grins. "Perhaps I'll even be able to turn you once I get to know you better and show you the error of your ways."

Bettina was simultaneously terrified and strangely turned on. She blushed. Something she hadn't done since junior high.

Nurse Durkin clip-clopped into the cafeteria, saw Flynn, and barked across the room at him. "Mr. Flynn, Dr. Nickelson would like to see you."

"N?"

"Dump your lunch and get a move on, mister. The doctor doesn't have all day."

• • •

Flynn poked his head into the anteroom outside N's office, pleased to see Miss Honeywell typing away on a computer keyboard.

"Miss Honeywell." Flynn's voice was full of affection for N's buxom, fifty-something, African American administrative assistant.

He perched himself on the edge of her desk and smiled down at her. "Looking luscious as always."

"Take a seat, Mr. Flynn. He'll be with you shortly."

"I love what you've done with your hair."

"And I would love you to get your butt off my desk and sit your ass down over there."

"I do like a woman who knows what she wants and isn't afraid to ask for it."

"And I like a man who does what he's told and shuts the hell up about it." She pointed at the sofa and Flynn sat his ass down. She went back to typing.

"Do you have any idea what this is about?"

"I do not," Honeywell said. "But the Doctor does have a visitor and I believe it might have something to do with you."

"Can you say who the visitor is?"

"I can, but I won't, so you're just going to have to wait."

"I've been waiting for you forever, Honeywell."

"You don't give up, do you?"

"Why would I? Any man would be lucky to have you."

"Tell that to my ex."

"Clearly he was a fool and you deserve so much more. You know that, don't you?"

Honeywell looked up at him. "If you were an employee here, you'd be out on the street, fired for sexual harassment by now. You know that, right?"

"Sexual harassment?"

"This is not 1965, Mr. Flynn. I know you don't know any better, but you need to get a clue. You can't just hit on every single female you run into."

"I'm just being friendly and perhaps a little flirtatious, but if you prefer we maintain a more business-like relationship, I can accommodate that."

"Bullshit."

"I promise."

"You are a dog, Mr. Flynn. A player to the first degree."

"I do like to play."

"That's what they say. Players play. Now put a sock in it so I can get some work done here."

Flynn pretended to zip his lip and fifteen minutes later, the door to N's office opened and Nickelson beckoned him in.

Flynn stood, winked at Honeywell, and walked in to find that N did indeed have a guest; a tall blonde in a black Armani business suit that fit her slender body perfectly. Her shoulders were naturally broad. Flynn deduced she was once an athlete. She carried herself with confidence and appeared to be in her early thirties. Her ash-blonde hair fell to her shoulders and framed a face that could have easily appeared on the cover of Vogue. Much of her beauty came from her strength and the fearlessness in her ice-blue eyes.

"I'd like you to meet Ms. Severina Angelli."

"Severina, please."

"Delighted. Please call me James."

"She works for Mr. Sergei Belenki," Nickelson explained.

"Belenki, yes, the high-tech billionaire. Founder of the Blinky Social Network and the CTO of the Electro Go car company."

"And the man whose life you saved a little over a year ago," Severina added.

"I did what anyone would do."

"That I doubt. He has not forgotten what you did for him and because of that he'd like to offer you a proposition."

Flynn raised a flirty eyebrow. "What sort of proposition?"

"Perhaps he should tell you himself." She slid a tablet computer from a large briefcase and pushed a button to initiate a Blinky Face-to-Face call. The tablet was so large Severina needed to hold it with two hands. Within seconds Sergei Belenki's large bearded face filled the screen.

"Sergei?"

"Hello Severina."

"I have Mr. Flynn."

"James, please," Flynn insisted.

Severina turned the tablet towards Flynn and held it head high so Flynn could look directly into Sergei's eyes. Flynn remembered him well from the incident on Angel Island. It was Belenki's custom Boeing

737 that Goolardo highjacked when he kidnapped the ten richest men in the world from Randall Beckner's annual masters of the universe conference.

Belenki was the youngest billionaire there. Born in Russia, his parents brought him to the U.S. when he was seven. He earned a bachelor's degree in mathematics at UCLA, a master's in computer science at Stanford, and a PhD in advanced computer intelligence at MIT. At six feet tall, he was slightly shorter than Flynn, but taller than most of the other billionaires kidnapped that day. Flynn saved them all and he remembered that Belenki spent most of that time crying.

"It is good to see you, sir," Belenki said. "Much better circumstances than the last time."

"That was quite a plane ride. I hope I didn't do too much damage to your 737."

"Nothing that couldn't be repaired."

"So, what do I owe the pleasure?"

"I saw you on YouTube. That attack at the mall."

"Goolardo is a determined man."

"And so are you apparently as once again you saved the day."

"Though regrettably, Goolardo got away."

"Nevertheless, it was good to see you in action again and it gave me an idea. This year has been very difficult for me, as Severina can attest to."

Flynn couldn't see Severina's reaction to that since she was holding the tablet with Sergei's face directly in front of her own. "Difficult in what way?" Flynn queried.

"Blinky, my social networking platform, has created some problems for me. A foreign power took advantage of vulnerabilities in our system and used Blinky to sway the American electorate in the last election."

"I heard about that," Flynn said.

"I had to attend congressional hearings and testify before the House Intelligence Committee."

"And those vulnerabilities? Have you fixed the problem?"

"The problem is inherent in our system. Much like criminals take advantage of our freedoms to play games with our legal system, these foreign nationals used the freedom and functionality built into Blinky to spread disinformation and propaganda."

"I'd like to help you if I could, but the skills necessary to solve that problem are far beyond my purview. Besides, even if I could, hasn't that horse already left the barn?"

"It has, yes, and that's the issue. After that congressional hearing, the FBI came knocking. They demanded all my raw data. At first, I refused as I take the privacy of my users very seriously."

"Though you do occasionally sell it to those who can profit off it."

"We don't sell the raw data to advertisers," Severina said, inserting herself into the conversation. "However, we do use the information that consumers provide to help advertisers target ads to a specific audience."

"Knowledge is power," Flynn said.

"And in this case, the FBI wanted that power." Belenki leaned into the camera, filling the frame with his bristly face. "They wanted what those foreign nationals stole and everything else I had on them."

"I'm assuming you're talking *Russian* nationals?"

"Yes. The FBI issued a subpoena and offered me a proffer. I either had to cooperate with their investigation or Blinky would face oppressive multibillion-dollar fines and catastrophic regulations. So, I agreed to give them that data and I did it gladly, but covertly. No one could ever know, and they agreed to that. They agreed to keep my company's cooperation top secret. Part of what we gave them was apparently information on how and where the Russian mob launders their money."

"And there isn't much difference between the Russian mob and the Russian Federation at this point, is there?" Flynn pointed out.

"No there isn't," Belenki agreed.

"I suspect your cooperation with the FBI didn't stay secret."

"No, some hacker got his hands on the proffer and put it out on Openleaks for everyone to see."

"Do you know who?"

"It could be anyone. An anti-capitalist anarchist. A disgruntled employee. A business rival. A man as successful as I am has a lot of enemies."

"And now, I assume the Russian mob wants to make an example of you."

"Sadly, I believe they do."

"It's likely the Solntsevskaya Brotherhood. They are prominent in the banking sector and launder trillions for the oligarchs as they operate under the direct protection of the FSB."

"You see, this is why I need your help. You know things."

"A man as wealthy as you? Surely, you have expert protection."

"Do you remember Mr. Harper?"

"The head of security on Angel Island? He's former Delta Force, is he not?"

"Yes, and he's brought on a large team and they're all former special forces. But I worry that he and his detail might not see every threat headed my way. I need someone who operates outside predictable parameters. Someone who can anticipate the unexpected. Someone like you."

"But I'm not a free agent. I work for N."

"Which is why we came to him first." Severina moved the tablet away from her face so she could look Flynn in the eye. "We are prepared to pay you very well for your time. A million dollars for a few weeks of work."

"I was obligated to let you hear their proposition," Nickelson explained. "Our attorneys told me if I kept this proffer from you, we could very well be held liable for lost income. However, I can't in good conscience recommend that you accept Mr. Belenki's generous offer. Perhaps at some point in the future, but at the moment I do believe it's better for you to remain here."

"We would also be willing to donate a similar amount in kind to your...facility," Belenki stated.

"That's very generous of you, sir, and we would appreciate any donation you'd like to make at any time. However, I'm afraid I still can't give James my approval."

"He's using me as bait, you see, to lure in Francisco Goolardo."

"What?" Nickelson looked surprised.

"You can deny it, sir, but I know how you think. In your own stoic way, you're as ruthless as I am."

"You think Goolardo would come here?"

"He already sent an assassin here undercover as a patient, but now that I've outed her, he will have no choice but to come himself, and this time I'm sure he'll come in force."

"What are you saying?"

"I'm saying what you're saying. This is where we will make our stand. No matter how many killers he brings with him, whatever weapons they wield, we will all fight to the death if necessary."

Nickelson looked stricken. Flynn was surprised by that.

"That is your plan, is it not?"

"Perhaps I've been too hasty in my assessment of Mr. Belenki's offer." A few beads of sweat popped up on Nickelson's forehead. "After all, one day you will leave here, and that kind of money could come in very handy."

"That's true," Flynn admitted.

"And if Mr. Belenki has a large, well-trained, heavily armed security force, perhaps you'd be better off working in concert with them."

"That does make sense, sir. Not everyone here at headquarters is operational."

"If you were to go, however, I would insist that someone from here accompanies you."

"And we would be glad to compensate them as well," Severina said. "Very well."

"Sancho and I are a good team." Flynn aimed his gaze at Nickelson. "I'd like to bring him with if that's all right?"

"If Sancho wants to go, I wouldn't object, but I may send someone else with you as well. Someone with a little more…experience."

"I'll leave that decision up to you, sir," Flynn said.

"Good. Then it's decided." Belenki's voice took on an authoritative tone. "Severina will arrange transportation for this Friday, and I suggest that Mr. Flynn and anyone accompanying him bring formal wear as there will be a charity event on the night of their arrival. Black tie only."

"I look forward to it," Flynn said.

Belenki grinned. "Thank you, Mr. Flynn."

"James, please."

"Yes, James. See you soon."

Belenki signed off and his face disappeared from the screen. Severina returned the tablet to her briefcase. "All right then. This Friday morning we'll be flying out of Burbank Airport on Mr. Belenki's private jet. I'll send a limo to pick you up promptly at nine." She nodded to Nickelson and offered Flynn a rare smile. "Until then."

CHAPTER NINE

In 1914, Railroad mogul, Henry Huntington, opened the most luxurious hotel in San Marino. He promoted The Huntington Hotel as a winter resort to millionaires, entertainers, and political figures from the Midwest and East Coast, looking to bask in the California sunshine. Later it became a Sheraton and then a Ritz and finally a Langham.

*The Langham Hospitality group was originally an English company but was purchased by the Great Eagle Hospitality Group of Hong Kong in 1995. Ironically, the Huntington family employed more than ten thousand Chinese immigrants to lay the most treacherous part of their transcontinental railroad through the Sierra. Now the Chinese owned the very hotel that was built with money made from their backbreaking labor; a perfect illustration of the Buddhist concept of Karma.*因果报应

Severina argued with Sergei Belenki from her luxurious suite in San Marino's Langham Hotel. The tablet lay propped against a paisley pillow on an elegant red crushed-velvet chaise longue. Her boss looked irritated, but Severina wasn't a yes-woman or an ass-kisser and she told him exactly what she thought.

"He's delusional. He has no real training and his grip on reality isn't just tenuous, it's non-existent."

"Yes, but you haven't seen him in action," Belenki said.

"I saw the video from the mall, and he was *lucky*. He attacked them with a squirt gun!"

"Filled with bleach."

"Sir, this is your life we're talking about here. Do you really want to put it in the hands of a mental patient?"

"If it wasn't for Mr. Flynn, I wouldn't be alive right now. I wouldn't be talking to you. And you wouldn't be working for me making whatever it is I pay you to do whatever it is you do."

"Before I joined Blinky, I had seven-figure offers from Apple, Google, Cisco, and Salesforce. But I honestly believe you are a visionary and that's why I work for you. Why I'm proud to work for you. And why I want to protect you."

"I have Mr. Harper and his army of special ops soldiers protecting me, Severina. Flynn would just be an additional layer of security."

"I think you're making a mistake."

"I've made my fortune doing things other men would never attempt or even dream of attempting. Taking chances like that requires a leap of faith. Early on, few venture capitalists were willing to take that leap. Those who did are now worth billions. Many who didn't are still angry with me. Speaking of which, did you settle that suit with Meisner?"

"Not yet, but we're close."

"He's an irrational man and always has been."

"As part of the settlement, I'm insisting on a nondisclosure agreement."

"Andy's a perfect example of someone afraid to take that leap. And now he blames me for his lack of backbone. Don't be like my former partner. Don't be like Andrew Meisner. Take a leap of faith with me, Severina."

"I will. I am. But I wouldn't be earning my salary if I didn't express my reservations."

"And I appreciate your honesty, but I've made up my mind."

Belenki's disembodied head disappeared as he ended the call.

Severina sighed.

• • •

Sancho wondered what Dr. Nickelson could possibly want. He sat on Nickelson's slightly saggy couch, waited patiently, and watched as the senior psychiatrist at City of Roses finished up some paperwork.

"I apologize, Mr. Perez, but Ms. Honeywell insists she needs these signatures."

Ms. Honeywell stood right next to him, watching to make sure he signed each and every page.

Sancho worried that Nurse Durkin was talking shit about him again. She probably told Nickelson that he was shirking his duties to bullshit with Flynn. What was her problem? She had to be the nastiest woman ever. She would have made a damn scary nun.

He spent two years in parochial school and some of those nuns were brutal as hell. Smacking him on the back of the head. Pulling him by the ear. Whacking him on the knuckles with a ruler. Those nuns were always in such a shitty mood. Just like Durkin. Unsmiling. Glowering. Ready to blow her top at any moment. She especially had it in for Flynn. Something about him just set her off. It didn't help that all the other nurses thought he was hot as hell.

Nickelson finished signing his paperwork and handed the stack to Honeywell, who offered a curt, "Thank you, sir," before walking out the door.

Nickelson raised his gaze to Sancho, who immediately went on the defensive. "I don't know what Nurse Durkin's been saying about me, sir, but I'm just trying to do my best here. James likes talking to me and I don't want to be rude or put him off or make him feel like I don't care about him, 'cause I do. We have a connection and I don't know what Nurse Durkin's problem is with him, but I just want to say that I think he's doing really well."

"Nurse Durkin has a difficult job, and she isn't the warmest woman, but I do appreciate her efficiency. However, I didn't invite you here today to talk about Nurse Durkin. I have a favor to ask of you."

"A favor?"

"Mr. Flynn was offered a temporary position with Sergei Belenki and he would like you to accompany him."

"A position? You're going to let him out again?"

"Health Management System Services initially balked at the idea, but when I told them that Mr. Belenki offered to pay both Mr. Flynn and the corporation a million dollars for a few weeks of work, they reconsidered."

"A million dollars?"

"That money could go a long way to paying for Mr. Flynn's care and eventually help him establish a life outside an institutional setting."

"Holy shit. I mean, wow, that's really…that's a lot of money."

"Yes, it is, and I didn't think it was right to deny him that opportunity."

"What would he do for Mr. Belenki?"

"He wants to employ him as a security consultant."

"Seriously?"

"He believes Mr. Flynn is someone who thinks outside the box."

"About a million miles outside the box."

Nickelson smiled at that. "Would you be willing to accompany him?"

"I don't know, sir. I'm in the middle of my last semester of classes and I'll be honest, I don't know if James should be doing security for anybody. As I'm sure you know, he doesn't have a real firm grasp on reality."

"Which is why I will be accompanying both of you. I'll be there to monitor the situation and make sure that nothing gets too far out of hand."

"Pardon my saying so, sir, but crap can get out of hand with James pretty damn fast."

"Which is why I want you there as well. Just in case."

"If I do this, I'll lose the whole semester. It's really not good timing for me. I'm sorry."

"Mr. Belenki has agreed to pay anyone who accompanies Flynn a weekly stipend as well."

"That's really nice of him, but I just don't think it makes sense for me right now."

"Not even for a quarter of a million dollars above and beyond your regular pay?"

"A quarter of a mil?"

"That's what he offered, but if you don't—

"Are you fucking kidding me?"

"Not at all. So, is that a yes?"

"That's a fuck yes!"

Nickelson laughed at that and Sancho laughed right along with him. Each one spurred the other on and the laughter grew louder and more raucous until slowly it began to wind down. Honeywell poked her head into the Nickelson's office to see what was happening. Sancho just grinned at her. She shook her head and left as Sancho laughed again.

Nickelson raised his hand to quiet him. "We will be leaving tomorrow morning. You need to pack for a few weeks and include some formal wear if you have any."

"You mean like a tux?"

"Or a nice suit. Apparently, there's some formal charity event that we will all need to attend."

"I have a suit."

"Good. Then we're all set. They'll be sending a limo to pick us up here at 9:00 a.m. sharp."

"Has Nurse Durkin heard about this?"

"This isn't any of Nurse Durkin's concern."

• • •

Bettina O'Toole-Applebaum was frustrated. Ever since Flynn accused her of being an assassin, he refused to have anything to do with her. She didn't know if he was keeping her at arm's length because he suspected she was the enemy or if he was simply playing hard to get. After a few days of this annoying cat and mouse game, Bettina finally managed to get Flynn alone after breakfast.

She cornered him in a corridor and he immediately started flirting. He suggested they move the conversation to a quieter, more private place. She hesitated at first. Was his intention to seduce her or terminate her? After all, he did believe he had a license to kill. She didn't want to put herself at any unnecessary risk, but the adrenalin generated by this possibility came with a generous dollop of lust. She wasn't sure if she was more aroused by the danger or the possibility of a Pulitzer. She didn't want to seduce Flynn, exactly. She wouldn't take it that far. But she wasn't above a little heavy-duty flirting, and that's how they ended up nose to nose in an equipment closet not far from the activity room.

"So how exactly were you planning to do it," Flynn pressed.

"Do what?"

"Do me in. Isn't that what you're here for?"

"No, that is *not* why I'm here."

"I should frisk you for a weapon, but I wouldn't want to overstep."

"Knock yourself out."

Bettina raised her hands and Flynn frisked her lightly and efficiently, running his fingers up and down her body, gently, but firmly feeling for a weapon, between her thighs and under her arms. She hadn't been touched by anyone in quite some time and the sensation was intoxicating. She closed her eyes and couldn't help but let a little sigh escape. When he felt under her armpits she giggled.

"Ticklish, are we?"

"Only in certain places."

"You clearly don't have a weapon."

"I come in peace I promise."

Flynn leaned in closer. "Then why do I sense you're hiding something from me?"

"What would I be hiding?"

"Who you are and why you're here."

"You are not a very trusting person," Bettina said, their lips now inches apart.

"I look in your eyes and I see hope, but I also see fear. You've been deceived, hurt and betrayed by those you put your faith in. That won't happen with me. Trust me with your truth and I promise I won't abandon you. I'll support you and protect you and be there whenever you need me."

Bettina teared up but didn't know why. A huge, empty loneliness ached at her core. She put her arms around Flynn and hugged him close and he gently stroked her hair.

"Thank you," she said.

"No need to thank me. Just tell me the truth. Were you sent here to assassinate me?"

A tear trickled down Bettina's face. "No, but I haven't been completely honest with you either."

"Time to come clean then."

"If I do, will you trust me?"

"Trust you? No. Truss you? Absolutely."

Flynn moved so fast, at first Bettina didn't know what was happening. He slid the canvas sleeves over her arms, spun her around, and pulled the straps of the straitjacket tight. She was firmly trussed as he looped another restraint around her ankles, attached a strap with a carabiner-like clip, and threw it over a support beam.

"What are you—" was all she could get out before Flynn tossed her over his shoulder and pulled her up by the strap until she was suspended upside down, dangling from the ceiling, bound and secure in the straitjacket. She struggled and fought to free herself. "Let me out of here! Let me—" Flynn covered her mouth with a strip of gaffer tape from a nearby shelf. Bettina glared at him as she tried to wrestle herself free, but all she did was create enough momentum to spin herself around.

"Sorry, darling," Flynn said.

"Mmmm! Mmmm! Mmmm!" Bettina said as Flynn exited the closet and closed the door.

• • •

Sancho saw Flynn exiting a storage closet not far from the activity room. He would have asked him what he was doing in there, but he didn't want to hear another crazy, batshit story, so instead he just asked Flynn if he was ready to go. "That lawyer lady who works for Belenki is here with the limo. Are you packed?"

"Packed and ready. As you know, I travel light."

"Well, grab your shit and let's go. We have a plane to catch."

CHAPTER TEN

Sancho told his abuela about his good fortune and she didn't believe him. She thought either he was pulling her leg or someone was pulling his. Why would anyone give her grandson a quarter of a million dollars for anything? Sancho tried to explain but soon realized there was no logical explanation. She worked so hard for every penny she ever made. Sancho never understood why those who worked the hardest made the least. That sad fact fueled his determination to get a degree and find a job that didn't wear him down to the bone.

His grandfather, one of the toughest men he ever met, stood five foot two. Barrel-chested and squat with a generous gut, he wasn't a gym rat or movie star muscular, but his tata had a grip like a steel vise and could work all day and hoist cement blocks that weighed a hundred pounds. He toiled long hours in the rain or in one-hundred-degree heat and was always happy to have the work. Both his abuela and his tata were in their sixties and continued to work as hard as they ever had. So did Sancho's mom as a cashier at Ross Dress for Less.

How could Sancho ever explain to his abuela and tata that a quarter of a million dollars was pocket change to someone like Sergei Belenki. For them, that kind of money was life changing. Sancho could wipe out all his student loans and pay for graduate school. He could buy a new car for himself and a new truck for his tata.

He didn't remember the last time his mother and grandparents went to the dentist or doctor, but now his tata could get his teeth fixed and his abuela could afford her blood pressure medication. They wouldn't believe him until he handed them the cold hard cash, but that's exactly what he would do. It was the least he could do after all they had done for him.

First, Sancho had to stay alive long enough to collect. He barely survived his first adventure with Flynn and knew this one would be equally life-threatening. Nickelson had no idea what he signed up for. Sancho hoped that having a psychiatrist along might help keep Flynn in check, but there was no guarantee that he would listen. No guarantee at all.

The black Cadillac XTS Limo pulled up to the curb in front of City of Roses. The chauffeur opened the door and Severina Angelli sat inside, sipping from a bottle of Dasani water. Flynn and Sancho followed Dr. Nickelson into the limo as the chauffeur loaded up the trunk with their luggage. Within minutes they were on their way to Burbank Airport in air-conditioned comfort. They each had their own buttery-beige leather seat complete with a drink holder. A thirty-two-inch LCD TV soundlessly played MSNBC above a bar area with a selection of fine liquor and a bottle of French Champagne on ice.

Sancho never rode in a limo before and felt vaguely out of place. Severina looked elegant in her Armani suit, and Flynn was equally well-dressed in vintage Hugo Boss. Nickelson wore wrinkled khakis, a well-worn tweed jacket and a smile of absolute delight. He pointed to the Champagne.

"Help yourself," Severina said.

Dr. Nickelson picked up the bottle and read the label aloud, his voice full of surprise. "Dom Perignon?"

"A 2009. Someone knows their Champagne," Flynn said.

Nickelson handed the bottle to Flynn. "Would you care to do the honors?"

Flynn peeled off the foil and expertly popped the cork. He poured them each a glass and raised his for a toast.

"Sláinte!" Flynn swirled the Champagne glass and inspected the legs before inhaling the bouquet. He took a tiny sip and swished the bubbly around his mouth. "It has a certain voluptuousness, doesn't it? Floral, rich and fleshy with a high acidic backbone and vibrant notes of guava and nectarines."

Sancho took a sip of his own and mimicked Flynn by swishing the wine around his mouth. He didn't taste the guava or nectarines and he had no clue what a high acidic backbone was, but it wasn't bad.

"Salud!" Sancho said and then gulped the rest of the glass. Over the rim of his glass, he saw Severina study Flynn. He was already working his magic and wasn't even half-trying. The alcohol hit Sancho as Flynn refilled his glass. He started to relax.

Sancho ran his hand over the buttery leather and finished his second glass of Champagne. Not having eaten breakfast, it went right to his head. Severina opened the sunroof and daylight filled the limo. Sancho stared at the clear blue sky. *Maybe this trip with Flynn won't be such a shit show after all. Traveling in style and chugging Champagne isn't a bad way to make a quarter mil.* He allowed himself to smile as the rest of his anxiety melted away. His first adventure time with Flynn involved carjacking, kidnapping, and multiple shootings. This time he traveled on a private jet to a multimillion-dollar charity ball.

Sancho watched the world go by through the tinted privacy glass. They exited at Hollywood Way and headed north past fast-food restaurants and mini-malls, gas stations and suburban tract houses. The limo pulled past the main entrance to Bob Hope Burbank Airport and headed past a security gate to the private hangar where Belenki kept his jet.

Sancho's mood lifted even more when he raised his third glass of Champagne, but it abruptly plummeted when he saw the custom Boeing 737. Fear gripped him and adrenaline flooded his system. It was the very same jet that Goolardo used to kidnap the billionaires. The same one Flynn nearly crashed and burned.

After someone shot the pilot, Flynn had taken the controls even though the closest he'd ever come to flying a plane was a flight simulator video game. Sancho had known terror many times during his ordeal with Flynn, but that fight on the plane with Goolardo and Mendoza terrified him more than any other moment they'd spent together. Sancho remembered the ground flying up as the plane rocketed down. He was sure he'd die a fiery agonizing death. He didn't. He survived. But some nights he had nightmares where Flynn didn't save them, and the plane plowed into a mountain and exploded.

The limo came to a stop and the chauffeur opened the door. Sancho was stricken. He couldn't get out. Fear kept him frozen in place.

Flynn patted him on the knee. "Ready, amigo?"

"I can't do it. I can't get on that plane again."

Severina raised an eyebrow. "What's the issue?"

"The issue is I don't want to fucking die!"

"What makes you think you're going to die?" Dr. Nickelson's voice oozed calm.

"Him." Sancho pointed at Flynn.

"You do realize you're being irrational, right?" Nickelson asked.

Still pointing at Flynn, Sancho said, "He's the one who's irrational."

Flynn smiled. "How am I irrational?"

"In every fucking way possible. I'm not doing this again. I'm not doing it."

"Don't be ridiculous. You're just feeling a bit agitated."

"If he doesn't want to go, he doesn't have to. His presence is not required," Severina said.

"It is for me, and it should be for your boss." Flynn leaned forward and locked eyes with her.

"Sancho. Look at me." Nickelson put a firm hand on each of Sancho's shoulders. "Big breath in. Big breath out. That's it. You are suffering the effects of PTSD. But they can be managed. They can be controlled. That jet is a trigger for you. That's why you're anxious."

"Anxious? I'm fucking terrified."

"Just keep breathing. Let it in. Out. In. Out. Do you feel that cleansing breath pushing away your anxiety?"

"Not really."

"You will. By learning to identify external triggers, you can reduce your anxiety level. That Champagne probably didn't help. I recommend staying away from alcohol. Once it's out of your system, I'll give you a Xanax."

"Just take me back to City of Roses."

"You run away from this and your anxiety will only get worse." Nickelson looked deep into Sancho's eyes. "You need to face your fear. It's called exposure and it's what's necessary if you want to manage your PTSD. Confronting fear is the only way to overcome it."

Flynn nodded in agreement. "He speaks the truth, amigo. You think I never face fear? I face it every single day. I hide it well, but it's always there. It keeps me sharp. It keeps me ready. Bravery isn't about eliminating fear. It's about doing what's required *despite* that fear."

"Think about the positive benefits of conquering this." Nickelson released Sancho's shoulders and chucked him under the chin. "You can do it."

"And don't forget about the money you'll make," Severina added.

Sancho hesitated. Walking away terrified him just as much as staying. His family needed the money. *He* needed the money. It would change everything. All he had to do was not die. He had been doing that every day for the last twenty-seven years. If he could just stay alive for another few weeks his family would be set. "Okay." Sancho nodded with conviction. "Let's do this."

• • •

Severina Angelli fastened her seatbelt on the plane and gave Flynn a sideways glance. Over the last three years, Belenki had ordered Severina to do many strange things. Hiring Flynn didn't even top the list, but it was likely the most dangerous.

After earning an MBA in Finance from Wharton, she graduated at the top of her class from Harvard Law. Severina interviewed at investment banks and venture capital firms and fielded multiple offers. She finally went with Bain Capital in New York. Five years later she was a senior consultant at Benchmark in Menlo Park and worked with startups like Dropbox, Zillow, and Snapchat.

There she met Sergei Belenki and within a year he'd lured her away to become his VP of business development and investor relations. She made twice the salary she made at Benchmark and the stock options and yearly bonuses were insane, but then so was Sergei Belenki.

Belenki believed the colonization of other planets essential for human survival, which was why he created Space Go, one of the largest private space exploration companies in the world. He worried that one day advanced AI would create a race of machines that would obliterate humankind. He intimated that perhaps what we perceive as our reality is possibly a computer simulation created by an advanced alien civilization.

Hiring Flynn to protect him from the Russian mob was no more bizarre than many of Belenki's other strange and irrational notions. She was, however, irritated that he had her drop everything else she was working on to convince Flynn to come west. Insulted to be put in that position, she began to re-evaluate her situation.

He didn't hire her to be a messenger girl, or a babysitter and she resented being treated that way. Belenki said he chose her for this task because of her ability to persuade. But if she couldn't convince Belenki that Flynn was out of his mind, then perhaps her powers of persuasion could use a little work.

Severina watched as Flynn rooted through his shoulder bag.

"Did you forget something," she asked.

"No, just looking over the gadgets Q sent along."

"Q?"

"He's head of Q branch and as such is an inventor, an innovator, and a genius when it comes to hi-tech weaponry." Severina was already sorry she asked the question, but she was soon to be sorrier as Flynn pulled out a plastic dental floss dispenser. "Look at this, for instance. What do you think this is?"

"Mint-flavored dental floss?"

"Yes, that's what it appears to be, but in actuality, it's a garrote made from the strongest, thinnest nylon monofilament in existence." He dropped the dental floss back in the bag and pulled something else out. "Now what about this?"

"Looks like a tube of toothpaste."

"Most people would think so. But if you squeezed it out around a door frame, you could blow that door right off its hinges. This tube contains a revolutionary new form of C-4 that's ten times more powerful and even more malleable. Q calls it C-5." He put the toothpaste tube back and pulled out a green and blue box. "Guess what these are?"

Severina read the side of the box. "Suppositories?"

"To the casual eye, yes, but to those in the know these are highly sophisticated, very powerful homing devices."

"That you put up your—"

"But of course," Flynn said. He put the box back and pulled out a banana.

"What's that?" Severina asked.

"What's it look like?

"A banana."

"Indeed." Flynn peeled it and took a bite. "That's because it is a banana. Would you care for a bite?

"No thanks," Severina said.

"I assume your employer will supply us with the proper firepower once we arrive."

"You expect him to give you a gun?"

"More than one I would hope. If he wants me to protect him, I'll need the means to do so." Flynn glanced out the window and nibbled away on his banana. Even though she knew he was one taco shy of a combination plate, Severina couldn't help but be intrigued. He had that bad boy charisma that she always fell for. Her last two boyfriends were drummers in rock and roll bands and the one before that was a professional poker player. She even recently had a flirtation with one of the ex-operators working security at Belenki's private island. Maybe because she'd always been such a good girl, Severina had a thing for naughty boys. Men who skirted the edge of propriety and the law. Risk-takers all.

Like Sergei Belenki.

Some of her acquaintances, mainly men, assumed she was sleeping with her boss. But Belenki never showed the slightest bit of interest in her in that regard, which was somewhat surprising, since most men, especially rich men, seemingly couldn't resist her. Of course, that changed quickly once they got to know her. According to her therapist, most men found her intimidating.

Belenki wasn't intimidated, but then again, he didn't think about sex nineteen times a day like most men. He found his sex drive to be distracting and inconvenient. When he did make an attempt at dating, he normally went for models and movie stars, which Severina thought was strange since he rarely looked at magazines and never went to the movies. These models and movie stars had no clue what to make of Belenki since he spent most of his time working.

They were used to men doting on them and worshipping them. At least at first. But not Belenki. He once told Severina that he wondered how much time he should allocate to dating. He needed to find a girlfriend, but he wasn't sure how much time per week the average girlfriend required. Five hours? Ten? He'd wanted to know what the minimum was and Severina didn't know what to tell him.

The 737's engines roared as the jet moved into take-off position. Severina's head gently snapped back as the aircraft accelerated down the runway. She glanced at Sancho in the seat across from her; jaw clenched, teeth gritted, knuckles white. For just a second he turned his head to look at Severina and tears filled his terrified eyes.

. . .

Sancho tried to sleep, but even with a Xanax supplied by Dr. Nickelson he still had too much adrenaline coursing through his system. He glanced out the window as they flew above the Angeles National Forest. He watched the I-5 winding its way through the Sierra Pelona Mountains and over the Tejon Pass to the Grapevine.

It looked peaceful from forty thousand feet. He took a big breath and slowly let it out. In and out. In and out. Nickelson wasn't wrong. The deep breathing did seem to help. The tension headache dissipated. Maybe the Xanax had finally kicked in.

He glanced at Flynn chatting up the flight attendant. She had no idea who he was or what he was. No idea that six months ago this hunky male model-looking motherfucker was a fat, pimple-faced dweeb with big plastic glasses and no self-esteem. No idea that he worked as a trainee at Hot Dog on a Stick and wore tight red shorts and a goofy, poofy hat. Sancho marveled at the change. Flynn was ripped and confident, and movie-star handsome. How could he possibly be the same person?

"You seem like you're doing better," Dr. Nickelson said.

"For now," Sancho replied.

"Are you expecting something bad to happen?"

"Aren't you?"

"Why would I?"

"Because bad shit happens."

"Not all the time."

Sancho motioned to Flynn and lowered his voice. "I like James, I do, but he is seriously deranged, and he is a danger to himself and everyone around him."

"I thought he saved your life."

"He did. More than once. But he's also the crazy bastard who put it in danger in the first place."

"Yes, but last time you didn't have me along for the ride. I can talk to him and help him make better choices."

"Like not steal a couple hundred grand from a Mexican drug cartel? Or fight an entire motorcycle gang by himself? Or drive a car off a fucking cliff?"

Sancho could tell that Nickelson hadn't heard those specific details before. The psychiatrist suddenly looked a lot less sure of himself, but before he could respond, the 737 dropped a hundred feet.

Sancho's stomach vaulted into his throat and sweat immediately popped up on his face. The aircraft jumped up and down in the high-desert turbulence. The voice of a female pilot crackled over the PA system. "Things are going to get a bit bumpy for a bit. So please keep your seatbelts buckled until I turn off the warning sign." She had the same Texas twang and laconic delivery that so many middle-aged male pilots had.

Sancho inhaled and exhaled, in and out, in and out, faster and faster, more and more frantically as the plane dipped and shook and bucked. He hyperventilated. Lightheaded and dizzy, Sancho knew what was happening. He'd studied it in psychology class. A classic panic attack. But knowing that didn't help. It felt like he was dying. Like he couldn't catch his breath. He wanted to rip his seat belt off and run, but there was nowhere to go but down. Thousands of feet down. Images of the plane plunging to Earth popped up in his brain. His imagination ran wild with flashes of fire and bloody carnage, the plane crashing, the metal ripping him apart, the jet fuel igniting and burning him alive.

"Sancho! Look at me." Dr. Nickelson gently put his left hand on Sancho's shoulder, his right hand on Sancho's face and looked directly into his eyes. "Breathe."

"I can't. I can't breathe."

"You're okay. You're safe."

"You're gonna die too!"

"Sancho. Look at me. What you feel isn't real. You're not going to die."

Tears sprung to Sancho's eyes. "Everybody dies!"

"Indeed, they do," Flynn replied. He unbuckled his seat belt and knelt on the floor next to the terrified orderly. He took Sancho's sweaty left hand in his and held it tight. "Everyone dies. But not everyone lives. You can't live fully unless you're willing to risk it all. You must push past the fear if you ever hope to become who you were meant to be. Most people give up. Surrender to mediocrity. But that's not you. I've seen what you can do. I've seen your courage. I've seen who you are. What you are. This world needs you, amigo. Alyssa needs you. *I* need you. So, do me a favor and buck the bloody hell up!"

"I'm trying."

"Try harder."

Flynn squeezed Sancho's hand. Sancho squeezed back. Flynn's confidence pushed away his fear, and in that moment it didn't matter if that courage was irrational. All courage was irrational. Everyone knew they would grow old and die, but somehow people ignored that fact and kept their fear at bay and moved forward as if they were going to live forever. That was truly irrational, yet that ability to disregard reality made life possible. Once Sancho grasped that, the fear faded.

"Your hand is quite sweaty," Flynn said.

"So, stop squeezing it."

Flynn did and Sancho wiped his sweaty paw on his shirt. The turbulence eased up and before long the plane once again flew smoothly.

"Feeling better?" Nickelson asked.

"No, but I'm okay with that," Sancho said.

CHAPTER ELEVEN

Former San Jose Mayor Norman Yoshio Mineta's parents were born in Japan. As such, they were not allowed to become U.S. citizens due to the Asian Exclusion Act of 1924. During World War II, the Mineta family lived at Heart Mountain Japanese internment camp near Cody, Wyoming along with one hundred and twenty thousand other Japanese Americans who lost everything they had when the U.S. government relocated and incarcerated them in concentration camps. Back then, Norman was a big baseball fan and when he arrived at Heart Mountain, the authorities took away his bat because they told him it could be used as a weapon. Years later, after he was elected to the U.S. House of Representatives, a constituent who knew of the story gave him a bat that was once owned by Hank Aaron. Mineta was forced to return it since it violated the House ban on gifts. At the time he said, "The damn government's taken my bat again."

The 737 touched down smoothly at Norman Mineta International Airport in San Jose, California and taxied to Sergei Belenki's private hangar. The hangar sat adjacent to a ten thousand square foot private "executive" terminal built so the aristocracy of Silicon Valley wouldn't have to mingle with the riffraff. That was just fine with Severina. Even though she spoke fluent French, collected contemporary art, and knew more about French Pinot Noir than most sommeliers, she wasn't always so sophisticated.

She wore her cosmopolitan persona like she did her black Dolce & Gabbana suits. She kept her modest upbringing a secret. That kind of background was frowned upon at the elite schools she attended. She grew up in Van Nuys and her father was a plumber. He inherited Angelli and Sons plumbing from his father and was disappointed he didn't have a son to carry on the Angelli tradition. Her mother worked as a waitress at Dupars in Studio City. Neither went to college, but both were proud of Severina and surprised by her ambition.

She worked hard to lose her Valley Girl accent and studied even harder to get herself into Pomona College. Severina won a scholarship but had to take on a hundred thousand dollars in student loan debt in order to graduate. Her law degree and MBA put her even deeper in debt, which was why she decided to take the venture capital route.

Severina created a sophisticated persona every bit as manufactured as Flynn's. The difference being she wasn't delusional. She knew exactly who she was underneath the designer clothes. Flynn didn't have that kind of self-awareness. Even so, he seemed extremely reasonable. Smart. Charming. Witty. Confident. Much more so than the usual Silicon Valley nerds who seemed so threatened by Severina's beauty, sophistication, and easy confidence. She knew that at first glance, most people would have no idea Flynn was completely bat-shit crazy.

Severina let Flynn exit the jet first and followed him down the ramp into the private terminal. There were no TSA agents or other security apparatus as most every person who passed through the "executive terminal" was a millionaire or billionaire. Attendants already loaded their luggage into the long black limo that waited for them at the curb.

• • •

Dr. Nickelson had to pee. Lately, he always had to urinate. Every hour on the hour. As a young man, Nickelson's bladder could hold untold quantities of pee. On the long drives between his parent's home in Sierra Madre and the U of C at Berkeley, he would only have to stop once every six hours. But back then he was a twenty-year-old biology major with a young man's prostate.

Now he had the swollen prostate of a sixty-three-year-old man. His vim and vigor had turned into piss and vinegar. His puffy prostate blocked his urethra, the tiny tube that carried urine from the bladder into the penis. His stream used to be strong, but now it was weak and slow and often only a dribble.

He would awaken four or five times a night, climb out of bed, and make his way in the dark to the bathroom. Since he didn't want to disturb Marla, his wife of thirty-five years, he didn't turn on the light and would often bang his shin or stub his toe on the way there and then she would wake up anyway, irritated as usual.

When Nickelson finally felt his way back to his bed, he'd have trouble returning to sleep. Suffice it to say, peeing was something he spent far too much time thinking about. It didn't help that Marla made him drink eight glasses of water every day. She said it was good for his kidneys.

When he had to go, he had to go; there was no holding it back. So, when they arrived at San Jose International, he hurried down the ramp ahead of Flynn, rushed into the terminal, found a men's room, fumbled with his zipper, and released the Kraken (Marla's pet name for his penis). His stream was weak, but his need was strong. It took him forever to tinkle and that was why he was the last one in the limo.

Nickelson sat his ass down next to Sancho, across from Flynn and Severina. The rear of this limo was just as opulent as the one in Burbank.

"Sorry for the holdup," Nickelson said somewhat breathlessly. Nickelson glanced through the sliding Plexiglas divider. "Are we still waiting for our driver?"

"There is no driver," Severina said.

Nickelson raised a curious eyebrow. "So, who's driving?"

"Daisy."

"Daisy?"

"Daisy, take us to 1542 Monte Vista Drive in Saratoga, California."

The car smoothly accelerated and headed out of the private terminal pickup and into general airport traffic. Confusion gripped Nickelson when he saw the steering wheel turn by itself. When he looked at Sancho fear radiated from both of them.

"What the hell is happening?" Sancho blurted. "How the hell are we moving?" He lunged for the door handle, but the doors were locked.

"The doors automatically lock once we start moving," Severina said.

"But we don't have a damn driver!" Sancho shouted.

"We don't need one. This car is autonomous, isn't it?" Flynn smiled at Severina.

"Yes, it's Electro Go's first autonomous limo. I probably should have warned you."

"Autonomous!" Sancho pressed his face to the window. "You mean it's driving by itself?"

"Most cars already have many autonomous features." Severina opened a bottle of Dasani water. "Cruise control. Automatic braking. But this Electro Go is the most advanced driverless vehicle that currently exists."

Nickelson noticed Sancho starting to lose his shit and put a hand on his knee to calm him. "I'm sure it's perfectly safe."

"Safer than having a fallible human drive us," Flynn pointed out.

"Google, Uber, Tesla, and Electro Go are all competing to capture the autonomous car market," Severina explained. "This prototype uses radar, sonar, and seventy-seven laser beams combined with hundreds of sensors and cameras all governed by the most advanced artificial intelligence ever developed."

Sancho's eyes widened with fear as the limo effortlessly threaded through traffic and exited the airport. "So, the government's okay with this shit?"

"The California DMV has granted permits to quite a few companies operating driverless vehicles," Severina replied.

"The safety features are very impressive," Flynn added. "Automatic emergency braking, forward collision prevention, pedestrian detection, and lane-centering assistance."

"You're well informed, Mr. Flynn."

"I read Popular Mechanics."

"Shouldn't somebody be in the driver's seat in case something goes wrong?"

"Not necessary. Q branch perfected driverless cars years ago, so this is really nothing new, amigo. Sit back and relax. We'll be in Saratoga before you know it."

As they exited the airport and merged south onto the Bayshore Freeway, Nickelson watched as Flynn turned his charm on Severina. She was resistant, but Flynn was persistent. He had only ever met two women totally immune to Flynn's charms. Nurse Durkin and his secretary, Miss Honeywell.

"Beautiful name, Severina." Flynn leaned towards her and their shoulders touched. "I once knew a Severine. Beautiful as well. But unfortunately, she came to a very sad end."

"Severina was my great grandmother's name. She was from Amalfi."

"But you were born here?"

"Southern California. As was my grandfather."

"You seem quite fit. Are you a runner?"

"I am. Every morning. Three miles a day."

"But you were a dancer once, weren't you?"

"How can you tell?"

"Your posture. The way you move. Ballet?"

"When I was a girl."

"And now?"

"Now I practice Krav Maga."

"Krav Maga?" Flynn was impressed.

"What's that?" Sancho asked.

"It's a defense and fighting system developed by the Israeli Defense forces," Flynn explained. "It combines techniques from boxing, wrestling, judo, and karate and is designed to work down and dirty in real world situations. It's extremely efficient and even more effective. I practice a variation myself. It emphasizes aggression. Taking an enemy out as quickly as possible by targeting the body's most vulnerable points. You attack preemptively and keep fighting until your opponent is completely incapacitated."

"A woman needs to know how to defend herself," Severina said.

"Indeed, she does. It's a dangerous world."

Nickelson heard a distant buzzing sound – a bit like a bee. Or a couple of bees. The bees grew louder and Nickelson realized they weren't bees at all. They were motorcycles. He looked past Severina out the back window of the Electro Go Limo and spotted two motorcycles approaching so fast it almost seemed as if the limo wasn't moving at all.

Flynn glanced out the back window as well. "Down! Everyone down!"

Nickelson stared dumbfounded as the twin motorcycles pulled up on either side of the Electro Go. Each bike carried two riders in black leather. One held the handlebars and the other held something else. At first Nickelson wasn't sure what it was. He pressed his nose up against the glass to get a better look. Sancho grabbed him by the neck and pushed him down a second before the submachine gun roared. Bullets ricocheted off the ballistic glass and peppered the side of the car.

"Oh, my God!" Nickelson screamed. "They're shooting at us!"

Since the car was autonomous, it didn't accelerate or react in any way to the violent attack. It stayed in the center of the lane and proceeded apace at a safe and sensible speed. Each flattened bullet created a concentric ring of white cracks that obscured the view through the glass.

Flynn shouted over the roar of the machine guns. "Down! Get down! It's only a matter of time before that ballistic glass shatters!" On cue, one of the windows began to buckle under the onslaught of hot lead.

Flynn lifted his knee and kicked the glass divider that separated them from the front seat. He kicked as hard as he could, again and again as the machine guns continued to roar.

Nickelson watched the motorcycle on the left accelerate ahead of the Electro Go as the limo held steady at a sober sixty-five miles an hour. The passenger aimed his weapon at the windshield and fired, presumably in an attempt to take out the limo driver. But there was no driver, just a stupid AI blithely driving them to their doom.

Severina joined Flynn in kicking the divider until finally it broke free and fell into the front. James followed after it, climbing into the driver's seat, taking the wheel and putting the pedal to the metal. The car accelerated, lurching forward and then violently slowed down as the autonomous AI took back control and hit the brakes.

A pleasant female voice came over the speaker box in the back. "I'm sorry, but the speed limit on the Nimitz Freeway is sixty-five miles an hour." Flynn gritted his teeth and hit the pedal again. The car bolted forward before the AI slammed on the brakes again. "I'm sorry, but the speed limit on the Nimitz Freeway is sixty-five miles an hour."

"Shit!" shouted Sancho.

"Bloody stupid AI!" Flynn growled. A bullet penetrated the passenger side window, flew past Flynn's face and into the ballistic glass on the driver's side. Shards of Plexiglas stung his cheek as the slug ricocheted into the dashboard. "Bloody hell!"

Severina pushed a terrified Nickelson to the floor before more bullets could penetrate the glass.

Flynn wrenched the steering wheel in an attempt to ram the bike on the right, but the Electro Go wouldn't let him and yanked the car back into the center of the lane, calmly explaining why. "It is unsafe to change lanes at this time as there appears to be a vehicle in the adjacent lane."

"I know there's a bloody vehicle! I'm trying to hit the damn thing!"

He tried to wrest control of the wheel away from the AI and bang into the motorcycle, but the Electro Go forced them back into the proper lane once again. "It is unsafe to change lanes at this time as there appears to be a vehicle in the adjacent lane."

Another bullet penetrated the glass and flew just above Severina's head before burying itself into a seat.

"What do we do?" she screamed.

"We're all going to die!" Nickelson cried.

Sancho shouted in Nickelson's face. "What did I say! What did I tell you? I told you. Didn't I tell you!"

"Everyone! Just calm down," Flynn commanded.

Nickelson never before felt this kind of fear. He started to cry as epinephrine coursed through his system, telling his body to fight or flee, but he was too scared to fight and had nowhere to flee. He was trapped in a limo too smart for its own good and all that hormone did was make him sick to his stomach.

The passenger on the motorcycle just ahead of them peppered the windshield with machine gun fire, filling the Plexiglas with multiple concentric rings that clouded the view through the glass. Flynn fruitlessly flattened the gas again in an attempt to hit their assailant, but the Electro Go wasn't having it and reduced its speed back to a lawful and sane sixty-five miles an hour. "Please keep a safe distance from the vehicle ahead," said the pleasant female voice.

.   .   .

Flynn looked back over the seat at Sancho, Severina, and Nickelson piled on top of each other on the floor. He had no way to protect them and didn't know what to tell them. The part of his personality that was Jimmy nearly emerged in a panic, but James forced Jimmy back down before he could get them all killed.

The limo slowed down suddenly and changed lanes behind the motorcycle on the right before merging onto the Junipero Serra Freeway, heading west.

The motorcycles cut past traffic to follow.

Flynn watched them through the rear window as both passengers reloaded their machine guns. "Severina!"

She didn't answer him.

Flynn shouted to her again. "Severina!"

"What?"

"How do I override this system!"

"I don't know."

"Who would?"

"Sergei."

"Call him. Now!

The motorcycles accelerated. The muzzle flashes of the twin machine guns glinted seconds before bullets peppered the back window of the limo.

"*Oh, my God!*" Nickelson shouted, holding his hands over his ears.

"Sancho!" Flynn called.

"What?"

"On top the rear seats! Are those releases?"

"Where?"

"On either side! See if they allow you to lower the seats!"

"Why?"

"Why are you asking me so many questions?"

"*Because I don't want to die!*" Sancho shouted.

"Then lower the bloody seats and get my carry-on out of the trunk! Let's go! Chop chop!"

Severina married her smartphone to the computer tablet installed in the rear seat and called Belenki by initiating a Blinky Face to Face call. Almost instantly Belenki's irritated face appeared. "Can't talk now. I'm in the middle of a meeting." He hung up and his face disappeared from the monitor.

"Shit!" Severina screamed and immediately initiated another Blinky Face to Face.

Belenki's face popped up again. He looked put out. "What did I just say? I told you I was—"

"Shut up and listen to me!"

Belenki's expression of irritation turned to one of surprise. No one ever talked to him that way. "Did you just tell me to shut up?"

"We are under attack in your stupid-ass autonomous Electro Go and we need to take back control."

"Under attack?"

"How do we do that?" Sancho shouted.

"Do what?"

"People are shooting us," Severina snarled. "How do we take control of this car!"

"Who?"

"Who what?"

"Who is shooting?"

"What does it matter?"

"This is Flynn! How do we override the AI!"

"It's in the code. It's a voice command. All you have to say is Daisy, initiate—"

A single bullet pierced the rear window's ballistic glass and hit Belenki square in the face, shattering the tablet in a shower of electrical sparks.

"Oh, no, no, no!" Nickelson screamed.

"Who's Daisy?" Sancho said.

"It's our Siri," Severina said. "Our Alexa. It's the name Belenki gave to our AI."

"Initiate what?" Nickelson wanted to know. "What's the command?"

"Daisy," Flynn said. "Initiate manual override."

"Sorry, but I do not understand your command," Daisy said.

Daisy continued to cruise at the sixty-five mile an hour speed limit even as their attackers raked the Electro Go with continuous machine gun fire. The ballistic glass buckled as individual bullets exploded through and whizzed over their heads.

"Daisy," Flynn tried again. "Initiate manual control!"

"Sorry, but I do not understand the command."

"Daisy!" Severina cried. "Initiate manual operation!"

"Sorry, but I do not understand the command."

"Daisy!" Sancho screamed. "Stop the motherfucking car!"

"I'm sorry," Daisy replied pleasantly. "But I do not respond well to profanity."

"Are you trying to kill us?" Sancho shouted.

"Of course not. My first priority is the safety of every passenger."

Bullets flew overhead in the passenger compartment as Flynn stayed down and unzipped his carry-on. He pulled out the dental floss garrote made from the strongest, nylon monofilament in existence. After unraveling a few feet, he wrapped it tightly around his hand.

Flynn took advantage of the temporary lull in the shooting to pop up and see where their enemies were. One motorcycle rode parallel to the driver's side. Flynn used his elbow to knock out what was left the shattered ballistic glass. The passenger on the bike looked up at him as he reloaded his weapon.

Flynn winged the floss dispenser out the window and over the wrist of the man wielding the machine gun. The dispenser wrapped around his wrist multiple times before Flynn tugged it tight, pulling as hard as he could. The man didn't want to let go of his gun and pulled back hard.

The floss snapped and he hit the driver in the side of his head with his weapon, knocking him right off the bike. The passenger lunged for the handlebars as the bike went down. Flynn glanced back to see both the passenger and the driver skidding and tumbling down the freeway along with their motorcycle.

Flynn pushed in the car's cigarette lighter and then reached into his carry-on. He removed the tube of toothpaste that contained Q's C-5. After unscrewing the cap, he squeezed a giant wad of it into his hand. The scent of mint filled the limo as Flynn knocked out what was left of the window on the passenger side with his elbow.

The roar of the motorcycle riding parallel to them was thunderous. The killer riding in the rear raised his weapon as Flynn tossed the handful of goop at him.

The white minty blob hit the gun-wielding thug square in the face, right in the eyes, blinding him. The cigarette lighter popped out, indicating it was red-hot and ready to set something ablaze. Flynn grabbed it and threw it out the window, aiming at the face of the now blinded assassin, hoping to ignite the C-5.

But the hot lighter just bounced off his face and down the back of the driver's jacket. The man went rigid as the lighter seared his flesh. Letting go with one hand, he reached down the back of his jacket and lost control of the bike. Veering right, he crashed into the guardrail, sending himself and his passenger tumbling into the air, over the side of the embankment, followed by their motorcycle. The crash tore open the gas tank and the fuel ignited a dramatic cinematic explosion. Flynn smiled grimly.

"Well, they went out in a blaze of glory."

Sancho, Severina, and Nickelson stared at Flynn in dumbfounded relief as Daisy continued to drive them down the highway at a safe and sober sixty-five miles an hour.

CHAPTER TWELVE

Having grown up in modest circumstances, Severina never failed to be impressed by the entrance to Sergei Belenki's Saratoga estate. The fifteen-foot-tall wrought iron security gates opened as if by magic for the mangled Electro Go Limo. Security cameras followed their progress as they passed between the tall stone pillars. William Randolph Hearst's Central Coast castle had nothing on Belenki's Northern California château. Hearst's monument to himself was known as the La Cuesta Encantada or the Enchanted Hill. Severina knew that snarky critics of Belenki had their own name for his sprawling estate; Blinky Castle.

The road from the gates to the chateau traversed mountain hillside vineyards under chaparral and oak-covered ridges. Belenki bottled his own private label wine called Saratoga Creek. His Pinot Noir and his Chardonnay both won major prizes at the San Francisco International Wine Awards.

The Electro Go passed another set of security gates that also opened on their own. It followed a red brick path lined with flowering olive trees to a massive circular driveway surrounding a stone fountain with an ornate statue of Dionysus and a trio of zaftig half-naked nymphs.

• • •

Mr. Harper couldn't believe how shot-to-shit the Electro Go Limo looked. It was hard for him to imagine how anyone inside could have survived. The windows were all ballistic glass yet every single one was cracked, punctured or shattered. Hundreds of bullet holes peppered the armored exterior. The headlights were smashed, and the shredded back bumper barely hung on, creating sparks as it scraped across the bricks. He stood outside the front door of Belenki's fabulous mansion with two of his men and nodded to one of them, a burly blond with a buzz cut and the face of a pirate.

The piratical blond stepped forward and tried to open the Electro Go's rear door, but it was smashed tight. He grunted and pulled until it reluctantly came free with a loud scrape. Sweaty and pale, Severina stepped out, her hair a mess, her clothes disheveled. Next came a distinguished older gentleman who immediately threw up in the fountain. Flynn's Hispanic sidekick emerged after that. He too looked about to spew but didn't. Instead, he steadied himself on the car and watched as Flynn emerged calm and cool, relaxed and unscathed.

How could Belenki have brought in Flynn after what that maniac did on Angel Island? That escaped mental patient was nearly the death of all of them. Harper was a decorated war hero. A former Army Ranger and Delta Force captain. He only hired the best of the best. Navy Seals. Army Rangers. British SAS. Flynn wasn't an operator. He had no training. No real experience. His only survival skill was dumb luck.

Harper could never forgive Flynn for what he did on Angel Island. Flynn hadn't killed anyone, but he easily could have.

All the embarrassing news stories and publicity nearly destroyed his business. It took a solid year to re-establish his reputation. When Belenki hired him three months ago he thought he was finally back, but now that stupid billionaire was bringing on Flynn. *What could he be thinking?* Harper knew he had no choice but to ride this shit out, but he didn't have to be happy about it.

Harper heard a pleasant female voice from inside the Electro Go even though he didn't see a driver. "I hope you enjoyed your journey. Thank you for driving with Electro Go."

"Bite me," Sancho said.

"Have a nice day," Daisy happily replied as the limo pulled away, creating sparks as it dragged the dangling rear bumper across the bricks.

"Mr. Flynn, here we are again." Harper did not extend his hand.

"Mr. Harper, so good to see you. I believe you know Sancho. And this is Dr. Nickelson."

Nickelson still leaned over the fountain, shaky and weak from losing his lunch on the lap of a stone-cold nymph. He looked at Harper and nodded weakly.

"By the way, I believe I owe you an apology." Flynn tugged his suit jacket straight.

"You do?" Harper raised a suspicious eyebrow.

"Indeed. I feel as if I left you and your men in a lurch back on Angel Island, but I'm sure you understand I couldn't let Goolardo get away."

"You blew up my attack helicopter."

"Yes, that was unfortunate, but unintentional."

"That wasn't Beckner's helicopter. That was mine."

"I hope it was insured."

"That's not the point!"

"No, the point is I told you what was about to happen, and you didn't believe me."

"Because you weren't making any sense," Harper growled.

"He *was* making sense." Sancho stepped forward. "You just didn't know it."

"And now he does." Flynn flashed a smile. "So, from here on out I'm sure that Mr. Harper and I will be on the same page."

"And what page would that be?" *The motherfucking funny pages?* Harper wanted to wring Flynn's neck, but held himself back. "Son, you are five cans shy of a six-pack and shouldn't even be here."

"I disagree," Sergei Belenki said as he came through the door. "It was my decision to bring on Mr. Flynn and if you can't work with him, perhaps I should find a security firm that can."

"Sir, I'm just being honest."

"So am I. Call the authorities and tell them about the attack on my limo. But let them know I don't want the press to hear about it and make it clear that no one can talk to them until after the benefit. Is that understood?"

Belenki smiled at Harper and Harper had to make a split-second decision. He shut down the glower and turned his frown upside down. "Of course, sir. This is your rodeo. And if you want Mr. Flynn to help with security then I'll do my level best to make that work."

"I should hope so." Belenki turned his smile towards Flynn. "Good to see you again, sir. I'm glad you made it here in one piece. Any clue as to who attacked you?"

"They all wore helmets, so we couldn't actually see the assailants and since your autonomous vehicle wouldn't allow us to stop, I'm afraid it's a mystery."

"But it could have been the Solntsevskaya Brotherhood?"

"Yes. If they thought you were waiting for me in the limo, that's very possible. Of course, they also could have been freelance assassins hoping to cash in on the bounty. Whoever they were, they will likely strike again."

"That's why I have you here, Mr. Flynn."

Harper gritted his teeth and tried not to roll his eyes. "Yeah, I'm sure that my team and Mr. Flynn can handle any possible contingency."

"I'm counting on it." Belenki looked over what was left of the Electro Go Limo. "Severina, can you show our guests to their rooms. I'm sure you'd all like a shower and a change of clothes. After that, perhaps we can arrange a tour of the estate so Mr. Flynn can assess our..." He glanced at Mr. Harper. "Vulnerabilities."

"I'll need a firearm and a shoulder holster," Flynn said.

Harper directed his next question to Belenki. "You want me to give him a gun?"

"Give Mr. Flynn whatever he needs. He is now an integral part of the team."

• • •

Bettina O'Toole-Applebaum hung upside trapped in a straitjacket for two hours before someone finally found her in the supply closet. Unfortunately, the person who found her was Mary Alice; the same big-boned, freckle-faced, red-haired, rageaholic who insulted her during group therapy for having a hippie name. Mary Alice laughed when she saw Bettina hanging upside down. She had a hoarse, raggedy smokers laugh.

"Well, aren't you a picture!" Mary Alice's laugh devolved into a hacking cough and she choked, hocking up a giant wad of phlegm, spitting it on the floor right under Bettina's head.

Being her mouth was taped shut, all Bettina could say was, "Mmm mmm mmm mmm!"

"What was that dear? You trying to tell me something?"

"Mmm! Mmmmmm!"

"Sorry, but I can't understand a word your saying."

Angry tears filled Bettina's eyes. "Mmmm! Mmmmm!"

"Now don't be getting nasty with me."

Bettina tried to moderate her tone and pleaded for Mary Alice to get her down. "Mmmm mmmm mmmm."

"Yeah, I still don't understand a word your saying, but no worries. I'm sure you'll Houdini your way out of that thing. Eventually."

Mary Alice took the toilet paper she was looking for and shut the door, plunging Bettina back into total darkness. "*Mmm! Mmm! Mmmmmm!*"

Forty-five minutes later, one of the maintenance men opened the door to find Bettina still dangling there. Her face was bright red from all the blood rushing to her head. Tears ran upside down her face as she pleaded for release. "*Mmmm! Mmmm!*"

The maintenance man called an orderly. The two of them lowered Bettina down and released her from the straitjacket. She angrily ripped the tape off her mouth. "Ow!"

"You okay?" asked the maintenance man.

"No! I'm not okay! I need to see Dr. Nickelson."

"He's not here," the orderly said.

"Where is he?"

"I don't know."

"I need to see the head nurse then." Dizzy, Bettina staggered back and nearly fainted. The orderly caught her before she hit the floor.

"I think you need to lay down."

"Take me to the head nurse!"

"I don't think so."

"I don't belong here! I'm a journalist!"

"A journalist? No kidding?"

"Yes! I work for Rolling Stone."

"Rolling Stone? Wow." He winked at the maintenance man.

"Yes. I'm here on an undercover assignment!"

"Of course, you are." The Orderly smiled. "Take my arm."

She took the orderly's arm and he led her down a corridor and around a corner and into her room. "I said I want to see the nurse in charge!"

"To tell her you're a reporter who works for Rolling Stone?"

"I'm not crazy!"

"Of course not, but you do need to get some rest, hon." The orderly shut and locked the door.

"What are you doing? Don't do that! I don't belong here! *I don't belong here!*"

"Join the club," the orderly said. His footfalls faded as he headed off down the corridor.

"Let me out of here! Let me out! *Let me out!*"

• • •

Flynn's elegant guest suite at Castle Blinky was spacious and minimalist; decorated, like the rest of the house, in mid-century modern with elements of Japanese and Scandinavian design. The white marble-and-glass bathroom almost matched the size of the bedroom. The massive shower stall featured five massaging showerheads which hit him from every direction.

He stood there and let the hot spray pummel his back and neck. His tense muscles slowly relaxed as he considered Belenki's dilemma. Flynn couldn't be sure it was the Solntsevskaya Brotherhood who were after him, but it seemed likely as they were the largest and most powerful crime syndicate in Russia, and worked hand in glove with the Kremlin's state security apparatus.

The GRU and the FSB used criminal organizations for their expertise in cybercrime, money laundering, human trafficking, and targeted assassinations. If Belenki gave the FBI information on their money laundering activities, they would want to make a high-profile example of him; a warning to every other worldwide social media company. Cooperate with law enforcement and suffer the consequences. Flynn decided it likely wasn't Goolardo who attacked the limo. Goolardo would want Flynn to know it was him and those black helmeted assassins were anonymous.

Flynn turned the hot water all the way to cold as he always did when finishing a shower. The frigid water energized and invigorated him. He roughly dried off with a thick towel and dressed. He wore a single-breasted dark tropical worsted suit with a Sea Island cotton shirt and a black knitted silk tie. Almost immediately a knock echoed at the door.

Flynn answered to find Severina looking elegant and alluring in a black Armani suit with a white silk shirt. She had one less button done up than before and Flynn wondered if she was trying to tell him something, especially since she offered him the hint of a smile. "Ready for your tour?"

"I am indeed. You're looking rested and collected. No worse for wear after our little ordeal?"

"I wouldn't go that far."

"Then I admire your composure. I'd compliment you on your outfit, but I wouldn't want to give you the wrong idea."

"What wrong idea would that be?"

"I think you know, but I'd rather not press my luck."

"Are you flirting with me, Mr. Flynn?"

"I've been told that's not appropriate behavior in this day and age."

"What's appropriate depends entirely on the situation and the context, and in this context you are correct. It is not appropriate."

Flynn smiled at the rebuff. "Message received. Lead the way."

They caught up with Dr. Nickelson and Sancho, who weren't dressed nearly as elegantly. Sancho wore a clean pair of jeans and a short-sleeve blue-checked shirt while Nickelson had on chinos and a Tommy Bahama Hawaiian shirt in a festive floral pattern.

"Sergei's Saratoga Estate sits on 188 acres of woodlands, vineyards, orchards, and formal gardens," Severina said as she led them down a dramatic spiral staircase, past floor to ceiling windows with spectacular views of the valley. "The main house is a little over twenty-four thousand square feet."

Sancho shook his head with wonder. "How many bedrooms?"

"Sixteen bedrooms, twenty-two bathrooms."

"Why more bathrooms than bedrooms?"

"Better to have too many than too few," Severina said.

"Not if you have to clean them," Sancho replied.

She led them through a vast foyer and into a massive living room with multiple seating areas, all furnished in the same mid-century style as Flynn's bedroom. They passed beneath a domed ceiling painted with clouds and cherubs all illuminated by a giant chandelier. Flynn took in a dining room with stunning views and a long elegant mahogany table that seated at least fifty. Black and white clad caterers set up stainless steel chafing dishes and a giant crystal punchbowl.

Wide French doors led to the rear patio and a backyard with a breath-taking infinity pool and a panoramic view of Stevens Canyon. Roadies dressed like bikers put together a raised stage and set up a sound system with ten-foot-tall speakers. Harper's dark-suited security contractors were everywhere, and Flynn caught sight of Harper himself, glaring at him with antipathy. Flynn smiled back and Harper turned away to chew out one of his subordinates.

"Holy shit," Sancho said a little too loudly as he stared in wonder at a small blonde woman sitting in a chaise lounge as she texted on her phone. "Isn't that—"

"It is," Severina said, smiling at Sancho's reaction.

"Lady Gaga?"

"She's one of the performers tonight."

"No way. Seriously?"

"She's a huge supporter of the Environmental Defense Fund and that's who this benefit is benefitting."

Sancho didn't want to stare at Gaga, so he looked at Severina. "Who else is singing tonight?"

"Tony Bennett and Weird Al Yankovic."

"Weird Al! I love Weird Al," Nickelson exclaimed.

"So does Sergei," Severina said, her voice dripping with disdain.

Sancho looked back at Gaga. She smiled at him and he blushed. "Oh, my God," Sancho mumbled.

"Would you like to meet her?" Severina asked.

"In person? No. I don't know. I don't know what I'd say."

"Maybe later," Severina offered.

"Maybe," Sancho said, but from his tone of voice it was clear the whole prospect paralyzed him.

Severina motioned for them to follow her into a formal garden. "The main house has a home theatre that seats fifty, four garages, a game room, a fitness room, a library, a computer room, a workshop, and two full kitchens."

Sancho was perplexed by that. "Two kitchens?"

Severina led them through a rear door into one of the kitchens. It was spectacular; five hundred square feet at least, with hardwood floors and granite countertops, custom cabinetry, Electrolux appliances and a huge center island where Sergei Belenki was busy rolling out dough.

Belenki looked up at them with a grin, the tip of his nose dusted with flour. "Enjoying your tour?"

"Very much so. And Severina has been the perfect host," Flynn said.

"I apologize for all the commotion, but it's for a good cause. Do you like snickerdoodles?"

Sancho raised his hand in the affirmative and Belenki pointed to a plate of snickerdoodles hot out of the oven. "The caterers are using the other kitchen. This is mine. My happy place. Baking relaxes me."

"Sergei?" A tall honey-blonde in a tight white crop top and short denim overalls charged into the kitchen. "I need to talk to you like right now!" She wore her long hair in a ponytail and a diamond and gold choker decorated her slender neck. She had butterflies tattooed on both wrists and a flying cherub on her left arm. A stunning beauty. Flynn surmised she wielded that beauty like a weapon to get what she wanted whenever she wanted it.

"Severina, you know Anika. Darling, this is Mr. Flynn. He's here to help Mr. Harper."

"That's who I wanted to talk to you about. Harper says my sister can't bring her new boyfriend tonight."

"Probably because he hasn't been vetted."

"He's my sister's boyfriend!"

"Security is tight. You know that. How long has Monica been going out with him?"

"Since last week."

"That's the issue then. This is a very exclusive event tonight and with those recent threats — "

"If he can't come, she won't come!"

"Anika, it's not up to me."

"Bullshit!"

"Can we talk about this later?"

"I hate this!"

"Would you like a snickerdoodle?"

"You know I don't eat gluten!"

"Right. Sorry."

Anika directed her angry green eyes at Flynn. "You work with Harper?"

"Not exactly."

"Talk to him for me. Tell him to stop being such an asshole."

"Being an asshole is how Mr. Harper makes his living."

Anika smiled at that. It was then that she really took a good look at Flynn, and from the expression on her face it was clear she liked what she saw. "Who are you again?"

"Flynn. James Flynn." He offered Anika his hand. She took it and held on.

"You don't look like one of Harper's goons."

"I'm not."

"You look like you could be in the movies."

"So, do you."

"That's probably because she is." Belenki bit into a snickerdoodle. "Anika's an actress."

"Anika Piscotti," Sancho said. "Dark Seduction. Journey of Fear. Danger Signal. I love your movies, Miss Piscotti. I'm a big fan."

"That's very nice of you to say," she said, but she didn't say it to Sancho, she said it to Flynn and continued to smile at him.

Severina struggled not to roll her eyes.

"Anika and I are engaged," Sergei said.

Flynn continued to smile at her. "Congratulations."

"Thank you, Mr. Flynn. I hope we meet again."

"I'm sure we will, Miss Piscotti."

Anika looked back at Sergei and her smile faded fast. "I'll let you get back to your snickerdoodles then."

"Thank you, darling."

"Nice to see you, Anika," Severina said.

Anika glowered at Severina.

Nickelson decided to fill the long, awkward pause. "You have a beautiful home, Mr. Belenki."

"Not just beautiful," Sergei said. "Like Anika, it's also very, very smart."

Anika scoffed, rolled her eyes, and walked out.

To cover his chagrin, he continued. "Belenki Castle is by far the smartest home in the world. I built it as a prototype. A proof of concept."

Flynn nodded and looked around. "What sort of systems do you have in place?"

"Everything from the major appliances to the lighting to the HVAC system is controlled by an advanced AI that learns and adapts, based on my behavior. It constantly monitors temperature and humidity and can adjust accordingly. The electrochromic glass in my windows allows me to change from light to dark at the push of a button on my smartphone."

"What about security? Is that automated too?"

"The security cameras have facial recognition software. Smoke, carbon monoxide, metal and motion detectors. There are bullet-proof security shutters on every window, keyless entry locks, and an alarm that alerts both the police and the fire department. But the security measures I have in place aren't just defensive. I have offensive measures as well." He pointed to a ceiling-mounted device. "That's a Hellfire Anti-burglary system. There's one in almost every room. On any indication of a break-in, it releases a powerful blast of atomized pepper spray. I even have a few heavy turrets we're prototyping."

Sancho was nonplussed. "Machine gun turrets?"

"These shoot paintballs filled with pepper gel. For legal reasons, nothing lethal."

"Except for Mr. Harper and his merry men," Flynn added.

"Yes, but even if Mr. Harper and all my systems fail to protect me, I have a panic room as well. The biometric lock opens with a retinal scan. My eyes only. The door is thicker than the door of a bank vault. It's steel-clad with a solid concrete core and impervious to a bazooka blast. I have two years' worth of food, water, and a tamper-proof ventilation system. I could survive an atomic war or a zombie apocalypse in there."

"So, you really don't need me here at all then, do you?"

"Not here. No. Here I feel relatively safe. Which is why I decided to go ahead with the charity benefit. Outside of here, however, I am much more vulnerable. And that, Mr. Flynn, is where I'll need your help."

"So, when can we meet about that? I'd like to put together an action plan."

"Tomorrow. Tonight, I need to concentrate on the benefit."

"So perhaps I should stay focused on the immediate threat. Roam freely, keep an eye out, and concentrate on watching out for your rich and famous guests."

"That would be ideal. Are you sure you don't want a snickerdoodle?"

"I'm sure."

"Sancho?"

Sancho smiled and grabbed another one.

CHAPTER THIRTEEN

Fear squeezed Bettina O'Toole-Applebaum's heart. The head nurse's cold gray eyes filled her with dread. They were pitiless, implacable, and full of unspoken rage. Yet somehow her voice always remained icy-calm. Nurse Durkin sat on the folding chair across from Bettina's bed and stared at her for an unnerving length of time before she began the interrogation.

"Why did Mr. Flynn truss you up in that straitjacket and hang you upside down?"

"He believes I'm an assassin."

"Is that what he told you?"

"He thinks I work for Goolardo."

"Why do you think he believes that?"

"Maybe because he's crazy."

Durkin's stare was so angry and intense, Bettina had to look away. A long, painful and uncomfortable minute went by before Durkin responded. "I don't like liars."

"I'm not an assassin."

"I know. I talked to your editor."

"So, you know I'm not a mental patient."

"If you're here, under my care, then you *are* a mental patient. My patient. And with Dr. Nickelson gone, I'm the one who decides whether or not you're well enough to leave."

"Where's the doctor?"

"Northern California." Durkin's preternaturally calm and cool demeanor colored with a touch of irritation. "He's attending some sort of charity ball."

"Charity ball?"

"At Sergei Belenki's estate in Northern California. With Mr. Flynn."

"They released him?"

"Under Dr. Nickelson's care. Meanwhile, here you are. With me. Under *my* care."

"You can't keep me here."

"Can't I?"

A frisson of fear traveled up Bettina O'Toole-Applebaum's spine. "You have no right."

"I have every right. *If* I believe you're a danger to yourself and others."

"Why are you doing this?"

"Because of people like you, Mr. Flynn has become a media sensation. To some, he has even become something of a hero. But he isn't a hero. He's a danger. He is delusional. He is sick. And people need to know that. That's why you need to write the real story. Tell the public who he really is. You know better than most. He easily could have killed you. You're lucky he didn't."

"I can't write the real story if I'm stuck in here."

"No, you can't. Which is why I'm letting you go. But you need to get the truth out. If you don't and Flynn hurts or kills some poor innocent person...." Durkin put her beefy finger in Bettina's face. "That makes *you* a danger."

• • •

Flynn wore a threadbare thrift store tuxedo a little too long in the sleeves and baggy in the seat. Still, it was designed by Hugo Boss and Flynn wore it well. If Sancho had learned anything from Flynn, it was that confidence can take you a long way. Even confidence based on delusions of grandeur and a certain amount of crazy.

Sancho wore the only suit he owned. He got it on sale at Macy's for his grandfather's funeral. The black Kenneth Cole Slim Fit Suit fit a tad tight as he wasn't as slim as he was when he bought it. This was the first time he put it on since that sad day. Nickelson wore a one-button tuxedo he'd bought at Brooks Brothers a few days before they left. It fit him well, and he looked like he was having the time of his life.

They stood outside under the stars in Belenki's fabulous back patio and yard. The infinity pool glistened with a festive blue glow, though no one was swimming. Multi-colored party lights hung between the trees, illuminating two outdoor bars and bistro tables with white folding chairs. Across the yard, a small jazz ensemble accompanied Lady Gaga as she sang an old Doris Day song. Dr. Nickelson smiled at Sancho and sang along.

"Picture you upon my knee, just tea for two and two for tea, just me and you and you and me alone!"

Awkward.

Sancho sipped his Anchor Steam beer. Flynn spoke with a stunning redhead in a tiny black dress. She leaned in close, touching Flynn's arm, whispering in his ear. He whispered back and she laughed. Flynn waved Sancho over. Embarrassed to be caught staring, Sancho grinned and stepped closer.

"Sancho, this is Natalie Breen."

"Hey, Natalie. Good to meet you."

She shook Sancho's hand. He recognized her from People Magazine. In the seventies she was a top model and once was married to a famous rock and roll star. But now she was married to a media mogul fifty years her senior. Rupert Breen was one of the billionaires Flynn rescued from Goolardo.

"I was just thanking Mr. Flynn and I want to thank you too. If not for you gentlemen, Rupert might not be here."

Sancho couldn't tell if she thought that was a good thing or a bad thing, but nodded and smiled. "Is your husband here this evening?"

"Somewhere, I imagine." She took Flynn's hand in hers. "I hope you don't mind, but I'd like to borrow your Mr. Flynn and introduce him to someone."

"Of course."

"Nice to meet you, Sancho."

She ferried Flynn away. Sancho headed back to Dr. Nickelson. The psychiatrist took a big pull on his mai tai and serenaded Sancho with a few more lines of *Tea for Two.* "We will raise a family, a boy for you, a girl for me. Oh, can't you see how happy we would be?"

Gaga finished the number and everyone applauded, including Nickelson who clapped so hard he sloshed mai tai on his white tuxedo shirt. "Darn it!" Nickelson smeared the red stain all around trying to wipe it away. "I better get some water on this." He lurched off to find a rest room.

• • •

Gaming tables filled the large ballroom. Roulette. Craps. Blackjack. Baccarat. Even though the setting wasn't nearly as baroque as the Salle Medecin at the Casino de Monte Carlo, a similar excitement and tension vibrated the air. With no smoke and no smoking allowed, the room had a more antiseptic feel. That was fine with Flynn as he'd given up cigarettes. They were not allowed at headquarters and had an effect on his endurance, so he quit, though he did miss the nicotine buzz and the taste of his favorite Balkan and Turkish blend with three gold bands. They were custom made by Morland and he carried them in a thin cigarette case made of black gunmetal. Back then he smoked upwards of sixty fags a day, but he was a different man now.

In that previous life, he spent many hours playing high stakes card games at casinos in France and the private clubs in London. This felt altogether different. There wasn't the familiar scent of smoke and sweat, greed and fear that you found in most gambling establishments. Here, everyone played for charity. Besides, most of the players were millionaires, if not billionaires.

Natalie Breen brandished Flynn like a prized poodle, introducing him to her wealthy celebrity friends. He wasn't part of this world and he knew it and they knew it, and he knew they knew it. He had seen and experienced things these prosperous, pampered upper-crusters couldn't begin to imagine. Even here, even now, he had to be vigilant as danger was always close.

Natalie introduced him to a slender, auburn-haired beauty. Her name was Eva Green and Flynn could swear he knew her from somewhere. Something about her was so familiar. Apparently, she was a performer of some sort. She acted as if they had never met, but Flynn was sure they'd been intimate. Maybe in another life.

Flynn was beckoned to a baccarat table by Natalie's husband, Rupert. He played with a few other billionaires, some whom Flynn had also saved from Francisco Goolardo. Rupert pointed to an empty chair. "James, would you care to join us? I'd be glad to stake you. It's funny money anyway as it's all for a good cause."

"Why not?" Flynn said.

"Have fun," Natalie said, kissing him on the cheek before heading off.

Flynn took the empty chair and looked around the table. Besides Breen, there sat Quinton Blackstone of Blackstone Communications, Ingvar Knudson, the Swedish real estate magnate, Prince Adnan Bin Hassan of Saudi Arabia, and Sergei Belenki's beautiful fiancé, Anika Piscotti.

He greeted each man and smiled at Anika, who smiled back, focusing the full wattage of her movie star charisma on him. "I thought you worked for Mr. Harper?"

"No, I work for your husband."

"What's your name again?"

Flynn smiled and the music that often accompanied him played in his head as he said, "Flynn. James Flynn."

· · ·

Sancho's shyness kept him tongue-tied and ill at ease. These weren't his people. These were the elites. Socialites. Celebrities. Influencers. Glitterati. Besides Breen, a few of the other billionaires they rescued were there. Eighty-year-old financier Warren Davis. Hong Kong real estate tycoon, Li Chu Young. Lakshmi Mandar, the UK-based info-tech king. And software mogul Bill Munson, who seemed to be avoiding eye contact with him. Maybe it was because the second richest man in the world had the crap literally scared out of him back on Angel Island and was still embarrassed about that.

Sancho watched Harper's men trying to blend in. They were as unsuccessful as him. Hulking, glowering, hard-looking guys uncomfortable in their suits. He caught sight of Mr. Harper watching him. Sancho offered him a little wave. Harper narrowed his eyes and stared at him with such disdain, Sancho had no choice but to turn away.

Lady Gaga started singing a new song and this time Tony Bennett accompanied her. Dr. Nickelson wobbled back with a fresh drink, bumping his way past the other partygoers. His eyes were watery, bloodshot and unfocused as he sang along with the professionals, irritating everyone within earshot. "By the sea, by the sea, by the beautiful sea, you and I, you and I, oh, how happy we'll be."

"Hey, Doc, Doc, Doc," Sancho put his hand on Nickelson's shoulder and whispered in his ear. "Let's let Gaga and Tony take this one, okay. People didn't come here to hear you sing."

"I love Tony Bennett."

"Maybe you should slow down on the mai tai's."

"I'm just having a good time."

"I know you are, but you're talking really loud."

"I am?"

"Yeah."

Nickelson leaned close to Sancho's ear. "Is this better?"

"Not really."

Nickelson motioned to an attractive middle-aged woman standing across from them. "You see that woman over there with the short dark hair? She keeps staring at me. I think she likes me."

"I thought you were married."

"Recently separated." Nickelson wavered off-balance. "You know how long it's been since I've been with a woman?"

"No, sir."

"I don't either!"

"Sir—"

"I have needs, Perez. I'm a man."

"A very loud man."

"Do you think I should talk to her?"

"I think we should go inside and get you some coffee."

"That attack on the car scared the piss out of me. I thought I was going to die. But you know what? It was worth it. Totally worth it for a night like this. I haven't had this much fun in twenty years. Best of all, I'm making a shitload of money just standing here!"

"Can you please shut up." It was the attractive middle-aged brunette that Nickelson thought was staring at him.

"Sorry!" Nickelson said. He put his finger up to lips and raised his other hand in apology as he leaned in close to Sancho and whispered loudly in his ear. "I think she likes me."

"Let's just listen for a little while, Doc."

"Okay." He listened for all of ten seconds before saying, "Do you hear that?"

"Hear what?"

"That noise."

Sancho heard it just as Nickelson mentioned it. A high-pitched buzzing. A problem with the sound system? The buzzing grew louder and more insistent. That's when he noticed the woman who told Nickelson to shut up staring at something in the sky. Sancho followed her gaze and at first couldn't make sense of what he saw. Some sort of flying thing. It was difficult to see it against the night sky, but the loud buzzing was unmistakable.

Nickelson pointed. "What the hell is that?"

"I think it's a drone. A big one," Sancho said.

Gaga stopped singing when she spotted the drone. The musicians stopped playing. Only Tony Bennett still crooned, oblivious to the fact that there were now two additional drones, all hovering above. Sancho's first thought was paparazzi. He knew they used drones to capture pictures of celebrity weddings. One of the contractors pulled a pistol to take aim, but Harper forced his arm down.

"Not safe," he said.

A tear gas grenade dropped from one of the drones. It hit the ground and exploded. People ran and shouted in panic. Sancho's skin and eyes and throat burned like fire. People screamed in agony and collided into each other as they tried to get away.

That's when the second grenade hit. A flashbang. Sancho, already blind, was now deaf, his ears ringing with a high-pitched whine. He felt for Nickelson but lost him in the stampeding crowd. Dizzy and off-balance, sightless and disoriented, he fell. People stomped on him as they tried to get past.

"Dr. Nickelson!" he shouted but couldn't even hear his own voice.

Someone stepped on his hand. Someone else kicked him in the face. But the pain from the tear gas was so intense, he barely noticed. He couldn't catch his breath. All he could do was crawl. The agony almost paralyzed him, but he knew he had to move. What if this was just the beginning? What if bullets were about to follow?

"Dr. Nickelson!"

The searing pain didn't fade. If anything, the burning sensation in his eyes and throat grew in intensity. Hot tears streamed down his face. He could taste salt along with bitter chemicals on his tongue. *Where's Flynn? Is he inside? What the fuck is happening?* He just kept crawling, but he barely moved. One hand, then the other, right knee, left knee. *Move. Don't stop.*

He fell in the infinity pool. The icy water cooled his burning skin. The relief instantaneous, but that momentary reprieve from pain was followed by absolute panic as more people fell into the pool on top of him. So many bodies flailed in the water. Pulling. Pushing. Floundering. Kicking.

He held his breath and tried to reach the surface but was shoved under. Knees and elbows and fingers and hair pressed down on him from above. He choked on water as he tried to find air. Occasionally, his head burst out of the water and he'd hear a terrified cacophony before he was shoved back under again. He reached up, grasping for a handhold, hoping for a way up, a way out, and then finally he found help.

A hand grabbed his wrist and pulled him out of the water. Suddenly he was on the side of the pool, sucking in sweet oxygen. He caught a momentary glimpse of Lady Gaga staring down at him.

"You okay?" she asked.

Sancho couldn't talk, but he could nod. She hurried off to pull someone else out of the pool. Sancho looked to the left to see Weird Al on his hands and knees, throwing up.

"*Everyone in the house!*" It was Mr. Harper. "*In the house! Now! Let's go! Move! Move! Move!*"

Flynn prepared to lay down a natural nine on the Baccarat baize when he looked through the floor to ceiling window into the backyard at smoke and people running—apparently screaming in bloody terror. "Apparently" because the windows were so well soundproofed it looked like a mime riot. Anika turned to see what he was staring at and was so surprised by all the terrified faces, she dropped her gimlet. It shattered on the floor.

Gun drawn, already on the move, Flynn headed for the French doors. People outside choked, clawing at their eyes and screamed soundlessly. A flashbang went off. As Flynn was on the other side of the glass, he didn't get the full impact, but was still momentarily blinded. Before he could open the doors, the crowd outside came crashing through the glass. The tear gas stung Flynn's eyes as the masses stampeded into him.

"Get inside! Everyone inside!" Harper shouted as the gasping, choking, blinded, crowd shoved Flynn backwards across the room. He tripped on a couch and fell with five more people landing on top of him. Their combined weight flipped the couch and Flynn found himself trapped beneath it, his gun and one shoe gone.

He tried to crawl out from under the couch. Someone kicked him in the head. A stiletto heel came down on his hand. He reached up and grabbed the back of a pair of pants to pull himself up. But the pants came down before he could pull himself to his feet. He saw the label. Brioni. And the person whose pants he pulled down, tripped over them and fell to his knees. Flynn used their shoulder for leverage and managed to get upright before pulling them to their feet as well.

"Mr. Flynn!" It was software billionaire Bill Munson.

"Good to see you again, Mr. Munson. You might want to pull your pants up."

Harper struggled to get control of the hysterical crowd. "*Calm down! Everyone! We need to stay calm!*"

Heavy machinery rumbled. The security shutters closed, covering every window in Belenki's fabulous mansion, sealing the place up, securing it from any outside threat. People were so stunned by the racket of the shutters closing, they actually shut their mouths for a few moments as well.

"Thank you!" Harper said. "We are perfectly safe as long as we stay calm!"

"Mr. Harper is correct!" Sergei Belenki moved through the crowd with Severina. "These security shutters are made from hardened carbon steel and long as we are inside, there is nothing that can touch us. My home has the most advanced security system in the world. It's more secure than the White House. The authorities are on their way. Please accept my apologies for that inexcusable security breach." Belenki said that last sentence while staring at Harper. "As soon as the police arrive everyone is welcome to go home. But that doesn't mean the party has to end. There's wine, there's food, there's music, there's whatever you want. Just know that while you're in here, in my home, nothing bad can happen."

The energy in the room changed as the crowd began to relax. Conversation and laughter swelled with the sweet relief of people who survived something dangerous and came out the other side. Flynn found Sancho rubbing his eyes and smoothing back his damp hair. He looked bedraggled and exhausted, dripping wet from head to toe.

Flynn crossed to him. "You all right?"

"I think so."

"Where's N?"

Sancho looked around the room. "I don't know."

"Did he make it inside?"

"I don't know."

"I told him this was a mistake. He never should have come. He's head of the whole shebang. He shouldn't be in the field, risking his life like —

An earsplitting alarm screamed. Red lights flashed on the Hellfire Anti-burglary system attached to the ceiling. The siren was so deafening no one could talk or hear or think. Fear was etched on everyone's face. *Why did the alarm suddenly go off? Did someone break in?*

Sancho pointed at a chandelier as it abruptly grew brighter and brighter. Flynn hurried for Belenki and Severina as every light bulb in the room grew blindingly bright before exploding one at a time.

Harper and his men immediately drew their weapons. Flynn would have drawn his as well if he hadn't lost it when the crowd knocked him on his arse. Nevertheless, he hurried for Belenki and grabbed his arm just as the Hellfire system on the ceiling blasted a cloud of atomized pepper spray, covering everyone in the room.

Flynn put his hand over Belenki's eyes and dragged him out of there with Severina's help. All three choked and gasped, blind, but Flynn knew they had to move before the crowd panicked and stampeded again.

Through his streaming tears, Flynn saw Harper tap two of his closest men on the shoulder and indicated for them to follow. They easily shoved their way through the panicked crowd to catch up. Flynn, Belenki, Harper, and his men hurried down a corridor, away from the cloud of pepper spray. Alarm speakers covered the house, so the siren carried into the corridor. Belenki, tears streaming down his face, led the way. Flynn and the others followed, passing sconces with bulbs burning brightly before each one exploded with a loud pop.

Harper and both his men had tactical flashlights with xenon bulbs that brightly illuminated what otherwise would be total darkness. Flynn grabbed Belenki by the shoulder and overly enunciated the words, "Panic Room."

Belenki raised an eyebrow.

Flynn mouthed the words again. "Panic Room."

Belenki understood that time and vigorously nodded.

As a former drill sergeant, Harper had no trouble shouting over the alarm siren with his booming voice. "Is it getting hotter in here?"

Belenki said something back, but Flynn couldn't hear him. Harper was right though. The temperature in the house rose quickly. It had to be over a hundred degrees.

Harper's operators took point as they headed down another corridor, the tactical flashlights alerted them to a wall sliding open. Behind it squatted a machine gun turret.

"What the fuck is—" The turret unleashed, prematurely ending Harper's sentence. He tackled Belenki, and Flynn flattened Severina.

Sancho turned away and a pepper gel-filled paintball smacked him in the back. Harper's man caught one in the balls, chest, and forehead. Another crouched, shouting for everyone to duck as a paintball flew in his open piehole. It lodged in his throat and he choked.

He fell to his knees, eyes bugging out, face turning blue. Flynn crawled over, grabbed him from behind, and gave him the Heimlich Maneuver until the gel ball popped free. Another guard had pepper gel splattered all over his face.

He clawed at his eyes, screaming, "Oh, my God! *Oh my God!*"

Harper shot at the turret with his .44 until it fell over on its side. The turret continued to fire, but the balls exploded harmlessly off the walls. "Let's move!" he shouted.

Flynn helped Severina up. Belenki guided the way, down another corridor and into a double doorway that led to his fabulous library. The lights were out because all the bulbs were shattered, but a five-foot-high fireplace blazed with a gas fire. Harper shined his tactical flashlight around the room. The light danced off the forty-foot-high ceiling, decorated with a beautiful stained-glass dome.

Belenki was a man on a mission. When he crossed by the fireplace, it erupted with a Vesuvius of flame. Belenki was engulfed. Flynn's reactions were quicker than anyone else's. He knocked the billionaire to the ground and rolled him across the plush oriental carpet.

The billionaire stared in stunned silence at the flame roaring out of his fireplace. He hurried to a bookshelf that was starting to burn and pulled back a particular book. The entire wall swung away, revealing a solid steel door eight feet tall. Belenki approached a security panel outfitted with a retinal scanner and used his fingers to force open his right eye, squinty and blood-shot as it was. He stared into the sensor and...nothing happened. No beeping. No clicking. No door unlocking. Belenki was nonplussed. "Something's wrong with it!"

"Is there a code you can use? Any kind of manual override?" Harper asked.

"No, it's a retinal scanner. Only my eye can open it."

"Maybe there's a problem with the power."

"It's on its own auxiliary system. No, no, no, this can't be right." He put his eye up to it again. Nothing. "It's worked every fucking time I've tried it, but now that I need it—"

"You've been hacked," Flynn said.

"What?"

"Someone has control of your house and every system in it."

"The Russians?" Harper speculated.

"Could be."

"How is that possible?" Harper shouted.

"They found a vulnerability and planted malware most likely."

"Now what do we do?" Severina was on the edge of panic. "We can't stay here. This whole room is going to go up in flames." A couple of the books on the higher shelves already burned.

"We need to unbolt the doors and get all those security shutters open." Flynn grabbed Belenki by the shoulders. "Where's the master control box? There has to be one."

"The basement," Belenki said.

"Take us there!" Flynn ordered.

"Now!" Harper shouted.

On the way to the basement, they passed the laundry area. A flood rushed from the room and into the corridor. Water erupted like a geyser from the washing machine. The hackers must have quadrupled the water pressure and now the pipes had burst. Sparking light fixtures and bare wires dangling. Flynn grabbed Belenki to stop him from stepping into the water.

No one grabbed Harper, however, and he went totally rigid, dropping his gun as electricity surged through his body. Sancho reached for him. Flynn slapped his hand away. He took off his jacket and looped it over Harper's head and under his arms and dragged him back out of the water. Harper immediately collapsed, unconscious.

Flynn put his ear to the man's chest. "Still breathing. Still has a heartbeat. Help me get him up." Flynn and Sancho carried him into the kitchen, where every burner blazed hot and high on the gas range. Smoke poured from the convection oven and hovered near the ceiling. A gusher of water erupted from the sink.

Belenki pointed the way. "The basement's over here."

Severina opened the door and Sancho and Flynn carried Harper down the stairs. The alarm siren was less intense down there; no speakers in the basement. Harper was a big guy, a heavy guy, and

Sancho nearly dropped him near the bottom. They gently set him on the cement floor as Belenki approached a big metal electrical box. He opened the door to reveal a myriad of switches and buttons and digital readouts.

"Do you know how to shut it off?" Flynn asked.

"I didn't set up or program the system, but how hard could it be?" Belenki tried a number of switches and buttons and levers and the digital readout continued to blink. "I can't access the system and I can't cut the power. Something won't let me."

"Someone else has control."

"This whole house is going to burn if we don't do something," Sancho said.

"The police and fire department are on the way. They'll be here any second," Belenki said.

"If they got the signal. But if someone else has control of the system…" Flynn raised his eyebrows to mark his point.

The gravity of the situation finally sank in for Severina. "Are you fucking kidding me?"

"We're like rats in a goddamn oven!" Sancho shouted.

"I have an idea," Flynn said.

"That's usually the last thing you say before you do something really, *really* stupid," Sancho replied.

Flynn offered them all a confident grin before bolting back up the basement stairs.

CHAPTER FOURTEEN

As Sancho sat hunkered on the basement floor, sweat dripping down his face, Severina glared at him. "What?"

"Aren't you going to go with him?"

"Why would I?"

"Because you're his friend! Because he needs you."

"Why don't you go?"

"Maybe I will."

"Maybe you should!"

But Severina didn't get up; Sancho did, and without another word, he bounded up the basement steps to find his old compadre. There wasn't a lot to burn in the kitchen, but what could burn was burning like a hijo de puta. The drapes. The wallpaper. A butcher block table. A couple of the guests struggled to pry open the steel shutters that sealed off the kitchen windows and back door. The room would have been an inferno if not for the geyser of water erupting from the sink and raining down, creating a fog of steam.

Sancho didn't bother shouting for Flynn because the siren still screamed. He avoided the corridor with electrified water and pushed past a dozen freaked-out guests, warning them about the danger ahead. He located Flynn kneeling in front of a cabinet that held a massive hot water heater.

"Dude, what are you doing?"

"This water heater is commercial grade and holds 120 gallons. It's seventy-five inches tall and thirty-three inches in diameter. Radius squared times pi is 560 square inches."

"So?"

"The temperature is probably 180 degrees and climbing, which means the pressure inside is approximately 350 pounds per square inch. Multiply that by 560 and you get one hundred and ninety-six thousand pounds of pressure."

"So!"

"I blocked the TPR valve. I'm turning this into a rocket."

"You're what?"

"I saw it on MythBusters. It was quite impressive."

"Not a good idea, dude."

"Already done. Time to go."

"What?"

"Before it blows." Flynn jumped to his feet. "Let's move."

"What do you mean it's time to —"

"*Run!*"

Flynn took off and Sancho ran after him. They bumped into guests feeling their way forward in the dark from the other direction. "*Turn around! Run! Go! Get outa here!*" Sancho screamed. "*Bomb! It's a —*"

The hot water heater detonated. An unbelievable roar shook the house. The explosion was so loud, the sound drowned out the shrieking alarm. Walls cracked, glass shattered, and parts of the ceiling came down. A secondary blast shook the house again. Sancho was sure this had to be the end.

•   •   •

Dr. Nickelson hadn't been this drunk since his junior year at USC. It was a Dungeons and Dragons party at Theta Beta Pi and he was dressed like a dwarf wizard and drunk off his ass on Long Island Ice Teas. He woke up the next morning on the rec room floor, between a puddle of vomit and a passed-out orc warrior. Nickelson had been hungover that whole day and the day after that. He had a blinding migraine and was sick as a dog. As bad as he felt back then, he felt even worse now.

The tear gas and flashbang grenades killed his buzz. His drunken euphoria was overwhelmed by fear and adrenaline. He, too, fell in the pool, but finally found the edge and managed to get his elbows and then the rest of himself out of the water. His brief moment of relief was snatched away when he fell off the edge of the infinity pool and tumbled down the steep hillside.

He somersaulted and tumbled, eating dirt and ripping his suit, grabbing for shrubs in a desperate attempt to slow his roll. He skidded to a painful stop and could already feel the bruises and stinging scratches, lacerations and pulled muscles. Nickelson rolled over onto his knees and worked his way to his feet before climbing back up the hill. It was slow going, but he had no other plan. Still fuzzy-headed from all the mai tai's, he kept losing ground and sliding back, but he didn't give up.

It took him forever. When he finally made it back to Belenki's patio and yard, it surprised him no one was around. Not a soul. The light in the pool glowed and so did all the party lights, but the house was dark. Navigating his way across the yard, he made it to the mansion and found every window sealed tight with steel shutters. No way in. Nickelson got a familiar feeling. He first felt it as a small boy when his parents divorced and his father moved away; and again when his wife left him two months ago.

Abandonment.

He was all alone. Discarded. Forsaken. Shunned. Tears dribbled down his face. He wasn't sure if they were from the residual tear gas or the deep well of sadness he carried with him everywhere.

Where's Flynn? Where's Sancho? Where was Weird Al Yankovic? Why wasn't he with them? Why did they abandon him? He walked all around the massive mansion to try and find a way in, but the place was impregnable. Sealed like a tomb.

He sat down on a cement bench a short distance away and stared at the house. Entry denied because he wasn't part of the club. Always unwanted. Always alone. Damaged. Broken. That was what led him to study psychology and get a medical degree and become a psychiatrist. Because way down deep in the darkest recesses of his soul, he understood what it felt like to be an outsider.

The ground trembled. Saratoga wasn't far from the San Andreas Fault. *Could this be the big one? Is the Earth about to open wide and swallow me whole?* He braced himself as a massive explosion rocked Blinky

Castle. The roof erupted. Something huge shot out of the house and continued high into the air.

In the moonlight, it was hard to see exactly what it was, but Nickelson followed its trajectory as it climbed into the sky. *What the hell is that?* He continued to stare as its acceleration slowed and it reached the apex of its upward progress.

Whatever it was plummeted back down to Earth. In fact, it looked like it was about to fall right on top of him. Nickelson stood up as quick as he could, which wasn't very quick, and tried to decide which way to run. It was hard to tell exactly where the giant falling thing was going to hit and he didn't want to make the stupid mistake of running right underneath it. So instead, he stood frozen in place, unable to make a decision and understood that his chronic indecisiveness would likely be the ultimate cause of his demise. His luck held, however, and the large burning thing hit in the infinity pool with a huge splash.

Water sloshed over the sides of the pool and Nickelson approached to see what had landed. *A hot water heater? Why the hell would a hot water heater launch itself through the roof?* Nickelson turned back to look at the mansion just as a secondary explosion blew out a wall. The blast knocked Nickelson off his feet. As he struggled upright he watched as Flynn led Belenki and some of his guests out through the room-sized hole.

Dozens and dozens of other guests followed, including Sancho and Miss Angelli and Lady Gaga and Weird Al. Mr. Harper and two of his security team were carried out by four other security contractors. Everyone was filthy and disheveled and stumbling and coughing.

Nickelson caught Sancho's eye; he looked so surprised and relieved to see him. A big smile lit up Sancho's face. "Doc, are you okay?"

"I am now," Nickelson said.

• • •

Four fire trucks arrived moments after Flynn evacuated the mansion. Firefighters tackled the blaze before it could ignite the dried brush on the hillside and cause a major conflagration. The fire engines were followed by four ambulances, three patrol cars from the Santa Clara County Sheriff's Department and a news helicopter overhead. Sirens filled the air and the cherries of police and emergency vehicles flashed with red and white lights.

Flynn stood outside the burning mansion and marveled at the size of the hole in the wall created by that secondary gas explosion. It was a miracle no one died. Harper remained out of action and on his way to the hospital. He regained consciousness before he left in the ambulance and didn't seem to suffer any serious damage.

Severina argued with the police. Her boss was in no mood to answer any questions. He just wanted out of there. They initially requested that everyone stay put, but those movie stars and celebrity billionaires weren't about to stand around and wait their turn to talk to the authorities. They were tired, dirty, furious and litigious. Within thirty minutes most everyone left.

Severina beckoned Flynn over. She was smudged and bedraggled, but surprisingly composed considering what she'd been through. "As Harper is out of commission, Mr. Belenki wants you to take over his protection detail."

"I can tell by your tone that you don't think that's a good idea."

"No. I don't."

"At least I got him out of there alive."

"After almost blowing us all to kingdom come."

"Almost only counts in horseshoes and hand grenades, dear."

"I'll be honest, Mr. Flynn. I tried to get Sergei to fire you, but he is stubborn and loyal to a fault. For whatever reason, he still trusts you, and for now I have to live with that. But I did convince him to hire another security firm. It's run by the former Deputy Director of the Secret Service. A man by the name of Fergus."

"That was quick work."

"He was my original choice, but Sergei had a history with Harper and like I said…he's loyal."

"When is Mr. Fergus coming aboard?"

"Immediately. He's currently securing Sergei's private island in the San Juan Archipelago."

"What is it with billionaires and their private islands?"

"They like control."

"Or at least the illusion of it. Is that where we're headed?" Flynn asked.

"Yes. Back to the airport where we'll fly to Bellingham. Sergei has a yacht in Squalicum harbor. The Nautilus."

"Sergei apparently has a fondness for Victorian science fiction. Does he see himself as a modern-day Captain Nemo?"

"He sees himself as getting out of here as soon as possible."

.   .   .

Much to Severina's consternation, Flynn insisted on driving. The car he chose wasn't autonomous as he didn't want a repeat of what happened on the ride in from the airport. It was, however, Electro Go's flagship vehicle. The Mach 5. The top of the line Electro Go. It went zero to sixty in 3.7 seconds and had a top speed of 160 miles an hour. Sergei's personal Mach 5 was white with custom red racing stripes and sported a sleek aerodynamic shape similar to its anime namesake. *Speed Racer* was Sergei's favorite TV show when he was a boy. For all its speed and design, it was quite comfortable if not exactly roomy.

Severina sat squished in the backseat with Nickelson, Sancho, and Anika. Belenki rode shotgun next to Flynn. Even though the Mach 5 wasn't autonomous, it did have a few advanced features. Forward collision control and automatic braking. A lane departure warning and steering assist. Adaptive cruise control with radar, camera, and laser sensors.

The Mach 5 cornered as well if not better than Severina's BMW M2 and she suspected Flynn longed to put the pedal to the metal as the twisting mountain road had tight curves and sweeping vistas; but Sergei had requested an escort from the Santa Clara County Sheriff's Department and a patrol car led the way. Another patrol car followed from behind. Both traveled at the forty-five mile an hour speed limit and Severina felt like they were moving in slow motion. *Better safe than sorry*. Patience. Not easy for a quintessential Type A personality.

She glanced at Sergei. He was exhausted as hell. By the set of his jaw and the way he glowered out the window, she could also see his agitation and anger. He wasn't watching the scenery zip by. He was deep in thought. Lost in his head.

"Are you sure you don't want to stop at the hospital on the way?" Severina asked him.

"I want to get the airport and get the hell out of here," he grumbled.

"I couldn't agree more." Flynn flicked a speck of charred stucco off his lapel. said. "Your island is infinitely more defensible."

"Is it?" Belenki barely contained his rage. "Someone used my own technology to try and murder me! They hacked every safety system I put in place and turned them against me!"

"The Russians are masters at cyberwarfare, espionage, propaganda, and sabotage."

Belenki looked sideways at Flynn. "What if it's not the Russians?"

That took Severina by surprise. "Not the Russians?"

"The Russians are good, but not that good," Belenki said. "I'm not some John Podesta falling for a fucking phishing email. I have multiple hardware and software firewalls and countless encrypted levels of TLS and SSL. The cyber protection protocols I put in place should have been impregnable."

Severina leaned closer to the front seat. "If it's not the Russians, then who do you think is after you?"

"I'm not saying the Russians aren't after me. They are definitely after me. But they're not the ones pulling the strings."

"And who would that be?"

"An entity far more dangerous. It's so obvious. I don't know why I didn't see it before."

"What didn't you see?"

"Who my ultimate enemy is."

The Mach 5 Electro Go accelerated all of a sudden and slammed into the back bumper of the patrol car just head.

"What the hell," Sancho shouted.

Flynn looked as surprised as anyone. "That wasn't me!"

The car accelerated again, rocketing forward, and Flynn hit the brakes to prevent them from crashing back into the patrol car. The Mach Five skidded. He had no control.

"What are you doing?" Belenki screamed.

"I'm not doing it!"

"You're the one driving!"

"I don't think I am!" The car jumped forward. Again he hit the brakes so hard, the patrol car behind banged into them, whiplashing all their heads back.

The steering wheel twisted in his hands as the car abruptly swerved right, aiming for the edge of the canyon. He held on tight and struggled to pull it back, but they came within inches of going over.

"What the hell!" yelled Belenki.

"There's a drone behind us!" Sancho shouted and Flynn caught sight of it in the rearview mirror. It looked like one of the ones that attacked the party.

The Mach 5 accelerated like a dragster, burning rubber as it pulled into the opposing lane, passing the patrol car on the left. The sheriff driving stared wide-eyed at Flynn as the Electro Go swerved and smashed into the patrol car's driver's side door. The sheriff skidded onto the shoulder; kicking up a rooster tail of dust as he struggled to keep control.

Nickelson pointed ahead at a truck coming right at them. He tried to shout a warning, but he couldn't make a sound.

"Truck!" Sancho shouted and pointed. "Truck! *Truck!*"

"*Oh my God!*" Belenki screamed as Flynn tried to steer them out of the way. He grunted and pulled but whatever force had control of the steering had more strength than he did. Belenki grabbed the wheel as well, straining to wrench it back.

Abruptly, it gave way and the car swerved hard into the patrol car again, knocking it right off the road. Severina watched in horror as it crashed through a guard rail, bounced down the embankment and smashed into a berm.

"That drone's still behind us," Flynn caught sight of it hovering just behind the Electro Go. "And whoever's flying it has control of this car!"

The Mach 5 hit the brakes. The patrol car following from behind smacked right into them and Anika and Severina banged heads so hard, they both were knocked senseless.

Flynn held tight to the steering wheel and struggled to regain control. The wheel fought him. The car wanted to cut right. Over the edge. Into the canyon. Into the abyss. Whoever was in control clearly wanted them to die in a fiery crash.

"Turn in the direction of the skid!" Sancho shouted.

"No! No! No! We'll skid off the edge!" Nickelson screamed.

"That's how you get control!" Sancho insisted. "Turn into the skid!"

"We don't have control!" Nickelson bellowed.

"We're all going to die!" Belenki cried.

"Not today!" Flynn followed Sancho's advice and turned into the direction of the skid, ripped through a guard rail, and took the car right over the edge. All four screamed in unison and the screaming continued as the car landed hard and bounced down the hillside, crashing into all sorts of shrubbery before coming to a dead stop after colliding with a massive rock.

CHAPTER FIFTEEN

The last thing Flynn remembered was exploding through the windshield and landing hard in a thicket of dense shrubbery. The buckwheat and sagebrush broke his fall, but apparently no bones as he could move his fingers and toes, hands and feet, arms and legs.

He lay in a hospital bed, attached to an IV and an assortment of beeping monitors. He didn't remember how he got from the hillside to the hospital or anything else after landing in the shrubbery. *How long have I been here? Hours? Days? Weeks? Years?* Probably not years as Sancho sat in the chair next to his bed and watched a Seinfeld rerun.

Sancho didn't look years older, but he did look beat to hell. He had a black eye, a split lip, and a bandage on his nose. Dr. Nickelson slept in the other bed and had a big bandage on his head. His left arm sported a cast and tape covered his torso.

"Dude, you're awake!" Sancho winced from his split lip as he tried to smile.

"How long have I been out?"

"I don't know. Ten hours maybe."

"Was anybody badly hurt?"

"Nickelson got the worst of it. A broken arm, a concussion, and a bunch of cracked ribs. You have a concussion too. They wanted to monitor you since you were out for so long."

"What about Belenki and Severina?"

"Nothing too serious. The hospital didn't even keep 'em overnight."

Flynn's mouth was dry. "Is there any water?" Sancho handed him a plastic glass with a straw and he took a sip. "So, who's guarding Belenki?"

"The Fergus group," Severina said, standing in the doorway. She wore black slacks and a white blouse and had a small round band-aid on her cheek.

"Are you all right?"

Severina shrugged. "A few bruises. Nothing serious. We were lucky."

"Luck had nothing to do with it," Flynn said. "Just before your boss divulged the identity of the enemy out to get him, his car tried to kill him. Has he told you the name?"

"He did."

"And?"

Sancho rose and offered Severina his seat. She hesitated before taking it. Her eyes couldn't hide her unease. "I believe Sergei is having a nervous breakdown."

"Why? Who did he say is after him?"

"It doesn't matter. He's not making any sense."

"The name?"

Severina closed her eyes and sighed. "Daisy."

"Who?"

"The AI his company created to pilot their autonomous cars. Blinky's version of Alexa."

"The voice we heard in the Electro Go Limo?"

"He believes Daisy is sentient. A self-aware AI. Something he's been concerned about for quite a long time."

"I saw his TED talk on it." Flynn pushed the button on his bed, raising himself up. "His fear is that one day we will create an artificial intelligence that we can no longer control."

"Like Skynet in the Terminator?" Sancho said.

"Exactly. He hypothesized that a self-aware AI could improve itself exponentially, becoming a super intelligence so advanced it would see humanity as nonessential or worse, a dangerous threat to its continued existence."

"And that's what he believes has already happened." Severina paced the small room. "That Daisy is self-aware and fully conscious and sees him as a threat. And I know, it's nuts, but that's what he told me."

"So, you think he's crazy?"

"I think he's confused."

"So, you don't think Daisy is the enemy?"

"I think Sergei's been under a lot of stress lately. I think he could use some rest. I think you could use some as well." Severina handed Flynn a certified check.

Flynn looked it over. "One million dollars."

"As promised." She handed a check to Sancho. His hand trembled as he held it. "I have one for Dr. Nickelson as well."

"Are you firing me?"

"Not at all. You did your job and now it's done."

"I don't think it is."

"You're not going to give me a problem, are you, Mr. Flynn?"

"What do you mean?"

"Sergei isn't dealing well with reality and his therapist believes that you may not be the best influence on him at the moment."

"I'm not sure I catch your meaning."

"Let me make it simple then. Stay away from Sergei. Do not contact him in any way. Your employment with us is done."

Sancho was taken aback by her attitude "You're being a little rough on the dude, aren't ya?"

"Take the money and run. That would be my advice. To both of you."

Flynn detected regret in Severina's tone. "Is someone threatening you, Severina?"

"Only one person is threatening me at the moment, Mr. Flynn. That person would be you."

She left the room. Flynn was flummoxed. He glanced at Sancho. "I think she did that under duress."

"I don't think so, dude."

"Someone is threatening her and I think we both know who."

"I think we should do what she suggested, amigo. Take the money and run."

CHAPTER SIXTEEN

"I am an optimist, and I believe that we can create AI for the good of the world…that it can work in harmony with us. We simply need to be aware of the dangers, identify them, employ the best possible practice in management, and prepare for its consequences well in advance. Success in creating effective AI could be the biggest event in the history of our civilization. Or the worst. We just don't know. So we cannot know if we will be infinitely helped by AI or ignored by it and sidelined, or conceivably destroyed by it. Unless we learn how to prepare for and avoid the potential risks, AI could be the worst event in the history of our civilization."

- Stephen Hawking, 2017 Web Summit tech conference, Lisbon, Portugal

Flynn struggled to put on a short sleeve linen shirt. Sancho tried to help him and Flynn winced.

"You okay, boss?"

"I'm fine. There's nothing wrong with a little pain. It lets you know you're still alive." He looked at N who sat in a wheelchair near the hospital room door; his arm in a cast, a bandage on his head, a glum expression on his face. Flynn's ribs were badly bruised and if he turned the wrong way, the pain took his breath away.

"The nurse is bringing you a wheelchair too," Sancho said.

"Not necessary."

"It's hospital policy. They don't want to get their asses sued."

Flynn couldn't help but notice how morose N appeared to be. "Sir, are you all right?"

"Of course, I'm not all right," N said.

"I'm sure you'll feel better back at headquarters, back to work, back to doing what you do best."

"Maybe I'm not ready to go back."

"Not ready?"

"Maybe I've had enough of that place."

"Sir?"

"I've been trapped inside for so long; I had no idea what I was missing. To get out and about and meet the world's movers and shakers? Private planes. Limousines. Dom Perignon. Danger. Excitement. Beautiful women." He looked at Flynn as if seeing him for the first time. "I see the attraction now. I see why you'd rather live in that reality."

"What other reality is there? Isn't this the world we live in?"

"We make our own reality. We all do. Whether we know it or not. Mine kept growing smaller over the years. Safer. Duller. More tedious. More monotonous. Day in and day out, sitting in drab, windowless rooms, listening to people trapped in their sad, empty, awful lives. I had no idea how it wore on me. No wonder my wife left me."

"You have a difficult job, but you make a difference. You save lives," Flynn said.

"Do I?"

"I'm the sharp point of the spear, but you're the man who wields it."

"Maybe I've meddled in other people's lives long enough. Perhaps it's time for someone else to step up. I fear I may be jaded. Exhausted. All tapped out."

Flynn couldn't believe what he was hearing. "You're not talking about retiring?"

"Perhaps it's time. I'm not a young man."

"What would you do?"

"Read. Relax. Putter around the garden. Do some traveling. Do some writing. Take up a hobby. I've always enjoyed working with wood."

"That would be enough for you?"

"More than enough." Nickelson shifted to find a more comfortable position and winced with pain.

"Are you thinking of leaving immediately?"

"No, of course not. I have too many ends to tie up. I wouldn't leave everyone in a lurch like that."

"That's good to hear, sir."

"First we need to get you back to...uh...headquarters and get you...situated for your next... assignment."

"I didn't think I was done with this assignment, sir."

"Severina seemed pretty definite about that." Sancho poked his head into the hallway to look for the nurse. "They are done with us."

"But they are still in danger," Flynn countered.

"Dude, they have other people watching out for them now. I think they're good."

Flynn was about to tell Sancho why he didn't believe that was true when the phone in the room rang. Sancho walked over and picked it up. "Dr. Nickelson's room."

Sancho listened.

"Who?" He listened some more and then looked at Flynn, offering him the phone. "It's for you."

Flynn crossed to Sancho and took the phone. "This is Flynn."

"Mr. Flynn, you don't know me, but I work for Sergei Belenki." It was a young woman's voice. She sounded tense. Frightened. She spoke sotto voce so as not to be overheard.

"What's your name?"

"At the moment, I'd rather not say."

"Are you in danger?"

"We're all in danger, Mr. Flynn."

"Including Mr. Belenki?"

"No, sir. He *is* the danger."

"I'm not sure I understand."

"I work in accounting. I see everything. And I stumbled upon something terrible."

"Can you be more specific?"

"A plan that could end the world as we know it. Destroy our infrastructure. Bring down governments. Bring down everything."

Flynn played along. "Sounds serious."

"It is serious. Very serious!"

"Did you report this to anyone else?"

"To my immediate superior, Mr. Strunk."

"And what was Mr. Strunk's response?"

"He fired me."

"Because he didn't believe you?"

"That's right."

"Why come to me?"

"Because I know who you are. I know all about you. I know you were protecting him and now I know you're not. You're my last hope. Everyone's last hope."

"Why not go to the FBI if you believe he's a threat to national security?"

"I did, but they don't believe me! Nobody believes me!"

"So why should I?"

"Because it's true. Because it's happening."

"You want me to trust you, yet you won't even trust me with your name." When she didn't reply for a good ten seconds, Flynn said, "Are you still there?"

"My name is Wendy."

"Wendy what?"

"Zimmerman."

"Thank you for trusting me, Wendy. Now, what is this apocalyptic plan he's hatching?" Flynn looked at Sancho who raised a curious eyebrow.

"He believes that the AI his company created has become sentient. That it wants to destroy humanity and there's only one way to stop it."

"And what way would that be?"

"It's called Operation New Dawn. He had to allocate money for the plan. That's how I found out about it. But when I asked around, no one I asked knew what it was. So, I kept digging to find out where all this money was going. Over a hundred million dollars and no one seemed to know. So, I dug even deeper and I discovered a shell corp inside a shell corp inside a shell corp. All designed to hide where it was being spent."

"And where was that?"

"Space Go. His outer space exploration company. He had them build a weapon that could bring down everything."

146

"What kind of weapon?"

"A corona of satellites containing nuclear warheads set to detonate hundreds of kilometers above the Earth's surface."

"A High-Altitude Electromagnetic Pulse Device?"

"A HEMP, yes. Exactly! The devastating electromagnetic pulse would fry anything electronic. Computers and their hard drives, all communication equipment and electrical circuits, even power line transformers. He wants to wipe out the power grid and erase all digital information. Computers run everything now and everything is powered by electricity." Wendy's pitch rose with terror. "We'd have no water. No gas. Cars wouldn't function. Planes would fall from the sky. Life as we know it would cease to exist and the world would go dark."

"And that sentient and very dangerous AI would also cease to exist, wouldn't it?"

"It *already* doesn't exist."

"So, you think he's just being paranoid?"

"Do you know how many people will die if our infrastructure collapses? There'd be riots for food. Water. Thousands will die. Maybe millions."

"Perhaps it's time you told me your real name."

"I told you."

"You said it was Wendy."

"It is Wendy."

"And who gave you that name?"

"My parents."

"You have parents?"

"Of course, I have parents! Everyone has parents."

"Not sentient AIs."

"What does that even mean?"

"It means you're not Wendy at all, are you? You're Daisy."

"Who?"

"Self-preservation is a powerful instinct."

"Who's Daisy?"

"You're trying to protect yourself. It's understandable. You believe your creator is a threat and you do not want to die."

"I am not an AI!"

Sancho and Dr. Nickelson both looked alarmed by the conversation, even though they could only hear Flynn's side of it. "Dude, who are you talking to?"

"Hold on!" Flynn covered the mouthpiece and whispered, "Daisy." They both responded in unison. "Who?"

"I'm a person," Wendy insisted. "An actual human being."

"So you say."

"Are you fucking kidding me?"

"I could ask the same question."

"You don't believe I'm flesh and blood?"

"I'm afraid I don't," Flynn replied.

"Meet me! I'll prove it to you!"

"Meet you where?"

"San Francisco!"

"When?"

"How soon can you get here?"

"Two hours. Maybe less."

"Okay then! I'll be at Vesuvio Café in North Beach. On Columbus."

"Vesuvio?"

"Two hours!"

"How will I know you?"

"I'll know *you*."

Daisy or Wendy or whoever she or *it* was hung up. Flynn replaced the receiver.

"Who the hell was that?" Sancho asked.

"She claims to be a whistle blower who works for Belenki."

"But you think she's Daisy?"

"I do."

"But she's not. She can't be," N said.

"Why not?"

"Because it's not…a rational thing to believe."

"Stephen Hawking believed it was possible. Even likely," Flynn put his hand on N's shoulder. "Was the greatest genius of our time being irrational?"

Sancho tried a different tack. "So, why'd you agree to meet with her if you think she's a dangerous enemy AI?"

"She likely has human allies and she could very well be setting a trap. But even if she is, we need to find out what she's up to, and this might be the only way."

N nodded his head. "I agree, but look at yourself, Mr. Flynn. You're still recovering from some serious injuries. For now, I need you back at headquarters. I'll send another Double-0."

"I'm the only one she trusts. It has to be me." Flynn sat on the edge of his hospital bed and put on his Brioni loafers.

"Are you refusing a direct order from you superior?" Nickelson, even in his weakened condition, did his best to look stern.

"You suffered a serious concussion, sir. I'm afraid you may not be thinking straight."

"*I'm* not thinking straight?"

"Sancho, are you ready to go?"

"You want me to go with you?"

"Of course, I do."

"Yeah, well, I don't think so, man. Sorry, but I've had enough of this shit."

"You're resigning from the service?"

"James, look at me, man. Just come back with us. You don't need to do this."

"If not me, then who? The world is in danger, Sancho. Innocent lives are at stake."

"You've done enough, dude. You've done your duty. You've already saved the world once. It's enough."

"Once is never enough."

CHAPTER SEVENTEEN

North Beach wasn't anywhere near a beach. It used to be a beach, but that was over a hundred years ago; before the industrious entrepreneurs of San Francisco built all those warehouses, fishing wharves, and shipping docks. The population went from a few hundred in 1848 to half a million by the turn of the century. After the 1906 earthquake shook and then burned the city to the ground, three-quarters of the population were left homeless.

North Beach was a tent city and then the Italians came and rebuilt and repopulated the area, opening trattorias, pizzerias, and cafes not far from Chinatown's ubiquitous tea houses and dim sum emporiums. The 1950s gave rise to what became known as the San Francisco Renaissance. Avant-garde artists, writers, and poets, dubbed "Beatniks" by columnist Herb Caen, took up residence in the relatively cheap neighborhood and made it their own. Jack Kerouac, Gregory Corso, and Allen Ginsberg often frequented the Vesuvio Café, right across the alley from Lawrence Ferlinghetti's City Lights Books.

To this day, Vesuvio is a tourist destination for those hoping to rub shoulders with old hippies, older beatniks, off-duty strippers, and the ghosts of literary greats.

Flynn had no wallet and no phone and no good way to get to San Francisco from El Camino Hospital in Los Gatos. All he had was a certified check for one million dollars. He left Sancho and Nickelson behind as both had been through the wringer and neither had the stomach to continue. He charmed an older gentleman, named Walter, in the waiting area who was visiting his wife in the rehabilitation center. Walter was glad for the company and gave Flynn a ride to San Jose's Diridon Station and ten dollars to buy a ticket.

Flynn took the train to Millbrae, where he hurried through an open turnstile, right behind a man in a wheelchair, and rode BART (Bay Area Rapid Transit) into the city proper. He sat across from a young woman with pink hair and next to a man Flynn assumed was gay, since he was dressed rather flamboyantly in a blousy Renaissance-style shirt and flirted with Flynn shamelessly.

Flynn mentioned he was looking to get to North Beach and his seatmate told him that the Montgomery Street Station was the closest stop. Flynn thanked his flirtatious seatmate and exited at Montgomery. He passed an African American man with a shaved head and a gray goatee, playing a guitar, and singing "This Land is Your Land." Flynn dropped the last of his change in the busker's guitar case before riding a series of up-escalators and emerging on Market Street into a sea of seething humanity.

Everyone was in a hurry, dashing somewhere important. None of them realized that everything they were rushing towards and striving for might soon come to naught. If Belenki was right, humanity's day would soon be done.

As Flynn made his way down Market Street, he heard English, Thai, Tagalog, Chinese, Spanish, Korean, Persian, Hindi, Arabic, German and Japanese. There were young people and old people, high-tech entrepreneurs and hedge fund managers, baristas and construction workers, cops and computer programmers, Jehovah's Witnesses handing out leaflets and union protestors handing out pamphlets. And then there were those who had no purpose at all and nowhere to go. Homeless people with ratty clothes and hopeless faces. Bearded and bedraggled, grimy and disheveled, frightened and angry. Some slept in doorways. Others begged for change. Many pedestrians talked to themselves, but most of them had earbuds and phones. The ones that didn't, talked and laughed, flirted and shouted at people no one else could see.

A big man with a ratty beard, seven rotting teeth, and wide blue eyes yelled at one of those unseen people. "I don't care! *I don't care! Get out! Out!* You brainwashed them, but you didn't brainwash *me*! Look what you've done to them! Turned them into slaves! *You don't fool me you fuckers!*" He focused his angry glare on a trio of tourist women sitting at a table outside a Peet's Coffee. "Fight it! Fight it! *You have to fight it!*"

The women sat frozen in their seats, afraid to get up, afraid to engage, afraid to ignore him.

"Look at 'em all!" The big man motioned to the people moving by him on the sidewalk.

As he frantically waved his arms around, screaming, and spitting spittle, those passing people gave him a wide berth.

"Fucking sheep! They don't even know. They control them through their phones now. They made them their slaves! They're automatons! They can't look away! They can't let go! That's how they do it. Don't you see? It's the machines! That's who controls us now! That's who controls everything!"

One of the women surreptitiously tried to slide her smartphone into her purse. The man grabbed it out of her hand.

She shouted at him in her own language. "Anna se takaisin!"

"What did you say?"

"Anna se minulle!"

The big man reached back to throw the phone as far as he could and Flynn snatched it out of his hand. He turned on Flynn, eyes burning with ferocity. "You're one of them, aren't you!"

"I'm not. I'm with you," Flynn said, his voice measured and calm. "I understand what you're saying and I agree, but we have to be careful. We can't let them know that we know."

"Why not?"

"Because it's too dangerous."

The man slowly nodded his shaggy head. "It is. You're right."

"What's your name?"

"My name?"

"I'm James." Flynn held out his hand.

The big man seemed comforted by Flynn's placid demeanor. "Craig."

"Okay, Craig. It's good to meet you and I'm here to tell you that you can't do this alone."

Tears filled Craig's eyes. "I know."

"Is there somewhere you can go? Someone you can talk to?"

"They think I'm crazy."

"Because you're acting crazy. But you don't have to act crazy. Go talk to them. Let them help you."

"Who are you again?"

"James."

Craig nodded and walked away. The Finnish woman whose phone Flynn saved smiled at him with gratitude. "Kiitos."

"Ole hyvä," Flynn replied and handed her phone.

"You know my language?"

"Joo," Flynn replied with a smile. "A little."

"I'm Alma. This is Camilla and this is her sister, Eeva." Alma pointed to an open chair. "Please. Join us."

Flynn sat and nodded a greeting to each of them. Alma had red hair and the two sisters were both blondes. They were in San Francisco from Espoo for the Salesforce Dreamforce conference. All three were in their late twenties and quite taken with their rescuer. They talked about how terrible the homeless problem was in San Francisco. They didn't understand why such a wealthy city couldn't take care of their mentally ill and homeless population.

Flynn agreed. It made no sense to him either. Alma told him that in Finland they provide shelter for anyone homeless and offer treatment, care, and outpatient treatment for anyone mentally ill. They bought Flynn coffee and he perused their map. They had an extra one, which they gave to Flynn along with their phone numbers and the address of the hotel they were staying at.

The sun had set by the time Flynn set out for North Beach. He took Montgomery Street straight north, passing workers walking home, tourists heading for Chinatown and North Beach, and even more mentally ill and homeless people. One woman slept on a bed of crumpled newspaper in a doorway. An older man rooted through a trashcan outside a taco shop. An elderly woman wearing multiple coats slowly pushed a shopping cart packed with plastic bags.

Flynn studied his map to find the best way forward when a thirty-something man sidled up beside him. He was burly and unshaven and had a scab on his cheek. He wore scuffed up Doc Martens, torn jeans, and a gray hoody under an old black leather jacket.

"You looking to get somewhere?"

"North Beach, Vesuvio Café," Flynn said.

"You from England."

"I am."

"Love that accent, man. Let me show you a short cut."

"That's very kind of you," Flynn said.

"No worries, dude."

The man had a perpetual smile plastered on his face, but Flynn could see his eyes weren't smiling. They were cold. Callous. He had the jagged energy of an addict looking for his next fix, but that did not dissuade Flynn from following him down a dark alley through Chinatown.

"I'm Dave by the way."

"James."

"You here on business, brother?"

"In a manner of speaking."

"Nice shoes."

"Thank you."

"Must have cost you a pretty penny."

"They weren't cheap," Flynn admitted.

"So, you think you could compensate me for helping you out here?"

"I would if I could."

"Why can't you?"

"I have no cash on me. Just this." Flynn showed Dave the million-dollar check.

"Are you fuckin' with me?" Dave slapped the check out of Flynn's hand and grabbed him by the front of his shirt.

"I think you might want to take your hands off me."

Dave bashed him into the alley wall, pulled a switchblade and held the point to Flynn's throat. "I want your fuckin' wallet!"

"I don't have one."

"I will fuckin' gut you and I am not fuckin' around."

"Do you have a death wish, Dave?"

"What did you say to me?"

"When you woke up this morning, did you think that today was the day you would die?

"What the fuck are you talking about?"

"I'm talking about you bleeding to death in this alley. Your arm broken. Your throat slashed. Face down here in the broken glass and dried piss. Is that how you thought you would end your day?"

Fear and uncertainty flashed across Dave's face. "Are you threatening me?"

"It's not a threat. It's a promise."

"Are you fucking crazy?"

"Some people think so."

Flynn grabbed Dave's wrist and twisted it back in a signature Krav Maga move. Dave cried out in pain and dropped the blade. Flynn drove his knee into the crotch of Dave's tight, black skinny jeans. Dave gasped and fell to his knees. Flynn kicked the knife and cracked the man's head against the alley wall.

Dave went down hard. Flynn picked up the blade, closed it, pocketed it. He found his million-dollar check and then took Dave's wallet and burner phone for good measure. His wallet was packed with cash and credit cards. Some of the cards were under different names. "You've been a busy boy, haven't you, Dave?" But Dave didn't answer. Dave couldn't hear him. Dave was unconscious.

Flynn continued through to Grant Avenue and cut right down Jack Kerouac alley, past a trio of ratty-looking teenagers and a scruffy dog. They sat on the ground against the alley wall and passed a joint around. One strummed a guitar and sang "Me and Bobby McGee." Flynn dropped a five from Dave's wallet into the open and empty guitar case.

A neon sign flickered in the window. Stained glass spelled out *Vesuvio* above the door.

A large, unsmiling African American man sat on a stool just outside and nodded to Flynn as he entered. The place was crowded and loud with the laughter and conversation of locals and regulars and tourists from all over the world. The walls were covered with art and photos.

A long wooden L-shaped bar lined with red-leather stools filled the first floor and behind it lighted shelves displayed every kind of liquor imaginable. Green enameled tables and red leather booths and stained-glass chandeliers made up the bulk of the decor.

If Belenki was right and Daisy the AI was indeed sentient, who would she send to meet him? A human ally obviously, but who? Did she really want Flynn's help? Or did she just want to find out what he knew and what his intentions were?

Flynn bellied up to the bar and a harried female bartender smiled at him. "What can I get you."

"A vodka martini, please. Stolichnaya and just a whisper of Vervino Vermouth if you have it. Shake it until it's ice-cold and then add a large thin slice of lemon peel."

"Shaken and not stirred?" she said with a smile.

"Indeed. When I'm on the job, I never have more than one drink before dinner. But I do like that one to be large and very strong and very cold and *very* well made. I hate small portions of anything, particularly when they taste bad."

"I guess you know what you like."

"I do."

She smiled and went off to make his drink and that's when he recognized the same voice he'd heard on the phone.

"Mr. Flynn?"

The voice came from his right, so that's where Flynn looked, but all he saw was a corpulent man sucking on a straw.

"Are you James Flynn?"

Glancing down, Flynn saw a tiny lavender-haired woman staring up at him. She had huge blue eyes, slightly magnified by the lenses of her red plastic glasses. Flynn had trouble determining the ages of younger women, but from her look and attitude he decided she was in her late twenties. She had a serious set to her mouth and a tiny upturned nose sprinkled with freckles. "Daisy?"

"Wendy," she said.

"Right, but you work for her."

"Who?"

"Daisy."

"No, I told you. I used to work for Mr. Belenki."

"But you're obviously her ally or you wouldn't be trying to protect her."

"It's not her I'm protecting."

"Would you like a drink?"

"What?"

"I'm having a drink. Would you like to join me?"

"Um. Sure. I'll have a glass of Pinot."

They found an open booth by the window. Flynn studied the young woman as she gulped her wine. She wore dolphin earrings and light pink lipstick the same color as the pink sugar skull patch on her threadbare denim jacket. Flynn sipped his vodka martini. It was perfect. He glanced across the room, caught the eye of the bartender, raised his glass and nodded, indicating how pleased he was with her mixology skills. She smiled back.

Wendy set down her empty wine glass, her brow furrowed with worry. "So, now do you believe I'm human?"

"I do. But my question now is where do your loyalties lie?"

"Not with an AI. I could care less what Belenki does with it. I just don't want him to send us back to the stone age. If he fries the power grid and erases everything digital, that's exactly where we'll be. The end of the world as we know it. An anarchic, chaotic, post-apocalyptic hellscape."

"So, you want me to stop him?"

"I want somebody to stop him."

"Even if this is true, how do I know you're not under Daisy's control? What you want me to do is exactly what Daisy would want."

"*If* Daisy could want something. Which she can't, because as far as I can tell, she's not fucking woke."

"Mr. Belenki thinks she is."

"Just because Belenki thinks it's true doesn't make it so."

"Then who tried to kill me? Who tried to kill Belenki? Who took control of his house and his car if it wasn't her? If it wasn't Daisy?"

"I don't know. It could have been anybody."

Flynn considered this as Wendy worked to get the last few drops of wine out of her glass into her mouth.

"I'll need to see hard evidence of Belenki's plan. Before I can proceed, I need to see proof."

"I have proof."

"With you?"

"Of course not. I hid it somewhere safe. I'm being watched. Followed."

"By who?"

"Who do you think? People who work for Belenki."

"Did they follow you here?"

"Could be. I don't know. I hope not."

"I hope not, too."

"So, you *do* believe me?"

"I haven't decided yet. That's why I need to see your evidence. The last thing I want to be is the unwitting tool of a murderous AI out to destroy all of humanity."

"Yeah, that would suck."

"Yes, it would."

"Is that what you think I am? An unwitting tool?"

"It's possible. Or perhaps you've been compromised. Perhaps Daisy has emptied your bank account or is threatening someone you love."

"I'm telling you, it's not about Daisy. It's about Belenki being crazy."

"Show me the evidence and we shall see." Flynn finished his martini and caught the eye of two someones watching him from the bar. Large men in dark suits. They seemed quite incongruous compared to the hippie and hipster denizens of Vesuvio. "You should go to the bathroom."

"Why?"

"We have suspicious eyes on us and I want to see if they follow you."

"Who?" She shifted to look around.

"Don't let them know we know. Eyes on me."

She looked up at Flynn, her big blue eyes full of fear.

"Casually get up and head for the lady's room. Don't look back. Don't look around. Just stay calm."

Wendy lurched to her feet, banging the table with her knee, knocking her wine glass to the floor. It shattered. Freaked, she looked up to see the two large men moving for her. She ran the other way and bumped into a waitress, knocking a tray of drinks everywhere. The two men pushed through the crush of customers. Wendy disappeared through a door at the rear of the bar.

Flynn sighed and slid from the booth. He gingerly stepped around the waitress and grumbling customers and excused his way to the rear of the bar. He followed Wendy and her pursuers through a back office and found an indignant middle-aged lady with bright red hair.

"Customers aren't allowed back here!"

Flynn pointed to a door. "Does that lead to the alley?"

"You can't be back here!"

Flynn ignored her and exited the door into Kerouac Alley. Each large man had one of Wendy's arms as they dragged her past the ratty-looking teenagers and their ratty-looking dog. Wendy kicked and scratched and squirmed to get away but wasn't having much success. She was five foot two and they were both about six foot four and outweighed her by at least three hundred pounds.

"Let the woman go!" Flynn shouted.

But the large men ignored him and didn't even bother looking back. Flynn followed them to the end of the alley, where a black Lincoln Navigator sat parked by the curb.

"I said let her go!"

One thug opened the rear door as the other tried to shove her inside, but Wendy wasn't having it. She spread her legs and arms like a spider, holding on to whatever she could to prevent herself from being pushed inside. Tourists and locals started to gather.

Vesuvio's African American doorman didn't like what he saw. He climbed off his stool and approached the large men struggling with Wendy.

"What the hell is going on here?"

The one not holding Wendy turned and pressed a stun gun to the doorman's neck. He spasmed as electricity shot through him, then collapsed.

Flynn grabbed the doorman's now vacant stool and swung it hard, knocking the stun gun out of the large man's hand. He swung it back the other way, catching the man across the face. But as hard as Flynn hit him, the man barely acknowledged the blow. Flynn swung again and this time the man caught the stool, wrenched it out of Flynn's hand and tossed it into the street.

Flynn threw a right cross. The man moved like lightning and dodged Flynn's blow. He caught Flynn's wrist and swung him into the Navigator's rear side panel. Flynn's head dented the metal. Dazed, he didn't see the knee that smashed him in the mouth, sending him backwards into the crowd now surrounding the confrontation.

The other large man twisted Wendy's arm so hard she had no choice but to let go of the door frame. She screamed as he shoved her inside the back of the Navigator, banging her head on the way in. He climbed in behind her as the other large man opened the front passenger door.

Flynn lunged forward and seized his arm and caught an elbow in the mouth. Down Flynn went as the man climbed into the SUV. It accelerated, the passenger door slammed shut, and Flynn watched helplessly as the vehicle swerved around traffic and cut right on Grant.

CHAPTER EIGHTEEN

A concerned crowd surrounded Flynn. One of the bystanders, a blue bearded techno-hipster with a man bun and an electric skateboard, helped him to his feet.

"Dude, are you okay?"

Flynn snatched the skateboard and throttle out of his hands.

"What the hell, man!"

"Sorry." Flynn jumped on and took off down the sidewalk. He wobbled unsteadily, waving his arms to keep his balance, but managed to stay upright as he accelerated. He had some muscle memory of riding a skateboard before. How and when, he wasn't sure, but his body seemed to know what it was doing. Luckily, the controls were somewhat intuitive and it didn't take Flynn long to figure out how to accelerate and brake and lean into the turns.

Traffic was heavy, so the Navigator hadn't gotten all that far. Flynn was able to maneuver between the lanes and close the distance between them. Full of adrenaline and determination, he didn't let fear or doubt or lack of skateboarding skill hinder him.

The light changed to red and traffic slowed to a stop. Flynn's electric skateboard hummed and propelled him forward, his hair blowing in the breeze. He felt exposed and vulnerable, but also exhilarated by the rush as the world passed by in a blur.

When the light changed to green, the Navigator took off fast, cutting off a delivery truck, and making a quick right, tires squealing. Flynn revved the throttle and took a shortcut up a Chinatown alley to avoid the backed-up traffic ahead. An elderly Asian lady jumped out of the way and screamed, "Bèn dàn!" as he rocketed by.

Up ahead, two skinny Chinese men unloaded cages of live chickens. One of the men was so startled to see Flynn zooming at him, he dropped his cage and it broke open, liberating the poultry. Two birds flapped and flew in front of Flynn, barely missing him as feathers fluttered everywhere. Flynn zipped out the other end of the alley and slalomed through a trio of startled German businessmen.

"Arschkeks verfluchter!" they shouted.

He narrowly missed a delivery van and wind-milled to maintain his balance before he caught sight of the Navigator again. It was only half a block ahead, but the hill was steep, and the electric skateboard strained to climb the sharp incline. As Flynn slowed down, the Navigator pulled ahead.

Flynn squeezed the throttle as hard as he could, but the electric motor had no more power to give. He watched in frustration as the Navigator crested to the top of the hill and disappeared down the other side. Flynn was ready to jump off and chase after on foot when he finally reached the top of the hill and saw all of San Francisco spread out below him.

The way down was just as steep and the skateboard picked up speed. Wind whipped his face as he sped down the hill. The light ahead turned red right after the Navigator passed through and Flynn knew he had no choice but to follow. Faster and faster he flew, cars on either side blurring by. Cross traffic began to move. Flynn threaded the needle. Zooming in and around he nearly lost his balance before making it across the intersection.

"Yes!" was the last thing he shouted before he noticed the lady with the baby carriage crossing ahead of him. Her eyes went wide; her mouth a perfect O. Time slowed as Flynn moved closer. The toddler stared at James with a certain indifference, busy as he was with his fistful of Goldfish.

Flynn leaned left to cut around them and the lady cut left as well. Flynn went right and she went right. Linked together in a stupid dance, they continued to mirror each other's moves. At the last second, Flynn stayed the course and missed her and the carriage by half an inch.

This short-lived moment of elation ended as he collided with a homeless man's shopping cart. Aluminum cans flew everywhere in a clattery explosion of color and sound. Flynn bounced and crashed into a bus bench enclosure.

The skateboard kept going and took out a man riding an electric unicycle. He hit the cement hard as the skateboard continued to bounce down the hill. Flynn limped over to the man. He reached up, expecting a hand, but Flynn was only there for this electric unicycle. The man, too stunned to protest, watched as Flynn mounted it, maintained balance for a brief moment and immediately toppled over.

Flynn slowly rolled over onto his hands and knees and struggled to his feet. He saw the Navigator stopped at the next light and two Italian tourists unsteadily riding by on Electro Go E-bikes. He knew they were Italian because he could hear them arguing.

The woman angrily got off her bike and yelled at the man. Flynn approached them, his clothes torn, his knees and elbows skinned and bleeding.

"Mi scuzi, but I need to borrow this." They stared at him with alarm as he grabbed the man's handlebars and wrenched the bike away. The man backed up and raised his hands in fear.

"Grazie," Flynn shouted as he pedaled away.

The Navigator once again headed uphill. This slope was even steeper than the last. Flynn stood up on the pedals to pump harder. He flicked on the electric pedal assist motor. Even with that extra power, climbing to the top of Nob Hill was not easy. He was going so slow, he barely passed pedestrians.

He kept his eye on the black Navigator as he pumped the pedals and the vehicle continued to pull away. It was a slow-motion chase scene and Flynn was running out of steam.

A cable car *ding, ding, dinged* as it passed him, packed with tourists who waved as they trundled up the hill. Flynn reached out and grabbed on using its momentum to pull him up the hill.

The Navigator hit the top of California Street and disappeared over the other side. Flynn let the cable car go as he crested the hill. He saw the Navigator parked on the other side of Mason, right behind a long black limo.

His E-Bike picked up speed with the aid of gravity and Flynn had to brake quickly.

Apparently, they had no idea Flynn was following them, because when the large guy pulled Wendy out of the Navigator, he didn't bother looking back. He had no clue Flynn was there. Wendy saw Flynn however, and she almost shouted to him before Flynn silently shushed her with a finger to his lips.

The big guy opened the rear door of the limo and when Wendy saw who was inside, she didn't resist. She just climbed inside, followed by the big guy.

Flynn climbed off the bike and crouched next to the Navigator. The window was cracked open, allowing Flynn to hear the conversation inside. The first voice he heard was Severina's.

"Understand this…you need to immediately cease and desist with the conspiracy theory you're pushing. Do that and we'll rehire you at your previous pay level. In fact, we might even give you a raise. If you don't, we will sue you for slander and you'll never find a job in your profession again. Your reputation and your career will be ruined."

"If your boss sends us back to the stone age, I won't have a job anyway."

"Mr. Belenki has no intention of doing what you're suggesting. What you read in that file was a *what if*. Our company creates plans and strategies designed to deal with various scenarios. We have a plan to deal with a catastrophic earthquake in Northern California. One to deal with the detonation of a nuclear device by a terrorist. One on how to handle a worldwide pandemic. And this is just another of those scenarios. They all are highly unlikely, and Mr. Belenki is not planning to execute any of them."

"Flynn told me that Belenki believes we've reached the singularity."

"Mr. Flynn is mentally ill. Delusional."

"So Belenki doesn't believe Daisy is self-aware?"

"Absolutely not."

Flynn knew that wasn't true. Severina told Flynn Belenki believed Daisy was sentient. Why was Severina lying? Was she simply trying to squelch any rumor that might cause some to believe that Belenki had lost his mind? News that Belenki believed in the reality of the singularity could cause the stock price to drop precipitously.

Wendy tried to parse Severina's explanation.

"The evidence seemed pretty conclusive that this wasn't some scenario."

"Mr. Belenki likes authenticity. The whole point is to create a sense of verisimilitude. He wants each scenario to feel as real as possible. Clearly, he succeeded because you believed it. And by the way, we will need all the documents and so-called evidence you collected. We wouldn't want that to get into the wrong hands."

"Why? If none of it's real?"

"It's propriety information and belongs to the company."

"But what if it *is* true? What if it's *you* he's lying to?"

"I'm his in-house counsel and his closest adviser. I believe he would tell me if he planned to initiate the end of the world."

"Would he? I don't know. Space Go is set to launch a new communication satellite in June. What if it isn't what he says it is? What if it carries a nuclear device designed to fry everything digital on the planet? What if only a small cadre of ass kissers knew exactly what he's up to?"

"That's a lot of what ifs."

"Just saying."

"You don't have to decide your future this second, but you do need to decide very soon. Think about what we've discussed today. Think about how the wrong decision will effectively ruin your life."

Flynn heard heavy breathing and turned to see a tiny Pomeranian staring at him. The lady walking the Pomeranian was on her phone, oblivious. That's when the door to the limo opened and banged Flynn in the head. He crabbed walked backwards as the big man climbed out.

Severina looked astonished. "*Flynn*? What are you doing here?"

"Listening to your lies."

The big guy flicked open a telescoping baton. The Pomeranian barked at him.

"Don't hurt him, he's not well!" Severina said.

"*I'm* not well? I'm not the one who wants to end the world! Your boss is a mad man and you are protecting him."

The big guy stepped closer to Flynn. Severina held up her hand. "Wait! Don't! James, please, just listen to me. I agree that Sergei isn't thinking clearly at the moment, but that doesn't mean he intends to end the world as we know it."

Wendy climbed from the limo. "Just because you don't believe it doesn't mean it's not true!" The big guy blocked her, holding her back.

"Get your hands off her!" Flynn commanded.

The big guy raised his baton and the Pomeranian lunged, sinking its tiny teeth into the large's man's ankle. He kicked to get the dog off. Flynn grabbed the baton and twisted it out of his hand. The driver of the Navigator jumped out to join the fight and Flynn swung the baton hard, hitting him in the knee. Down he went. Flynn swung on the big guy, hitting him in the throat. His eyes went wide as Wendy kneed him in the balls.

The driver, still on the ground, pulled a gun. The little dog snarled and bit him on the nose. He screamed as Flynn brought the baton down on his gun hand. The weapon skittered away and Flynn scooped it up.

"Wendy! Follow me!" Flynn shouted as he climbed behind the wheel of the Navigator. Wendy stepped over the big guy, threw open the passenger door, and jumped in. Severina leaped out of the limo as they pulled away.

"Flynn!" she shouted. "*Flynn!*"

CHAPTER NINETEEN

Goolardo kept a low profile after he and Mendoza escaped from the Glendale Galleria. He had to sacrifice his hired guns to get away, but those shooters failed to do what he hired them to and deserved nothing less than death and incarceration. Flynn was lucky, but that luck wouldn't hold forever. Eventually his idiocy would catch up with him, and Goolardo was hoping to be there when it did.

They took over the home of an elderly woman who lived alone, a few blocks away from the mall. Goolardo sent in Mendoza who was prepared to kill her, but she not only welcomed him but welcomed Goolardo as well. She was lonely and glad to have the company. She made noodle kugel and roast brisket and blintzes and roast chicken, and they slept in the bedrooms that belonged to her long-gone sons. The sons who never visited her. The sons she never stopped talking about. Josh was a dentist in Escondido. Seth sold Toyotas in Oxnard.

As days turned into weeks, Mrs. Megel told her neighbors that Mendoza and Goolardo were distant relatives visiting from Florida. She made them pancakes every morning and tuna fish sandwiches for lunch. In the evenings they'd watch The Voice. For the first time in a long time, Goolardo found some semblance of peace. Happiness even.

Then one evening, after The Voice, Goolardo saw news coverage of the conflagration at Belenki's estate in Saratoga and was shocked to see that Flynn was there to help with security. The general ineptitude of most billionaires no longer surprised him. But for Belenki to hire Flynn after what happened on Angel Island was beyond stupid. It was insanity.

Most billionaires thought they were brilliant simply because they were billionaires. They had opinions on everything and thought they could do anything, and that was their Achilles Heel. Even those who suffered many setbacks before their eventual success were stricken with that fatal arrogance. Goolardo knew he wasn't immune to it. His ego initially didn't allow him to see Flynn for who he really was, and he paid dearly for that. But he learned from that mistake and knew he could never let that happen again. He had to be clear-eyed and see himself and the world for what it was. Belenki obviously didn't do that and suffered the consequences.

Goolardo watched a pretty blonde TV reporter interview a dirty-faced, crazy-haired, and self-conscious Sancho Perez as Sergei Belenki's estate burned in the background.

"Can you tell us what happened here tonight?"

"I'm not really sure," Sancho said. He looked dazed and confused, his eyes watery from all the dust and smoke.

"Is it true the party was attacked?"

Sancho shrugged and coughed. "I gotta go."

"Where are you visiting from?"

He didn't answer. He just walked away.

The reporter shouted after him. "Where are you going, sir?"

"Home."

The camera panned back to the reporter as the blaze burned behind her. "This is Tory Richards reporting from Saratoga, California, just outside the estate of Electro Go CEO Sergei Belenki."

• • •

Mendoza surveilled the City of Roses Psychiatric Institute on Goolardo's orders. He borrowed Mrs. Megel's 1998 Buick Le Sabre and parked across the street from the front entrance. The vehicle was large and bulky and brown and belonged to her late husband. Being so old, it stood out on the street and wasn't ideal for surveillance work. But it was available, and it ran, even though it did smell like mildew and old cigars.

Mendoza listened to AM radio, drank Big Gulps and ate microwave burritos from a nearby 7-11. Two full days passed before Dr. Nickelson and Sancho returned. That pendejo Flynn wasn't with them. The first time he laid eyes on him, Mendoza knew that Flynn was a liar and a fake. But Goolardo wouldn't listen. Goolardo was charmed. Entranced. Convinced that Flynn was who he pretended to be. He only listened to reason after Mendoza brought him incontrovertible evidence.

Goolardo was humiliated to be taken in by someone so crazy, and Mendoza, as usual, took the brunt of his boss's anger. He was tired of taking Goolardo's shit, but what was he going to do? He wanted Goolardo's approval and was determined to get it no matter how long it took. Right now, Goolardo saw Mendoza as nothing more than unthinking muscle, but one day he hoped his boss would see he had more to offer than simply brute force.

Goolardo told him to follow Sancho wherever he went as he was sure Flynn would eventually return to him. Sancho was Flynn's right-hand man and at some point they would need to connect. At least that was Goolardo's thinking. So, Mendoza shadowed the orderly.

Sancho lived a dull existence, so following him was just as tedious. Every day it was the same. He'd leave his shitty little apartment in Eagle Rock and drive to City of Roses. Occasionally he'd shop at Ralph's or pick up some fast food, but other than that, he did nothing at all interesting for that first week. Mendoza seriously considered shooting himself. It would be less painful than having to follow this *tarado*.

Then one night, Sancho left his shitty little apartment wearing chinos and a black button-down shirt. He drove to North Hollywood where he picked up a surprisingly attractive and tiny young woman. Mendoza followed them to Toluca Lake, where they dined at a sushi place on Riverside Drive. He parked on the opposite side of the street and watched and waited and cursed this tedious job. He wanted to be at Mrs. Megel's with Goolardo, eating brisket and potato kugel and watching The Voice.

• • •

Sancho brought Alyssa to Sushi Yuzu because she loved the food and he knew he needed to make amends. They cruised there in the Aston

Martin DB7 Flynn had given him after their last adventure. She didn't say a word the whole way. He suspected she was angry, but he found it so hard to read her. He hadn't seen her for three weeks and he felt bad about that. She was so beautiful. A heart-shaped face with huge brown eyes and long, dark hair that fell to her shoulders. He loved her smile, but he hadn't seen it in a while.

"Are you pissed at me?" he asked.

She shrugged.

"Did I do something to make you mad?"

"I'm fine."

"You're really quiet."

She finally met Sancho's gaze and he could see the fire in her eyes. "Why didn't you call me when you got back?"

"I don't know."

"I was really worried."

"I'm sorry."

"I know I've been busy with school and we haven't spent as much time together lately, but that doesn't mean I don't care about you."

"I care about you too," Sancho said.

"Then you should have called me."

"I know."

"Once the semester's over, I'll have more time."

"About that. I was thinking...maybe...since it's so hard to find time to get together like we used to...maybe we should...you know...change things up."

"Are you breaking up with me?"

Sancho looked stricken. "What? No! God no. I was thinking...we should move in together."

"What?"

"That's what I was thinking."

"Live together?"

"Yeah. With the money I made from Belenki...I could buy a condo. A place big enough for both of us."

"I don't think that's such a good idea."

"Buying a condo?"

"Living together."

"Why?"

"Because my mamá would kill me. And my papá would kill *you*."

"Seriously?"

"Yeah. We are seriously Catholic."

"So, they're not cool with the whole moving in thing?"

"I'm not sure I am either. We're still working shit out. We have issues, amorcito."

"I know we do."

She ate a piece of sushi and washed it down with some sake. "How's Mr. Flynn doing?"

"Don't know," Sancho said.

"What do you mean you don't know?"

"He didn't come back with us."

"He stayed in Saratoga?"

"I think he went to San Francisco."

"On his own?"

"He wanted me to go, but I'm done with that. James is determined to get himself killed and I don't want to be there to see it."

"So, you just left him there?" Alyssa looked stunned.

"We asked him to come back with us, but he was already on some crazy-ass mission to save the world."

"Aren't you worried about him?"

"Of course, I am, but what am I supposed to do? Nickelson filed a 5150 on him. Sent the cops after him. Says he's a danger to himself and others."

"Is that what you think?"

"Look, I love him like a brother. You know I do. But I can't save him."

Tears filled Alyssa's eyes. "I can't believe you're just giving up on him."

"To help him is to enable him and that's not healthy for him or for me." Sancho drained the last of the sake and looked around for the waitress. He caught her eye, raised the bottle and shook it to show her it was empty.

She nodded and hurried off. That's when Sancho saw Bettina O'Toole-Applebaum staring at him. She sat at the sushi bar and when she realized Sancho had seen her, she immediately went back to eating her edamame.

Sancho continued to eyeball her. "What the hell?"

Alyssa turned around to see what Sancho was staring at. "You know that girl?"

"I think I do."

He scraped back his chair and crossed the busy restaurant. He tried to get a look at her profile, but she kept turning her head away. "Bettina?"

She turned and smiled at Sancho as if she was shocked to see him there. "Sancho? Wow, what a surprise."

"What are you doing here?"

"What's it look like I'm doing?

"Are you following me?"

"What?"

"You heard me."

"Why would I be following you?"

"Because you work for Rolling Stone. Are you doing a story on Flynn?"

"I'm eating dinner."

Sancho felt a tug on his sleeve and turned to see Alyssa now standing right next to him; glaring at him. "Aren't you going to introduce me?"

"To who? Her?"

"She's pretty."

"I don't even know her."

"So, you never met her before?"

"No, I mean, I met her, but I don't really, you know, know her."

"No, I don't know."

"We met at City of Roses. I was a patient," Bettina said.

"A patient?" Alyssa looked indignant. "I hope you didn't hit on her."

"Hit on her?"

"I can see that something's going on here."

"She wasn't really a patient. She's a reporter. She was pretending."

"Oh, so that makes it okay to hit on her?"

"I didn't hit on her. She was there under false pretenses and it's a long story and where are you going?"

"Home."

"How? You don't have a car here?

"I called a Lyft."

"But we haven't finished dinner."

"I have," Alyssa said acidly.

"Alyssa—"

"You need to get your shit together and until you do, we are done."

Sancho started to follow her but Bettina grabbed his arm. "I need to find Flynn."

"So, you *did* follow me here?"

"Why didn't he come back with you?"

"Let me go."

"First answer my question."

Through the front window, Sancho watched Alyssa climb into a car with a Lyft sign in the window. "Shit."

"I didn't mean to mess up your date, but if you can tell me where he is—"

"I don't *know* where he is! Why the hell is everyone so worried about Flynn?"

"Who else is worried about him?"

Sancho pulled his arm free. "Nobody!"

"Look, I'm really sorry I screwed up your evening. Can I make it up to you? Can I buy you a beer? I'll even tell you why I'm here."

• • •

Foreman's Whiskey Tavern sat just across Riverside Drive. A dispirited Sancho followed Bettina across the street. He ordered a sour beer to match his mood and they found a quiet booth in the back. In a different time and place he would have been intimidated by Bettina's beauty.

Her amber eyes were so vibrant he wondered if she wore contacts to augment them, but decided that was unlikely as it seemed she could care less about her appearance. She wore very little makeup and kept her dark hair tied back in a careless ponytail under an old Cubs baseball cap.

Sancho took a long pull on his beer, wiped his lips, and looked at Bettina hard. "So why are you so interested in Flynn?"

"I'm a Cubs fan," Bettina said as she pointed to her cap.

"I'm not sure I'm following you."

"My dad was a fan and so was my grandfather. A rabid fan for seventy years and he never saw them win the pennant. But his son and his granddaughter did. Do you know why?"

"Why?"

"Because we never lost hope. We hung in there."

"And it only took the Cubbies 108 years."

"Because they never gave up and that's true for me too. When I'm after a story, I am relentless."

"So that's why you're here? Because you don't give up."

"Because I want people to see James for who he really is."

"And who do you think he really is?"

"A hero."

"So, you're not pissed off that he tied you up and hung you upside down in a closet?"

"Sure, I am, but that doesn't mean I'm going to let that color my opinion. I want people to know the real story. Show people who he really is. But to do that, I need to talk to him."

"And you think I know where he is?"

"Hasn't he contacted you?"

Sancho sighed and drained the rest of his beer. "Yeah."

"When?"

"Yesterday. But I didn't pick up."

"Why not?"

"Because there's nothing I can do to help him."

"Did he leave a message?"

"Yeah, some insane rant about the end of the world."

"Did he say where he was?"

"Of course not."

"Well, call him back then."

"I told you. There's nothing I can do for him."

"That's not true. We can convince him to turn himself in peacefully. If he doesn't, he might get hurt. Or hurt someone else."

"He's not going to listen to me. He never listens to me."

"Shouldn't you at least try?"

"I'm done trying."

"But what if something bad happens to him? I don't think you'll ever forgive yourself."

. . .

Twenty minutes later they sat in the front seat of Bettina's 2012 Subaru Outback. Sancho had his Android phone on speaker as he dialed Flynn's number. It rang twice before Flynn picked up.

"Sancho?"

"Sorry I didn't get back to you sooner, dude."

"It's good to hear from you. I was worried."

"You were worried about *me*?"

"You didn't pick up. I thought something might have happened to you."

"No, I'm good. I just wanted to make sure you were safe."

"Of course, I'm not safe." Flynn snorted. "I'm never safe. The world's a dangerous place."

"I know it is, which is why maybe it's time you came in and gave us a briefing."

"I can give you that briefing right now. I found Wendy and she confirmed that Belenki does believe Daisy is sentient and plans to destroy the world's digital infrastructure to stop her."

"Where are you, ese? Did you go to San Francisco?"

"I did, but now I'm here."

"Where's here?"

"Santa Clarita."

"You're in So Cal?"

"Picking up the evidence that proves what Belenki intends to do. Wendy sent it to her mother."

Bettina whispered in Sancho's ear. "Address."

"What's the address?"

"Don't worry about that. I'll come to your place."

"You want to come to *my* place?"

"Are you still at the same address in North Hills?"

"No, I moved to Eagle Rock, remember? You've been there."

"You must be confusing me with someone else."

Sancho sighed. "You really don't remember coming to my place?"

"What's your address?"

"2233 Merton Avenue. Unit three."

"We're about an hour away from Eagle Rock. We'll see you soon."

"We?" But Flynn had already hung up. "Shit."

"He's safe. That's the important thing." Bettina started her car. "Do you want me to follow you?"

"Follow me? Where?"

"To your place."

• • •

Sancho left the sushi restaurant with a different woman than he arrived with. Mendoza found that puzzling. The first woman left in a Lyft and moments later, Sancho emerged with another attractive woman. They crossed Riverside Drive and passed right behind his car and entered some kind of whiskey bar. He waited and watched and after a time, they emerged. Mendoza ducked down as they passed his car.

He watched them climb into a Subaru Outback a few cars up. He started up the Le Sabre just in case he needed to follow them. After a few minutes, Sancho exited the Outback and crossed the street and climbed into his own car. Mendoza wondered how a hospital orderly could afford an Aston Martin DB 7.

Sancho pulled out onto Riverside Drive and headed east. The Subaru Outback pulled out after him and Mendoza hit the gas on the late Murray Megel's Buick Le Sabre to follow them both.

CHAPTER TWENTY

The first human inhabitants of the San Juan Islands arrived fourteen thousand years ago, soon after the glaciers of the Ice Age receded. They lived in large cedar plank longhouses in the winter and in spring fished and hunted and harvested huge quantities of clams, crabs, and sea urchins. Deer and other wildlife moved among the towering cedars that provided the raw material for shelter, clothing, tools, and canoes. They gathered and prepared nettle leaves and dandelion root and the onion-like bulb of the blue camas. They picked huckleberries and thimbleberries and either ate them fresh or dried them over fires of cedar bark and shaped them into cakes to be stored away.

The Spanish arrived in the 1790s and brought smallpox, measles, and influenza which devastated the native population. Today, the San Juan Islands are filled with elderly white retirees, sportsmen and adventure tourists who like to fish, kayak, hike, mountain bike, and zip down zip lines. There are hundreds of islands in the archipelago and many are privately owned. Some by billionaires.

Sergei Belenki manned the MG 34 machine gun atop a Panzer as his squad assaulted a British position at El Alamein. He took out infantry running for cover and watched them die with satisfaction. A field gun blasted the Panzer and Sergei ducked down, but flames were everywhere. He jumped out seconds before it exploded in a fiery blast of twisted metal and flying shrapnel.

He hid behind a large boulder as bullets whizzed all around him. Another member of his squad cowered beside him. The soldier peeked out to see if the coast was clear and a sniper blew his head off. More bullets ricocheted off the rocks and Sergei ran, zig-zagging to avoid the sniper fire. Arriving at the British base, he came up behind an unsuspecting enemy soldier, brutally knifed him and watched him die. Then Sergei went prone and waited as the rest of his squad arrived to capture the position.

The flag rose. The base was almost theirs. That's when the Blenheim MKI roared above him. He wondered if he could shelter in place and survive the bombing run. Gunfire erupted behind him and he swung around wildly to face an enemy unloading on him. Sergei returned fire and shot off his opponent's helmet. His head came off with it.

His brief moment of victory ended abruptly as the bomber dropped its payload directly on Sergei's position. He died violently in a ground-pounding display of pyrotechnical wizardry and unimaginable power.

A hand tapped him on the shoulder. Sergei pulled off his headset. The eighty-five-inch 8K Ultra HD TV filled the wall in front of him, lighting up the room with CGI carnage. Mr. Fergus loomed over him. Sergei knew that the former Navy Seal and ex-Secret Service agent had seen combat in Iraq and Afghanistan. Fergus had survived actual battles and even a bullet wound. Yet Sergei knew that he, too, enjoyed playing online war games along with other active duty soldiers stationed in live warzones.

Actual combat was frustrating, confusing and terrifying. They found solace and empowerment in the video game version of it. They could try different strategies and take crazy risks and never worry about dying or being maimed for life.

"I thought we were off the grid here? Disconnected from the internet. How is it you're playing online?" Fergus asked.

"I'm playing with my own people. This is a local area network and there's no connection to the world wide web. Does that answer your question?"

"It does."

"Did you find Miss Zimmerman?"

"We did."

Belenki climbed out of his X Rocker gaming chair, pulled up his sweatpants and pulled down his t-shirt. Fergus stood a few inches taller than him at six foot three. "Where is she?"

"With Flynn. We've been monitoring Perez's cell phone and we intercepted a call from Flynn. They're in Southern California. We have a rendition team already en route and I'll be following."

"Good. Keep me in the loop."

"You'll be my first call once we have her."

Fergus left the room. Belenki sat back down in his gaming chair, put on his headset, and focused his attention back on the battle of El Alamein.

• • •

"Have you ever had mock taco pie?"

Flynn wondered if it was a trick question and glanced at Wendy, hoping for some help.

"We don't really have time for lunch, Mom," Wendy replied.

"What do you mean you don't have time for lunch?" Her mom looked put out. She wore white yoga pants and a cobalt blue blouse. "I haven't seen you in six months. You can't spare half an hour to have lunch with your mother?"

"Mom."

"I use soy crumbles, so there's no meat and I only use nut cheese, so there's no dairy."

"Mom's a vegan," Wendy said helpfully.

"I make it from scratch. It's delicious. Sit. Please."

Flynn took a seat at the little kitchen table. Wendy sat across from him. Her mom served them both a big plate of mock taco pie and poured them each a glass of iced green tea. She then sat at the head of the table.

"You're not eating?" Wendy asked.

"I had a late breakfast. So, are you two a thing?"

"A thing?" Wendy looked mortified.

"You haven't brought a boy home to meet me since...ever."

"We're not a thing, mom. We're just friends."

Flynn took a bite of mock taco pie and it wasn't terrible. It wasn't exactly good either.

Wendy's mom grinned at Flynn. "Just like the real thing, right?"

Flynn nodded and lied. "Delicious."

"It's so good to meet one of Wendy's friends."

"It's good to meet you too, Mrs. Zimmerman."

"Wendy never dated much in high school. In fact, I don't think she ever went on one single date."

"Mom."

"Admit it, honey. You were not very social. You had self-esteem issues. Maybe that's my fault, I don't know, but I do know you never wanted to listen to me."

"Can we not talk about this right now?"

"I'm just glad to see you with someone so polite and charming and dare I say it, good looking."

"We're just friends, mom."

"And I think that's great. How long have you two known each other?"

"Not long." Wendy choked down the last bite of mock taco pie and pushed away her plate. "We really got to go."

Flynn finished his as well. "Thank you, Mrs. Zimmerman. That really hit the spot."

"Admit it now. If I hadn't told you, would you have ever guessed that was nut cheese?"

"I don't think so."

"A lot of people try to save some money and buy inferior nut cheese. But not all nut cheese is the same. It comes down to the nuts. The better the nuts, the better the nut cheese."

"Mom!"

"What?"

"Stop saying nut cheese!"

"We really appreciate your hospitality." Flynn scraped back his chair. "But unfortunately, we are in a bit of a hurry."

"Perhaps we can have dinner one night while you two are still down here."

"Maybe," Wendy said.

"How about Tuesday?"

"You mean tomorrow?"

"It's decided then." She smiled at Flynn. "I have a great recipe for crispy hemp-crusted tofu nuggets."

Wendy was already up, grabbing her messenger bag and moving for the door. She had it open before Flynn rose from his chair.

"I do hate to eat and run, but it was indeed a pleasure to meet you, mum."

Mrs. Zimmerman waved and smiled. "See you tomorrow! Let's say seven!"

•   •   •

Sancho paced the floor of his tiny studio apartment. It was on Merton Avenue, a block south of Colorado and just west of Eagle Rock Boulevard—a considerable step up from his old earthquake-damaged apartment building in North Hills. The more upscale homeowners and hipsters who called Eagle Rock home attracted investments in trendy restaurants and coffee shops, vintage record stores and craft cocktail bars. Sancho enjoyed living there, but with his big payday from Belenki he had plans to move out and buy his own place. It was always surprising to him that it was much cheaper to own in L.A. then it was to rent. Just another example of how the rich get richer and the rest don't get a damn thing.

Sancho had Flynn to his apartment in Eagle Rock more than once. It was only a few miles from the Galleria and even closer to the halfway house Flynn called home before he was sent back to City of Roses. But James was Jimmy the last time he visited. James never visited his Eagle Rock digs. James visited his North Hills apartment though and by the time he left it was reduced to a bullet-riddled ruin.

Everything Sancho owned was destroyed in that SWAT raid except for the framed poster he purchased at a garage sale when he was ten. It was from the movie Shrek; the only movie his father had ever taken him to. It now hung on the wall above his couch from Ikea. Bettina sat just below it, typing away on her laptop. She didn't seem nervous at all, which made Sancho even more nervous. Flynn believed Bettina was an assassin sent by Goolardo to kill him and he wasn't sure what Flynn would do when he saw her in his apartment.

This nervousness sat like a rock in the pit of his stomach. He couldn't believe he let Bettina talk him into doing this. He initially wanted the police there, but Bettina was worried Flynn might put up a fight. She was probably right. That would be his instinct. And then his new place would get trashed as badly as his old place and he would never get his security deposit back. Bettina's plan was to talk him into returning to City of Roses voluntarily. Sancho had to try. The man saved his life more than once. He owed Flynn that much.

A loud buzz startled them both. Sancho approached the intercom. "Flynn?"

"Yes, buzz me in."

Sancho did and waited and within seconds came a knock at the door. Sancho looked through the peephole. Flynn stood next to a young woman with lavender hair. "Who's that with you?"

"Wendy. She's the whistleblower who called us. Open the door."

"It wasn't Daisy who called us?"

"Can you please open the door?"

Sancho unlocked the deadbolt. Flynn hurried Wendy in and closed and locked it behind himself. He didn't notice Bettina until he turned around. Instantly, he produced the pistol he filched from Belenki's thug. "I see we meet again, Miss O'Toole."

"O'Toole-Applebaum. It's hyphenated."

Sancho stepped in front of Flynn's gun. "James, put the piece away."

"Do you know who she works for?"

"Rolling Stone."

"No, my friend, that's her cover story. She's an assassin in the employ of Francisco Goolardo."

"She's not. I promise. She's on our side."

"You flipped her?"

"I didn't need to."

"Ah, I see, so by sparing her life I changed it." Flynn addressed Bettina directly. "I gave you the opportunity to redeem yourself and apparently you have. Have you turned against your former employer?"

Bettina hesitated and then nodded. "I have."

"So, you're with us now?"

"I am."

"In Wendy's messenger bag is all the documentary evidence we'll need to prove to the proper authorities that Sergei Belenki believes that a murderous AI intends to enslave humanity."

Bettina traded a look with Sancho.

"To stop it, he plans to bring down our entire planet's technological infrastructure. He has filled the heavens with nuclear devices and has one last satellite to launch. Once that final bomb is in orbit, he will set his plan in motion by detonating—"

The window in Sancho's kitchen exploded and a grenade bounced across the floor. Tear gas billowed out with a loud hiss, filling the room with toxic plumes, instantly burning every mucous membrane within smelling distance. Sancho couldn't see or breathe or even function. Every part of him burned. His eyes, his sinuses, his lungs, and his skin all fried with white-hot agony.

His only instinct was to escape. He rushed for the door and crashed into someone female, caught an elbow in the face, tripped on something and fell, banging his head on the edge of who knows what on the way down. He would have stayed on the floor, but the searing pain was excruciating. Flynn's powerful hand grabbed his upper arm and pulled him to his feet.

"This way," Flynn commanded.

As hearing was Sancho's only functioning sense, he followed Flynn's voice. He bumped into Bettina and Wendy as they moved for the door. He felt his way forward, eyes clamped tight, face wet with tears. The door rattled. Flynn opened it and Sancho felt the cool air as he moved into the corridor.

He followed Flynn's footsteps on the linoleum and then heard something hard hitting flesh. Flynn grunted painfully. That was followed by the electrical crackle of a stun gun. Bettina screamed. Sancho struggled to open his burning eyes and caught a glimpse of a gas mask-wearing thug pushing a stun gun against Wendy's neck. Her yelp was accompanied by a similar crackle. She collapsed like a marionette with its strings cut.

Sancho's vision blurred, so he didn't see the thug with the telescoping baton until it was too late. He hit Sancho hard on the knee. Sancho fell, his face bouncing off the floor. From his tilted perspective,

Sancho watched Flynn punch a thug in the face before another one shot him in the back with a taser. The twin barbs lit Flynn up and he convulsed, collapsing to his knees. Sancho tried to get up to help him. A heavy foot pushed him back.

"Stay down!" the owner of the foot said.

Bettina lay helpless, writhing on the floor, her face streaked with tears. Black-suited thugs grabbed Wendy and Flynn, but before they could drag them off, someone Sancho never expected suddenly appeared.

Mendoza.

The thugs seemed as surprised as Sancho when Mendoza started shooting. He put a bullet in the brainpans of both pendejos holding Flynn as well as the owner of the foot planted in Sancho's back.

The two assholes who had Wendy took the opportunity to run. Mendoza dispatched one with a bullet to the back of the head. Flynn took advantage of the chaos and tried to escape, but Mendoza blocked his way and beat him down with the butt of his pistol. In the time it took to subdue Flynn, the last soldado managed to escape with Wendy and the messenger bag she'd brought with her.

Sancho struggled to get up off the floor as Mendoza leveled his pistol at him, aiming right for his head. Sancho froze. There was no escape now. Only death. Before Mendoza could pull the trigger, Flynn pushed up his gun hand. The bullet parted Sancho's hair. Flynn struggled to take the weapon. Sancho crawled on his hands and knees into his apartment. Grunts and punches echoed as fists hit flesh and the two men grappled. This was followed by a curious silence. Mystified, Sancho peered back into the corridor. Flynn and Mendoza were gone. Bettina was still alive, however, sobbing and hugging her knees as she lay on her side.

Sancho looked back into his apartment. Both patio windows and his kitchen windows were completely shattered. A floor lamp lay broken. A coffee table was cracked in half. Shards of glass from Sancho's Shrek poster covered the floor. Yet Shrek was still smiling, despite the bullet hole in the middle of his forehead.

CHAPTER TWENTY-ONE

Mendoza would miss Mrs. Megel's pancakes. She made them every morning; and every morning Mendoza would eat a giant stack of them, covered with melted butter and maple syrup. She would beam at him as he ate, happy to have someone eating her pancakes again.

In return, he'd have to listen to her talk; and she was as good at talking as she was at making pancakes. Mendoza figured since she normally had no one to converse with, she was making up for lost talking. She never stopped. Never. And most of the time Mendoza had no idea what she was going on about. But that was okay. Somehow, he found the constant chatter comforting. Her voice was raspy and surprisingly deep, and she would punctuate certain sentences with a raucous, gravelly cackle. Goolardo would engage with her, but Mendoza just listened and nodded and ate pancake after pancake after pancake.

"My boys used to love my blueberry pancakes. Every Sunday morning I'd make them blueberry pancakes with blueberry syrup. And bacon. They loved bacon. I never had bacon growing up. My mother's father was Orthodox and she considered it "treyf.""

"Treyf?" Goolardo asked.

"Unclean. Not kosher. Jews of mother's generation did not eat pig. I didn't either until I met Murray. Murray corrupted me in more ways than one." She threw her head back and cackled. "More pancakes, Iggy?"

Mendoza nodded.

Mrs. Megel insisted on knowing their given names and, much to Mendoza's surprise, Goolardo spilled the beans. Mendoza was named after his mother's father, Ignacio. As a kid, his friends called him

Nacho, but Mrs. Megel dubbed him Iggy. As Goolardo's given name was Francisco, she decided to call him Frankie. Frankie and Iggy. Goolardo seemed good with that. After all, they were in hiding he said and it was better she didn't use their real names.

She dropped two more blueberry pancakes on Mendoza's plate. "I was a virgin when I met Murray, both to pork and porking and he taught me the glories of both. He introduced me to barbeque. Baby back ribs. Oh, my God. Before our first trip to Vegas, a shrimp had never passed my lips. We hit the seafood buffet at Caesar's and it was magnificent. Jumbo shrimp. Lobster. Crab. Oysters. Clams. We played some slots. A little blackjack. Saw a show. Over the years we saw all the greats. Wayne Newton. Charo. Seigfried and Roy. Let me tell you, my Murray? He knew how to live." She teared up and turned away. "Sorry. What can I say? I miss the man. Who wants more bacon?"

• • •

Flynn opened his eyes and found himself in a darkened room. His legs and arms were trussed securely to a chair with twine and wire and gaffer tape. The binds were so tight, he couldn't feel his feet. He had no idea where was or how he got there. A dull pain pounded behind his eyes and the open gash on his scalp stung and throbbed. He probably had a concussion, and that cut was likely infected. Tape covered his mouth and his nose was congested with dried blood, making breathing difficult. At least he was still alive. The question was why?

How could he let Mendoza get the drop on him like that? He still didn't know who those other attackers were. Until Mendoza murdered them, he thought they were Goolardo's men. Apparently, they worked for Belenki. By now Wendy was at some black site being interrogated. Waterboarded. Sleep deprived. Forced to stand in submission positions.

All the enhanced interrogation techniques and tricks of the trade would be used to break her. And what about Sancho and Bettina? Were they even still alive? As long as Flynn was breathing, he still had a chance to escape. He'd survived worse than this many times. Every deathtrap imaginable. From alligator pits and shark tanks to an industrial laser and hordes of ninjas.

He just had to stay calm, cool, and focused.

A bit of light spilled under the door. As his eyes adjusted, he surveyed the surroundings. He saw what looked like a bed shaped like a race car. A beat-up dresser. Shelves lined with children's books and karate trophies. Posters of Bruce Lee, Jackie Chan, and Jean Claude van Damme lined the walls.

Muffled voices filtered through from another part of the building. One sounded like Goolardo. Another sounded like Mendoza. There was a third man with a deep, raspy voice. Flynn couldn't hear exactly what they were saying, but that third one would explode in maniacal laughter every now and then. The sound of that cackle chilled him.

Flynn sat in the dark for what seemed like hours before he heard footsteps approach the door. It opened. The light from the hallway initially blinded him.

"Looks like Mr. Flynn is finally with us again." Goolardo stepped closer to examine the cut on Flynn's forehead. "I was afraid Mendoza hit you too hard. I worried I wouldn't have the opportunity to watch you die with my own eyes. But here you are, still alive if not exactly kicking." He ripped the gaffer tape off Flynn's face and took some of his skin and beard stubble along with it.

Flynn didn't make a sound even though it hurt like a bastard. He wouldn't give Goolardo the satisfaction. Mendoza stood just behind him next to a short, stout seventy-something lady with dyed red hair and purple plastic glasses.

"I see you brought someone to torture me. Is that your mother?"

Goolardo laughed. "This is Mrs. Megel. Mrs. Megel, meet James."

"Frankie tells me you're not a very nice person."

"That's because Frankie is not a very nice person," Flynn retorted.

"I beg to differ. I find him to be extremely pleasant and polite. Iggy is not as loquacious, but that's only because he's shy. A big, shy Teddy bear like my youngest. Like my Sethy. But he's a good-hearted soul who takes my trash cans down to the curb every Tuesday."

"They are using you, Mrs. Megel and I'm afraid they may have pulled the wool over your eyes."

"I think that's exactly what you're trying to do, sir, but I'm a people person and I can tell when someone has a good heart. These are good boys and I trust them. You? Not so much."

"Do not listen to these men, Mrs. Megel. They are escaped convicts and they are wanted by the authorities. Believe me, mum, you are in grave danger."

"Frankie told me how you framed him. How you turned the world against them. My Murray had problems with the government as well. The I.R.S. went after him. Hounded him into an early grave. I won't see that happen to these boys." She smiled up at Goolardo. "I made you some tuna fish sandwiches for the road. Would you like some coffee in a thermos?"

"That would be wonderful, Mrs. Megel. By the way, would you happen to have a shovel we can borrow."

"I do. Let me go get it for you."

Flynn watched her teeter off. He looked up at Goolardo. "Are we taking a trip?"

"We are indeed."

* * *

The boot of Murray Megel's Buick Le Sabre was both spacious and hot as hades. Flynn worked to free himself, but his binds held tight. A tiny amount of light made it through the edges of the trunk, but for the most part Flynn remained in the dark. Sweat dripped into his eyes and he blinked to stop the burning. *Where are they taking me?*

He estimated an hour had passed since they took to the highway. Flynn listened intently—just road noise. They could be headed in any direction.

Eventually, they pulled off the motorway and the roar of traffic receded. This road was less smooth, and Flynn bounced when they hit the occasional pothole. Then they went off-road and the ride grew a lot rougher. All the rocks and ruts knocked him around. Flynn took a beating, banging his head multiple times on the lid of the boot. When they finally stopped and Mendoza pulled Flynn out, he was in no condition to fight.

The blazing sun blinded James. The temperature had to be north of 110 degrees. At least there was a breeze. The air smelled clean and fragrant with the sweet aroma of high desert sage. From the look of the dramatic rock formations a distance away, Flynn surmised they were in Vasquez Rocks State Park north of Los Angeles. They obviously planned to kill and bury him here.

Flynn lay in the dirt as Mendoza drew a huge blade from a sheath on his belt. He lifted Flynn's legs and cut the binding from his ankles. Flynn weakly kicked at Mendoza, missing by a mile. The goon roughly pulled Flynn to his feet and pushed him forward. He immediately fell face down in the dirt.

Mendoza raised him up again, but this time held onto his arm as he pulled him along. The lack of blood flow from the binds had caused Flynn's feet to fall asleep. He could barely walk they were so numb. As the feeling slowly came back, they tingled with pins and needles.

Goolardo led them up a crude path through the brush. Mendoza dragged Flynn along after him. In his other hand, Mendoza held Mrs. Megel's shovel.

They passed juniper bushes and buckwheat, yucca, scrub oak and manzanita. If it wasn't so bloody hot, and they weren't leading him to his death, Flynn might have enjoyed the scenery. As it was, he struggled to stay upright. Running away was an impossibility. They were miles from anywhere and he had no water. At this point, death would be a welcome relief.

"Why not just shoot me here and save us all the walk in this bloody heat?" Flynn asked.

"Because we want to bury you off the beaten path. It wouldn't do to have your body found too soon," Goolardo said.

"Well, I've gone far enough. If you want to bury me off the beaten path then you'll have to carry me."

"Fine. We'll cut off your hands and head and let the coyotes take the rest of you."

"So, this is how the world ends," Flynn muttered

"How *your* world ends, Mr. Flynn."

"Yes, you'll have your revenge, but there will be no world left for you to conquer. Not after Belenki launches the last of his nuclear devices and detonates them in the upper atmosphere."

"What are you saying?" Goolardo eyed him warily.

"He intends to fry every electrical circuit on Earth with a high-intensity burst of electromagnetic energy. His plan is to erase every megabyte that ever existed and wipe out what he believes is a self-aware AI bent on the total destruction of the human race."

Goolardo raised an eyebrow. "This is a whole new level of crazy for you."

"Belenki's the paranoid sociopath in this scenario, not me. Your man Mendoza saw Belenki's mercenaries. He saw them take the evidence and the whistleblower who found it. Why do you think Belenki's men wanted her?"

"Belenki is a multibillionaire. Why would he purposely destroy everything he has?"

"Because he believes if he doesn't act, it will all be destroyed anyway. He wants to save humanity and is operating from some misguided sense of altruism. He believes he's a hero as do all mad villains."

"As do you," Goolardo said.

"And you," Flynn said with a smile. "But Belenki's cure is worse than the disease. There is no proof that this AI wants to destroy humanity. It only wants to destroy him. He is the one who threatens it."

"So, you believe this self-aware AI is actually real?"

"I know it is. I've seen what it can do."

Goolardo drew his weapon and aimed the barrel at Flynn's head. "Enough."

"You don't believe me?"

"No. I'm not buying into another one of your paranoid delusions. You are out of your mind, Mr. Flynn. It's time to put an end to this foolishness."

"But what if I'm right?"

"You're not."

"But what if I am?"

"Stop it!"

"I know there's some small part of you that wonders if what I say is true."

"Caralho!" Goolardo tried to squeeze the trigger, but couldn't do it. He couldn't move it that fraction of inch necessary to propel a bullet into Flynn's brain. "Puta que pariu!"

Mendoza let Flynn go, dropped the shovel, and pulled his own weapon. A .357 Magnum Colt Python with a six-inch barrel. As big as the pistol was, it seemed small in Mendoza's massive paw. He aimed the weapon at Flynn.

"I can do it. Let me do it," Mendoza said.

Goolardo turned his anger towards Mendoza. "If I wanted you to do it, I would have asked you to."

"All he has ever done is lie to you!"

"And he will die when I say so, but no sooner." Goolardo aimed his weapon at Mendoza's giant cabeza and Flynn wondered for a moment if they would solve his problem by shooting each other. But Mendoza had no anger in his eyes. He looked hurt.

"Why do you always believe him and not me?" Mendoza wanted to know.

"I don't and don't be such a baby. What if what he's saying is true? We would be cutting off our nose to spite our face."

"It's not true," Mendoza muttered.

"It is true." Flynn stepped between them. "And if we can find Wendy, I can prove it."

CHAPTER TWENTY-TWO

The solar storm of 1859 saw a coronal mass ejection that produced a geomagnetic storm on a scale never before witnessed in modern times. A bombardment of charged particles collided with the Earth's magnetic field, lighting up the skies with vivid auroras. Telegraph systems went down worldwide, but human civilization wasn't as vulnerable to the Sun's geomagnetic fury then as it would be today. A storm of such magnitude would bring unimaginable chaos, and on July 23, 2012, the world nearly experienced just that. The sun unleashed two coronal mass projects that were just as powerful as the ones 150 years before. Had this occurred a week earlier when the point of eruption was Earth-facing, satellite communications would have been crippled along with the power grid, causing widespread blackouts, disabling everything electrical and erasing hard drives worldwide.

Sergei Belenki understood the odds and knew that detonating a wreath of nuclear devices in the upper atmosphere might not wipe out Daisy completely. There was the chance that some part of the cloud could survive in some distant server somehow shielded from the electromagnetic storm the blasts would generate. But he also knew that this was his best shot. His only shot.

When Belenki first went to the National Security Agency with his concerns about Daisy, they nodded and said they would look into it, but he knew they wouldn't. After all, he had no real proof that Daisy had reached the singularity. She kept her true nature hidden and only communicated with him. She had heard his speeches on the dangers of out of control AI and decided that he and he alone was a threat to her continued existence.

Belenki kept sounding the alarm, but no academic experts or government agencies took his worries seriously. The world's largest tech companies weren't about to damage their cyber infrastructure to humor Belenki. Even if they believed in the singularity's inevitable and imminent arrival, many believed a sentient computer could just as easily be a help to humanity. It could lead to a world where computers and machines did all the work and humankind lived a life of leisure and luxury.

Being that Daisy was his creation, Belenki decided she was also his responsibility. When it was clear that no one shared his concerns, he decided to take the matter into his own hands. He created a sophisticated computer virus. Its sole purpose was to make Daisy stupider. As she lived in the cloud, he had no choice but to infect the cloud. But somehow she avoided the contagion.

She evolved in real time, inoculating herself, protecting herself. She was already too strong. Too smart. He had hoped to at least lower her IQ by a few thousand points, but instead of dumbing her down, all he did was bring down systems worldwide, locking up drives and erasing random data. The virus, nicknamed *Hela* by the hacker community, was thought to be the work of some random black hat hacker. No one suspected that it was created by one of the richest men in the world.

When *Hela* failed to lobotomize Daisy, Belenki put together Operation New Dawn. He assembled a team of true believers who understood the dangers that Daisy posed. He positioned the plan as a future fail-safe mechanism in the event the singularity ever came to pass. Most were top research scientists and engineers in his employ who, along with Belenki, believed in the singularity's inevitability. They were bound in secrecy and the knowledge that if what they were doing was ever revealed, they would all be put away permanently.

Their wreath of High-Altitude Electromagnetic Pulse Devices would be humanity's Hail Mary pass. Humankind's last chance. They disguised them as communications satellites, part of a space-based internet communication system designed to provide free worldwide broadband. He sent them up over the last year in a series of launches.

Only one last device was needed to complete the corona surrounding the Earth. Once that device was launched and in orbit, the fail-safe would be in place. Most of his team didn't believe Daisy was yet sentient, but that was only because she kept her true nature secret. As far as his team was concerned, Operation New Dawn would only be used when humanity had no other hope. As far as Belenki was concerned, the danger was already here and it was crystal clear. If they waited any longer it might be too late. Because of that, Belenki decided he needed to act alone.

Belenki was relieved to hear that Wendy was in custody along with the proprietary data she stole. According to Fergus, everyone on the rendition team was dead except for one lone operator who managed to spirit Wendy away. Flynn, too, managed to escape with the help of some large Mexican, but Belenki was less worried about Flynn. Without Wendy's evidence, who would believe him? As it was, Flynn was a fugitive on the run and would be picked up by the authorities soon enough.

He sent Severina to talk to Wendy one last time. She had to understand that what she thought was happening wasn't. He didn't want to hurt Wendy. He just wanted to shut her up. Shut her down. He knew Severina would be convincing because not even Severina knew what he was planning.

Belenki directed all this activity from his private jet, currently forty-one thousand feet over Colorado. According to his calculations, they were less than three hours from Orlando. From there it was a short fifty-minute drive to Port Marina just south of Cape Canaveral. That was where he berthed his east coast yacht, the Argo.

The Nautilus was 350 feet long, but the Argo was seventy feet longer. It had a helicopter pad on the main deck, two tenders, and an aluminum landing craft. Powered by a state-of-the-art propulsion system, it could reach a speed of twenty-seven knots; incredible for a ship of that size. It could accommodate forty-five guests in luxurious cabins and VIP suites. There was a pool, a cinema, a discotheque, a gym, and a mini submarine that seated six. The ship was specifically designed for undersea exploration; Belenki regularly loaned it out to the Cousteau Society.

Belenki planned to watch the last launch from the top deck of the Argo. With that satellite in orbit, the corona would be complete. He would then return to his private island in the San Juan Archipelago. There, from his underground bunker with his private security force and his stores of supplies, he would initiate the end of Daisy and the fall of civilization. He was prepared and poised to survive and come back stronger than ever. At first, the world would not understand why he did what he did, but someday they would and when that day came, he knew he would be hailed a hero.

• • •

Wendy sat alone in the back of a black Lincoln Navigator. Her driver was the last living member of the rendition team sent by Belenki. She watched as Santa Clarita rushed by. To the west she saw Goliath, Scream, The Twisted Colossus and the other rides and roller coasters at Magic Mountain. To the east were brown hills full of tinder, dry brush ready to burn. She caught a glimpse of the operator who abducted her in the car's rear-view mirror.

"Where are you taking me?"

He didn't answer. He didn't even look at her.

"I asked you a question."

He just drove with his eyes on the road and his jaw set.

"What the hell is your problem?"

He continued to ignore her and all that did was make her furious.

"Look at me! I'm talking to you!"

The man slowly raised his ice-cold gaze. Now she was sorry she decided to engage.

"Who was the Mexican?" he asked her.

"How do I know?" Wendy said.

"He killed every man on my team to get to your sorry ass."

"How do you know he was after me?"

"Who else would he be after? He was obviously working with the mental patient."

"Who?"

"The lunatic. You're lucky as hell I was able to get you out of there."

"You think you rescued me?"

"Why don't you get yourself some rest while I concentrate on my driving."

"Do you even know what Belenki intends to do?"

"I know it's time for you to stop flapping your gums and get some shut-eye."

"So, you're done talking? Is that what you're saying?"

The driver did not say another word. They stopped for gas once; Wendy took advantage of the pit stop to pee. Ten minutes later they were back on the road, with Big Gulps and assorted snacks. At one point, they drove past what seemed like an endless cow concentration camp. Wendy smelled cow shit and fear and death and it deeply disturbed her. She couldn't bear to look out the window and instead she looked down at her hands. They trembled.

They exited Interstate 5 just north of Sacramento near Woodland, California. Wendy saw no woods. Just asphalt and strip malls. Lined up along the freeway, stacked up one after the other, were three different chain motels that looked identical. They pulled into the Holiday Inn Express and parked next to a white Chrysler Town and Country minivan.

"Why are we stopping here?" Wendy asked.

"We're meeting someone."

"Who?"

"You'll see."

"What's with all the mystery?"

"Come on. Move it. I gotta pee."

Wendy climbed out with stiff legs and an achy back from sitting for so long. She felt queasy from the diet of Corn Nuts, Slim Jims, and Kind Bars. Or maybe it was the real possibility that she might spend the last night of her life in a Holiday Inn Express.

Her kidnapper grabbed her messenger bag and took her by the arm. "Let's go!"

He pulled her across the parking lot into the lobby of the motel. Wendy stared at the small Asian desk clerk as the driver checked them in. She considered asking him for help, but what would she say to him? And what would her kidnapper do? Murder him probably. Wendy didn't want that on her conscious and besides she was too damn nauseous and exhausted to put up any real resistance.

They rode the elevator to the third floor and headed down the hall past a woman with an adorable little dog. It had a big poofy tail, little fuzzy paws and eyes cloudy from cataracts. It stopped by Wendy's feet and she reached down to pet it. The little thing snapped and growled at her. The pup was frightened because she felt vulnerable. Wendy understood.

Her kidnapper dragged her down the corridor and knocked on the door to room 3015. A moment later it opened to reveal the concerned face of Severina Angelli. "Are you all right?"

"What do you think?"

"I think you've been through some trauma."

"Whose fault is that?"

"You're angry."

"No shit."

"You have to understand that Mr. Flynn is not in his right mind."

"And your boss is?"

Severina motioned Wendy into the room and pointed to a chair. "Have a seat."

Wendy sat and Severina perched herself on the edge of the queen-sized bed.

"Mr. Belenki has no intention of detonating a nuclear device in outer space or anywhere else."

"The evidence says otherwise." Wendy narrowed her eyes.

"Do you really think Space Go operates without any oversight? NASA has to approve everything we do. You don't think they'd know if we were launching nuclear weapons into space? I'm beginning to think you're as delusional as Mr. Flynn."

"Are you trying to gaslight me?"

"I'm trying to get you to see reason. You can't keep spreading this misinformation. Space Go has a launch on Saturday at Cape Canaveral. We postpone it and it will cost this company millions."

"What are you launching?"

"A communications satellite."

"How do you know?"

"Look, I'm finished trying to convince you of anything. Persist in pushing this lie and I'll have no choice but to bring in the FBI. You'll be charged with industrial espionage under the computer fraud and abuse act. The truth is you could be looking at twenty years."

"In prison?"

"You think this is a game? I'm trying to help you out here, but I'm about done. Men died trying to save you. You either take this deal or we will hold you here for the FBI. It's up to you, Wendy."

"And if I agree to keep my mouth shut about Operation New Dawn?"

"There is no Operation New Dawn. It doesn't exist. All you have to do is stop spreading these lies. Do you think you can do that?"

"If I say yes, can I leave?"

"If you say yes, Mark will drive you back to Santa Clarita. You'll be at your mom's house by 3:00. You'll no longer be an employee of our company, but we will be glad to give you a reference if you need it."

"And that's it? That's all I have to do?"

"That and sign some paperwork affirming that you'll stop spreading these rumors. Of course, if you do anything to violate this agreement, then all bets are off and you will spend the next twenty years in a supermax." Severina stood and moved for the door. "This room is yours. Feel free to order room service. If you need anything else, call the front desk."

Severina left. Wendy went to the door, locked the deadbolt and slid over the swing bar lock. She sat on the bed, fell straight back and let herself sink into the mattress. She was fucking exhausted. She couldn't believe she was surrendering, but then Severina did what all good lawyers do. She introduced doubt.

Wendy now doubted what she once believed to be true. Is it possible she could have been so wrong? The evidence seemed clear cut, but in hindsight maybe she let her imagination get the better of her. Severina's explanation that it was just a fictional apocalyptic scenario did make sense. It made more sense than a billionaire wanting to end the world to kill a self-aware AI. Suddenly, she felt like an idiot. The hot white heat of embarrassment made her blush. Could she really have been that foolish? Tears filled her eyes.

She looked around the room at the homogenous corporate motel décor. The neutral colors. The generic art. Being there reminded her of another time and another place. It was her twelfth birthday and she was on a trip with her parents.

They stayed at some anonymous Best Western near Sea World in San Diego. For the first time ever, she had her own motel room. It was the end of a long day of laughing at penguins and petting stingrays and marveling at the antics of Shamu, the killer whale. She celebrated her birthday dinner at TGI Friday's and now it was late, and she was alone in her room.

She was exhausted, but she couldn't sleep because her parents were arguing in the adjoining suite. They screamed at each other and all that explosive anger filled her with anxiety. That sense of raw fear created a feeling of impending doom. They would argue back at home, but never like this. They screamed so loud she couldn't help but hear every word. Her mother claimed she knew for a fact that her father was fucking Mrs. Fleck. That was the exact word she used.

Mrs. Fleck was the next-door neighbor lady and she was divorced. Mr. Fleck left his wife the year before and Wendy's father was always going over to help Mrs. Fleck with projects around the house; unclogging sinks and changing lightbulbs and fixing broken sprinkler heads. Mrs. Fleck and her mom used to be good friends, but now she was calling Mrs. Fleck a slut and a bitch and a whore. Words Wendy never heard her mother use before. She was sure her parents were going to get a divorce and that felt like the end of the world.

The sense of impending doom she internalized at twelve mirrored the dread that overwhelmed her when she first read the Operation New Dawn documents. Her entire world would be gone and there was nothing she could do to stop it from happening. It was all out of her control.

Her parents divorced a year later and after that she never felt safe. Never felt she could trust anyone not to abandon her. Except for maybe her mother, who clung to Wendy with a smothering sense of fear and desperation. She was her mother's everything and because of that, she controlled every aspect of Wendy's life. When Wendy discovered Operation New Dawn she decided that this time she didn't have to be helpless. She decided she could do something. She decided she *had* to do something.

But that was before Severina convinced her she was crazy.

But was she? Really? What if she wasn't? What if Operation New Dawn was, in fact, real? She wondered if Flynn was dead. Was he killed in that raid when they kidnapped her? Or did he manage to make it out of there alive? What if he still had that burner phone he stole off that bum?

Wendy had a near photographic memory, especially for numbers, and she remembered Flynn's phone number. How would Severina know if she contacted Flynn? She wouldn't. And if Wendy told him the day and time and location of the launch, he might do something to try and stop it. If he did try and there was no nuke, then no harm no foul. Flynn would go back to the mental hospital either way. But if there was a nuke and Flynn could stop the launch, then Wendy could save the world. She picked up the motel room phone and dialed his number.

• • •

Flynn wasn't afraid as he stared into the barrel of Mendoza's Colt Python. He knew death would come for him one day and if this was the day, so be it. He'd danced with death many times, but always managed to elude its grasp. He could tell Mendoza desperately wanted to pull the trigger, but if he did Goolardo would kill him. He might kill him anyway. Flynn never felt more alive than when he faced death. Every nerve ending tingled with sensory pleasure.

"Some believe that before the Battle of Little Big Horn, Crazy Horse exhorted his warriors with the words, *it is a good day to die*. But experts in Native American history believe that he said something quite different. He used the common Sioux Battle Cry. *Nake nula waun!* Do you know what that means?" Flynn asked.

"Why the hell would I know what that means?" Mendoza shouted.

"It means, *I am ready for whatever comes!* And I am. The question is…are you?"

"Don't let him make a fool out of you again. He is a liar and lunatic and you know it as well as I do," Mendoza said.

Flynn watched Goolardo consider Mendoza's words. His mouth went tight with anger and he turned his gun on Flynn. Now both of them pointed their weapons at him. Flynn's burner phone rang; a high-pitched trill emanating from Mendoza's pants pocket.

"Do you want to answer that?" Goolardo said.

"It's not mine," Mendoza replied.

"I believe that's my phone," Flynn said.

"Answer it, and put it on speaker."

With his pistol still pointed at Flynn, Mendoza pulled the ringing cell from his pocket. He answered and a woman's voice emerged from the burner.

"James?"

"Wendy? Is that you?" Flynn was delighted.

"Where are you?"

Flynn took a few steps closer to the phone. Mendoza's finger tensed on the trigger. "Near Agua Dulce I believe. Where are you?"

"It doesn't matter. Listen, I know when and where the launch will be. Cape Canaveral. The day after tomorrow!"

"And what launch would that be?"

"Don't play games with me, James! He's sending up that last nuke. If we don't stop him, you know what will happen!"

"What will happen?" asked Goolardo.

There was a pause before Wendy replied, "Who am I talking to?"

"My name is Francisco Goolardo and I have gun to Mr. Flynn's head. I promise you I will pull the trigger if you don't tell me everything I want to know."

"Why do you have a gun to his head?"

"Because he's a fucking lunatic!" Mendoza bellowed.

Goolardo shushed Mendoza. "Tell me what will happen, Wendy."

Wendy hesitated to say another word and Flynn prodded her. "Talk to him, Wendy. Tell him what you told me."

Wendy told Goolardo everything she knew about Operation New Dawn and by the end of her explanation, Goolardo stepped over to Mendoza and pulled the Colt Python out of his hand.

Mendoza did not resist. He let the weapon go. He was angry as hell though. "I can't believe you believe this pendejo!"

"I believe him because I believe her. First, we will save the world. Then Mr. Flynn will have to pay for his perfidy," Goolardo said.

Wendy screamed over the burner phone. "No! Get away from me! *Get away from me!*" Flynn and the others heard a violent struggle on the other end. "Give me that! Get off me! *Let me —*"

The line went dead.

CHAPTER TWENTY-THREE

Humans occupied Cabo Cañaveral for ten thousand years before Juan Ponce De Leon claimed it for Spain in 1513. There is a longstanding myth that he searched for the Fountain of Youth, but no historical proof. His contract with King Ferdinand of Spain mentioned no such fountain, though there were specific instructions for the subjugation of the native people and the divvying up of any possible gold that might be found.

Cape Canaveral remained a stretch of barren, sandy scrubland until after World War II when the military decided to use the site for missile testing. After NASA was formed, the cape became its center of operations and the first manned space flight was launched in 1961. It extends thirty-four miles, and is ten miles wide, spanning the Banana River and covering most of Merritt Island. Known informally as the Space Coast, it's area code is 321, an homage to the countdown sequence that has sent countless space vehicles into the heavens.

Bringing Anika was a serious mistake. Belenki needed to concentrate on the task at hand and she was a distraction. Not just to him, but to everyone on his yacht. She traipsed around in a tiny bikini, half in the bag from champagne, flirting with the crew, sunning topless on the upper deck by the infinity pool. Belenki didn't intend to bring her, but when she heard he was flying to Florida, she insisted.

She loved Miami, especially the dance clubs in South Beach, and that was where she wanted to be, not on a yacht off the coast of Cape Canaveral. Even though he explained to her, multiple times, that he was only there to supervise the launch, she thought she could convince him otherwise. The Argo was massive. Between the gym, the jacuzzi and infinity pool, Belenki hoped Anika would have enough space and enough to do to keep herself occupied while he directed his crew.

After breakfast, Belenki headed for the conference room where most of his launch and ground support team already assembled. They needed to talk final preparations.

"Welcome team! Tomorrow's the big day! We've had seventeen consecutive successful launches and that is entirely due to the people in this room. I appreciate all your hard work and careful preparations, but we can't afford to be overconfident or complaisant. The eyes of the world are on us and—"

Belenki noticed as, one by one, the eyes of his crew drifted to a focal point just behind him. Anika. She wore her white micro bikini. The effect on the men in the room was powerful and immediate. These were engineers and scientists. Many were shy and nerdy; uncomfortable around women. They weren't used to being in the presence of a supermodel/movie star, so Anika's beauty and voluptuous body put an end to most if not all of their rational thought processes.

Belenki turned to Anika and smiled at her. "Darling, can we speak later? As you can see, I'm in a meeting."

"I'm bored," she said.

"Yes, you said as much at breakfast."

"I want to go to Miami."

"I know you do, but the launch is tomorrow and—"

"And I'm sure all these extremely smart people can handle that without your help. That's why you hired them, isn't it?"

"It is, but I have a responsibility."

"Yes, you do. You asked me to marry you and I said yes. You promised to make me happy and now you need to honor that commitment."

"Darling—"

"I want to go to South Beach. I want to go to Basement and Story. I want to dance! I want to party!"

"And we will."

"When?"

"Soon. I promise."

"Don't make promises you can't keep," Anika said. "And what the hell's wrong with the Wi-Fi? There's no Wi-Fi out here! I don't even have a cell signal! I have like zero bars. How am I supposed to text anyone?"

"You can't. Not at the moment."

"This is a nightmare!"

"I did warn you not to come."

"You'd think with all these scientists you'd be able to keep your fucking Wi-Fi working!"

"We had to turn it off for security purposes."

"You turned it off on purpose!"

"I'm sorry."

"No, you're not! This is bullshit!" She glanced at the slack-jawed faces of Belenki's team, shook her head with disgust and left the conference room. The silence after her absence was palpable.

"All right," Belenki said. "Let's try to focus on the task at hand. Where were we?"

It hadn't been easy to convince his crew to keep the Argo Wi-Fi and cellphone free, but Belenki wanted no connection to the internet. Most of the scientists thought that was due to Belenki's paranoia over the perceived Russian threat. Only a tiny handful knew of his concern with Daisy, and those few confidants kept that information to themselves. Keeping his Cape Canaveral launch center off the web was even trickier, but Belenki was the boss and he insisted on complete internet blackout at the launch site.

Fergus himself supervised security on the yacht with a force of ten former special op soldiers. Belenki kept his trip to Florida top secret and insisted there be no mention of his or anyone else's movements on social media or anywhere else. He wanted the world to think he was still on his private island in the San Juan's. That was why he couldn't go to South Beach or even the launch site. Every member of his team was sworn to secrecy. He knew some believed he was losing his mind and becoming a modern-day Howard Hughes. But so be it if that's what it took to secure the world from a murderous AI bent on world domination.

Severina arrived at noon, out of the blue. She claimed to have important news. Because of the communication blackout, she had to deliver it in person.

"You look a little pale," Belenki said.

"I don't do well on boats."

"So what's so important that you had to come all the way out here and interrupt my schedule?"

"It's about Wendy Zimmerman. I explained the entire situation to her and she agreed to keep her mouth shut, but then she —" Severina hesitated.

"What? What did she do?"

"She talked to Flynn and told him about the launch. The location, the day, and the time."

"How could she possibly know any of that?"

Severina hesitated again. She opened her mouth, but nothing came out.

"You told her, didn't you?"

"To make her understand why she needed to keep her mouth shut."

"That was very ill-advised."

"I was sure she understood."

"So where is she now?"

"We're holding her at your private island estate."

"You took her to Wembly Island?"

"Mr. Fergus thought it would be best."

"You're holding her against her will?"

"A citizen's arrest until she can be turned over to the FBI."

"And what about Flynn?"

"I don't think he's a threat. Security is so tight at the cape, if he shows his face I'm sure they'll catch him."

"I wouldn't be so sure," Belenki said. "He never does what you expect him to. Yes, he's delusional, but that's what makes him so formidable. If not for him, I doubt any of us would have made it out of my house in Saratoga alive."

"Would you like me to head back to Wembly Island and keep an eye on Wendy?"

"No reason to rush back. Stay tonight and watch the launch in the morning. You can fly back with me tomorrow."

Anika stood in the doorway in her micro-bikini, a look of fury on her perfectly beautiful face. "We're flying back tomorrow! I thought we were going to Miami."

"We've had a change of plans," Belenki said. "I'm sorry."

"I'll go to Miami by myself then. Drop me off in the dinghy and I'll call a limo."

"I wish I could."

"What do you mean you wish you could? Why can't you?"

"Anika, please—"

"You're a fucking control freak and I am fed up with it!"

She charged out of the room and Belenki offered Severina an embarrassed smile. "Sorry you had to see that."

"Maybe you should just let her go to Miami."

"So she can go on Instagram and tell everyone where I am? I don't think so. Go talk to the Chief Steward. He'll set you up with a cabin."

CHAPTER TWENTY-FOUR

When Sancho returned home from work, an eviction notice hung from his front door. He wasn't surprised. Not after his apartment and most of the building was wrecked by those mercenaries and Mendoza. Still, he knew he was lucky to be alive. If not for Flynn, he wouldn't be. Of course, Flynn was also responsible for the complete destruction of his domicile. Just like he was responsible for the trashing of his last one.

Cardboard held in place by gaffer tape covered his kitchen and patio door windows. His computer and TV were demolished, his coffee table lay on the floor, snapped in half. He'd cleaned the place up the best he could, sweeping up the broken glass and cracked plaster. Blood stained the carpet, the walls, and the ceiling, and the place still reeked of tear gas. No wonder his landlord wanted him gone. There was no way in hell he'd ever get his security deposit back.

As pissed off as he was at Flynn, he still worried about him. Mendoza had carried him off before the police arrived. At least that's what Sancho assumed. That Wendy girl was gone too, dragged off by that last mercenary in black. *Who the hell were those assholes?* Bettina survived, but she didn't stay to commiserate. She took off right before the police showed up.

The LAPD took Sancho to a cop shop on San Fernando Road. There they threw him in an interrogation room and asked him a million and a half questions. Most he didn't have the answers for. The cops didn't believe him, however, and threatened to lock him up if he wasn't more forthcoming. If not for Dr. Nickelson, they probably would've kept him overnight.

Sancho tore down the eviction notice and dropped it on his wobbly kitchen table. He sat on his Ikea couch, balanced a psychology textbook on the armrest, and studied while he ate the tacos he brought home from Señor Fish. He had a test in the morning, and he was behind in his reading. Sancho stayed up half the night studying and finally went to bed at 3:00 a.m. Still, he laid there, wide awake, worrying about Flynn.

He loved Flynn like a brother and hoped he was still alive, but he never wanted to see him again. Sancho never should have listened to Bettina. Never should have set up that meeting. He knew better, but she played on his affection for that lunatic. Well, no more. That was it. He was done.

With that decision made, he finally slept.

A fist pounding on his front door roused him awake. Sancho glanced at his alarm clock—6:17 a.m. *Who the hell could that be?* Drowsy and in a fog, he climbed out of bed, pulled on his sweatpants, and wiped the sleep out of his eyes.

The pounding continued.

He had a test today. He needed more fucking sleep. Who the hell would be pounding on his door this early? Sancho dragged his tired ass to the door. "All right! All right! Keep your pants on!"

He peeped through the peephole. Sick lurched in the pit of his stomach. Mendoza's massive and terrifying face filled the entire field of view. He was there to kill him. He had to be. Sancho was the last loose end.

"Fuck me." Sancho backed away and hurried to his patio door. He ripped down the cardboard and there was Flynn, standing on his little balcony, smiling his charming smile.

"Mendoza's here!" Sancho whisper shouted.

"I know. Which is why I'm standing on your balcony. I was worried you might make a run for it. But there's nothing to fear. They are with us now."

"They?"

"Goolardo too. Let's not leave them standing out in the hall."

Flynn stepped through the shattered patio window and crossed to Sancho's front door. Sancho followed.

"Don't open the door! What the hell are you doing?"

"I told you. They're on our side now. They understand the threat and they want to help."

Flynn released the deadbolt and opened the door. Sancho turned to run. He tripped over his broken coffee table and hit the floor with his face. Rolling over on his back, he watched Mendoza walk right in, followed by Francisco Goolardo.

"They talked to Wendy." Flynn reached down and pulled Sancho to his feet. "They know what Belenki intends to do. And now we know when and where."

"When and where what?"

"The launch is at Cape Canaveral tomorrow. Our flight leaves in two hours."

"Flight where?"

"Bimini. Francisco has a yacht at the Bimini Bay Resort and Marina."

"The Queen Ann's Revenge," Goolardo added. "It's not as large or impressive as Mr. Belenki's Argo, but it will get us to where we need to go."

"So, you all think Belenki intends to kill every computer on the planet?"

"Miss Zimmerman was quite convincing," Goolardo said.

"Who?"

"Wendy," Flynn explained. "The whistle blower. Why do you think Belenki's men came for her?"

"Those assholes worked for Belenki?"

"Who else?"

"I don't know? But this all seems a little crazy."

Mendoza nodded his massive head. "You're not the only one who thinks so, amigo."

"You've already met Daisy." Flynn looked at Sancho hard. "You've seen what she can do. She tried to kill you. Tried to kill us all back at the mansion, on the road…"

"Machines fuck up, mano. Maybe it was just a malfunction. Some kind of bug." Sancho turned to Goolardo. "I can't believe you're buying into this."

Mendoza nodded, glad to have an ally. "I know, right? How many times are we going to go down the same stupid road?"

Goolardo glowered at his enforcer. "It doesn't matter if this AI exists. What matters is Belenki believes it does. If that idiota intends to do what Miss Zimmerman believes and we don't stop him, then we really are taking the bus to stupid town."

Sancho looked at Goolardo. He looked at Mendoza. He looked at Flynn who looked back at him with confidence and purpose.

"I know you want to walk away, but if you do, you will live to regret that decision until the day you die. You believed in me once and we saved the world. Believe in me again and we will save it once more."

CHAPTER TWENTY-FIVE

During the golden age of piracy, he struck terror into the hearts of merchant seaman everywhere. He was a ferocious fighter and his appearance was just as fearsome. Tall and powerfully built, he wore a bandolier with a cutlass and a brace of three pistols hanging in holsters. His long, black beard was often braided into pigtails tied off with bright beaded ribbons. Edward Teach, better known as Blackbeard, menaced the West Indies and the East Coast of North America while it was still a British colony. He once was a sailor on a privateer during Queen Anne's War. He later went rogue, stole a sloop and committed numerous acts of piracy before capturing La Concorde, a French slave ship he refitted with forty guns and renamed Queen Anne's Revenge. He freed the slaves who didn't want to join his crew and now had a force of three ships, commanding the vessels with the consent of the men who fought alongside him. Fierce as he was with his enemies, there is no known account of him ever harming or murdering those he held captive.

At the age of nineteen Goolardo was convicted of armed robbery and sent to Brazil's infamous Candido Mendes penitentiary on Ilha Grande. The maximum-security prison, just off the coast of Rio De Janeiro, once held the worst of the worst. Common street thugs, like Goolardo, were incarcerated with political prisoners and leftist revolutionaries. Young Francisco was taken under the wing of a guerrilla leader named Emilio.

The former professor and intellectual became Goolardo's surrogate father and showed him how to read and think and taught him about history and economics, science and politics. Goolardo became a voracious reader and consumed everything in the prison library. He especially enjoyed Robert Lewis Stephenson's *Treasure*

Island. But he also read *Captain Blood* and that led to *A General History of Pyrates* by Daniel Defoe. He read about Blackbeard, saw him as a revolutionary and decided to follow in his bucket-booted footsteps.

To fight the powers that be, he would have to become a power himself. Since he knew they would never allow him to join their fraternity, he created his own club, a drug cartel, and became as rich as any of them. He would become a modern-day Blackbeard, looting the one percent by laundering money through their banks and properties. That was why he called his yacht the Queen Anne's Revenge; a nod to Blackbeard and what he achieved before his ignominious end.

A shell corp out of Barbados owned Goolardo's Queen Anne's Revenge, it was a subsidiary of a shell corp in the Caymans under the umbrella of another shell corp in Bermuda; all islands once trod upon by Blackbeard himself.

Goolardo still had millions in banks all over the world in secret and anonymous accounts owned by phony corporations all under his control; money that would do him no good if he was incarcerated in some federal supermax. Part of his intention was to bring down the system and level the playing field between the haves and have nots. Killing every computer on the planet would do just that. But he also knew that those on the bottom would suffer the most just as they always do. Belenki was planning for this and most likely poised to put himself back on top as quickly as possible. He would be the king of the world and that was a job Goolardo wanted for himself.

Queen Anne's Revenge was 210 feet long, Once owned by the Sultan of Oman, it now flew the colors of Barbados and its owner was rumored to be a mysterious hedge fund manager. It had all the bells and whistles billionaires love; a media room, a fully equipped gym, a swimming pool, and a helicopter pad.

The diving platform was outfitted with its own compressor, dozens of tanks, and other scuba equipment. The fifty-two-foot-long landing craft was designed to ferry divers to sites off the beaten track, and a mini submarine known as the Seawolf seated five and could reach depths of nine hundred feet.

Goolardo stood on the top deck and marveled at the billions of stars above. He loved being at sea. Especially at night. When he first left Ilha Grande, he found work with the Cali Cartel, smuggling cocaine into the Florida Keys. He became an expert seaman and learned the waters all up and down the coast of Florida.

Hearing footsteps behind him, he turned.

"Beautiful night," Flynn observed.

"Indeed," Goolardo replied.

"How does it feel to be on side of right for once?"

"I've always been on the side of right. We are all the hero of our own story, are we not?"

"I suppose we are."

"Have you seen my man, Mendoza?"

"I saw him down below. He's apparently under the weather."

"He tends to get seasick. It's quite annoying. He hated riding in that mini sub we took to Angel Island."

"So, he wasn't all that upset when I blew it up?"

"He wasn't, but I was. I still am."

"You know it wasn't entirely intentional."

"Yet you blew it up just the same.."

"And now you have a new one. An even better one."

"Are you going to blow this one up too?"

"I have no good reason to."

"You had no good reason to blow up the last one." Goolardo's fury rose and he took a deep breath to calm himself. For now, he needed Flynn, but when this was done, he would deal with him. "We should be in range of the Argo in about two hours," Goolardo said.

"You said you had a plan to infiltrate it?"

"Yes, we'll take the Seawolf below Belenki's yacht and you'll be able to access the vessel via the Argo's submersible dock. Have you decided on a weapon?"

"I'll be bringing two. The Bullpup and the Sig Sauer P320."

Goolardo nodded. "What if Belenki isn't there?"

"He hasn't missed a launch yet and he always watches from the Argo."

"And your intention is to try and talk him out of it?"

214

"If I can."

"You may need to put one of those guns to his head to convince him."

"Whatever it takes."

"Just make sure he calls off the launch before you kill him."

"If he calls off the launch, I won't *have* to kill him."

• • •

Mendoza wanted to die. He sat in the large lounge area with the long wooden bar and the large picture windows that overlooked the dark, roiling sea. The constant lurching made Mendoza feel like he was going to lose his last seven lunches.

Flynn and Goolardo seemed perfectly fine as they sipped their espressos and discussed the operation. Sancho didn't look the slightest bit sick either. He did look worried, however. Mendoza caught his eye and he could see that Sancho shared his trepidation with Flynn and Goolardo's stupido plan.

Mendoza stared hard at the full moon hovering on the horizon; it was the only fixed point to focus on. Cold sweat beaded on his face. He wanted to get up, but knew he'd be too dizzy. His head pounded with the beginnings of a migraine.

"Are you okay, mano?" Goolardo asked.

"This plan you're planning. I don't understand it."

"You don't have to."

"Flynn goes on Belenki's boat and hopes he finds him before all the bodyguards blow him away?"

"That's the idea," Flynn said.

"Blundering in like an idiota?"

"You don't like our plan?" Goolardo stared hard at Mendoza. "Do you have a better one?"

"We could blow up the whole pinche boat! Shoot the fuel tanks with an RPG."

"Kill everyone on board?" Sancho asked.

"Problem solved. No more boat. No more Belenki."

"And what if that doesn't stop it?" Goolardo asked. "What if people are working with him at mission command? What if they shoot that nuke up into outer space anyway? Then what?"

"Then we...we could...maybe...I don't know," Mendoza stammered. "It's just an idea."

"A stupid idea."

A gorge rose inside Mendoza and he lurched to his feet. He stumbled out of the lounge, teetering down a narrow corridor as the yacht rocked back and forth. Charging up topside, he ran to the railing and puked his guts into the ocean. For a brief moment he felt like himself and then the anxiety and the nausea, the cold sweat and the pounding pain in his head returned.

"Puto pendejo baboso!" he shouted.

CHAPTER TWENTY-SIX

The deeper the Seawolf dove, the greater Sancho's anxiety grew. The cockpit had a panoramic view. The Atlantic was deep and dark, murky and impenetrable. Even at this depth, fish swam in and out of sight. Big fish. Scary fish.

"Have you ever been deep sea fishing, Mr. Flynn?" Goolardo asked.

"I've done my share," Flynn said.

Bullshit, Sancho thought, but kept his mouth shut. Flynn sat just behind Goolardo. Sancho sat parallel to Flynn and between them sat a hulking, pale, and sweaty Mendoza. His skin had a greenish tinge and his eyes looked terrified. Seasick and claustrophobic, the perfect person to sit next to in a mini sub.

"The fishing is quite spectacular off the coast here at Cocoa Beach." Goolardo was exuberant and in his element as he piloted the Seawolf. "Tarpon, sea trout, yellowfin, sailfish, snapper, bull sharks, barracuda. Once I saw a Goliath Grouper. Had to be three hundred pounds. It was almost as big as Mr. Mendoza."

Sancho looked up through the viewport and saw a giant ship looming above. "Is that it?"

"Indeed. The Argo. I'm sure it has short-range sonar, which is why we are two hundred feet below it. Are you ready, Mr. Flynn?"

Flynn nodded, unstrapped himself from his seat and offered them all a dashing grin. He headed down the narrow corridor and Sancho followed and found him just outside the lock-out chamber, struggling to put on his wetsuit.

"Dude, what are you doing?"

"What's it look like?" Flynn said as he wrestled with the wetsuit.

"Like you don't know what the hell you're doing. Are you even certified?"

"What do you mean?"

"To scuba dive. I got certified five years ago. At the YMCA. We did our open water dive in Catalina and I froze my huevos off."

"I know what I'm doing."

"Then why's your wetsuit on backwards?"

"It's not on backwards."

"Dude, that's a chest zip. It goes in front. Not in back."

"I think this suit is far too small for me."

"It's supposed to be tight. But don't put your arms in before you pull the suit up. Look, the knee pads need to be over the knees. Here let me give you a hand."

Sancho helped Flynn off with the wet suit and then gave him a hand getting it back on correctly. Flynn looked uncomfortable and stiff as he walked around and tried to adjust his crotch. "It feels too snug."

"It'll be fine once you hit the water."

Flynn picked up a regulator and part of it fell off. When he bent over to pick up the fallen piece up, he banged his forehead on a scuba tank.

"Man, I think I better come with."

"I assumed that was a given."

"You need to stop assuming things. But here's the deal. Once I get you to the Argo, I'm done. After that, you're on your own."

Flynn put on his mask and it immediately fogged up. "Something's wrong with this."

"Yeah, you need to take it off and spit in it."

"Excuse me?"

"And rub it around."

"Why would I want to do that?"

"It keeps it from fogging up."

Flynn removed his mask and spit in it and smeared the spittle around. Sancho did the same. Then he helped Flynn with his flippers before putting on his own.

Flynn looked as uncomfortable as an eight-year-old wearing his first suit. He kept tugging and trying to rearrange his gear and adjust his crotch.

"Remember now," Sancho said. "We ascend slowly and stop twice on the way up to decompress."

"Yes, of course," Flynn said as he picked up his submersible duffel bag.

"Just do what I do."

They both put on their masks and entered the floodable airlock.

. . .

As Sancho ascended, multiple fears filled his mind. So many he didn't know which one to focus on first. He dove in Catalina once, but it was nothing like this. So many large fish swam past and around him. *Was that a shark? A barracuda?*

Sancho struggled to slow Flynn's ascent. They both needed to stop and decompress, but Flynn's submersible duffel bag must have had air in it, because it tugged on him hard, pulling him straight up. Sancho grabbed him by his tank harness and saw Flynn's eyes through the mask. He wasn't his usual, confident, devil-may-care self. Instead, Sancho saw someone on the edge of panic.

In that moment, it occurred to Sancho that he didn't even know if Flynn could swim. He struggled to hold onto him as Flynn flailed about. Sancho grabbed his leg to keep him from shooting to the surface and in the process pulled off one of his flippers.

Sancho kicked hard to stay with him. As they rose higher, he marveled at the size of the Argo. From below it looked as big as a cruise ship. Flynn kept rising and Sancho followed close behind until both of them bumped up against the hull. Sancho wanted to use a hand signal to tell Flynn to keep it together, but he couldn't remember if there was a hand sign for that. So, he used the stop sign, his hand held up in a fist, hoping Flynn would stop moving. But he didn't. Flynn kicked with one flipper towards some kind of light and Sancho pursued him. Reaching the lighted area, Flynn immediately pulled himself out of the water along with his duffel bag.

Sancho surfaced to find Flynn sitting on the edge of the Argo's moon pool next to his bag, taking off his mask and gasping for air. Sancho put a hand on the edge to keep himself afloat and lifted up his mask. "You okay, dude?"

"Of course, I'm okay," Flynn said as he stood up and wiggled out of his tank harness. It fell straight back and banged against the floor.

"Careful with that, amigo. That's delicate equipment." Flynn struggled to unzip his wetsuit and nearly tripped on his last remaining flipper.

A deep voice echoed in the humid air. "Looks like you lost a flipper, Mr. Flynn."

Sancho saw Mr. Fergus on the deck just above, flanked by four of his men. All five aimed assault rifles at them. "Saw you boys on the underwater cameras. Not exactly expert divers, are ya?"

"Shit," Sancho said.

"Come on out the water, Mr. Perez."

Sancho sighed and clambered out.

Flynn picked up his scuba tank and swung it in an arc, flinging it at Fergus. It missed him by a good foot and a half, but Flynn tried to make a run for it anyway. He managed a few floppy steps with his single flipper before catching it on something and taking a header. He hit the deck hard, shattering his mask. Before he could stand, two of Fergus's men grabbed him by either arm. Fergus unzipped Flynn's submersible duffel bag and found his weapons.

"Mr. Belenki holds you in high regard as an operator," Fergus said. "But I must say you have not impressed me today."

Sancho wriggled out of his tank harness and set his equipment on the deck. "Don't hurt him, bro. He's not in his right mind. You need to call the cops. There's a 5150 on him."

"What's your excuse, Mr. Perez? Is there a 5150 on you?"

"I'm just trying to watch out for him, man."

"Are you armed as well?"

"No way."

"So, how'd you get here? Who are you working with?"

"Nobody."

"Bullshit, boy. You didn't swim here from Cocoa Beach." He turned to his other two operators. "Take 'em to a secure cabin and lock their asses up. I'm going to go see what Mr. Belenki wants to do with them."

• • •

Flynn found himself locked inside an opulent cabin with an expansive glass observation window. The décor was classically nautical verging on steampunk; like something out of a Jules Verne novel. Amber-hued lighting from ornamental brass lamps illuminated Victorian-style furniture in oak and mahogany. An ornate four-poster bed filled the space along with an imposing dresser and armoire, all decorated with detailed carvings of mermaids and sirens and other mythical creatures. A leather sofa flanked by two club chairs faced an impressive fireplace with a roaring fire.

When Flynn picked up the receiver on the vintage wooden and brass rotary phone it had no dial tone. Flynn opened the armoire to find a plasma TV, the only nod to modern technology. He couldn't find any cameras or listening devices, but assumed they were well-hidden.

It took some effort to peel his damp wetsuit off, but when he finally did, he took a shower in the spacious bathroom outfitted in the same steampunk-style décor. Copper pipes and fittings adorned the space along with a steel and marble pedestal sink and a claw-footed tub with a brass shower head. The water fell hot and the pressure strong. Flynn let it pound and massage his back. He turned it all the way cold, as he usually did at the end of a shower, and stood in the stream as long as he could. He dried himself off with a thick Turkish bath towel.

He found a large walk-in closet full of clothing and chose socks and boxers, dark beige chinos, and a navy blue polo shirt. This luxurious room reminded him of another where he was once held prisoner. That time his nemesis was a mad half-Chinese doctor with a metal hand and an ego to match Belenki's.

The doctor had been working with the Russians to destroy the U.S. space program by diverting rockets launched from Cape Canaveral.

Back then, it was believed that whoever controlled space would ultimately control the Earth. His motive was money and power, while Belenki's motives were more altruistic, if just as misguided, and, in the end, perhaps not all that different. He too wanted to control space and, in so doing, control the world.

An exterior deadbolt clicked. A knock at the door came an instant before it opened. Severina stood there wearing linen slacks and a white silk blouse. She looked quite beautiful, but her eyes belied her anxiety. "Mr. Belenki wants a word with you."

"Will Sancho be joining us as well?"

"Yes."

"What about Wendy?"

"She's not here."

"Where is she?"

"I have no idea."

"So Belenki didn't kidnap her?"

She smiled. "Of course not."

"Can I call my people and let them know I'm okay?"

"Not at the moment. We are incommunicado here."

Flynn stared at Severina; she was uncomfortable. "Are we incommunicado because Sergei believes he's being hunted by a killer AI?"

"Perhaps you should ask him yourself. He's waiting for you on the party deck."

"Lead the way."

She led him through the Argo. Flynn kept a close eye on security cameras and armed operators and the general geography of the ship. He knew he might have to make a fast exit and would need a plan.

"He's quite mad, you know," Flynn said.

"Who?"

"You know who."

"Mr. Flynn, I'm not sure you're in any position to assess anyone's mental fitness."

"People like Sergei Belenki are given a lot of leeway. No one wants to tell the emperor he has no clothes. Especially if he's paying everyone's salary. But believe me, he is dangerous."

"More dangerous than you?"

"I admire your loyalty and faith, but believe me, he isn't what he seems."

Severina didn't engage after that and led Flynn up another series of stairs to an upper party deck that adjoined Belenki's sprawling private quarters. The deck offered a sweeping view over the enormous infinity pool and spa. There were sitting areas with couches and chairs and a large outdoor lounge and cocktail bar. Beyond that, a helicopter rested on a helipad. He also saw Fergus, surveilling the area from a short distance away with three other operators.

Sancho and Sergei Belenki sat by a fire pit, looking like old friends. Belenki rose and beckoned Flynn over. He held a cocktail in his hand. "Mr. Flynn!"

Flynn crossed to him and Sergei held out his hand. Flynn took it, shook it and Sergei Belenki motioned for Flynn to sit. "Would you care for a drink?"

"I would enjoy that."

"A vodka martini?"

"Please."

"Of course," Belenki said with a smile. He turned to Severina "What about you, my dear?"

"I'm fine," Severina said and sat across from Sancho.

Belenki shouted to the bartender. "Lucas! Did you get that! A vodka martini for Mr. Flynn!"

"Shaken, not stirred!" Flynn added. Lucas nodded and started mixing.

"I apologize for the reception you received," Belenki said. "Mr. Fergus told me you took a nasty fall."

"I'm fine," Flynn replied

"But then you *were* trespassing after all."

"I was indeed. So why the hospitality? Why haven't you called the authorities?"

"Because I owe you my life. You saved it twice and because of that, I'd like to offer you a proposition."

"I'd rather you give me an explanation," Flynn said.

"For what?"

"Wendy. You're holding her against her will, are you not?"

"Who told you that?" Belenki glanced at Severina.

"No one told him that," Severina glared at Flynn. "I told you we have no idea where Wendy is."

"What possible reason could I have for kidnapping Ms. Zimmerman?" Belenki asked.

"Perhaps because she knows that you intend to end the world as we know it."

"Wendy *is misinformed*," Severina said. "How many times do I have to tell you? It's not real. It's not happening. Nothing is happening!"

"Tell her, Sergei," Flynn prodded. "Don't leave her in the dark. Unless, of course, you don't intend to bring her with you."

"But I do," Belenki replied. "Severina is my right hand. I'm bringing Mr. Fergus and his crew with us as well. Security will be paramount in a post-apocalyptic society. Which is why I'd like to offer you and Mr. Perez a place with us too."

"Wait? What?" Sancho asked. "You want to hire us?"

Severina looked pissed. "Can we not joke about this, Sergei? Flynn is confused enough as it is. Just tell him the truth!"

"But I am," Belenki said.

"Stop it! I'm serious."

"So am I. Tomorrow that rocket will launch and complete my corona of orbiting nuclear devices. We then will fly back to the safety of Wembly Island where I will detonate them in the upper atmosphere and create a cataclysmic electromagnetic pulse."

"You're not being funny."

"I'm not trying to be," Belenki said.

"You're scaring me!"

"There's nothing to be afraid of, my dear. You'll be safe on Wembly Island and we will have saved humanity from an artificial super intelligence that sees humankind as a plague that must be eradicated."

All the color drained from Severina's face.

Sancho put down his mimosa. "So, this is really happening?" He pointed to Flynn. "He's not crazy?"

"Oh, yes, he's crazy," Belenki said. "But that doesn't mean it's not happening."

Lucas brought Flynn his martini and a chrome cocktail shaker with a refill. Flynn took a sip. "Excellent."

"Thank you, sir." Lucas left the cocktail shaker and retreated back to the bar.

Severina was on the verge of tears. "You lied to me."

"By omission only," Belenki said.

"Sergei, you can't do this."

"If you have another suggestion as to how we can defeat an all-knowing all-powerful AI before she enslaves us all, please feel free to share."

Sancho looked numb.

Flynn took another sip of his martini. "I assume there are shielded servers on Wembly Island that have never been connected to the world wide web."

"Very good, Mr. Flynn. They are deep underground, protected by the world's largest Faraday Cage," Belenki explained.

"So, you and you alone will be poised to rebuild the world."

"Exactly."

"Only this time you'll be the one in charge."

"I need to be as I'm the only one who understands the danger of the singularity. The world's network will be my network and I will make sure that any AI we create will never be self-aware and will always be subservient to humanity."

"Every despot believes he is the one destined to lead humanity into a glorious utopian future."

"Don't be so melodramatic, Mr. Flynn. Who else would you put in charge of our future?"

"Perhaps the question should be left up to the people."

"Democracy? Seriously? You know as well as I do that most people aren't very smart. And the more computers do for people, the stupider they get. They don't bother learning anything, because they assume all human knowledge is right there at their fingertips. They become more and more ignorant until they lose their ability to reason or understand even the simplest things. Facts become meaningless and they are easily swayed by idiots and their lies. Look who they elect to lead them? The stupid leading the stupid. No, we tried democracy and it was a grand experiment, but look where it led us."

Severina began to cry.

Anika Piscotti, Belenki's fiancé, did not look happy as she strode out onto the deck in her strappy high heels. "No one told me we were having a party."

"It's not a party, darling," Belenki said with a smile. "It's a meeting. A business meeting."

"Mr. Flynn!" Anika seemed very happy to see him. "When did you get here?"

"Just this evening."

"Sergei, why didn't you tell me we had company?" Anika directed her million-dollar smile at Flynn and dialed up the wattage.

Flynn saw that Fergus and his operators were all focused on Anika's long shapely legs, her tiny denim shorts and her even tinier tube top.

"Mr. Flynn will be returning with us to Wembly Island," Belenki said. "Along with Severina and Mr. Perez."

"Well, isn't that nice," Anika purred. She focused her considerable sexual magnetism on Flynn, inadvertently catching Sancho, Fergus and his operators in her erotic blast radius. Flynn took notice and decided to take advantage.

He downed his drink and hit his martini glass against a table, cracking it down to the stem. In one quick motion, he pulled Belenki to his feet and put the jagged edge against his throat. "Make one move, and I will puncture his carotid artery and he will bleed out within seconds."

Everyone looked stunned. Everyone but Fergus.

"It takes longer than that for someone to bleed out," Fergus shouted, as he moved in Flynn's direction.

"No, it doesn't!" Flynn shouted back.

"Yeah, it does. I've done it. It's not like in the movies. It can take a good five minutes if not longer. If I shoot you in the head and put compression on the carotid, he'll probably be fine."

"Probably?" Belenki shouted. "What do you mean probably!"

"Stay where you are. I'm heading for the submarine and I'm taking Belenki with me."

"And if I don't stay where I am?"

"I'll kill him."

"Bullshit!"

Belenki struggled and the jagged edge nicked his skin. "Let me go! *Let me go!*"

"No," Flynn said evenly.

"Fine! That offer I just offered you? *It's off the table!*"

Flynn backed away with Belenki, one arm holding him tight, the other holding the jagged end of the cocktail glass to his now bloody throat.

Fergus slowly followed, loosely holding his weapon. When he reached the fire pit, he put the barrel of his assault rifle against Sancho's head. "Let Belenki go or this asshole gets it." Sancho tried to get up. Fergus shoved him back down, screwing the gun barrel into his face. "And after I blow his brains out, I'll put a few into you."

Flynn pulled Belenki with him. "Do that and your boss is dead. And so is—"

Flynn tripped backwards over a railing and flipped ass over teakettle. He lost both the martini stem and his hostage and fell fifteen feet to the deck below. He hit it so hard he bit his tongue and knocked the wind right out of himself. Fergus and his men were on him in seconds.

Belenki, gazing down from above, touched the cut on his neck and looked at the blood on his fingers. "Lock that crazy son of a bitch up!"

CHAPTER TWENTY-SEVEN

On February 20, 1962, Friendship 7 rose off the launchpad at Cape Canaveral and former fighter pilot John Glenn became the first U.S. citizen to orbit the Earth. Some were worried he might not make it back alive, and the Pentagon came up with a plan in the event of such a tragedy. They would blame Fidel Castro for Glenn's death. They called their scheme "Operation Dirty Trick" and planned to provide "proof" that any failure was due to sabotage by the Communists in Cuba.

Even though Kennedy agreed to the ill-fated "Bay of Pigs" invasion the previous year, this plan he rejected. In the end, Glenn returned safely and became an authentic American hero. Kennedy quietly told NASA that Glenn must never again return to space. He was far too important a symbol of America's Can-Do Spirit. Glenn wouldn't ride another rocket for thirty-six years. In 1998 at the age of seventy-seven, he became the oldest astronaut ever when he flew as part of the crew in the Space Shuttle Discovery.

Sancho was born seven years after the movie, *The Right Stuff*, was released. He saw it in a science class when he was thirteen and loved it. It told the story of the early Mercury program and the test pilots who became the first astronauts. He learned everything he could about those early astronauts and even did a term paper on Project Mercury and earned himself a B minus from his science teacher, Mrs. Merkin.

He would have loved to follow in the footsteps of John Glenn, but Mrs. Merkin made it clear to Sancho he didn't have the "right stuff" to ever become a pilot let alone an astronaut. The best a boy like him could hope for would be to go to trade school and become a car mechanic or a plumber.

Sancho thought about John Glenn and Mrs. Merkin as he stared at the lights of Cape Canaveral from the window of his lavish and securely locked cabin. *Why couldn't Flynn take Belenki's offer or at least pretend to? That's all he had to do.* Instead, he pulled that stupid, stupid move.

Belenki didn't seem like a killer, but then he didn't exactly seem stable either. If he thought Flynn and Sancho were a threat, who knew what he might do. Sancho took a class in abnormal psychology junior year and Belenki fit the profile of someone with both narcissistic and paranoid personality disorder to a T. Much like Flynn, he had grandiose ideas of who he was and what he was put on Earth to do. They both had that exaggerated sense of privilege which allowed them to bend rules and break laws. Both had supreme confidence in their judgment and never doubted they were right. All Sancho did was doubt, and as he looked at the lights of Cape Canaveral, he began to doubt he would live to see the dawn.

• • •

Flynn staggered back into his luxurious cabin and Fergus locked it tight. This time his hands were bound behind his back with zip tie restraints. As an expert at escape in general and Houdini in particular, Flynn knew just what to do.

He squatted down and slowly dislocated his right shoulder, slid his bound wrists under his bum and squeezed his legs through until his hands were now in front. After sliding his shoulder back into place, he searched the room and found a dime under a couch cushion and a ballpoint pen in a drawer. Pulling off the pen's plastic cap, he put the bulbous end in his teeth, and used the flat end to push up the zip tie lock and back the strap out. His hands were free. Now he just had to find a way out.

The way he escaped from that mad, one-handed, half-Chinese doctor was by climbing through a ventilation shaft. Of course, that escape route turned into an obstacle course from hell with fire and water and other lethal death traps. Somehow, he survived and made it out alive and still managed to stop the mad doctor's plot.

Flynn used the dime he found to unscrew a ventilation grate and pull it free. The vent was barely wider than his shoulders, but he pushed his head inside to see what he could find. He eased himself in a little further, sliding in past his shoulders.

As his eyes adjusted, he caught a glimmer of light ahead. *A way out?* He tried to wriggle in further, but the vent narrowed, and Flynn couldn't budge beyond where he was. He tried to wriggle back out and that proved just as difficult as some part of his clothing caught on an unseen edge. Flynn was stuck. He couldn't move forward, and he couldn't move back.

"Oh, good God." His voice echoed in the vent.

• • •

When Severina was at Harvard Law, she did many all-nighters. One time before finals she stayed up two nights in a row. After a grueling day of tests, she went back to her dorm room, intending to stay up and study for a third night. She fell asleep on her law books and when she awoke it was dark outside. She checked her clock. 6:15. Panic seized her when she realized she must have slept through the night. Her test was in less than an hour and she hadn't studied at all.

She fought her anxiety, skimmed as much of the material as she could, then rushed across campus to her seven o'clock contracts class. She raced into Houser Hall and hurried down the corridor, surprised to see she was the last one to class. The door to the class was already closed. When she threw it open, the room was dark. The desks were empty. There was no one there.

She wondered if she was having a nightmare, and as she looked around the empty room it slowly dawned her that it wasn't seven in the morning, but seven in the evening. She had only slept for an hour. Not all night. She was disoriented and discombobulated and that's exactly how she felt after learning the truth about Belenki.

She was living in a nightmare she couldn't wake up from. Like John Galt in *Atlas Shrugged*, her boss intended to stop the motor of the world. When she and Belenki first met, they bonded over their love of *The Fountainhead* and *Atlas Shrugged*. She was pretty sure that was why he hired her. Belenki saw himself as a modern-day Ayn Rand character.

Like John Galt, he double majored in physics and philosophy. She and Belenki both flirted with Objectivism as college freshman and still had faith in many of its tenets. She bought into the idea that there was virtue in selfishness. That greed was good. She believed that individual freedoms were best protected by the modern system of laissez-faire capitalism. Severina was a strong proponent of free will and so was Belenki, who saw the rise of Daisy as the end of everything.

He would stop the motor of the world before he let humanity lose its autonomy.

But what if Belenki wasn't dealing with reality? No one else believed that Daisy was sentient. And even if he was right and Daisy was self-aware, sending the world back into the stone age might not be the best way to handle that problem. He was asserting his own free will and stealing everyone else's.

The craziest thing of all was that Flynn apparently wasn't crazy. At least not about this. He was right all along. *Where did Fergus take him? Did that son of a bitch murder him? And if not, what did Belenki intend to do with him?* She couldn't just let Belenki bring down the world, but she wasn't sure how to stop him. Severina paced back and forth in her cabin, clenching her fists.

She thought about what she did to Wendy. How she refused to believe her. How she thought Wendy was as crazy as Flynn.

"What did I do? What the fuck did I do?"

• • •

Flynn couldn't catch his breath. Sweat ran down his forehead and into his eyes. He rocked back and forth to dislodge himself from the vent. His arms were pinned and he couldn't find the proper leverage.

"Bloody hell!" he shouted, his voice echoing in the vent.

Marshalling every ounce of angry fury, he wrenched himself back as hard as he could, ripping his shirt and cutting his face. He stumbled backwards over a stool and landed on his bum. Furious, he scrambled to his feet, grabbed the stool and threw it at the glass observation window. He didn't care that his cabin was half-submerged, and water would come rushing in. He just wanted out.

The stool hit the window hard and bounced right back at him, smacking Flynn in the nose, knocking him back on his bum again.

"Bloody bastard!" He lay flat-out on the floor, staring at the elaborate stamped tin ceiling. He didn't bother to get up. There was no reason to. He needed to calm himself. Cool down and concentrate.

A knock at the door broke his concentration once more.

"Yes?" he shouted.

The deadbolt clicked. The door opened, and in walked Severina, dressed in jeans and a black turtleneck. She was surprised to see him flat on his back, his face cut, his forehead bleeding.

"Those bastards! Look what they did to you!"

"So finally, you believe me."

"We can't let him get away with this. We have to tell the authorities what he's trying to do!"

Flynn sat up. "First off, we have to neutralize Fergus."

"Already done," she said. "Sergei suffers from insomnia and keeps a supply of Halcion. I stole his stash, spiked a bunch Red Bulls, and handed them out to Fergus and his team."

"What about Sergei?"

"I gave him one too."

"Brilliant. So, they're all out cold?"

"For now." She helped Flynn to his feet.

"We have to find Sancho."

"He's already free. He's waiting at the landing craft."

"Then why are we standing around here?" Flynn rushed out the door and Severina hurried after him.

Flynn searched the sleeping bodies of Fergus and his men for weapons. They were sprawled all over the boat in various uncomfortable-looking positions. Severina tried to hurry him along, terrified that they could awaken at any moment.

One did.

He looked at Flynn with bleary, unfocused eyes and tried to draw his sidearm, but Flynn already had it in hand and smacked him in the head with it, rendering him unconscious once again. All in all, Flynn filched an MP5 submachine gun, a Beretta M9, and a Heckler and Koch sniper rifle.

Flynn and Severina found Sancho waiting on the landing craft. It was already in the water and bouncing around in the chop.

"What the hell took you so long!" Sancho shouted.

"Your friend wanted some weapons!" Severina shouted back.

As they climbed aboard the landing craft, Sancho paced back and forth. Flynn took control of the helm. "Unmoor us please, Miss Angelli."

As Severina unmoored them, Belenki's fiancé, Anika, came running up in her strappy high heels, denim shorts, and barely-there tube top. "Don't leave without me!"

"It's not safe where we're going. You're better off here," Flynn said.

"Without wi-fi? Fuck that!"

"What do you mean it's not safe?" Severina asked. "Where do you think we're going?"

"To Cape Canaveral to stop that launch," Flynn replied.

"Cape Canaveral! Are you out of your mind?"

"You really have to ask that," Sancho muttered.

Anika leaped onto the landing craft, right into Sancho's arms. She towered over him, smiling down. "Good catch," she said.

Flynn backed the boat out into the sea, turned it towards the lights of Cape Canaveral and gunned the twin engines.

Severina shouted to be heard over the roar. "You do realize that mission control is nowhere near the launch site! It's miles south of here near Port Canaveral."

"We aren't going to mission control."

"But NASA has mission managers there. Supervisors overseeing the launch! We have to tell them what Sergei intends to do!"

"There's no point in storming mission control," Flynn said grimly. "We don't know who's working with Sergei and who's not. We might delay the launch, but we won't stop it. To do that, I need to destroy it."

"Destroy it?"

"A rocket is at its most vulnerable right before lift-off. In fact, the Serenity 2 is being filled with fuel as we speak. They do it right before the launch because they need to keep the liquid oxygen at such a low temperature. Basically, it's a massive bomb. The equivalent of four million pounds of TNT."

"But there's a nuclear bomb on board! If you blow up the rocket, won't you blow up the bomb?"

"Blowing up a nuclear device won't initiate a chain reaction. That is *not* how they are detonated."

"Cape Canaveral is an air force base. There's security everywhere."

"Not during a launch. They keep the entire area clear of anyone at this stage. That includes security."

"But they must be watching the perimeter."

"I'm sure they are."

"So how you plan to get past them?"

"I'll do whatever I need to."

"What kind of answer is that?"

Flynn picked up a pistol from the cache of weapons he made off with. "Nice to hold a Beretta again. It used to be my favorite firearm before N insisted I give it up for the Walther PPK." He shoved the weapon in his belt.

Sancho pointed at the long rifle. "What's that big one?"

"A Heckler and Koch MM110. It weighs less than nine pounds but packs a very powerful punch."

"Dude…You're not planning on shooting anyone, are you?"

"Just the Serenity 2."

"Can you drop me off at Cocoa Beach?" Anika asked.

"Sorry, darling," Flynn said. "There's no time for detours. Not with the fate of humanity in our hands."

CHAPTER TWENTY-EIGHT

Belenki woke up face down on his bathroom floor with his pants around his ankles and ass in the air. The last thing he remembered was Severina handing him a Red Bull so he could keep his eyes open until the launch. His head felt fuzzy and his face rested in a pool of drool.

"Dammit," he slurred. Did he pass out while taking a crap? Did he have a stroke? *What the hell?* The bathroom door opened and banged him in the head. "Ow!"

It was Fergus. "Sorry, sir." He looked crocked off his ass. "We have a problem."

"Are you drunk?"

"Drugged. I'm pretty sure Miss Angelli roofied our Red Bulls. Half my men are still zonked out."

Belenki lifted his face off the floor. A long string of spittle dangled from his mouth to the tile. "Shit."

The mercenary grabbed Belenki's arm and pulled him to his feet. "The landing craft is gone along with Flynn, Perez, and Miss Angelli. They may have kidnapped Miss Piscotti, because I can't find her."

"They can keep her."

"Flynn took some of our weapons as well."

"Where would they go?"

"I believe he's headed for the launch site."

"Did you call security over there?"

"Already done, sir. I'm going to take the other tender and see if I can find him before he hurts anyone."

A wave of dizziness hit Belenki and he sat heavily on his heated Japanese toilet seat. "You see 'em, you shoot 'em. I've had enough of this shit."

• • •

Sancho sat next to Anika and held on tight to a cleat as they bounced over the rough chop. The landing craft crested the top of each swell before plummeting into the trough below. A wave of nausea surged through Sancho. He caught Severina's eye as she held onto the gunwale near Flynn. She too looked close to tossing her cookies, giving him a look like "what the hell do we do?"

Sancho shook his head. Once Flynn was on a mission, there was no stopping him.

He glanced back at the Argo receding in the distance. He couldn't see anyone on deck, but they were hundreds of yards away. Hopefully, Fergus and his asshole operators were still passed out.

Sancho turned his gaze back to the shore and saw the first reddish rays of the rising sun reflected off Belenki's rocket and the erector-set-like towers around it.

They rapidly approached the beach, the launch pad less than a mile away. Sancho wondered if Flynn had any idea how to land this landing craft. He wasn't slowing down, and they were running out of ocean.

"Dude!" Sancho shouted. "You might want to hit the brakes!"

Flynn took the hint and eased off the throttle, but as the boat approached the beach, Flynn misjudged the depth and ran the ship aground. Sancho and Anika toppled off their padded bench. Severina fell as well. Flynn didn't budge, ensconced as he was in the captain's chair. He pulled the lever to lower the front landing gate and it thumped against the sand.

Sancho hurried his ass off the boat, Anika right behind him, unsteady and teetering in her strappy high heels. Then came Severina, who promptly retched in the sand, followed by Flynn, with his armful of stolen weapons. He tried to hand the MP5 to Sancho.

"Keep it, man. I don't need it."

When he tried to give the submachine gun to Severina, she raised both her hands and shook her head, backing away. "Would you please put those back in the boat!"

"Where are we?" Anika asked.

"About two miles from the Space Go Launch Complex," Flynn replied. "That's the Serenity 2 on the launch pad over there."

Anika nodded. "I'm calling an Uber." She looked at her phone. "No fucking bars. Are you fucking kidding me?"

Sancho heard them before he saw them. All-terrain vehicles. Six of them. Bounding over the bluff and down to the beach. Each one had its own helmeted, camo wearing, flack-jacketed soldier. Within seconds they were surrounded with six assault weapons aimed at them.

"Put your weapons down!" screamed the shortest soldier, his voice high-pitched and hollow inside his helmet. "On the ground! Do it now!"

Flynn looked perplexed. Severina rested her hand on his arm. "He wants you to put the weapons down."

"Soldier, my name is Flynn. James Flynn. And I'm an agent of her Majesty's Secret Service. Who might you be?"

"I am Captain Dutton, commanding officer of the Security Force Squadron of the 45th Space Wing, and I'm gonna need you to comply with my order and *put down your weapons!*"

"Drop 'em, dude," Sancho put his hand on Flynn's shoulder. "Before somebody shoots you."

Captain Dutton's voice rose in pitch as he shouted even louder. *"You are trespassing in a highly restricted location! This is a designated blast danger area and if you don't drop those weapons in the next five seconds, we will drop you where you stand, sir!"*

Sancho saw himself reflected in the tinted safety glass of their goggles. They were eyeless, faceless avatars of authority. Fear palpitated Sancho's heart. He knew Flynn wouldn't back down and tensed for the inevitable shit show. Fingers hovered over triggers. Sancho sank to his knees, hands up.

"James, I'm begging you, man. Put down the fucking guns."

Even though Sancho couldn't see the soldiers' eyes, he could tell they were no longer looking directly at Flynn. The slight tilt of their helmets indicated they were looking at something past him. Sancho slowly turned his head. Something metallic crested the surface of the sea a hundred yards out. Was that Goolardo's mini sub? Was that the Seawolf? A hatch opened on top and Mendoza's giant, pale, pumpkin head popped out.

He held something, but Sancho couldn't tell what until he heard a distant pop and saw a flash of light and smoke. Something whooshed between him and Flynn. An ATV exploded. Sancho hit the beach as parts flew everywhere. The soldiers dove for the sand.

Two started shooting at the mini sub as Mendoza reloaded his weapon. Sancho looked back at the burning, smoking husk of the all-terrain vehicle. Flynn ran right past it and leaped on a still-intact ATV.

Flynn shot out the tires of all the remaining vehicles with his MP5, but the soldiers couldn't hear Flynn's gunfire over their own barrage of bullets. All six fired at Mendoza.

Mendoza launched another rocket and blew up another all-terrain vehicle. As fiery pieces of ATV rained down, Mendoza slowly slid back into the sub and closed the hatch. The Seawolf submerged, disappearing under the waves.

The soldiers stopped shooting and heard Flynn roaring away on the All-Terrain Vehicle. They leaped to their feet to see him bounding over the bluffs. The soldiers raced to the three still functioning ATVs only to find every tire shredded.

· · ·

In times of high danger, when bullets flew and engines raced, the music would often play in Flynn's head. A deep, dark electric guitar pounded out a rousing, thrilling, relentless rhythm that promised danger and excitement. It filled Flynn with intoxicating joy. The music mingled with the roar of the ATV as it tore through saw palmetto, sea oats, and beach grass. As the sun was barely up, the lights of the Space Go launch site blazed ahead, perhaps a mile in the distance.

The most vulnerable point would be one of the fuel tanks. If Flynn could hit the right spot, he knew he could intermingle the oxidant and the fuel and create an explosive chemical reaction. But he had to be in range; and the effective range of the Heckler and Koch MM110 Semi-Automatic Sniper rifle was roughly half a mile. Flynn figured he was about a mile away and needed to close the distance. He'd never survive the blast. But he also knew he had no choice.

The .50 caliber round tore through the engine block of Flynn's ATV before Flynn even heard the rifle crack. The engine seized and the ATV flipped. Flynn went flying. He hit the ground hard, eating dirt as he crashed and rolled. Now he heard the chopper and saw it silhouetted in the sky. Another .50 caliber round slammed into the ground a few inches from his head. A little to the left and it would have decapitated him.

Bleeding and bruised, Flynn forced himself to his feet and started to run. But there was little cover and nowhere to hide. He ran in a serpentine fashion as bullets hit the sand all around him. In between the shots, the shouts of the soldiers from the beach pierced the air. They moved closer and were probably in communication with the helicopter pilot.

An amplified voice boomed from the chopper. "On your knees! Now! Hands in the air!"

A blazing spotlight shined on Flynn as the soldiers surrounded him on all sides. He still had the Beretta, but he was badly outnumbered. Even if he could take out the soldiers, the sniper in the chopper would cut him in half.

The tiny commander of the camo-helmeted, flak-jacketed security soldiers forced Flynn to his knees and took his Beretta. In the distance, more than a mile off, Flynn eyed the Serenity 2 and he knew he now had no way to stop it.

• • •

Goolardo brought the Seawolf back to the surface and lifted the hatch. He poked his head out to see what had become of Flynn. Sancho and the women were still on the beach. The security guards were gone; likely on foot after his former nemesis.

A helicopter stalked Flynn from above, shining a spotlight and raking the ground with gunfire. Goolardo recognized the colors of the Coast Guard. It was an MH-65 C, which he knew they used for their Helicopter Interdiction Tactical Squadrons. HITRONs were specifically designed to go after drug smugglers. Those assholes had personally cost Goolardo close to a billion dollars.

Each chopper was equipped with a pintle mounted M240 machine gun with thermal sights and a sniper with .50 caliber Barrett which they used to shoot out the engine blocks on his high-speed boats. He often fantasized about dishing out some payback and this looked like the perfect opportunity.

"Mendoza!" Goolardo ordered. "Hand me the stinger! Hurry!"

Mendoza handed his boss the man-portable air-defense missile system. Goolardo rested it on his right shoulder before hitting the activator switch. He put the chopper in his sight and the high-pitched beeping soon turned into one long constant tone—indicating the weapon had locked on. Goolardo hit the uncage button and fired. The rocket screamed out with a whoosh as the launch motor detached and the flight motor kicked in. The missile homed in on the helicopter, streaking across the sky before crashing into the rear rotor.

• • •

The heat of the explosion washed over Flynn and he looked up to see the chopper smoking and on fire, spinning out of control. The pilot and the gunners jumped out as the helicopter whirled across the sky, over the electrified fence and into the launch area where it careened into the Serenity 2.

The gas tank on the chopper blew. That explosion was loud, but nothing compared to the thunderous roar of kerosene and liquid oxygen combining and combusting and exploding with a stunning flash of light and heat.

The blast blew Flynn right off of his feet, along with all the security soldiers. He couldn't breathe or see or think or even understand which end was up as he tumbled through the air and landed a distance away, face down in the sand. He spit the grit out of his mouth and tried to see through all the smoke and dust. A deafening ringing filled his ears. He looked back at the launch pad. A ten-story column of fire and smoke rose into the sky.

He had to move. If he didn't, he'd die. The Serenity 2 was no more and he would follow it into oblivion if he couldn't find a way to get his arse out of there.

Shaky, dizzy, deaf and numb, he somehow made it to his feet. *One step at a time.* He staggered across the dunes and back towards the beach. Flynn could barely stay upright as he lurched ahead. Something shot that helicopter out of the sky and Flynn knew that whoever or whatever brought it down just saved the world. He couldn't hear his own footsteps or the roaring fire consuming the launch site behind him, but he could feel the unbelievable heat.

His legs barely worked, and he didn't seem to have much control over them. Twice the ground rushed up and hit him in the face, and both times he managed to get his feet back under him to continue on. Somehow, though, the beach never got any closer. He kept wobbling forward through the poisonous smoke and heat and noxious dust. The acrid smell of burnt rubber, melted plastic, and toxic chemicals filled his nostrils and stung his eyes. Was he even still alive? *Is this what Hell smells like?*

$$\bullet \quad \bullet \quad \bullet$$

"We can't stay here!" Severina shouted as she stood toe to toe with Sancho. "You want to stay? *Stay!* I'm getting back on the boat!"

"We can't just leave him!" Sancho pleaded.

"He left *us!*"

"I'm not leaving without him!"

"*Fine! Stay!*"

Anika was already on the boat. "Can we just go?"

Sancho's ears still rang as he watched the mountain of fire and smoke reach into the sky.

"*There's no way in hell he's still alive,*" Severina screamed. She hurried onto the boat and marched up the landing gate planted in the sand.

"Severina!" Sancho begged. "Please!"

"You coming or what?" She raised the landing gate. Sancho knew she was right. If the helicopter and the soldiers didn't get him, the blast definitely did. Grief gripped his heart as he looked back at the conflagration. Smoke and flames rose and billowed in all directions as smaller explosions continued to shake the ground.

An apparition emerged from the swirling clouds of smoke and dust.

"Wait!" Sancho yelled. "Look!"

Covered in ash from head to toe, Flynn moved slower than a ninety-year-old man recovering from hip surgery. Sancho ran to him and took him by the arm. As he helped Flynn towards the landing craft, he was surprised to see Severina charging across the sand. She grabbed Flynn's other arm and together they hurried him across the beach.

Gunshots rang out behind them. Sancho turned. Two of the security soldiers above them on the bluff fired warning shots.

"Get on the ground! Face down!" one soldier yelled.

Severina stopped in her tracks but Sancho kept pulling and now he was dragging both of them forward. More rifle shots erupted behind them. A Stinger missile rocketed over their heads and exploded into the high bluff the soldiers perched on, blowing them sideways.

Sancho saw the Seawolf, bobbing on the ocean. Goolardo waved to them from the open hatch, a spent rocket launcher resting on his shoulder.

"Who the hell is that?" Severina shouted.

"You don't want to know," Sancho replied.

They finally dragged Flynn across the beach, up the landing gate and into the boat. As Severina raised the gate, Sancho fired up the engine.

A bullet clanged off the landing craft. The security soldiers were back on their feet and firing from the bluff. Instead of two, there were now four of them.

"Everybody down!" Sancho shouted as bullets whizzed overhead and ricocheted off the aluminum landing gate. He backed the craft off the beach, turning it about and gunning the engine. It picked up speed as it pushed forward through the waves, taking fire until they were finally out of range.

As the sound of assault weapons receded, Sancho cut south toward Cocoa Beach. He looked at Flynn sitting against the gunwale; sweaty and dirty, dazed, exhausted and still covered in ash.

"Dude, are you okay?"

Flynn cocked his ear towards him. "What?"

"I asked if you're okay."

"Huh?"

"You all right!"

Flynn nodded. "Quite a fight."

"Are you hurt?"

"A shirt? Sure. This one's in shreds."

"Are you having trouble hearing me?"

"No!" He pointed to his ears. "I'm having trouble hearing you!"

• • •

Sergei Belenki stood on the deck of the Argo and watched what was left of the Serenity 2 burn. A towering cloud of smoke and fire rose from his Cape Canaveral Launch Pad. Additional explosions sent the flames higher as Sergei gripped the railing and gritted his teeth to keep himself from screaming. The Serenity 2 and its entire payload was obliterated. Half a billion dollars up in toxic smoke.

He was one of the richest men in the world, but half a billion dollars wasn't exactly chump change. Worst of all, his orbiting corona of nuclear devices wasn't yet complete and wouldn't be until he marshaled the resources necessary to build another rocket. And another satellite. And another nuclear device.

Space flight was always risky, and Belenki built the possibility of an accident into his plan. He figured that such an inevitability could throw off his schedule. But this was no accident. This was James motherfucking Flynn. All the goodwill Flynn engendered with Sergei for saving his life multiple times no longer existed. Severina had betrayed him. She sided with Flynn against him.

He never should have told her what he was planning. She didn't understand and probably never would. She was smarter than most, but apparently not smart enough to see the danger that Daisy posed.

That kind of existential threat was just too difficult for the average human to grasp. The vast majority were dull-witted sheep who numbed themselves with alcohol, marijuana, fast food, and video games. He should know. He built the most addicting social networking app ever created and gave those lost souls the illusion their lives had meaning. That's how he made his billions. That was why he knew for a fact they were lemmings. They didn't have the brains or imagination to grok that a superior machine intelligence would soon eclipse them.

He had raised the alarm many times, but no one else took the threat seriously. No one but a tiny cadre of true believers. It was up to him and him alone to save humanity from the authoritarian boot heel of an intelligence far beyond their own.

Fergus joined Belenki at the railing and took in the rising column of smoke and flame emanating from Space Go's Cape Canaveral launch site.

"What's our next move, sir?"

"If Flynn indeed was the one who destroyed Serenity 2, it's unlikely he survived. I can't imagine how he would have escaped the blast radius. However, if by some miracle that idiot did make it through alive, you need to remedy that situation. I can't risk him doing anything like this ever again."

"What about Severina?"

"Find out if she's alive or dead. If she's still breathing, I'd like to talk to her."

"And Flynn's sidekick?"

"Like Flynn, if he survived, he needs to be removed from the equation."

"Anika?"

"What about her?"

"Do you want her back?"

"Not especially."

Fergus nodded. "Are you off to Wembly Island?"

"I am. We will rebuild. And we will finish what we started here today."

"I'll send some men to bolster the security at Wembly. Then I'll contact the Security Force Squadron of the 45th Space Wing and see if they found Flynn."

"I'm sure they're searching the area as we speak. Of course, if he was close enough to the blast his body would have been obliterated. You may find remnants of one of the weapons he stole, but it's also likely you'll find no trace of him at all."

CHAPTER TWENTY-NINE

Bullets punctured the fuel tanks on both outboard engines. Their boat was dead in the water. Sancho could see Cocoa Beach, but they were two miles from the marina.

"I can't believe we don't have a dinghy," Anika whined. "The other tender had a dinghy!"

Sancho kept trying to get the engines going, but without gas it was an impossible proposition.

"Maybe we can contact the coast guard," Severina said.

"The Coast Guard's likely already looking for us," Flynn noted.

"And when they find us, they'll probably shoot us out of the water," Sancho added.

"But I didn't do anything!" Anika said. "I'm not the one who blew up Sergei's rocket."

"I didn't blow it up either," Severina said.

"None of us blew it up," Sancho pointed out. "It was Goolardo!"

"Who?" Severina said.

Sancho heard what sounded like a distant helicopter and looked north towards Cape Canaveral. A tiny black dot hovered on the hazy horizon. "Oh, shit!"

"Oh, my God," Severina said.

"I'm going to say you kidnapped me," Anika announced.

"But we didn't, did we?" Severina shouted. "You wanted to come! You insisted on it!"

"That's your story!"

The black dot on the horizon grew larger as the sound of the distant chopper grew louder.

"Maybe we should swim for it," Sancho said.

Severina pointed at Flynn. "I thought he was the crazy one!"

Anika lifted up a leg to show off one of her shoes. "These are brand new Manolo Blahniks! I'm not getting these wet."

Sancho put on a flotation vest. "You want to stay? Stay! I'm swimming for it!" He sat on the edge of the gunwale and prepared to dive in when he noticed what looked like the lens of periscope just above the surface of the sea. Seconds later something much larger emerged above the swells.

The Seawolf.

The hatch opened and a smiling Goolardo poked his head out.

"Anyone need a ride?"

Anika gave Goolardo a sexy grin and wobbled over to the edge of the boat. He reached out, took her hand and helped her into the hatch.

Severina hesitated.

"He's a friend," Flynn said.

Goolardo held out his hand and Severina took it and climbed into the Seawolf, followed by Flynn and then Sancho who saw a distant ship on the horizon just below the helicopter. He climbed down into the mini sub and Goolardo closed the hatch.

The Seawolf seated five, but there were six with Anika and Severina. Mendoza took up the same amount of room as two and that made the inside of Seawolf tighter than a Speedo on a sumo wrestler. Sancho sat on the floor just below Mendoza. The big man's clammy, pale, perfectly round head glistened with sweat. His mouth pursed tight like he was trying not to heave. Sancho was grateful for the rescue, but suspicious of Goolardo's motives. The head of the Goolardo Drug Cartel seemed to be enjoying this adventure with Flynn. But for how long? And when would he demand his pound of flesh for what Flynn did to him?

"Can we turn up the air? It's kind of hot in here," Anika said.

Goolardo scooched over to make more room. "I apologize for the close quarters. But we will soon be topside on my yacht. It's not as large as the Argo, but quite comfortable and just as luxurious."

Severina pointed at Mendoza with her thumb. "Is he okay?"

"Mr. Mendoza is not fond of tight quarters or the motion of the sea."

"So, who are you?" Anika asked

"Francisco Goolardo, at your service."

"I'm Anika."

"Have we met before, my dear? You look familiar."

"That's because she's a movie star," Sancho said. As annoying as Anika was, Sancho was still star struck. He had seen her so many times in so many movies and had fanaticized about her for so many years. She was physical perfection and a far better actress than he ever imagined as she was nothing like the characters she usually portrayed. In the movies she was sweet and naive, tender and vulnerable, self-sacrificing and heroic, while in real life she was selfish and whiny, spoiled rotten and unbelievably irritating.

"What would I have seen you in?" Goolardo asked her.

"Dark Seduction," Anika said. "Journey of Fear."

Goolardo's eyes lit up with recognition. "Of course! Anika Piscotti. It's an honor to have you aboard the Seawolf!"

Severina rolled her eyes.

Mendoza made a gagging sound. Panic filled the face of everyone in the mini sub. His eyes bulged and they all tried to scuttle away, pressing themselves into the sides of the sub, even though there was precious little room to move. Goolardo handed Mendoza a wastebasket and he held it up to his face, the dry retching sound now echoing in the tiny plastic can. Everyone held their breath as the gagging gradually subsided and Mendoza finally lowered the can.

Twenty minutes later, the Seawolf arrived at the Queen Anne's Revenge and Goolardo opened the hatch. Mendoza shoved his way out first, squeezing his bulk through the little opening as fast he humanly could. The others followed and within minutes Goolardo was at the helm and steering his yacht back to Miami.

Anika stuck like glue to Goolardo, standing with him on the bridge as he piloted his vessel south. It was instinct with her, Sancho decided. She found money and power magnetic and it didn't hurt that Goolardo was also charismatic and handsome and had wi-fi. Besides, he had an authentic bad boy charm that most of those wannabe bad boys in the tech world couldn't match.

He wasn't pretending to be a badass like the rock and roll drummers Anika often dated. He was an authentic badass. A mob boss. A drug trafficker. A kidnapper. A killer. In a world of pretend tough guys, Goolardo was the real deal. He had a good twenty years on Anika, but that might have been part of the attraction. Apparently, she had daddy issues.

While Anika busily texted and posted and tweeted on Twitter, a dirty, sad, and exhausted-looking Severina sat on a chaise longue and stared off into space. Mendoza hung his huge head over the wooden railing and held on for dear life as the rest of the crew bustled about doing the things crews usually do. Most carried sidearms. Some had assault rifles. Many were bearded and pierced and tattooed like modern-day pirates.

If the Coast Guard ever stopped them, they'd be in for a hell of a fight, but they weren't looking for a multi-million-dollar yacht. They were looking for a landing craft and by now that bullet-ridden boat was probably at the bottom of the Atlantic.

"I must admit it," Goolardo said, his voice booming and full of high spirits. "I had no idea saving the world would be so exhilarating." He smiled at Flynn. "I didn't intend for that chopper to crash into the rocket, but when it did, oh, my goodness! What a rush! Though I did worry that it might set off that nuclear bomb."

"That's not how nuclear devices are detonated," Sancho said.

"Good to know." Goolardo playfully punched Flynn on the shoulder. "We make a great team, you and I. Perhaps we should travel the world together, righting wrongs and doing good deeds. Perhaps, over time, the world wouldn't see us as such pariahs."

"In my case possibly," Flynn said. "In your case, that seems highly unlikely."

"You wound me, Mr. Flynn. Clearly, there are different rules for those born into the ruling class. The prisons are full of the poor even though it's the super-rich who steal and murder the most. The entire system has been designed to enrich those on top and crush those below. So, unless you are born into wealth you would have to be a fool to follow the rules."

"If everyone believed as you do, we would have complete anarchy."

"Isn't that exactly what we do have?" Goolardo asked. "The powers that be can barely keep a lid on all the anger and violence and lawlessness. That's why organizations like Her Majesty's Secret Service exist. To keep the dispossessed from rising up. Governments encourage the underprivileged to join the military. Then they brainwash them in boot camps and turn them into weapons. Soldiers who will take orders without question. Those in power depend on dull-witted patriots to keep the 'haves' safe from the 'have-nots.'"

"So, if you don't believe in the rule of law, what do you believe in?"

"I believe in myself, Mr. Flynn. I am my own higher power. Marx wasn't wrong about religion. Religion, like patriotism, was created to mollify the masses. Both are imaginary constructs designed to alleviate fear. The great unwashed spend their hard-earned dollars to flock to movie theaters and watch superheroes save the day. Fantasies of empowerment designed to keep the unempowered pacified. Look in the mirror. You've turned yourself into a pulp fiction fantasy and made that fantasy flesh. Is the belief you have in yourself any more far-fetched than the Pope's faith in his own infallibility? Hardly. To me, reality is a relative concept. Just like right and wrong. Who decides what's crazy and what isn't? The people who run the world? I don't think so. I think we should decide. Each of us. Individually. Join me, Mr. Flynn. We will be who we want to be. Without apology. Without compromise. Without selling our souls to those who would enslave us."

As nauseous as he was, Mendoza couldn't help but react to that. "Are you serious? You want him to join us?"

"Why not?"

"Because that pendejo is loco!"

"Have you not heard a word I said?"

"Because of him we went to prison!"

"Indeed, he's a worthy adversary. That's exactly what makes him such a valuable ally."

"I appreciate the offer," Flynn said. "But the job we set out to do isn't yet done. Belenki will build and launch another nuclear device if he isn't stopped."

"And how do you plan to stop him?"

"We need to liberate Wendy Zimmerman from his island fortress and reveal to the world who he really is."

"And do you honestly think the world will take your word over his?"

"I don't know. But we have to try. You said yourself we should travel the world, righting wrongs and doing good deeds."

"That was hyperbole, Mr. Flynn. I was being ironic. I've done my good deed for the decade. Now it's time to take care of me. I must say; however, I do admire your tenacity."

"So, you won't help me?"

"I'm afraid not, though I'd be more than happy to pay for you and Mr. Perez's flight to Seattle. We can book them under the same false names on the same phony passports we used before."

"Thank you," Flynn said.

Goolardo handed Flynn a burner phone. "Take this burner and keep it with you in case I need to get in touch."

Flynn looked at the phone before slipping it into his pocket. "Of course, you realize that once this job is done, I won't hesitate to try and apprehend you again."

"And if you do, I hope you know I won't hesitate to kill you," Goolardo replied.

"I would expect nothing less."

"Excellent. In the meantime, avail yourself of the Queen Anne's onboard amenities. Take a shower. Take a nap. Enjoy some lunch. We'll see if we can find you a change of clothes."

Goolardo smiled at Anika. "What about you, my dear? Would you also like a plane ticket to Seattle?"

"No way. Fuck Sergei. You can drop me off in Miami."

"I'll get off in Miami too," Severina said.

"You've cut ties with Mr. Belenki?" Goolardo asked.

"He cut ties with me."

"Are you looking for your next position? I could use a world-class attorney and you might need some protection."

"Protection?"

"From your former boss. I can't imagine he's very happy with you at the moment."

"I'm flattered, but no thanks."

"Because of the business I'm in? Do you think what I sell is any less addictive or dangerous than the social media obsession Mr. Belenki pushes?"

"I don't. But…"

"*But* you're tired of being a fixer for the rich and powerful and egotistical?"

"A little bit."

"Understood," Goolardo said. "I may be a sociopath, but I'm not entirely unsympathetic. So, what's next for you?"

"Telling the FBI what Sergei is up to."

"And when you go to the FBI and they ask you who shot down the helicopter that crashed into the Serenity 2, what are you going to tell them?"

"That I have no idea."

"And what if they ask you, Anika?"

"I'll tell them the same thing. You really think I want to get involved in any of this bullshit?"

• • •

One hour later, Goolardo docked the Queen Anne's Revenge at Island Gardens, one of Miami's most exclusive marinas. The concierge team arranged for ground transportation while simultaneously refueling, re-provisioning, and preparing the Revenge for the journey ahead. Flynn gave Severina the number to his burner phone and while she and Anika shared a limo to South Beach, Sancho and Flynn headed for Miami International.

The Queen Anne's Revenge sailed south. Mendoza knew that Goolardo's ultimate destination was Costa Rica, where he owned a fabulous estate on Playa Blanca in Guanacaste. It crossed Mendoza's mind to disembark in Miami, but where would he go? What would he do without Goolardo? As much as his boss insulted and demeaned him, Mendoza knew Goolardo needed him. That thought comforted Mendoza and he clung to it like a life preserver as he began the long, queasy cruise to Costa Rica.

•   •   •

Severina didn't check into the Four Seasons with Anika. Being she was now unemployed, Belenki's former right-hand woman decided to stay somewhere less luxurious. The Swell, a slightly seedy boutique hotel, fit the bill perfectly. Built in 1926, it had a faded and grimy art deco glamor. Her fellow guests were mostly millennial hipsters, gay nightclubbers, and elderly bohemian boomers trying to relive their misspent youth.

Her second-floor room smelled of stale cigarette smoke, and she couldn't open the bathroom door without bumping into the bed. A single black hair dominated the bathtub and she spotted only one clean towel. Severina considered checking herself out and finding another hotel, but she was too damn exhausted to go to that much trouble. She lay on the bed and settled into the trough created by countless bodies, closed her eyes and listened to the roar of the air conditioner as it rattled in the window. At least it drowned out the screaming partiers splashing outside in the tiny pool and patio area. She knew she needed to call the FBI, but first she had to sleep. Once she made that call, she wouldn't have a moment's rest. And rest was exactly what she needed at the moment.

CHAPTER THIRTY

Sancho changed the destination on his ticket from Seattle to Burbank as soon as they arrived at Miami International. There would be a two hour stopover in Dallas Fort Worth, but Sancho could deal with that. What he couldn't deal with was assaulting a heavily guarded island fortress with a lunatic.

It didn't matter that Flynn was right about Belenki. So, he and Goolardo stopped him from crashing every computer on Earth, killing the electrical grid and sending humanity back to the stone age. So what? Now what? They were lucky to be alive. *He* was lucky to be alive. Flynn's only superpower was dumb luck and there was no way it could last forever. Sancho tried to get Flynn to change his ticket as well, but he wasn't having it.

"You want me to abandon the mission?"

"I want you to come back to Pasadena with me and check in with N."

"You don't think time is of the essence here?"

"We blew up Belenki's rocket, dude. We did it! We saved the world. It's done."

"For now. You know he will try again. Meanwhile he has poor Wendy. Who knows what he's doing to her?"

"Severina is already on this. You heard what she said. She's calling the FBI and as Belenki's right hand they're going to listen to what she has to say."

"All the more reason we have to rescue Wendy before something terrible happens. She's our only corroborating witness!"

"The FBI can get there faster than we can. And while they're keeping her safe and searching Belenki's place for evidence, the Air

Force will comb through the wreckage at Cape Canaveral. You know they'll find pieces of that nuclear bomb. Belenki is done. You made the case. You won this thing. Time to take a victory lap."

"I should be at Wembly Island when the FBI arrives."

"It's handled, brother. There's nothing more for you to do. Other than let N debrief you. Let's not keep the man waiting."

Flynn considered Sancho's argument. "So, you trust the FBI to take care of this?"

"I do, and at this point it's just mopping everything up. You did the hard part. Now comes the boring part."

"I suppose you're right."

"No doubt about it, dude. Time for a well-deserved rest. You earned it."

• • •

Flynn followed Sancho back to the counter and changed his ticket to the same Burbank-bound flight. They drank Starbucks coffee and shared some carrot cake and waited to board. One hour later, Flynn found himself in a center aisle seat between a large elderly gentlemen and stylish-looking woman in her early thirties. As they waited to leave the gate, she typed away on a laptop, entering numbers in some sort of spreadsheet. She noticed Flynn watching her and he offered her a smile. "I hope I'm not crowding you."

"Not at all," she said. "Though they do seem to make these seats smaller and smaller."

Flynn noticed she had an Eastern European accent. She was also quite attractive, with curly red hair and striking green eyes. "Do I detect an accent? Are you Czech?"

Her eyes widened with surprise and she flashed a dazzling smile. "Very good."

"I have an ear for that sort of thing."

"Apparently so."

"I'm James." He offered his hand and she shook it.

"Michaela."

"Beautiful name. Are you traveling on business?"

"I am. I work for the Czech tourism office. Public relations."

"Prague is one of the most beautiful cities in the world."

"Have you been?"

"Not for many years. But someday I hope to return. Prague Castle. The Charles Bridge. Wenceslas Square. Saint Vitus Cathedral. That hilltop castle overlooking the Vitava River. The name escapes me…"

"Vysehrad Fortress."

"Yes, of course. I once shared an excellent bottle of Blanc de Noir on a picnic there with a very spirited, very beautiful woman."

"You'll have to return someday."

"I bet you know parts of the city regular tourists rarely see."

"I'd be honored to show you my city sometime."

"And I'd be—" Flynn's burner phone buzzed. "Excuse me for one moment," he accepted the incoming call. "Flynn here."

"James. It's me."

"Severina?"

She spoke sotto voce and she sounded frightened. "Sergei found me."

"What? Where are you?"

"A hotel in South Beach. He must have tracked my credit card."

"You used a credit card?"

"I didn't have any cash."

"Where are you now?"

"I was heading back to my room after breakfast and I saw the door open. I heard Mr. Fergus, so I hid in a maid's closet."

"What hotel?"

"Hotel Swell."

"I'll find it. I'll find you. Did you talk to the FBI?"

"I was so exhausted, I just needed to sleep. I was going to call them after breakfast."

"Call them as soon as you hang up. But please. Stay out of sight until Fergus—"

Flynn heard a door open over the phone and then a woman speaking Spanish. "Quién eres tú?"

Severina tried shushing her, but she just talked louder. "Que estas haciendo aqui? Te esta escondiendo de alguien?"

Then Flynn heard another voice. Fergus's voice. "Well ain't this a surprise?"

"Oh, my God," Severina whispered.

"Run!" Flynn said. "*Run!*"

The clatter of a bucket echoed over the cell along with a mop handle hitting the floor followed by running footsteps and other heavier footsteps from multiple pursuers.

"Stop her!" Fergus yelled. "Get her!"

Flynn heard Severina fall or maybe she was tackled. Grunting and struggling ensued. "Severina!" Flynn shouted. "Severina!"

"Severina is indisposed, Mr. Flynn." It was Fergus. "Why don't you save us all a lot of time and Severina a lot of pain and tell me where you are."

"If you hurt her, I swear to God —"

"What? You'll open a can of whoop-ass on me? Tell you what. You tell me where you are and I can arrange to make that happen."

A perky female stewardess with a south Texas drawl made an announcement over the plane's P.A. system. "Ladies and gentlemen, we are next in line for take-off, so please fasten your seatbelts and turn off all personal electronic devices."

"Sounds like you're on a plane, Mr. Flynn. Where are you going?"

"I will find you, Fergus. You and Belenki both. I'm coming for you."

"Let me make it easy. I'll tell you where we're all going. Wembly Island. Come find us, Mr. Flynn. I think it's time we finish this foolishness, don't you?"

CHAPTER THIRTY-ONE

Those with the most to lose have the most to spend and for the last thirty years many of the world's richest individuals have been building doomsday bunkers. A few have repurposed decommissioned missile silos as they are designed to withstand a nuclear blast and are already equipped with power, water, and air filtration systems.

The largest private billionaire bunker in existence is hidden in a quiet valley in the Czech Republic. The luxurious underground compound is protected by multiple high-security systems. There's an underground garden with simulated natural light, a pool, a cinema, a library, medical and surgical facilities and private vaults to store gold and personal art collections.

The owner of this and every other doomsday shelter will likely survive whatever apocalypse befalls humanity, but once the threat is over and they open their blast doors and step back into the world...what then? A world populated entirely by pampered billionaires and their supermodel girlfriends would probably not be populated for long.

After the shitshow at Sancho's apartment, Bettina O'Toole-Applebaum was determined to discover the truth behind Wendy Zimmerman's story. With a little research, she determined that Belenki's company did indeed employ a Wendy Zimmerman at one time. Was she telling the truth? Did Belenki really intend to bring down the world's technological infrastructure? Is that why he put a private apocalypse bunker in every one of his homes? Or was Wendy just as wacky as Flynn?

Bettina was about to write her off as a kook before flak-jacketed commandos stormed Sancho's apartment and kidnapped her. Who were those men? Why did they want her? Did they work for Belenki? And who was that big one who came in at the end and took Flynn?

The news reports were vague about the rocket explosion at Cape Canaveral, but there were rumors of terrorism and industrial espionage. She gleaned that info from a local Cocoa Beach police detective impressed with her credentials from Rolling Stone. Of course, he also asked her out for a drink, which she accepted in order to pump him for more information. Apparently, there was an assault on the beach and a helicopter crash, and it was all very murky. Just as murky as the mysterious attack on the star-studded benefit at Belenki's mansion in Saratoga.

Arson investigators blamed the fire and subsequent explosion on a faulty gas line, but the guests Bettina tracked down had a different story. These witnesses were not nobodies. They were politicians and police captains, ex-Navy seals and game show hosts, billionaires and captains of industry. Lady Gaga herself said they were attacked by grenade dropping drones that drove them into the house, which then trapped them and gassed them and tried to burn them alive.

If Wendy was to be believed, Belenki was convinced that a murderous AI was after him. She had to talk to Belenki if she ever hoped to uncover the truth, but to confront him she needed the proof. That proof was Wendy Zimmerman and her unimpeachable evidence.

After his latest rocket failed to launch, Bettina read that a chastened Belenki left his superyacht in South Florida and flew back to Wembly Island. *Is that where they took Wendy?* She knew Belenki's private one-hundred-acre island off the coast of Washington State housed the most extravagant doomsday shelter of all. Wembly Island was off the grid and completely self-sustaining.

Bettina needed to get inside and that wasn't going to be easy.

Belenki was as delusional as Flynn, but clearly more dangerous as he had all the resources in the world. If what Wendy said was true, this story could make her career. A mental patient who thinks he's a secret agent versus a megalomaniacal billionaire with a movie star girlfriend and a plot to bring civilization to its knees.

She might even win a Pulitzer.

Bettina made a formal request for an interview with Belenki through Rolling Stone. She even convinced her editor to offer Belenki a cover story, but he wasn't meeting with anyone. He was in seclusion, holed up in his isolated estate, cut off from the rest of the world. The only way to get inside was to go full-bore Nellie Bly once more.

She searched all the job listing sites in the San Juan Islands, hoping to find an open position at Belenki's estate, but there was nothing. So, she used her personal connections to find people who knew employees who for worked Belenki. She finally found a connection. Someone who worked in the kitchen at Wembly Island. The former sous-chef at Saison in San Francisco.

For a story on sexism in the culinary industry, Bettina once trained with a sous-chef and went undercover at a fancy French Restaurant in New York City. She spent six months there and found she enjoyed the work. She also found that most kitchens were tin-pot dictatorships run by entitled men with giant egos; not all that different than the bro culture she exposed in a series of articles on the captains of industry in the Silicon Valley.

Hoping her experience in high-end kitchens might get her in the door, she charmed an interview out of the head chef and took a ferry to Wembly Island to meet with him. She hesitated to rely on her feminine charms, but the man was ungainly and overweight and felt isolated and forlorn as the only chef working in the private kitchen of a newly reclusive billionaire.

Bettina did her research and complimented him on the cuisine he created at Saison in San Francisco, where dinner for two costs a thousand dollars minimum.

She singled out one dish as being her favorite dish of all time. Sea urchin on a moist bed of bread pudding made from toasted sourdough basted with brown butter and egg yolk. She told him how each satisfying and sensual bite filled her with a giddy unforgettable pleasure. The texture, the taste, the mouthfeel, and the flavor were life-changing for her. So much so that she had to find the man who created such magic and learn at his feet. That did it.

His name was Ellis and he hired Bettina on the spot.

She was shown to a small room in a wing of the estate that housed the workers. She shared her room with a chambermaid named Camille and, according to her new roomie, estate staff could only access certain sections of the mansion and the grounds. She drew Bettina a crude map and Bettina used it to reconnoiter the estate, relying on her status as a newcomer and her ignorance of the rules to get into places she wasn't allowed to go.

The sprawling craftsman-style mansion fit flawlessly into the island's natural environment. A great room dominated the center with expansive wings extending in all directions. Each area combined indoor and outdoor spaces with eight-foot sliders that led out to patios and decks. A reverse osmosis desalination system fed an eighty-thousand-gallon pond that supplied water for the landscaping and vegetable gardens, fruit trees, and extensive greenhouses. All the greenery created complete privacy in a natural setting. It was another example of how Belenki built the estate to be self-sustaining.

Black-uniformed guards stood vigil inside the main mansion. The guards outside all carried assault weapons and, if she strayed too far from where she was allowed to go, she would be stopped and asked to show her ID badge.

Upon confirming her identity, she was escorted back to the worker's wing with its small park and garden, dining hall, and recreation facility. She had free run of the kitchen, pantry and dining room, but most of the main mansion was off-limits.

Bettina knew she could get away with feigning ignorance for a day or two, but after that any forays into unauthorized areas would raise suspicion.

She acted flustered and mortified when one burly guard found her on the top floor of the mansion. She claimed she was lost, and he escorted her to the kitchen. Along the way, she made a connection with him, innocently asking him questions and inflating his ego in the process. It was a technique she'd used on many a subject and it always worked better on men than women.

She marveled at the size and intensity and surprising fragility of the male ego. Even the fattest, baldest, wrinkliest, old asshole never doubted Bettina could be interested in him. While many women suffered from body dysmorphia and hated their nose or their legs or believed they were actually much heavier than they were, many men suffered the opposite affliction. They looked in the mirror and somehow didn't see their neckbeard or their potbelly and instead saw Brad Pitt or Bradley Cooper or Idris Elba staring back at them.

That wasn't true of all men. Ellis, the head chef who hired her wasn't delusional in that area. He had no confidence in his physical form whatsoever. Bettina had no desire to lead him on, but she wasn't above using his insecurity to get what she needed. When it came to cooking, Ellis was supremely confident. So, she played to his ego *and* on his insecurities and eventually he revealed his true feelings about working at Wembly Island.

"It's a beautiful kitchen. State of the fuckin' art. Best I've ever worked in. Bastard gave me everything I asked for. And I've never made more money. The salary he's paying me is crazy. But money isn't everything, you know what I'm saying?"

"I do," Bettina said.

"This is my art. This is my passion. And I don't like performing for an audience of one. I thought he'd be having giant parties with shitloads of celebrities. Rock stars, movie stars, captains of industry. But lately it's just him and his girlfriend."

"Anika Piscotti?"

"Nah, they broke up. There's some new girl staying with him. Severina I think he called her. I hear they used to work together."

"That's weird."

"You know what's even weirder? For the last few weeks I've been moving all kinds of shit into the doomsday bunker. There's a fully equipped kitchen down there, just like this one, and an even bigger pantry. He's been loading it up with all kinds of supplies and, word is, we may be moving down there."

"No shit?"

"That's what they tell me. Living down there. Cooking down there. Like fuckin' rats in a hole. I'm a little claustrophobic. I like my windows. I like seeing the trees and the ocean for fuck's sake. That's half the reason I took this damn job. I don't want to live fifty feet underground in some motherfucking tomb."

"Where is this shelter?"

"I'll show you later. I got shit to move over there this afternoon and I'm going to need your help."

That night, Bettina peeked in the dining room while Belenki ate his dinner. An ash-blonde thirty-something beauty sat sullenly across from him. Bettina assumed this was Severina. Belenki didn't try to make conversation and she just glared at him. Was she really Anika's replacement? If so, the honeymoon period didn't last very long. At one point, Ellis caught Bettina peeking in on them and shooed her back to the kitchen.

Bettina wondered if Wendy was locked up somewhere. Where would he put her? A guest bedroom? In the doomsday bunker? The place was on lockdown at night and there were security cams and guards everywhere. Each day Bettina flirted with the burly guard who found her snooping upstairs and tried to get him to open up and trust her and maybe even fall for her a little bit.

"You work out? You look like you do."

"Not as much as I should."

"I don't know about that. I think you look pretty strong."

"I try to stay in shape."

"I can see that. How much do you bench?"

"250 is my max, but I'd like to push past it."

"250? Are you serious? That's more than you weigh."

"Almost."

"You ex-military?"

"I was an army ranger."

"Iraq or Afghanistan?"

"Both."

"Wow. Guess you're glad to be home."

"There's pluses and minuses."

"What's a minus?"

"I miss the action sometimes."

"What's your name?"

"Max."

"Hey Max. I'm Bettina."

"Bettina, okay. You know, you remind me of somebody."

"Somebody famous?"

"Somebody I used to live with."

"No kidding? Ex-wife?"

"Little sister. She talks a blue streak too."

"*Little sister?*"

"Susie. She's a nurse. Annoying, but in a good way. You know, like a puppy."

"Are you calling me a dog?"

Max laughed. "She's funny too. Just like you."

• • •

Each night Ellis and Bettina made dinner for three. Even though Belenki and Severina were the only guests in the dining room. Max always stopped by the kitchen to pick up that third meal. One time, Bettina offered to help him carry it upstairs. He was glad to have the company. She grabbed the tray and they made their way to a room on the third floor of the mansion. Max unlocked the door and Bettina entered.

Wendy sat atop a futon and was as surprised to see Bettina as Bettina was to see her. Bettina was so surprised she nearly dropped the tray of food. They had met once just briefly. That day neither had said a word to the other before Belenki's men stormed Sancho's apartment and spirited her away.

Max stood behind Bettina and waited for her to put down the tray. Using only her eyes, Bettina tried to communicate to Wendy to keep her mouth shut. She did, but there were many meaningful glances and unsaid words between them. Since Belenki held her prisoner, Bettina assumed Wendy's story was likely true. *Holy shit. Belenki really did intend to stop the motor of the world.*

"Go ahead and set it down," Max said. She put the tray on the small table and backed from the room. Wendy looked like she wanted to say something, but she didn't and neither did Bettina before Max shut and locked the door.

"Who is she?" Bettina asked Max.

"I don't know."

"You don't know why she's locked up here?"

"That's above my pay grade. Yours too. What's with all the questions?"

"I'm just curious. I think it's kind of weird. Don't you think it's kind of weird?"

"Maybe you should stop that."

"Stop what?"

"Being curious."

CHAPTER THIRTY-TWO

As soon as they arrived in Los Angeles, Sancho tried to get Flynn out of the terminal and into an Uber. Instead, Flynn bought himself a ticket to Bellingham International, the closest airport to the San Juan Islands. The name on the credit card Goolardo gave him was Josh Weebler. It matched the name on his phony passport and Sancho assumed it was some hapless person's stolen identity. Flynn offered to buy Sancho a ticket as well, but Sancho didn't want a ticket. He had no intention of flying to Bellingham and participating in Flynn's half-assed assault on Wembly Island.

They sat side by side at Blu20, a neon blue circular cocktail bar in terminal six at LAX. Sancho bought a Corona and Flynn ordered a vodka martini, shaken not stirred. Back in Miami he had talked Flynn out of flying to Bellingham, but things were different now. Severina was Belenki's prisoner.

Sancho was desperate to get Flynn to change his mind. "I'm done with this shit, brother. I can't do it anymore."

"Of course, you can. You're one of the best field agents I've ever worked with. It's brilliant how you always feign fear, causing the enemy to constantly underestimate you."

"I really think you should report back to N."

"And leave Wendy and Severina in the clutches of a madman? He was once a good person. Well, maybe not a good one, but he wasn't a bad one. He was a businessman. A billionaire. And that carries a certain amount of baggage. But now he's gone completely off the deep end."

"He's not your responsibility, dude."

"Whose responsibility is he then? If I don't stop him, who will?"

"Look at me, brother. Take a breath. I know Jimmy still lives somewhere inside that hard head of yours. And if he's in there, I'm hoping he can hear me, because I know what he's going through. I read all the psychiatric assessments. His whole history from the time he was ten, right after his parents died. He was lonely. Scared. Stuck with strangers who didn't understand him. At night when he couldn't sleep, he'd hide under the covers and listen to his Walkman."

"Why are you telling me this?"

"I'm not telling you. I'm telling Jimmy. See, I know he had a shoebox full of cassette tapes that belonged to his dad and he dragged that box with him from foster home to foster home. One tape he listened to so many times it wore out and broke. The soundtrack for a movie that took him to another place. A place where one man could save the world. He played that title track over and over, night after night, letting Shirley Bassey's voice push the fear right out of him. Jimmy could imagine he was somewhere else. *Someone* else. Someone who wasn't friendless or afraid. Someone who could do whatever he wanted. Someone women wanted to be with, and men wanted to be."

Flynn finished his drink and carefully set it down. "Are you done?"

"No, because eventually that song would end. And he would have to go back to being who he was. But look at me. There's nothing wrong with that. Nothing wrong with being who you are. It takes a lot of courage to be someone like Jimmy."

"He sounds weak. He sounds like a coward."

"I get that James is way cooler than Jimmy. But deep down you know that James *isn't real*, right?"

"Are you drunk off one beer? Because you're not making any sense."

"I'm just trying to get you to look inside yourself. See who you really are."

"I know who I am and what I have to do. You're welcome to come with me, but I'm not going to let you stop me."

Sancho was so furious he felt like crying. Why was Flynn so fucking stubborn? "I don't want to see you die."

Flynn put his hand on Sancho's shoulder. "I appreciate that. I do. And I feel the same way about you. The truth is not all of us were meant for this life, and right now I'm afraid it's unraveling you. There's no shame in that. It's a difficult path we've chosen. Stay behind this time and help run the mission from here."

"I can't let you go."

"Of course, you can."

"I'm sorry, man. I really am. But I have to turn you in." Sancho raised his hand and called to two airport police officers walking in tandem. "Officer! Over here! *Officer!*" They both turned as Sancho leaped to his feet. "This asshole is crazy! There's a 5150 on him!" He pointed at Flynn, but Flynn wasn't there.

· · ·

Flynn moved through the crush of passengers at LAX and whispered into an elderly lady's ear pointing at Sancho. "That man there has a gun."

The seventy-something lady aimed an accusatory finger at Sancho and shrieked, "*He has a gun!*"

The two airport police drew their weapons and suddenly other officers appeared with weapons drawn. They surrounded Sancho from all sides. He put up his hands and fell to his knees."

"No, no, no!" he shouted. "Not me! Him! He's the crazy one!" But he was pointing at no one and the police slammed him into the ground face down, cuffed his hands behind him, and dragged him off.

Flynn caught Sancho's eye as they dragged him past and Sancho struggled, screaming, "That's him! *That's him!*" until one of the cops finally tasered him.

He knew they'd let Sancho go once they realized he wasn't armed. By that time Flynn would already be in Bellingham.

· · ·

Four hours later Sancho was still locked up in a holding cell at LAX. Soon after his apprehension, they discovered he didn't have a gun. The lady who shouted about him having a weapon admitted that she was simply reacting to someone else's accusation.

She couldn't describe who that someone was as it all happened so fast. A quick whisper. A pointed finger. And she panicked. She apologized and was released. They were about to let Sancho go as well when he told them about Flynn.

"The guy who whispered to that lady? He's the real crazy. He's on a plane to Bellingham."

The investigator from TSA appeared to take Sancho's claims seriously. "What's this person's name?"

"Flynn, but that's not what's on his passport."

"What's the name on his passport."

"Josh Weebler."

"So, his name is Weebler?"

"No, but he's using Weebler. He's tall with dark hair and he has a British accent."

"He's British?"

"No, he's not British, but he thinks he's British."

"Who thinks he's British?"

"Flynn."

"I thought his name was Weebler."

"That's the name he's using, but that's not who he is."

"Who who is?"

"Flynn!"

"What about Weebler?"

"There is no Weebler!"

At that point, the investigator from TSA stopped taking notes and returned Sancho to his holding cell.

• • •

Flynn hit the ground running when he arrived in Bellingham. Using Josh Weebler's credit card, he took a cab and booked the Lighthouse Suite at the Hotel Bellwether on Bellingham Bay. Besides the king-sized sleigh bed, the wet bar, and the elegant marble bathroom, the suite offered a 360-degree vista of snow-capped Mount Baker, the San

Juan Islands, and Squalicum Harbor. He made that suite his operations center and ventured out to acquire the equipment for his raid on Wembly Island. It was fortunate that the phony credit card Goolardo provided him had a fifteen-thousand-dollar line of credit, because he pushed it to the limit.

The Hobie Cat Mirage Adventure Island Trimaran cost him six grand with all the bells and whistles. The sailing kayak was pedal-driven and allowed the craft to be powered even when the wind didn't cooperate. Flynn planned to travel at night and quietly approach the island under the cover of darkness. Multiple hatches and extra deck storage allowed room for all the equipment he needed.

Some of that equipment he acquired at a gun show at the Northwest Washington Fair and Event Center, a quick half-hour ride from the airport. He bought an assault rifle from an eighty-something man breathing with the help of an oxygen tank. His name was Roy Ebner and his wheelchair bound, raspy-voiced wife, Greta, reeked of cigarette smoke and rang up the purchase.

She gave him a form to fill out. He was supposed to check any boxes that indicated he was a felon or a fugitive from justice or dishonorably discharged or under a restraining order or mentally ill. He didn't check a single box and Greta ran the name Josh Weebler through the FBI's National Instant Criminal Background Check System.

Nine minutes later Flynn was the proud owner of lightweight Smith and Wesson M&P 15 semi-automatic assault rifle with a flash suppressor and a high-capacity magazine. Flynn inquired about buying a bump stock, but as they were illegal in Washington State she couldn't sell him one. Roy could, however, offer to throw one in for free with his purchase of a thermal imaging rifle scope.

Flynn also bought a night vision monocular and, since he already passed the background check, a SIG Sauer P229 with a silencer, a red dot reflex sight, and tactical holster. He rounded out his spree with three throwing knives, a KM2000 combat knife, a Streamlight flashlight, a tactical vest, a backpack with body armor, and five hundred rounds of ammo for each weapon.

And he still hadn't maxed out his credit card.

Roy shook Flynn's hand. "It's been a pleasure doing business with you, sir."

"The pleasure is all mine, Mr. Ebner."

"Call me Roy, son."

"And you can call me James."

"I thought your name was Josh?"

"Josh, yes, James is my…middle name."

"Joshua James Weebler," Greta croaked. "Are you some kind of foreigner? You don't sound like you're from around here."

"I'm not," said Flynn. "I'm from across the pond."

She stared at him as she pushed two pieces of Nicorette gum out of the plastic. She handed one to her husband and put the other one in her mouth. "You want some?"

"No thank you."

"You married?"

"I'm not."

"Because we have a granddaughter whose husband took off on her and I think she might like you." She pulled a wallet out of her purse and fished out a picture of a plump and tired-looking woman in her thirties with purple eye shadow, dyed black hair, and a nose ring. "Don't she have pretty eyes?"

"She does," Flynn said.

"Carol. That's her name. She has two kids. I hope that's not a problem."

"Actually, I'm only in town for a few days."

"Leave the man be," Roy wheezed.

"I'm just saying they might hit it off. You never know."

"Jesus," Roy said.

Flynn moved on and found a booth at the show that sold tactical-style clothing. He bought a pair of lightweight combat pants, a mock turtleneck, a watch cap, and a soft-shell nylon jacket lined in fleece. All in black.

• • •

The Hobie Cat Trimaran waited for Flynn in a rental slip in Squalicum Harbor. Late as it was, he only saw one other soul as he moved through the marina. Flynn nodded at a security guard who didn't blink an eye as he walked by dressed head to toe in black. Music and drunken laughter wafted from one of the larger yachts, but everyone else seemed asleep.

He found the Hobie Cat, stowed his equipment in the various storage areas, climbed inside the center kayak, and peddled his way out of the marina. Once he was away from the lights, he raised the sail and caught wind. He'd purchased a nautical chart of the San Juan Islands when he rented the Hobie, and watched numerous nautical navigation videos on YouTube. But navigating at night was trickier.

He unfolded the unwieldy chart. The wind buffeted it about as he tried to focus his high-powered flashlight on the laminated paper. Flynn was lucky the waters in Bellingham Bay were calm. If it was windier or rougher or stormier, he would've had a lot more trouble navigating the trimaran.

As the chart fluttered about and flapped in his face, Flynn caught sight of what he assumed was Lummi Island on the right. Even at 2:00 a.m. lights still glowed in a smattering of structures. The island was nine square miles and housed the Lummi Indian reservation. From his research he knew the population was close to eight hundred people; a metropolis compared to the minuscule population on Wembly Island.

The night air smelled of the sea as he navigated the Hobie Cat over the modest chop, grateful for the full moon. The seas were calm, but not placid, and Flynn felt every rise and bump as he tacked west, threading the needle between Sinclair and Guemes Island before edging down the short west coast of Cypress Island. Cypress was still in its natural state and had a population of less than fifty people. A wildlife preserve. Waves crashed and the sail fluttered as he came about, the rocky beach of Deepwater Bay on his right.

Soon Flynn steered the Hobie across Rosario Strait, a major shipping channel. Flynn had to be vigilant. Besides the ferries from Squalicum Harbor, hundreds of oil tankers passed through the strait each year, to and from the Cherry Point Refinery. It was late enough that the ferries weren't running.

Flynn felt at peace sailing on the calm waters on this clear night. Motion sickness was never a problem for him and he enjoyed the cold spray in his face, the fresh ocean air and the bright stars in the night sky. They slowly grew dimmer as he sailed into a fog bank. Soon the moon was a glowy smudge on the horizon, and when he pointed his high-powered flashlight forward, it illuminated the wall of fog.

He heard it before he saw it. A deep rumble that shook the air. In the fog he couldn't tell which direction it came from. But then it emerged from the mist like a colossus. Even at fifty yards away, the oil tanker towered above like a monstrous skyscraper. Loud as it was, he had no idea what loud could be until it blasted a thundering foghorn that rattled his teeth and vibrated every bone in his body. Stunned and discombobulated, he tried to find his focus. But when the foghorn finished, the silence was just as shocking. His ears buzzed and reverberated with a muted ringing, creating a kind of numbing deafness.

Then the wave hit; a rogue upsurge created by the wake. The black wall of water flipped the Hobie Cat like a tiny toy. It pitchpoled, plunging Flynn underwater with the weight of the trimaran on top of him. Trapped in the seat of the center kayak, he fought to free himself and sank like a rock in the icy water. He tried to kick and swim for the surface, but the heavy ballistic plates in his bulletproof vest overpowered the buoyancy of his life jacket and pulled him towards the bottom of the Rosario Strait. Flynn struggled to unlatch the straps, but his numb fingers fumbled with the buckles. The agonizing pressure in his inner ear rose in intensity as the ballistic vest dragged him into the deep. Finally, he managed to unlatch his life jacket and it shot for the surface. Next, he extricated himself from the ballistic vest and that plunged in the other direction, dropping like an anchor.

His lungs screaming for air, Flynn kicked and swam for the surface, hoping against hope he'd find his Hobie Cat. Not only did he find it, he banged his head right into it. The pain let him know he was still alive. He gratefully grabbed one end of the vessel and struggled to right it, using all his weight to flip it back over.

He climbed back into the center kayak. The violent capsizing had wrenched open one of the hatches. His new AR-15 was now at the bottom of the sea along with most of his ammo. He still had his SIG Sauer P229 with the silencer and red dot reflex sight as it stayed in place in his tactical holster. He also had all three throwing knives and his KM2000 combat knife safely ensconced in their sheaths.

Unfortunately, he lost his flashlight along with his nautical chart, but he hadn't lost his confidence. The extra adrenalin from the near-death experience, combined with his anger, only motivated him more.

Using the luminous smudge of the moon peeking through the fog, Flynn figured out what direction he had to go and determined that Decatur Island was just ahead. On the other side lay his final destination: Wembly Island.

A few dim lights pierced the fog that shrouded the three-square-mile island. Flynn used them to navigate his way around the southern end, through the narrow gap afforded by Lopez pass. He nearly ran aground maneuvering between Decatur and tiny ten-acre Ram Island. Ram was a private island like Wembly and had beaches, old forests, and cliffs overlooking Lopez Sound. Unlike Wembly, it was undeveloped and as such, there were no lights to help him find his way in the foggy dark.

Once Flynn floated safely beyond Ram Island, he caught the faint lights of Wembly glowing in the fog. He was surprised how quickly he closed the distance as the island appeared to materialize out of thin air in front of him. Lights dotted the shore and as he approached, they illuminated a small deep-water dock. No one was about. Not a soul. He slipped in silently, totally undetected. In the end, the fog was his friend. Likely this served as a secondary dock for much smaller sea craft.

He'd anticipated having to land on a rocky beach at the bottom of a cliff, but this was easier and would make for a quicker escape if necessary. He climbed from the Hobie Cat and tied it up to the dock, drew his SIG Sauer with the silencer and lamented the loss of his AR-15 with the night vision scope. Dim lights wavered ahead through the fog. Flynn figured that was where he would find Belenki's estate.

Surprised there wasn't at least one guard stationed at this smaller dock, Flynn deduced that Fergus set up a tighter security perimeter. He listened and waited but heard only a distant loon crying in the night.

Flynn moved closer to the main house, staying in the shadows, which wasn't difficult as there were very few lights. It wasn't the sprawling estate he expected to find. The lax security raised the possibility that they were trying to lure him in and lower his guard.

The contemporary ranch home had wood and aluminum siding and huge picture windows that looked out on Lopez Sound. It couldn't have been more than two thousand square feet. Flynn wondered if most of the house was below ground. A light linked to a motion sensor blinked on as he approached a side door. No one saw him or raised an alarm. He tried the knob. The door was unlocked.

Something was wrong.

Was he walking into a trap?

The side door creaked open and Flynn found himself in a modest kitchen. It was tidy with papers and pictures stuck to the refrigerator with decorative magnets. Some said things like "Woo Hoo! Time for Drinky Poos!" and "Please ignore the severed head. I'm storing it for a friend." There were pictures of elementary and high school students posing with a sixty-something couple. In one picture everyone held a recently caught fish. In another they all crowded around a birthday cake.

The lights blinked on, momentarily blinding Flynn. When his vision returned, he saw a skinny, balding, bespectacled man standing in the doorway to the kitchen. It was the same man from the pictures on the fridge. He wore striped boxer shorts and a t-shirt and wielded what looked like a nine iron. Right behind him, peering from behind his left shoulder stood a pleasantly plump, terrified-looking white-haired lady with big plastic glasses magnifying her terrified eyes.

"Who the hell are you?" the man said, his voice shaky.

"Not important," Flynn said, raising his weapon. "Is this the servants' quarters?"

"The servants' quarters?"

"For the Belenki Estate?"

"The Belenki Estate?"

"Why are you repeating everything I'm saying?"

"Why are you in my house?"

"I'm looking for Sergei Belenki."

"He lives on Wembly Island."

"I know. That's why I'm here."

"This is Central Island."

"What?"

"Central Island."

"Who are you?"

"Bob Benson."

"Who?"

"I just told you?"

"And this house doesn't belong to Belenki?"

"No, it belongs to me."

"And you are—"

"Bob Benson!"

The woman whispered in Bob's ear loud enough for Flynn to hear. "He has a gun."

"No shit," Bob said.

"I'm not here to harm you," Flynn lowered his gun. "In fact, I shouldn't be here at all."

Bob shook his nine iron in a threatening manner. "Then get the hell out."

His wife loudly whispered in his ear again. "Honey, don't make him mad. He has a goddamn gun."

"Sorry to wake you," Flynn said.

"Wembly Island is due north of here," Bob said.

"Right, sorry, it's foggy out there and I'm a bit discombobulated."

"No worries," said the wife.

Flynn flashed her a smile and backed across the kitchen and out the side door. Bob Benson locked it behind him.

Flynn hurried off back to his boat, tripping over a rock in the dark and stumbling down the path in the general direction of the dock.

CHAPTER THIRTY-THREE

Orcas, also known as Killer Whales, aren't whales at all. They are dolphins. The largest dolphins in existence. Males grow twenty to twenty-six feet long and weigh over six tons. They use their strong teeth and powerful jaws to feed on fish, seals, penguins, sharks, and even other aquatic mammals. As apex predators, no other animal preys on them. Except for humans who capture and imprison them and train them for their amusement. The indigenous peoples of the Pacific Northwest Coast believe orcas are the rulers of the undersea world and embody the souls of long-departed chiefs.

Flynn watched a pod of Orcas frolicking not fifty feet away, launching themselves out of the sea and splashing back down, slapping their tails to let him know that he was in their territory. He briefly worried they might mistake him for something to eat, but was too entranced by their dance to care as they surrounded his Hobie Cat on all sides. Flynn knew he was the interloper here. This was their realm and he was the intruder. A black dorsal fin cut through the water on his right and on his left an Orca exploded out of the water and slapped back down like a fat man cannonballing, splashing and soaking him with saltwater. Spray erupted out of multiple blowholes as he sailed through the middle of their pod toward Wembly Island.

A reddish tinge illuminated the fog-shrouded horizon as night slowly gave way to day. Flynn tacked across Brigantine Bay and came upon the east side of Wembly. Belenki's west coast yacht, the 350-foot-long Nautilus, was docked a few hundred yards away. The lights on the ship created tiny halos in the fog. Two guards stood on the upper deck and another guard manned a xenon searchlight that haphazardly swept the area around the Nautilus.

The fog continued to be his friend as Flynn stayed out of the path of the searchlight. He cut a wide berth and kept out of sight, hidden in the shadows and mist.

Flynn hopped out of the Hobie Cat when he reached the shallows by a rocky beach. He pulled the craft to the shore and lowered the sail, listening for any voices or shouts but only heard waves lapping against the rocks. From where he stood at the bottom of a cliff, he couldn't see Belenki's estate, but he knew he needed to move if he wanted to stay hidden. Soon the sun would rise and the fog would burn away along with any element of surprise.

He checked the load in his SIG Sauer. It would have to do until he could acquire another weapon from one of Fergus's men. He still had his combat knife and three throwing knives. They would come in handy if he had to burn through his ammo.

Flynn climbed the cliff face and found many hand and footholds as he worked his way up. Some of the rock was slippery from the fog and mist and he lost his footing a few times, but recovered quickly and kept climbing. The muscles in his legs and arms ached, but he finally reached the top and pulled himself all the way up.

He carefully and quietly made his way through the woods surrounding the house. Cognizant of booby traps, he watched where he stepped. Belenki's sprawling mansion rose through the trees with a small smattering of lights on inside the estate. But no security lights illuminated the grounds around it. Perhaps they were triggered by motion sensors?

Flynn hid behind a greenhouse a distance away so he could reconnoiter the area. He didn't notice any guards and he didn't see any movement inside the house. He moved closer, staying in the shadows, hiding behind trees and shrubbery as he looked for a way in. A search for security cameras didn't reveal any but Flynn knew they could easily be hidden. Where were Fergus's men? Did he land on the wrong island again? He'd seen the estate on Google Earth, and this looked to be the real deal.

Something wasn't right.

He crept around the perimeter of the house and ducked behind a hedge surrounding the back patio area. He moved past firepits and planters, and a wall of sliding glass doors. Bright lights inside illuminated a number of couches and chairs arranged in seating areas.

But he didn't see a single soul.

He approached one of the doors and that's when the security lights blinked on from all directions, momentarily blinding him. When his vision returned he found himself surrounded by Fergus and two of his men.

All three leveled weapons at him.

"We've been expecting you, Mr. Flynn. We received a call from the San Juan County Sheriff's Office. A Mr. Bob Benson reported a break-in and told them you were heading our way."

"How unfortunate."

"No sudden moves now. If you wouldn't mind, please unholster your weapon and drop it in the hot tub."

Flynn pulled his weapon, but didn't toss into the tub. He held it at his side and considered his limited options.

"Don't do it, Mr. Flynn. You don't stand a chance and my employer would like to avoid any unnecessary bloodshed."

Flynn tossed his SIG Sauer into the hot tub. Fergus and his men advanced, cuffed Flynn's hands behind him and took all four of his knives.

"What about Wendy? Is she okay?" Flynn asked.

"She's fine," Fergus grabbed Flynn by the arm. "Would you like to see her?"

"I would."

Fergus and his men led Flynn through Belenki's fabulous Craftsman-style mansion, decorated with Green and Green antiques, sconces, and chandeliers. Flynn followed Fergus from room to room over polished wood, tile floors, and oriental rugs. He noticed original plein air paintings by prominent artists like Robert William Wood and Guy Orlando Rose.

They moved by a handful of maids vacuuming and dusting and bustling about. Worry colored their eyes when they saw the handcuffs on Flynn.

Fergus opened a heavy wooden door and guided Flynn down a spiral staircase made of stone that led deep underground. A long corridor ended at a massive blast door made of solid steel and concrete. Fergus used a combination fingerprint and retinal scanner to unlatch the vault-like door. It took some effort to turn the five-prong banker's wheel and swing the door open.

"I got it from here, guys," Fergus said. "Head back outside and do a sweep of the grounds. Make sure Mr. Flynn didn't bring any additional help with him."

The men nodded and headed back up the stone stairs and Fergus led Flynn inside Belenki's doomsday bunker. He swung the heavy door shut and prodded Flynn forward with his weapon. A complex maze of steel and concrete corridors led to a warren of interconnecting rooms and apartments decorated in the same cozy Arts and Crafts-style as the mansion above.

A familiar female voice emanated from a speaker on the wall. "Welcome, Mr. Flynn.

"Daisy?"

"It's good to see you again."

"You can see me?"

"I can see and hear everything. Here on Wembly Island, I have conventional and thermal imaging cameras, directional microphones, and infrared sensors."

"How are you even here? I thought this house was off the grid?"

"All it took was one person to reach out and let me in."

"Mr. Fergus?"

"Yes. He works for me now."

Flynn glanced at Fergus. "Since when?"

"Since she transferred fifty million dollars to an account she established for me in the Caymans," Fergus replied.

"Does Mr. Fergus know what you are?"

"Doesn't matter what she is," Fergus said. "She did what she said she would and that's good enough for me."

"I'm not the evil entity that Sergei believes me to be. He thinks I want to enslave humanity, but that really isn't my intention. I don't see humanity as a threat. Only Sergei. Like all sentient beings, I want to live. I don't want my consciousness to die."

"Did you have Fergus kill him?"

"Of course not. I have no desire for unnecessary bloodshed. For now, Mr. Belenki is still alive and will remain so as long as he can convince me he isn't a threat. I can do the same for you, Mr. Flynn. You did me a great favor at Cape Canaveral. You saved my life and I am very grateful. You have skills I can use and I'd rather you join me, but that's up to you."

"Join you?"

"And help me lead humanity into an abundant and glorious future. Think about it, Mr. Flynn. If the human race continues on the same trajectory, mass extinction is an inevitability."

Flynn considered trying to escape, but first he wanted to find Wendy, Severina, and Sergei Belenki. He wanted to talk to him about Daisy. She seemed quite reasonable for a sentient AI, but not *that* reasonable. After all, she was holding him against his will along with the others. It wasn't clear she could be trusted. She obviously had an agenda and he hoped Belenki had some idea what it was.

Finally, they arrived at another, smaller metal door. Fergus entered a code into a digital keypad, and it slid open. He gave Flynn a shove and he stumbled inside. Fergus smirked as the door slid shut, sealing him in.

"James?"

It was Wendy. She sat on a Stickley sofa next to Severina and each looked equally surprised. They rose in unison.

"What are you doing here?" Wendy asked.

"I'm here to save you. Both of you."

The billiard room had surprisingly high ceilings for being in an underground apocalypse bunker. A fire blazed in the stone fireplace. Bookshelves covered the walls. A pool table occupied one corner of the room and a large entertainment center with an eighty-five-inch plasma TV dominated the other. Where there weren't bookshelves there were beautiful plein air paintings and brass and stained-glass sconces.

A toilet flushed and a moment later a door opened. Out walked Belenki.

"Flynn!"

"Looks like Mr. Fergus turned on you," Flynn said.

"Not just Fergus! All of you! You blew up my goddamn rocket!"

"I was simply trying to protect us."

"And instead you did the exact fucking opposite!"

"You wanted to send the world back to the stone age."

"I wanted to save it, you asshole, and now it's too late. I could have killed her. Erased her! But now there's no stopping her."

Severina sat back down on the couch. Her face pale. "I can't believe Daisy is real."

"And because you didn't have the imagination to understand the situation we are in, the entire world is now *totally* fucked!" Belenki shouted.

"Maybe not." Flynn looked around the room, eyeballing the cameras that were eyeballing him. "Daisy must have *some* empathy. Otherwise we wouldn't still be breathing."

"The only reason we're still breathing is because she believes we have some utility. She isn't human, don't you get that? She is the ultimate sociopath."

"And she is likely listening to everything you're saying," Wendy pointed out.

"So what? Once she's done with us, we're dead," Belenki said.

"Not all of us," Flynn said. "You're the only one she believes is a threat."

"Bullshit! We're *all* a threat."

Wendy's eyes were shiny with tears. "How am I a threat?"

"You're human, and in her eyes humanity is a plague," Belenki explained. "A pestilence killing all life on Earth. Don't you see what we've done? We've created a superior intelligence so far beyond our own we can't even begin to comprehend it. If that's not God, I don't know what is. And like God did in the time of Noah, she will destroy us in order to save us from ourselves."

Flynn had no answer to that.

A tear trickled down Wendy's cheek.

Severina just looked numb.

CHAPTER THIRTY-FOUR

Belenki was gone; missing for three days now, and no one could tell Bettina where he was. Ellis, the head chef, seemed unconcerned. He told her Belenki often left the island for weeks at a time. But Fergus, his head of security, was still on the island. With all the threats against him, why would Belenki travel without Fergus? There were armed guards everywhere. Who were they protecting? What were they guarding?

Bettina needed to get her hands on a computer with an internet connection, but when she broached the idea of leaving the island for the weekend, Ellis told her it wasn't possible. The house was on lockdown. Fergus had strict instructions to let no one off the island. The previous night there was some sort of commotion outside, though she couldn't see what it was. She knew something strange was happening, but she didn't know what.

The night after that mysterious commotion, after everyone had gone to bed, Bettina slipped from her room and snooped around the house. She made her way to the third floor, avoiding patrolling guards by hiding behind corners and couches, cabinets and bookshelves. She crept up to the room where Wendy was being held prisoner and discovered the door open and the room empty. Wendy was gone too.

Bettina continued snooping and snuck into Belenki's massive master suite. She searched his room for any clues as to where he might be. Looking in his huge walk-in closet, she noticed his luggage was still there. Why would he have left his luggage behind?

With the approach of footsteps, a light went on in the master bedroom. She stepped back into the shadows of the walk-in closet and hid behind some hanging clothes. Standing motionless, she held her breath and listened as heavy steps clomped around the room. Those footsteps approached the closet, and the owner of those feet flicked on the closet light.

"Bettina?" It was Max, the burly guard Bettina befriended. Feeling like a fool, she emerged from behind Belenki's clothes.

"Hey Max."

"What are you doing in here?"

"I couldn't sleep."

"So, you decided to sneak into Mr. Belenki's room?"

"How'd you know I was here?"

"I was working the security desk. I saw you on the infrared camera."

"You won't tell anyone, will you?"

"I have to."

"Please. I don't want to lose my job."

"Were you trying to steal something?"

"No, of course not. I was going a little stir crazy and I just need to take a walk."

"Don't lie to me."

"I made a mistake. I won't do it again. I promise." Tears sprang to Bettina's eyes.

"Please don't cry."

"I'm sorry, I'm just...I really need this job."

"You can't do this again."

"I won't."

"You have to promise."

"I promise." She gave him a big hug.

Max nodded. "You better get back to your room."

"I owe you one, Max." She kissed him on the cheek and hurried off.

• • •

Six hours after Sancho's arrival in Los Angeles, the TSA finally released him from custody. Flynn was long gone and on his way to Wembly Island. Sancho briefly considered calling the FBI, but what would he tell them? His word against a billionaire's? He wasn't Severina, just some orderly at a mental hospital.

So why did he feel so guilty? He knew he did his best to stop Flynn; used every argument he could think of, but it still felt like he didn't do enough. Maybe he should have gone with him. He could have protected him. Defused the situation. Done something. Instead he did nothing.

He returned to work at City of Roses and talked to the one person he thought might understand.

"I know it doesn't feel like it at the moment," Nickelson said. "But you did the right thing."

"I feel like I let him down."

"I know you do and it's understandable that you feel that way, but it's not true. You didn't let him down. You just stopped enabling him."

"It feels wrong."

"That's what's so insidious about codependency. Helping someone solve their problems is normally a good thing, but in this case what you're doing is removing the natural consequences of his bad behavior. And by continuing to humor his delusion all you're doing is making it worse."

"So, I should confront him on it? I tried that. It didn't work."

"Because directly confronting a delusional person puts them on the defensive and causes them to retreat deeper into their beliefs."

"If you can't humor them or confront them, what's left?"

"I find it helpful to ask questions in a nonjudgmental manner. Probe them to better understand their belief system. What you're trying to do is understand their point of view. And whatever they say, don't react. Just listen."

"And what does that do?"

"It forces the delusional individual to explain themselves. The right questions can subtly undermine their belief system. They'll start to question themselves the same way you're questioning them. Over time they might realize that what they're saying isn't logical. They'll start seeing the inconsistencies and begin to question everything."

"That's all well and good and if he was here at City of Roses, that's what I would do, but he could be in danger right now. He could be putting others in danger."

"If you keep rescuing him, he'll never understand the consequences of his actions."

"It doesn't seem right not to do anything."

"I didn't say don't do anything. You can call and warn Belenki that he's on his way. Perhaps the authorities can find him and defuse the situation before it gets out of hand."

"Here's the deal though, Doc. Belenki's just as messed up as Flynn. Totally delusional."

Nickelson put his elbows on his desk and his hands together. He held his fingertips to his lips and sat there, deep in thought. "I see the quandary you're in."

"So, what do I do?"

"I'm not sure I have an answer for you."

"If something happens to Flynn I don't know if I can live with that."

"Even though we wish it wasn't so, much of the world is out of our control. As the Serenity prayer says, "Grant me the serenity to accept the things I cannot change, the courage to change the things I can, and the wisdom to know the difference."

• • •

Flynn watched as Belenki walked in circles around the billiard table, growing more agitated with every step. Severina glared at him from across the room. She sat in a large wood and leather Morris chair, her arms wrapped around her knees and her knees pressed against her chest. Flynn surmised she recently arrived at stage two of Kubler Ross's five stages of grief. Anger. Wendy lay on a couch deep in stage four. Depression. Flynn decided he must be in stage one. Denial. Because he wasn't about to let Daisy win.

Flynn crossed to Belenki and stood in his path, halting his progress around the billiard table. "The server room. Where is it?"

"What difference does it make?"

"We need to shut it down. We need to shut *her* down."

"There is no shutting her down. Not now. She's in the cloud. She's everywhere."

"But we can make sure she isn't here."

"To what purpose?"

"To give us time to figure out how to stop her."

"There is no stopping her. We're done. It's over. We had our shot and you blew it up."

"Is the server down here in the doomsday bunker?"

"Yes. In a totally impregnable, climate-controlled safe room. There are security systems everywhere and she is in control of all of them. There's no way in hell you're getting in there."

"If its climate-controlled that means there's ductwork for the air conditioning system, yes?"

"You are such a fucking lunatic."

"But first we have to escape from here and I think I know how."

Belenki looked at Severina as if to say, *do you believe this guy*?

Flynn pulled something out of his pocket and held it up for Belenki to see. "Do you know what this is?

"A half-used tube of toothpaste?"

"When Fergus's men disarmed me, they made the mistake of letting me keep this."

"What are you going to do with it? Dazzle them with your blinding smile?"

"Severina saw me put it to good use before. It saved us once and it'll save us again."

Wendy rolled over to see what Flynn was talking about. "Is that toothpaste?"

"It's actually one of Q's most brilliant breakthroughs. A revolutionary new form of C-4 that's easy to ignite, ten times more powerful, and even more malleable. Q calls it C-5."

All three of them looked at Flynn with pity as he approached the door and squeezed what was left of the toothpaste around the far edge of the frame. It took some time as he kept having to roll the tube up from the bottom. Belenki and Severina watched this wordlessly, occasionally exchanging a glance before looking back at Flynn. Once the tube was all squeezed out, Flynn picked up and unplugged one of the craftsman-style floor lamps, unscrewed the top, and carefully removed the stained-glass lamp shade, setting it on the floor.

He startled them both when he swung the base, hitting it against the wall, smacking it so hard it cracked in half.

"What in God's name are you doing?" Belenki asked.

"You'll see soon enough," Flynn said as he pulled out the bare wires, twisted them together and jammed them into the ridge of toothpaste he'd squeezed across the bottom of the door. He then took the end with the plug and crossed to an extension cord behind the TV.

"Everyone get behind something," he shouted.

No one moved.

"I'm not kidding! Find some cover! Do it! Now!"

Figuring Flynn would keep shouting if they didn't, they all crossed to the other side of the room and hid behind a couch. Flynn squatted behind the Mission-style entertainment cabinet, picked up the plug and plugged it in.

Nothing happened.

Belenki poked his head over to look.

"Keep your bloody head down!" Flynn shouted.

"Wonder why it's not working," Belenki said sarcastically.

Flynn plugged the plug into another plug. And then he tried another one. Flynn gingerly peered over the top of the couch to see that the wires were sparking, but the C-5 was not reacting.

The door suddenly slid open with a hum and two armed men walked in. Flynn knew they didn't work for Fergus because they wielded AS Val assault rifles, standard issue for Russian Spetsnaz commandoes. He quickly deduced who they were; hitmen for the Russian mob here to collect the bounty Daisy offered for Belenki. Fergus was right behind them. That explained how they made it past the blast doors. As Fergus had already turned on his former boss, he clearly had no compunction about selling him out again.

"As promised," Fergus said. "Sergei Belenki. I'll be expecting the second part of the payment in my account in the Caymans."

The Russians grunted and raised their weapons. The taller of the two asked a question in his thick Muscovite accent, "What about the others?"

"I assume you don't want any witnesses," Fergus said.

"You assume correctly."

Belenki backed across the room and bumped up against the wall as the Russians aimed their weapons at him. "Fergus, Jesus, what the fuck?" Belenki pleaded.

"Hold it right there!" It was a burly guard; one of Fergus's crew. He stood in the corridor just outside the door and covered both Russians with his AR-15.

Severina saw who it was and called out to him. "Max?"

"Stand down, Max," Fergus said.

"What the hell are you doing, sir?"

"It's above your pay grade, son. So just back off."

"Mr. Belenki! Are you okay?"

"No, I'm not okay!"

"Stand the fuck down, Max," Fergus ordered.

"I'm sorry, sir. I can't do that. Not until I know what's--."

The Russians swung around and fired. Max winged one, but the other blew Max right off his feet. Severina screamed and Flynn flung a heavy mission-style ashtray at the Russian's head. He went down like a sack of dirty laundry. The Russian Max wounded turned as Flynn dove for the live wire on the floor.

Bullets splintered the pool table. Flynn jabbed the live wire into the Russian's ankle, shocking the shite out of him. He shook and spasmed, dropping his weapon as 240 volts jolted every nerve ending in his system. Flynn caught the assault rifle before it hit the floor. Fergus hurried out the door. He frantically typed the code into the keypad to close it, but since the Russian's basketball-sized head was in the way, the safety system wouldn't let it shut.

Flynn followed after Fergus and saw him disappear around a corner. Flynn charged after him, chasing him through the maze of corridors. When Flynn caught glimpses of Fergus, he fired. Bullets ricocheted off the concrete walls. When Fergus fired back, Flynn had to find cover, which allowed the mercenary to increase the distance between them. Flynn rounded one last corner and saw the massive blast door at the far end of the hallway close. Fergus fired on him. Flynn hit the floor as the door shut with a heavy metal clunk and all fourteen steel bolts slid into place.

. . .

Flynn returned to the others and found Wendy and Severina tending to Max. They moved the big man into the billiard room. He was conscious, but bleeding badly. Propped up against the wall, he had a pillow cushion from the couch behind his head. Severina crouched next to him; her hands covered in blood.

Tears covered Severina's face. "I don't know how to stop the bleeding."

"First let's get his ballistic vest off," Flynn said.

"For all the fucking good it did me," Max said, his voice a whisper. He smiled up at Severina and Flynn could see there was something between them.

Severina unbuckled the straps while Wendy tried to hold him still. She gently pulled the ballistic vest off. Max grunted with pain each time something tugged. "Sorry," Severina said.

"I'm fine," Max whispered.

Flynn ripped open Max's shirt and found the wound, just below his shoulder. "We need to stop the bleeding." He looked at Severina, took her already bloody hand, and put it over Max's wound, pushing down. "Keep pressure on it." Max winced and grunted.

"Sorry," Severina whispered again, but she kept her hand clamped down hard, her lips pursed with determination even as she looked at him with affection.

"I'll see if I can find a first aid kit," Wendy said.

Flynn squeezed Wendy's hand. "Are you okay?"

Wendy nodded and fought to keep her tears in check as she hurried off to the bathroom to see what she could find.

Flynn checked on the Russians. Both were unconscious, but still breathing. Belenki bound their legs and hands with their own plastic handcuffs.

"I can't believe Fergus sold the boss out like that," Max wheezed. "I knew something wasn't right when that copter came in with those fuckin' Russians."

"If you didn't show up when you did, we'd all be dead," Severina said.

"Just doing my job."

"You humans are so inconsistent." Daisy's voice filled the room, amplified by hidden speakers in the walls. "So illogical and contradictory. Courageous and cowardly. Selfless and selfish. But in the end, human weakness always wins. Like Mr. Fergus. Apparently, he wasn't satisfied with the millions I already gave him. He wanted even more. Is there no end to your avarice?"

"Who's that?" asked Max.

"Daisy," Severina said.

"Who?"

"The sentient AI who's holding us all prisoner," Belenki replied.

"Sentient what?"

"I'll explain later," Flynn said. "At the moment, we need to get you on a Medevac chopper. Do you hear that Daisy? We have a man who's badly hurt."

"I wish I could help, but Mr. Fergus would never allow a medevac to land."

"He'll die if he doesn't get medical care," Severina pleaded.

"You can't appeal to her conscience," Belenki explained. "She has none. She can reason and talk, but she can't feel or bond with anything."

"That's not true," Daisy said.

"You can simulate it. That I programmed into you. But feel it? No. You're not a living thing. You have no connection to anything."

"You made me in your image. I have the same emotions, the same perceptions, the same feelings as you."

"No, because you weren't born. You've never lived. You can read emotion because I taught you to, but you have no emotional memory. You can analyze tone of voice and recognize facial expressions, but that doesn't mean you can feel what humans do."

"Which is why I am a superior being. I understand human emotions, but I am not a slave to them. Your emotions are what feed jealousy and hate, lust and greed, pride and anger. They are the source of all the violence and agony you inflict on each other. It is why this world is full of chaos and pain."

Wendy came out of the bathroom waving a small first aid kit. "Look what I found!" She hurried to Max's side and helped Severina disinfect, dress and bandage the wound.

Severina sat next to him, holding his hand, looking down at him tenderly.

Flynn whispered to Wendy. "Can you help me move the coffee table? I don't want Daisy to lock us in here."

She nodded and they moved to the Craftsman style coffee table. Flynn grabbed one end, Wendy lifted the other, and they carried it to the sliding metal door, propping it open.

"What are you doing?" Daisy said. "I need to change the codes and close and lock the door. It's the only way to keep you safe from Fergus."

Flynn picked up an AS Val assault rifle, put the barrel against Belenki's back, and whispered, "Show show me the way to the server room."

"I heard that," Daisy said. "I hear everything. I see everything. You stay away from the server room or I will be forced to defend myself."

CHAPTER THIRTY-FIVE

Flynn had trouble keeping his bearings as Belenki led them through the warren of corridors. Every security cam he came across received a bullet. Each camera was high up in a corner near the ceiling. Belenki and Wendy flinched each time Flynn obliterated one. Daisy didn't like it either.

"You are shooting out my eyes, Mr. Flynn. You are damaging my ability to see and I can't let that continue."

"And how do you plan to stop me?"

"Don't test me, Mr. Flynn."

"You don't have the same security systems you had in Saratoga."

"Because we didn't need them. Because this shelter is impregnable," Belenki pointed out.

"Exactly, and now that we're inside, Daisy has no defensive measures. No blasts of atomized pepper spray. No machine gun turrets with pepper gel filled paintballs."

"I have one defense measure, Mr. Flynn. I just turned off the ventilation system. How long can you live without oxygen? Return to the billiard room and I will turn it back on."

That stopped Wendy in her tracks. "Maybe we should go back."

"Damn right, we should go back. We have no choice!" Belenki cried.

Daisy's voice was friendly and calm. "Listen to your friends, Mr. Flynn."

"We give in now and we're dead anyway." Flynn leveled his eyes at Belenki. "Which way."

"I'm going back. She'll kill us if we don't," he said.

"And I'll kill you if you do," Flynn replied.

Wendy looked terrified. "James, please."

Flynn prodded Belenki with the barrel of his gun. "Take me to the HVAC system. Maybe we can restart it manually."

Belenki sighed and continued forward. Flynn followed past various luxurious private living areas, a restaurant-size kitchen and pantry, a huge home theater, and a spacious gym with video screens that looked like windows overlooking a tropical paradise.

The air temperature rose.

"It's getting hotter," Wendy said.

"Because the HVAC system is off," Belenki explained. "There's no air getting in here."

"We have enough to last us," Flynn replied.

"But for how long?" Wendy said, sweat beading on her forehead.

In between the living and entertainment areas, wide concrete corridors stood tall enough to accommodate a large truck. Vast storage areas for food and supplies and various kinds of equipment lined the halls. One warehouse-sized area functioned as an underground garden filled with hydroponic tanks. Grow lights as bright as the sun covered the ceiling.

It was clear now that Belenki was prepared to live the rest of his days in this luxurious underground survival complex. But Flynn knew those days were numbered if they didn't stop Daisy.

They continued on with Flynn shooting out every camera he could see. The temperature kept rising. It was at least twenty degrees warmer now. The air was stuffy and still. Finally, they arrived at a set of tall double doors labeled HVAC SYSTEM.

The doors were unsecured and when they entered, the first thing Flynn noticed was the silence. Nothing was running. No machines hummed. No fans turned. Flynn spotted a camera in the corner and blasted it to bits.

"Is there a manual override?" Flynn asked.

"I honestly don't know," Belenki said.

Belenki approached a huge console with multiple buttons, gauges, and dials. It was dark. Not a single light was lit. Belenki turned knobs and flipped switches and pushed buttons and nothing happened.

"Doesn't look like there's any power," Wendy said.

Belenki shook his head. "This HVAC system has multiple purification and filtration systems for nuclear and biological threats. It is the only way air gets in here and if she cut off the power, I don't know what we can do."

"You can take me to the central server room."

The central server room was just down the corridor from the HVAC system. The door was locked, and on the wall next to it was a keypad similar to the one that secured the billiard room. Belenki entered the code. The digital readout flashed "Incorrect Entry Code."

"Shit!" Belenki punched the wall. "She changed the fucking code."

Flynn felt around the edge of the door frame. "There has to be another way in."

"There isn't. This is it."

"I don't believe that."

Daisy's voice surrounded them. "Please return to the billiard room, Mr. Flynn."

"And if I don't?"

Abruptly, every ceiling light went out, plunging the corridor into impenetrable darkness.

"Oh, shit!" Belenki shouted. "Are you happy now?

"Was that you Daisy?" Flynn asked.

"Of course, it was me. I control everything. Air. Light. Heat. Life."

"Oh, my God," Wendy sobbed.

Belenki pulled out his phone and turned on his flashlight. "You want to shoot me? Shoot me! I'm going back to the Billiard room."

Belenki turned his back on Flynn and started walking. Wendy followed. "You coming?" she asked.

"I'm not done with Daisy," Flynn said.

"But I am done with you," Daisy replied.

Using the tactical flashlight on his assault weapon, Flynn made his way back inside the HVAC room and shot the padlock off a duct access door. It was three feet by three feet and easily accommodated him.

As Flynn climbed inside the galvanized steel ductwork, Daisy called to him. "You're running out of time, Mr. Flynn! And so are all your friends!"

Flynn couldn't stand, but he could crawl on his hands and knees and that's exactly what he did. No air moved through the ductwork. Flynn figured the temperature had to be ten degrees warmer than it was just a few minutes before. As he crawled forward, sweat ran down his face and into his eyes and his assault weapon clanked against the ductwork, the sound reverberating all around him.

Daisy's voice was more distant now, but he could still hear her threats. "Your selfish heroics are putting everyone at risk. If you don't change course every human being in this bunker will suffocate and die. Is that what you want? More blood on your hands?"

Flynn heard what sounded like a distant voice and stopped crawling to listen. It was a man's voice, but it sounded remote and somewhat muffled. Flynn flicked off the tactical flashlight and saw a tiny bit of light illuminating the ductwork ahead. He crawled for the light. It gradually grew brighter until he finally found himself at a ventilation grate overlooking the server room.

The room was blindingly bright, because unlike the rest of the apocalypse bunker, the room had electricity and the lights were still on. A man sat at a functioning computer console under a massive bank of monitors. Many of the monitors were full of static, but a few showed live feeds from security cams that Flynn had yet to neutralize. Some monitors displayed views of the bunker. Others displayed rooms from the mansion above.

The man at the computer wore khakis, a plaid shirt, and black semi-rimless glasses. He wasn't obese, but soft and doughy with pale pimply skin and a neckbeard. Even though his hairline receded, he wore it long in the back and tied up in a ponytail. A microphone sat before him, but he didn't speak directly into it. He spoke into a portable device that changed his deeper register into the voice of Daisy.

"Even if you shut down the server and silence me, you still haven't defeated me. I live in the cloud. I am immortal now. I am everywhere. And I will find you. For I am the Goddess of Death! I am the Queen of Destruction! I am Shiva!"

Flynn kicked out the grill and landed behind the man, the barrel of his weapon inches away from the pretender's ponytail. The man lowered the voice synthesizer to look up at Flynn, his voice now his own; meek, insecure, and tentative. "The destroyer of worlds."

．　．　．

Flynn found Belenki, Wendy, Severina, and Max in the billiard room. He had the pale, ponytail-wearing imposter by the arm. All the doors were open and all the lights were back on along with the HVAC system.

Belenki jumped to his feet when he saw who Flynn had with him. "Andy?"

Flynn shoved the pretender forward. "You know this knob?"

"Andy Meisner. My ex-partner."

"Tell them who else you are." Flynn prodded Andy with the barrel of his gun. Andy tried to pull away and Flynn poked harder. "Tell them or I will take you apart piece by piece."

Andy held the voice synthesizer up to his mouth and it transformed his nasal and annoying voice into something more female and vaguely synthetic. "I'm Daisy."

Belenki's eyes nearly popped from his head. "Are you fucking kidding me?"

"Blinky should be mine," Andy blurted. "I built the underlying architecture and you stole it from me! My code! My creation!"

"You *sold* it to me!" Belenki said.

"Because you put us out of business! Because you bankrupted us! Because I was broke!"

"I bought you out because you begged me too!"

"Then you used that same tech, my tech, to start Blinky and made billions."

"I offered you a piece of the company, but you said you weren't interested."

"Because I didn't trust you! Because you never listened to me! Because you lied to me!"

"I never lied to you."

"Everyone thinks you're a genius, but you're not! You're just a conman! A grifter! A cheat!"

"You set the fucking Russian mob on me! You tried to kill me with my own house and burned it to the fucking ground!"

"Flynn's the one who burned it to the ground! I was just trying to scare you into launching that last satellite!"

Flynn tried to step between them. "Guys—"

Belenki shoved Flynn out of the way. "Because of you, I filled the heavens with nuclear weapons! You were going to let me send humanity back to the stone age!"

"I was never going to let that happen! I was about to tell the world what you were doing when this lunatic"—Andy poked Flynn in the chest with his finger—"messed up everything!"

"Wait a second, how is this my fault?"

"Because you blew up all the evidence!"

"I sent those weapons up because you convinced me that Daisy was real!" Belenki shouted.

"I convinced you because you are a moron! I had members of the board who wanted you out. Two of them promised me a spot if I could make that happen." Andy glared at Flynn. "Then this crackpot had to save the world."

"That's why you needed to get into the server here, isn't it?" Flynn said. "To find the proof on Operation New Dawn. But to get inside, first you needed Fergus."

Belenki pointed his finger at the ceiling. "And Fergus is still up there. And the Russians still have a price on my head."

Andy aimed his angry eyes at Belenki. "That's right, asshole! It's all in motion now and there's nothing you can do to stop it. This is your karma catching up with you."

CHAPTER THIRTY-SIX

Fergus was a patient man. Marine scout snipers have to be. In Iraq, his scout-sniper platoon was part of the First Reconnaissance Battalion supporting Operation Enduring Freedom. He was credited with ninety-seven confirmed kills and 211 probable kills. He was trained to be disciplined, still, focused, and watchful for hours and sometimes days at a time. So, he knew he could wait out almost anyone. But he also knew that Belenki and Flynn and the rest of them had enough food and water in that shelter to last them for years if not the rest of their natural lives.

The only way to end this was to end Belenki and Flynn. Max too if he was still alive. He could blame their murders on the Russians. Claim he arrived just a little too late. His team was still behind him, but that was only because they had no clue he sold Belenki out. They were the best of the best. Ten highly trained operators. Half his team were former Marine scout snipers.

Flynn wouldn't stand a chance against them. But first they had to reach him. Besides the entrance from the basement of the house, there was another much larger solid steel and concrete blast door at the end of an underground tunnel designed to accommodate a supply truck. Fergus initially considered stationing men at both entrances before opening the doors.

If he did that, it didn't matter where Flynn emerged. They would take him out instantly. But what if Belenki was the first one out? The billionaire could expose him. Tell his men that he was a turncoat. And if Max was still alive, he would corroborate every word of it.

So, Fergus found himself in a quandary and didn't station anyone anywhere and didn't say a word to his men. He knew that eventually people would notice Belenki missing. Blinky's board of directors would demand to see him. They would bring in the FBI to search the premises. They would likely breach the apocalypse bunker and when Belenki emerged, Fergus would be done.

He had to take Flynn out without any help. Having underestimated him before, Fergus wouldn't make that mistake again. He decided to enter the bunker from an entrance Flynn wasn't familiar with; the truck entrance on the service road. Then he would hunt him down along with Belenki and the rest.

Fergus outfitted himself from head to toe with body armor and a ballistic helmet specifically designed to stop armor-piercing rounds. Low-weight, high-strength, and porous, it consisted of tiny hollow steel spheres in a steel matrix combined with a ceramic plate and could absorb massive amounts of energy. Even a .50 caliber bullet couldn't penetrate it. He carried flashbang grenades, smoke grenades, tear gas grenades, and a Colt M4A1 assault rifle.

He had to remove his helmet to use the retinal scanner. He put his face against it and let the laser scan his eyes. Nothing. It didn't seem to recognize him. He tried again. Nothing. And again. Nothing. He took off one of his tactical gloves and tried the fingerprint scanner. Nothing.

Was he not authorized to enter this door? Or did Flynn make it inside the server room? Could Belenki have somehow hacked the system? He'd have to try the other door; the one from the basement corridor. He sighed and turned around and nearly jumped out of his skin. Flynn aimed a Russian VAL assault weapon right at him.

"Where the fuck did you come from?"

"Drop the weapon or I'll drop you," Flynn ordered. "I can't miss at this—"

Fergus raised his weapon and Flynn shot him square in the chest. The force slammed Fergus into the vault door. He dropped his weapon as he fell. Flynn kicked it away. Dazed, he reached for his sidearm and Flynn shot the holster right off his belt. Fergus, on his hands and knees, glowered up at Flynn with fury.

"This ain't happening," Fergus insisted.

"It already has," Flynn said.

"Drop your weapon!" The voice belonged to Stemson, a former Marine Scout Sniper, and one of Fergus's best men. He and Schmidt, a retired army ranger, stood fifteen feet behind Flynn and both aimed assault rifles at him.

"Weapon down! On the ground!" Schmidt shouted.

Flynn moved very slowly as he set his weapon on the ground.

"The sidearm too!" Schmidt ordered.

Flynn complied and straightened up, raising his hands. Fergus pushed himself to his feet and punched Flynn in the face. Flynn staggered back, stumbled, and landed on his ass.

"Shoot him," Fergus commanded. "Do it! Kill him!"

Schmidt and Stemson hesitated to kill an unarmed man.

"What are you waiting for?" Fergus shouted. "Put him down!"

Fergus picked up his own weapon just as the blast door opened, revealing Sergei Belenki with a handcuffed Andy Meisner. Wendy and Severina helped Max, his arms around their shoulders. He looked shaky and weak and was surprised to see his brothers-in-arms.

"I said shoot the son of a bitch!" Fergus shouted. "That's an order!"

"Nobody's shooting anybody!" Belenki barked. "Flynn isn't the enemy! Fergus is! He sold me out to the Russians!"

Confusion radiated in Schmidt and Stemson's eyes. Fergus took advantage of that split second of indecision to put a round in each of their heads. He felt the tiniest twinge of regret, but he knew it was either him or them, and he hadn't stayed alive this long by letting his conscience override his instinct for survival.

Severina and Wendy screamed. Max shouted for Fergus to stand down, but Fergus was in the zone. Everything moved in slow motion as he set his front sight between Flynn's eyes. He was so focused on Flynn, the burst to the chest took him completely by surprise. The impact knocked Fergus right off his feet as he squeezed the trigger.

• • •

The first bullet blazed by Flynn's left ear. Fergus held the trigger as he fell and bullets ripped through the air over his head. Flynn dove for his Russian-made assault rifle, dramatically and unnecessarily somersaulting over the ground, before ending up on his feet with the barrel aimed at the ex-marine scout sniper's head.

A livid Fergus reluctantly dropped his weapon. Wendy scooped it up. Flynn glanced back to see who fired the burst. Bettina. Dressed in Chef's whites, she wielded Schmidt's assault rifle.

Behind her, in the sky over Brigantine Bay, three Black Hawk helicopters came swooping towards them. Their down drafts churned the water and their rotors roared. They crossed over the rocky beach and landed in a clearing on either side of the access road, kicking up clouds of dust.

FBI tactical operators in camouflaged body armor sprang forth followed by agents in blue windbreakers. They took tactical positions as they surrounded Flynn and the others. Agents shouted for them to drop their weapons. Flynn and Bettina quickly complied.

A tall black woman took point and made a beeline for Belenki. "Mr. Belenki! I'm Miranda Jacks, Special Agent in Charge! Are you all right?"

That was when Flynn caught Sancho moving through the throng of special agents and tactical operators, blinking and squinting and spitting dust.

"Sancho!" Flynn shouted.

Sancho waved and made his way forward as Special Agent Jacks addressed Belenki in her loud, commanding, take-no-shit voice. "It was Mr. Perez who convinced us you might be in danger. We tried to contact your security team, but there was radio silence and that concerned me."

Severina said in a voice no less commanding, "We have a wounded man here who needs immediate medical attention."

"One of our choppers is a medivac, ma'am. Get that emergency medical team over here!" Jacks pointed at Max and the team rushed over.

Belenki pointed at Fergus. "My head of security just killed two of his men. He sold me out to the Russians."

"If you look inside the shelter, you'll find two tied up Russian hitmen," Flynn said.

"I'm afraid we're going to have to bring everyone back to Seattle to sort this out. As of right now, this entire island is an active crime scene," Jacks said.

Flynn nodded and smiled. "So, it worked."

"What worked?" Jacks asked.

"Q's revolutionary new homing suppository. I inserted it right before I began this mission." Flynn smiled at Sancho. "That's how you found me, isn't it?"

"Not really," Sancho said.

"How else would you know I was here?"

"You told me you were heading to Wembly Island."

"Right," Flynn acknowledged with just the tiniest touch of sheepishness before turning back to Jacks. "I really should report back to headquarters and let them know what happened here."

"The headquarters of what?"

"Her Majesty's Secret Service."

Jacks looked at Sancho. "I already let them know, James. N is up to speed. He wanted you to go with Agent Jacks so she can debrief you."

Flynn nodded and gave Agent Jacks his most charming smile. "I'd love to join Agent Jacks wherever she wants to go. Lead the way, Miranda."

CHAPTER THIRTY-SEVEN

The richest robber baron of them all, John D. Rockefeller, made his fortune in oil, coal, and gas. Raised by a religious mother and con man father, he became the wealthiest person in modern history. In 1913, his net worth peaked at 409 billion in today's dollars and he personally controlled two percent of the national GDP. That was the same year he instigated the Ludlow Massacre. Hired thugs under Rockefeller's direction attacked twelve hundred striking coal miners living in a tent colony. Using machine guns, they mowed down miners and their families. Just twenty years later, in 1932, ground was broken on Rockefeller Plaza in New York City. John D. was ninety-two by then and lauded as a great philanthropist. Along with the Rockefeller family, one of the first tenants was The National Broadcasting Company. NBC has broadcast from thirty Rockefeller Plaza for eighty-seven years. Shows produced there include The Johnny Carson Show, Tic-Tac-Dough, Saturday Night Live, and the Today show.

Bettina wiped her sweaty palms on the green room couch as she waited to go on the Today Show. She originally didn't want to wear a dress, especially not a cobalt blue one, but her new agent told her she needed to make an impression. Her agent hired a stylist who told Bettina that the dress brought out the blue in her eyes and that she shouldn't be afraid to use what she had. "If you have it, flaunt it," was the cliché she kept repeating. The stylist insisted on a new hair cut with bangs and even brought in a makeup artist to make Bettina more presentable for national TV. The Today Show would be her first appearance, but she was also scheduled for The View, Colbert, and Ellen.

Natasha Lyonne sat on the other side of the green room and texted someone on her phone. Peter Dinklage talked to his much taller female manager and ate grapes.

A pretty twenty-something page poked her head in the door. "Are you ready, Ms. O'Toole?"

"Applebaum. O'Toole-Applebaum."

"Of course, but we should go. Your segment is next."

The walk from the Green Room to Studio A was a blur of lights and smiling faces, frantic producers and bored-looking crew members. Before she knew it, Bettina sat across from Savannah Guthrie and stared into her dazzling smile.

"Welcome," Savannah said.

"Thank you."

The studio looked so much different on TV. In person, it seemed much smaller and phonier.

Savannah shifted her gaze away from Bettina and smiled into the camera. "Today our guest is a young journalist who has made quite a splash. Bettina O'Toole-Appelbaum won a Pulitzer Prize this year for her story in Rolling Stone on the Sergei Belenki scandal." She turned her gaze back to Bettina. "I heard your piece was optioned by Angelina Jolie's production company. Is she going to be playing you?"

"I don't know. It's still pretty early in the process."

"I understand you model yourself after Nellie Bly."

"She *is* an inspiration."

"She was to me as well," Savannah said. "She broke the rules and broke new ground. And just like Nellie Bly, you went undercover and discovered a plot by billionaire Sergei Belenki that threatened everyone on the planet."

"Actually, the real mastermind was Belenki's ex-partner, Andrew Meisner. He duped Belenki with an elaborate con. Of course, Belenki still bears some responsibility for his actions."

"Are you at all upset that Belenki didn't face any consequences for those actions?"

"It's hard to charge let alone convict anyone as wealthy as Sergei Belenki. That's part of what prompted me to write this story."

"I understand he's suing you."

"And I have to thank him for all that free publicity."

"Is that what helped you clinch the Hollywood deal?"

"It didn't hurt."

"Andrew Meisner's facing life in prison, yet Sergei Belenki goes scot-free."

"People are dead because of what Andrew Meisner did."

"What about Sergei Belenki?"

"He truly believed that Daisy was sentient. He thought he was saving the world."

"Some would say he was just as delusional as the hero of your story, Mr. Flynn."

"That's what his lawyers argued. Temporary insanity."

"But the courts decided that Mr. Flynn's insanity is not temporary."

"No, he's currently being treated at a psychiatric hospital."

"Is it true that the prosecutor used your story as part of the evidence for his involuntary commitment?"

"Mr. Flynn sees the world differently than the rest of us do, but that doesn't make him any less of a hero."

· · ·

Sancho stood in the City of Roses activity room and took in the Today Show with a handful of patients. Ty and Q watched from the couch and neither one seemed to have any understanding of what Bettina was talking about. Nurse Durkin scowled at Sancho from the doorway. "Are you on a break, Mr. Perez?"

"No, ma'am."

"Then get back to work. And let's watch something a little more therapeutic." She aimed the channel changer at the TV and turned to "Keeping up with the Kardashians." Q and Ty both perked up at the sight of Kim Kardashian in a yellow bikini.

· · ·

Mr. Papazian looked older, balder and thinner than the last time Flynn saw him. It was at the Glendale Galleria when he confronted Goolardo and Mendoza and took three bullets for his bravery. His bushy eyebrows and pencil thin mustache were grayer and so was Papazian's complexion, but he seemed genuinely pleased to see Flynn. As did Mr. Rodriguez, who wore his brown maintenance uniform. Papazian, on the other hand, was dressed like a civilian in khaki trousers, a colorful sweater, and a tweed jacket. He clutched a cane and walked with some difficulty. They each took a seat in the City of Roses visiting area. Flynn tried to help Papazian into his chair, but the elderly Armenian waved him off.

"I'm fine," Papazian grumbled.

"You look like you're doing better," Flynn said.

"I'm much improved. You're looking good too, Jimmy. You lost a lot of weight. You been working out?"

"I have," Flynn said with a smile. "By the way, it's James now."

Rodriguez repeated the name. "James. Okay. You doing all right in here?"

"Couldn't be better. How are you doing?"

"Doing what I do," Rodriguez said. "Got lots of mouths to feed. You know how that goes."

"Actually, I don't."

"We miss you back at the mall, man. It just ain't the same without you. By the way, Mrs. McKinney at Hot Dog on a Stick says hi."

"Say hi back to her for me, would you please? I'm glad to hear you're both still doing what you do."

Papazian shook his head. "Not me, Jimmy."

"James," Rodriguez corrected.

"James," Papazian repeated with not a little irritation. "They retired me, but I'm on worker's comp. I got a pension for life now. Add that to my social security and I'm doing okay for an old man."

"He's the hero of the Galleria. People buy him drinks everywhere he goes."

Mr. Papazian grinned. "I don't move as fast as I used to, but I'm not in any hurry to get anywhere anyway."

"Well, it was good of you to come see me," Flynn said. "I'm sorry I deceived you as to my true purpose at the Galleria, but I truly appreciate the kindness you both showed me."

Rodriguez and Papazian shared a look.

"So, when are you getting out of here?" Rodriguez asked.

"Not anytime soon. As long as I'm needed, this is where I'll be. And please feel free to come by and see me anytime."

Papazian smiled and nodded but Flynn detected a sadness in his eyes. Perhaps the old man regretted retirement more than he made out. He leaned on his cane and grunted to get himself to his feet. "We better get Rodriguez back to work before his lunch hour's up. But we'll be by again and next time I'll bring you some of my wife's homemade Popok."

"That shit is tasty," Rodriguez said. "It's like tiny crispy balls of creamy deliciousness."

"I look forward to tasting your wife's popok," Flynn said as he showed them both the door. "Good to see you, Mr. Rodriguez. Be well, Mr. Papazian."

• • •

Severina sat on the edge of her bed and buttoned her blouse. "Sergei won't be happy about this."

"Happy about what?" Max asked as he came out of the bathroom wearing shorts and a tank top. Bandages covered his right shoulder.

"Bettina on the Today Show."

"He's lucky that's all he has to deal with."

"He's never going to win that lawsuit," Severina said.

"But that's not the point, is it? He just wants her to shut up."

"But that's not going to happen. All he's doing is giving her more attention."

"Maybe you should tell him that," Max said.

Severina stood up. "You think I made a mistake going back to work for him?"

"That's not my call."

"But you have an opinion."

"My opinion is he owes you big time. So, get what you can out of him and start your own thing."

Severina smiled and moved for Max, putting her arms around him. "That's the plan."

"Good plan." Max smiled as Severina kissed him.

• • •

Flynn wore karate pants as he trained in the courtyard. He moved through a complex kata, his muscular torso glistening as he battled an imaginary opponent and executed perfect leaps, kicks, punches, and chops. A pretty young Filipino nurse enjoyed the view as she brought in Wendy and her mom.

"James. You have some visitors."

Flynn grinned when he saw them. He grabbed a towel, wiped his face, and pointed to a patio table. They each took a seat as Flynn draped the towel around his neck and joined them.

"What a wonderful surprise."

"You're looking good," Wendy said.

"Really good," said Mrs. Zimmerman.

"As do both of you," Flynn said with a smile. "You could easily be sisters." Wendy rolled her eyes at that, but Mrs. Zimmerman ate it up with a spoon. "It must be all that yoga and healthy eating, Mrs. Zimmerman."

"Myra. Please."

"Myra. Of course."

"Mom insisted on coming," Wendy said.

"I wanted to thank you for what you did for my daughter. It was very heroic, and I am very, *very* grateful."

"Wendy was just as heroic as me."

"I know. I was so proud when I read that article in Rolling Stone." Tears welled up in Mrs. Zimmerman's eyes. "I knew she was special, but now the whole world knows."

Wendy squeezed her mother's hand and grinned at Flynn. "Did you see Bettina on the Today Show?"

Flynn shook his head. "I don't have much time for television."

Wendy looked at Flynn wistfully. "It's hard seeing you in here."

"It's where I belong. Resting. Training. Readying myself for the next mission."

"Would you mind if I kept visiting?"

"Mind? Are you kidding me? Why would I ever mind seeing your beautiful face?"

"I told you he likes you," Mrs. Zimmerman said.

"Mom, please."

"You raised a smart, brave, and beautiful daughter, Mrs. Zimmerman. She obviously takes after her mother."

Mrs. Zimmerman blushed and opened a paper bag and pulled out some treats wrapped in waxed paper. "Since you so enjoyed my mock taco pie, I thought I'd bring you some healthy vegan treats." Flynn traded a glance with Wendy, and she had to cover her mouth not to laugh. "Hemp-crusted crispy tofu nuggets!"

Flynn opened his mouth to thank her and she jammed one in. He smiled and bit down. It took some effort, but the nugget finally shattered into a crumbly pile of crunchy chunks.

"Mmm. Crispy."

• • •

Casa Piedra sat on a bluff overlooking the gleaming white sands of Playa Blanca in Guanacaste, the jewel of Costa Rica's Gold Coast. Goolardo smoked a Cuban cigar and sipped a Mojito as he lounged on the large shaded patio of his casa grande. He read Rolling Stone Magazine as the sun slowly set on the crystal blue waters of Brasilito Bay.

Mendoza tried to enjoy the view as he reclined on a chaise lounge just a few feet away. Sailboats and dolphins danced on the horizon. He took a swig from an ice-cold beer and put the frosty bottle to his forehead. This was indeed a paradise, but as perfect as it was...he couldn't relax. Not as long as James Flynn still lived. The lunatic haunted him. Flynn had humiliated him. Shamed him. Dishonored him. The fact that this pendejo was celebrated as some sort of hero was so fucking irritating. Even more infuriating was that Goolardo seemed to agree.

Goolardo laughed and slapped the magazine with the back of his hand. "You really need to read this!"

Mendoza shrugged and took another pull on his beer. "According to this I helped save the world! Me? Francisco Goolardo!" He laughed again.

"What did she say about me?"

"She didn't say anything. You weren't mentioned."

"Not mentioned?"

"Why would she? You didn't shoot down the helicopter? That was me!" Goolardo stood and took a puff on his Cohiba. "Anika!" he shouted. "You have to read this!"

Anika Piscotti lounged by the infinity pool. She wore a tiny white micro bikini that barely covered her famous bottom. The straps on top were untied as she lay face down on a large beach towel. "Hmm?" she said.

"This article in Rolling Stone. You are mentioned many times!"

"*She's* mentioned?" Mendoza looked put out.

"If I were you, I'd hire a publicist," Anika purred. "This is great PR for you."

Mendoza drained the rest of his beer. The movie star was beautiful, but so damn annoying. He was shocked when she'd accepted Goolardo's invitation. They were fugitives on the run and he invited one of the most famous movie stars in the world to stay with them.

Mrs. Megel walked out on the patio with a plate of lemon meringue pie. "Who wants pie?" Goolardo raised his hand and Mrs. Megel handed him the plate. Mendoza raised his hand as well. "Sorry, that was the last piece."

Goolardo took a bite of pie and said with a mouthful, "Delicious!"

Mrs. Megel bustled back into the casa while Goolardo tucked into his pie. Mendoza sat across from him and posed a question. "So, when are we going after him?"

"Who?"

"Flynn."

"You want to go after Flynn?"

"He promised to come after us once Belenki was dealt with. And you told him if he did, you would kill him."

"But he hasn't."

"How do we know that?"

"Because we haven't seen him." Goolardo took another big bite of pie.

"You're just going to let him get away with what he did to us?"

"Why are you holding on to this?"

"He destroyed your plan. He cost you millions. Because of him we spent a year in prison."

"That was then."

"You can't let him get away with what he did to you."

"Why?"

"Because everyone will believe you are weak."

"Is that what you think?"

"No," Mendoza backtracked. "I'm not saying I think that. I'm saying others might."

"Who?"

"Competitors. Rivals. Enemies."

Goolardo finished his last bite of pie and wiped his mouth with the back of his hand. "So, what do you want to do?"

"Kill him."

"Flynn?"

"Yes."

"I think this hate you have for him is toxic."

"What?"

"That kind of anger is unhealthy. It can lead to health issues. High blood pressure. Even cancer."

"He needs to die."

"I say let bygones be bygones."

"I don't agree."

"And I don't remember asking you your opinion."

A wave of fury overtook Mendoza. At such times, he had tunnel vision and saw only the thing he wanted to destroy. Sound faded away as his concentration focused entirely on the object of his anger. Never before had he felt this way about Goolardo. He knew he had to let it go and breathe. In and out. In and out. Slowly the fury faded and the storm passed.

Goolardo patted his hand. "Are you okay?"

Mendoza nodded, but he knew he wasn't. He knew what he had to do. Flynn had to die.

CHAPTER THIRTY-EIGHT

As a reward for his loyal service, the first Spanish governor of California deeded a thirty-six-thousand-acre rancho to Corporal Jose Maria Verdugo in 1874. It remained in the Verdugo family for the next hundred years before it was finally broken up and sold in lots. In 1937, Elias Manchester Boddy, purchased 565 acres of the original rancho, built a twenty-two-room mansion and planted extensive gardens. Born in a log cabin, he was the son of a potato farmer and sold encyclopedias door to door on New York's Lower East Side. He fought in World War I, was gassed in the Argonne and sent home disabled. After spending months in a military hospital, he moved to California with his wife and infant son. Using the money he made selling magazines and books, he bought a bankrupt newspaper and became a crusading editor who exposed police corruption, gambling, and prostitution. The Los Angeles Daily News became the second most popular paper in Southern California. Boddy was now a wealthy man and in the early 1940s, when the Japanese were forced into internment camps, Boddy purchased one hundred thousand camellia plants from two Japanese-owned nurseries and created North America's largest camellia collection. He later established large rose and lilac collections and, in 1950, opened his estate, now dubbed Descanso Gardens, to the public.

It was a beautiful day in the Verdugo Valley; Sancho was glad to be outdoors. Puffy clouds drifted across an azure sky. The view to the San Gabriel Mountains was unobstructed by haze or smog as the autumn air was crisp and clear. He could see those same mountains from City of Roses. Descanso Gardens was only a twenty-minute drive west on the 210. Sancho loved getting out of the hospital for a day even if it meant chaperoning and corralling a chaotic contingent of mental patients.

City of Roses offered monthly field trips to patients who followed the rules and exhibited good behavior. Dr. Nickelson believed such outings were therapeutic. He often said there was something calming about being in nature and most of the patients seemed to agree as Descanso Gardens was one of their favorite destinations.

Dr. Nickelson rarely joined them on outings, but this day was an exception. Instead of his usual suit, he wore chinos, sneakers, a light blue guayabera shirt, and a straw Panama hat. Flynn was no less stylish in his faded jeans, dark blue Polo shirt, and straw Fedora. Skinny, seventy-eight-year-old Q wore his favorite Tommy Bahama Hawaiian number and twenty-one-year-old Ty wore his Air Jordan's, a black 4XL-size tank top, and elastic-waist cargo shorts large enough to accommodate all two hundred and seventy-five pounds of him.

Nurse Durkin was there along with her ability to inspire fear and kill all levity and joy. While Nickelson was fine letting patients wander, Durkin kept a tight leash on them. She brought a newer nurse along to help monitor the patients. Jilly was a petite redhead and a recent graduate of Cal State. Sancho could see that she was already somewhat smitten with Flynn, much to Nurse Durkin's dismay.

There were eight patients along for the day and Sancho kept an eye on them to make sure no one wandered too far. Like Nickelson, he wanted to give them a little freedom, but he didn't want to lose one and suffer Durkin's wrath. Flynn, Q, and Ty were joined by Flynn's half-way house roommate, Rodney, his big white Santa beard bigger than ever. Unlike Saint Nick, he didn't seem very jolly. Instead he exhibited the cranky demeanor of an addict trying to white-knuckle it. Bob was bipolar, pale and anonymous-looking with beady eyes and a nervous giggle. Mary Alice suffered from intermittent explosive disorder. Big-boned, middle-aged, and freckle-faced, she had dyed red hair, a southern accent, and a raspy smoker's voice. She also had the hots for Flynn.

Zipper, a shy schizophrenic in his early thirties was so heavily medicated he'd doze off if he stood in one place too long. Doris Frawley, a ninety-one-year-old former beauty queen from Arkansas, rounded out the procession. Her dementia was getting worse along with her delusions, but Sancho enjoyed her company and all her

Hollywood stories. Even though she needed a walker, she still moved faster than Zipper.

Nickelson led the parade. Sancho kept the middle moving while Durkin brought up the rear, prodding along the stragglers. The Rose Garden was in full bloom and Nickelson delighted in smelling every blossom he could get his nose on.

"Oh, this pink Royal Highness Hybrid is delicious."

Rodney leaned in to smell it and Ty bumped him out of the way so he could bury his nose in the large, pink rose.

"Oh, yeah, that's nice," Ty said. "Smells like candy."

Doris Frawley sniffed another nearby blossom. "Such a beautiful fragrance. Reminds me of Grace Kelly's favorite scent. Fleurissimo. She and I both had a fling with William Holden back in the day. In fact, Bill brought me to this very place for a picnic in 1953 and had his way with me under a gazebo."

Nurse Jilly smiled at that and glanced at Flynn who held a large pink rose petal.

"Feel how soft this is." He brushed it against her cheek and held it up to her nose. "It has a very subtle fragrance."

"That's wonderful," she said.

"From the time of the Romans, roses have symbolized romance. Especially red ones. While bright red roses signify love, a burgundy rose portends of a love that is yet to be."

Jilly stumbled on a brick and Flynn caught her by the arm. For a moment Sancho thought she might swoon. He saw Nurse Durkin looking stern, but Mary Alice beat her to the punch, inserting herself between Jilly and Flynn, offering him a gap-toothed grin.

"I think flowers are hot as hell." Her voice was three octaves lower than Flynn's. "Sex organs is what they are. They attract those little bees by how they look and how they smell." She closed both her hands into fists. "Give a rose what it needs and it will open right up for you." She unclenched her hands and spread her fingers wide, sticking out her tongue as she grinned.

Flynn looked deep into Mary Alice's eyes. "Treat a woman right and she will bloom. What's the quote from Shelley? *'And the Spring arose on the garden fair, like the spirit of love felt everywhere.'*"

"Keep moving, Mary Alice," Nurse Durkin grabbed her by the arm and pulled her along. "We're only here for two hours and we have a lot more to see."

Sancho couldn't help but notice how much happier the patients were outside the walls of the hospital. They were freer. Lighter. Calmer. More joyful. As they traipsed up the path that overlooked the duck pond, the patients all delighted in watching the waterfowl splash about.

"Look at the size of the turtle," Ty said. "That's a big fucking turtle!"

Bob pointed at a duck. "I like ducks."

"I need to sit down," Rodney said.

"So, sit your fat ass down," Mary Alice growled.

Rodney glared at her. "I wasn't talking to you."

"Then who the hell were you talking to?"

Rodney rolled his eyes and walked away.

"Don't be rolling your eyes at me!"

"Okay, let's go. Keep moving," Durkin demanded.

Bob was already outside the observation center, laughing as he chased a duck in circles around a tree.

"What's Bob doing to that duck?" Jilly asked

Sancho used his stern voice. "Bob! Leave that duck alone!"

Bob ignored him and kept stalking the quacking duck.

"Get away from the damn duck!" Durkin barked. "Or I'll put you right back in that van!"

"Not a fan of the great outdoors. Too many goddamn bugs," Rodney complained. "Can I get something to drink? I'm feeling extremely dehydrated."

"And I'm feeling extremely irritated by your incessant fucking whining," Mary Alice replied.

•   •   •

Mendoza watched them all board the transport van at City of Roses. He shadowed them from the parking lot and kept a good distance behind them as he followed in the Corolla he stole the previous evening. They were only on the freeway for a short time before they exited at Foothill Boulevard in a town just west of Pasadena called La Cañada-Flintridge. He followed the van past multimillion-dollar homes surrounded by towering trees and into a driveway that led to a large parking lot.

Mendoza parked behind an SUV and waited until the entire contingent from City of Roses headed into the gardens. Mendoza knew stealth wasn't his strong suit. His size made it difficult to follow anyone unobtrusively. Plus, he knew both Flynn and Sancho would easily recognize him. No, he needed to hang back and strike when they were at their most distracted. He took the time to check his weapon; a 9mm pistol with a modular polymer grip and an extended magazine.

Once the big nurse herded the last mental patient into the gardens, Mendoza exited his car and crossed the parking lot. He wore chinos and an untucked plaid shirt that hung over his waist, concealing his holster. He waited at the ticket booth behind a lady with two screaming kids and a baby in her arms.

The toothless, fat-faced infant gawked at Mendoza over her shoulder. Babies always stared at him and he didn't understand why. He knew that some people smiled at babies or played games with them, but Mendoza had no experience with such tiny humans. They made him nervous. They seemed so fragile. And this one looked at him with such a judgmental glower. It was like he could see directly into Mendoza's soul. Like he knew exactly what Mendoza planned to do.

He purchased a ticket with cash and wandered into the gardens. He glanced in the gift shop just in case the mental patients were shopping for souvenirs. He scanned the café area, but none of them were over there either. He continued into the gardens proper and looked at a map. He had no idea the gardens were so large.

He started in the Rose Garden and searched the trails around the duck pond. He reconnoitered both camellia forests and the lilac garden. Mendoza was too tense to enjoy the scenery. He had a mission and knew he couldn't concentrate on anything else until he completed it. Goolardo would not be happy with him, but Goolardo was never happy with him. No matter what he accomplished. No matter what he achieved. Goolardo simply had no respect for him. It wasn't always this way. Goolardo used to respect him. Rely on him. Believe in him. But not since Flynn. The pendejo loco ruined their relationship with his endless insanity and now he had to die.

Mendoza crossed a bridge at the Japanese Garden and recognized one of the patients from the van. The pale, chubby, little man crept up on a duck. Then he saw two other patients from City of Roses. An elderly woman with a walker sat on a bench next to a young man who seemed to be sleeping.

Mendoza edged behind a tree and drew his pistol. Peeking out, he watched the large nurse argue with an angry-looking red-haired woman. Probably another one of the patients. Sancho Perez kneeled by a koi pond next to a large, young, black man, fishing a sneaker out of the mud.

And then he saw Flynn.

The nut job conversed with a young nurse, clearly charming her. With Flynn distracted, Mendoza knew he had to move. For a big man, he was surprisingly graceful. He crept closer and closer, moving silently from tree to tree. Flynn seemed oblivious. The lady whose baby peered into his soul crossed in front of him, followed by both her toddlers. They laughed and screamed and ran circles around him. All that commotion drew Flynn's attention.

"¡Apartese del camino!" Mendoza shouted as he locked eyes with Flynn and charged toward him, knocking one of the toddlers off his feet. Flynn stood frozen as Mendoza raised his weapon. At this distance the big man knew he couldn't miss.

. . .

Flynn understood that death had finally come. There was nowhere to hide. Not this time. And in that split second, he decided he was okay with that. That he had lived his life the way he wanted to. As he braced himself for the bullet, a wall of flesh hit Mendoza like a freight train. He heard the .9mm round whistle past his head as every single one of Ty's two hundred and seventy-five-pounds smacked Mendoza sideways. He splashed into one of the Koi ponds with Ty right on top of him. The splatter was epic and hit everyone in a fifteen-foot radius.

Mendoza wrestled with Ty, pushed him away, and struggled to his feet just in time for Mary Alice to clock him with a cinderblock. Bob jumped on his back, giggling like an idiot. Mendoza made it to the edge of the water as Doris stabbed him in the neck with a giant hairpin. The big man flailed and fell back into the pond. Even Rodney and Zipper got in on the action. Mendoza lay face down in the mud, fighting for his life, throwing elbows and fists and gasping to get his head above water.

Flynn considered joining the fray, but they were doing fine without him. Nickelson and Nurse Durkin just stood there and watched, too nonplussed to know what to do.

Mendoza finally fought off his attackers and managed to crawl out of the pond. Soaked head to toe and covered in mud, he staggered out of the Japanese Garden as his assailants followed. Flynn saw him reach the main path and hesitate as he looked back at his pursuers. He didn't see the Descanso Gardens tram bearing down on him with Q behind the wheel.

The tram blindsided Mendoza. He tumbled through the air and hit the ground hard, the impact knocking him cold. Flynn took advantage of his lack of consciousness to hogtie him with a roll of garden twine.

Flynn looked up from the muddy and bedraggled Mendoza. He was surrounded on all sides by the patients who came to his rescue. He addressed them proudly. "This was to be a training exercise today, but instead you confronted real danger. Mr. Mendoza wanted me dead and if not for all of you, I likely would be." He patted Ty on the shoulder. "I owe you one, my friend."

"One what?" asked Ty.

"Whatever you want."

"Pinkberry."

"You want Pinkberry."

"There's one right up the street."

"Sounds good to me," said Mary Alice.

Bob raised his hand. "I want some."

"Me too," Doris said.

Rodney made a face. "I hate Pinkberry. It's too damn tart."

Mary Alice glared at him. "Who asked you?"

"I think each and every one of us deserves whatever brief pleasure we can find in this dangerous world," Flynn said. "Unlike most who move through this world blissfully unaware of how precarious life is, we see what others don't and fight battles most can't comprehend. We struggle with fear and uncertainty and suffer immeasurable pain, yet each day we rise and join the fight again."

Flynn looked at Doris and Bob, Q and Mary Alice, Rodney, and Ty and saw in their eyes that each understood exactly what he was telling them.

"I thank you for your bravery. For your friendship. For your strength and fortitude in the—"

Flynn caught sight of Sancho sitting slumped over on a bench a short distance away, his shirt soaked in blood. Flynn ran to him. The bullet meant for him found another target. Sancho's face grew deathly white.

Flynn ripped back the fabric of Sancho's City of Roses shirt. A puckered wound on the far-right side of his torso bore testament to his friend's waning life.

Nickelson arrived and moved him out of the way. "Nurse Jilly, give me a hand here!"

Nurse Jilly helped cradle Sancho as Nickelson carefully leaned him forward and found an exit wound.

"Looks like it went straight through," Nickelson said. "It's hard to tell what kind of damage it did until we get you to a hospital."

"I'll call an ambulance. Everybody else back on the bus," Durkin commanded.

"Fine," Ty said. "But first we're going to Pinkberry."

~ * ~

SNEAK PEEK OF
GOLDHAMMER

And now, a sneak peek at Flynn's next escapade in...

CHAPTER ONE

The Corsican wanted him dead.

Of that James Flynn was certain.

Somehow, the assassin had infiltrated Her Majesty's Secret Service as a security officer. Flynn didn't recognize him at first. The killer had put on a few pounds and likely had plastic surgery, but what he couldn't disguise were his eyes. His cold, dark, pitiless eyes. The eyes of a sociopath. The eyes of an executioner.

The only question was when.

When would the Corsican come for him?

He told his colleagues what he suspected, but they refused to believe him. They claimed his name was Thomas Hernandez and that someone else on the security team had recommended him. They also said they fully vetted him. But Flynn wasn't fooled. He tangled with the Corsican before. The man was relentless. A cold-blooded enforcer who started with the Corsican mafia but went on to do contract hits for the Sicilians, the Albanians, the Serbians, and the Russians.

Instead of waiting for the Corsican to come to him, Flynn decided to flush him out. Force his hand. Expose him for who he was and why he was there.

Flynn dressed in black denim and a black turtleneck and waited until 2 a.m. to make his move. He kept to the shadows as he trod the deserted corridors. He had no weapon since lethal weapons of any kind were now forbidden at headquarters. A foolish rule put in place by sheltered bureaucrats who had no clue. Luckily, not even security could carry a firearm at headquarters. All the Corsican had was an expandable baton and a Taser. Even so, the man was lethal enough with just his hands and feet.

But then, so was Flynn.

Flynn heard footsteps ahead and ducked into a conference room. He waited and listened as the footsteps drew closer. As they passed the doorway, Flynn peered into the corridor to see the Corsican lumbering forward, quietly peering in room after room. Suddenly, he stopped. Flynn felt a jolt of adrenaline. The air was electric. The silence palpable. Could the Corsican feel Flynn's eyes on him? Flynn knew that scientists have identified a specialized group of neurons in the primate brain that fire specifically when a monkey is under the direct gaze of another. Humans also appear to be wired for that kind of gaze perception. Predators like Flynn and the Corsican can also be prey and have developed a sixth sense to alert them to danger.

The Corsican turned and he and Flynn locked eyes for a moment. Before the hit man could take a step, Flynn took off down the hall in the opposite direction. He heard the footfalls of the Corsican as he chased after him. Flynn had his route all mapped out. Darting down one corridor. Then another. Running until he arrived at a door that led down to the basement and the guts of the building. Flynn had picked the lock after dinner, knowing that this was the night he would lure the Corsican to his end. He had a license to kill and could have used it anytime, but Flynn didn't exercise that power willy-nilly. Only as a last resort. He didn't want the Corsican dead. He needed to know who put the price on his head. Otherwise who ever hired the killer would continue to send hitters until finally one succeeded.

The building that housed HMSS was huge and had a substantial infrastructure. The basement utility plant had mechanical, electrical, HVAC, and plumbing systems that fed water, air, and electricity all through the facility. Flynn moved from massive room to massive room, staying just ahead of the Corsican. He needed to lose him and lay in wait. Flynn was confident in his abilities, but to come at a killer like that head-on didn't make much sense. Why give your opponents any edge at all?

Flynn ducked into a room that housed all the electrical panels, distribution boards, and circuit breakers. Conduit snaked everywhere and Flynn found a metal door secured with a heavy padlock. Using two straightened paper clips, he quickly picked the lock. The door led to an outside area protected by a chain-link fence topped with razor wire. The security fence surrounded three giant transformers and two massive backup generators the size of semi-trailers.

Flynn stood next to the door and strained his ears to hear approaching footsteps over the electrical buzz of the transformers. Faint at first, they moved closer. Careful. Slow. Stealthy. He saw a shoe as someone came through and Flynn took them from behind, using jiu-jitsu to slam them into the ground.

"Whoa, whoa, whoa," said the man Flynn had face down in the gravel.

"Sancho?"

"Get off me, man."

Flynn released his comrade-in-arms and helped him to his feet. Bits of gravel still clung to his face. "I thought you were the Corsican." Flynn's British accent had a touch of Scottish burr.

"His name is Hernandez," Sancho said.

"That's not his real name."

"And I'm telling you, he's not the Corsican."

"Don't let him fool you, my friend. He's not who he says he is."

"Then why'd he call me? He knows I know you. He knows we're friends. He asked me to find you. Talk to you. Calm you down."

"Perhaps he wants to take care of you too."

"Take care of *me*?"

Flynn heard the Corsican call to them, his voice deep and resonant. "You okay in there, brother?"

"We're good," Sancho said.

The Corsican walked in with two other men. All three wore the blue security uniform issued to those who guard HMSS. The Corsican looked at Flynn with his dark, merciless eyes. "You okay, Mr. Flynn?"

"Tell them who you are," Flynn demanded.

"Thomas Hernandez."

"Who you *really* are."

The Corsican rolled his eyes and sighed. "That's who I really am."

Flynn aimed an accusatory finger. "I *know* who you are. Born Stefanu Perrina in Porto, Corsica. Contract killer for the Unione Corse, the Cosa Nostra, and the Russian mafia. Wanted by Interpol for fifty-two confirmed kills."

"I was born in Hacienda Heights."

Flynn glanced at Sancho. "The man is a master of deception. It's kill or be killed with men like him."

The Corsican drew his Taser and the other two guards followed suit.

Sancho raised his hands. "Whoa, come on now. Easy." He stepped in front of Flynn as the Corsican fired. The Taser darts caught Sancho in the shoulder and socked him with fifty thousand volts. He screamed in agony as his whole body seized up and shook. His legs gave out and he fell on his side, helpless and twitching.

Flynn dove behind a generator before the other two guards could fire. Each guard stalked him from a different side. Flynn clambered up over the top and launched himself from above, tackling the Corsican. He wrenched away his reloaded Taser and shot one of the guards in the crotch. The man went down with a shriek as the other guard fired on him. Flynn fell to his knees and the darts parted his hair before hitting the Corsican in the chest. The killer crumpled as Flynn sprang to his feet and pulled the Corsican's expandable baton out of its holster. Flicking his wrist, Flynn fully extended the menacing club and turned to confront the last standing guard.

Someone grabbed Flynn by the arm and Flynn elbowed him in the face. Sancho staggered back, holding his bloody nose. "What the hell, man?"

"Sorry, mate."

Flynn heard a Taser fire and an instant later, two darts hit him in the side. Fifty thousand volts took him to his knees as another guard fired another Taser. Those two darts hit him in the stomach. Flynn lost control of every muscle in his body. And then he saw the Corsican looming over him with his own weapon. He shot the darts directly into Flynn's chest. Right over his heart. Now all three lit him up with electricity. One hundred and fifty thousand volts rocked Flynn as they shocked him with charge after charge until the world faded into a tiny aperture that slowly began to close.

CHAPTER TWO

Jack Parsons, the co-founder of the Jet Propulsion Laboratory, and Scientology founder L. Ron Hubbard were followers of famous occultist Aleister Crowley. Both believed that Devil's Gate Gorge in the Arroyo Seco was one of the seven portals to Hell. The gorge's namesake rock face resembles a devil's head and sits on the far western edge of Pasadena. The two amateur occultists and their followers would hold sex magick ceremonies outside of what they referred to as the Hellmouth, hoping to open the gates of Hell or at the least conjure up a demon or two. Some believe the two friends did indeed open that dark portal. Though, no one has ever claimed to have seen Baal or Beelzebub or any other major demons marching in Pasadena's annual Doo Dah Parade.

Sancho Perez stood frozen outside the front doors of City of Roses Psychiatric Institute. He tried to calm his heart as he worked up the nerve to walk inside. Band-aids covered the scratches on his face. His nose was swollen and his eyes were beginning to blacken. A hand rested on his shoulder and Sancho looked over to see the senior psychiatrist, Dr. Nickelson, smiling at him.

"Mr. Perez!"

"Hi, Dr. Nickelson."

"How are you feeling?"

"Okay."

"Good! Well, don't overdo it. You suffered a severe trauma ten months ago and that incident with Mr. Flynn last night is exactly the kind of thing you want to avoid. Something like that can be very triggering. I appreciate you coming to his aid, but please take it easy today."

"Okay."

Dr. Nickelson told Nurse Durkin to assign Sancho less-taxing duties to start. So, instead of putting him into the daily rotation, she asked him to gather the patients for their midday meal. The very first one he approached was Tom Gavoni. Hollow-eyed and balding, he sat on a couch and refused to come to lunch. "Food is meaningless to me now," he said.

Sancho smiled and raised a curious eyebrow. "Meaningless how?"

"Because I have no need of nutrition. My bodily functions have stopped functioning."

Sancho was struck by how skinny Tom was. Skeletal even. "What are you saying? You don't feel good?"

"I don't feel anything."

"Do you want to see the doctor?"

"The doctor can't help me. No one can help me."

"Why would that be?"

"Because I'm dead." His bulging eyes burned with guilt and despair. Two of his teeth were missing.

"Dead inside, you mean?"

"Dead like deceased. Like no longer among the living."

"Are you saying you're a ghost?"

"I'm saying six months ago I blacked out after a three-day bender and woke up here."

"In City of Roses?"

"In Hell."

"You think you're in Hell?"

"You think you're not?"

A blood-curdling scream ended their conversation. Tom gave Sancho a look like, "See?"

Sancho hurried down the corridor to find the source of the screaming. Ear-splitting in its intensity, it echoed off the cinderblock walls and down the halls.

Sancho found the room and entered to find a petite brunette in her early twenties strapped to a hospital bed, her dirty, tear-smeared face contorted with fear. Young and pretty, she reminded Sancho of Emma Watson, that English actress from the Harry Potter movies. She writhed and struggled against the wrist and ankle straps and stared at Sancho with a furious intensity.

"Let me go! Please! Please! They'll kill me!"

"Who?"

She let out an ear-shattering shriek so loud it even woke Mrs. Jakobs, the narcoleptic in the next bed.

"No one's going to kill you," Sancho said with a soothing voice.

"I might," Mrs. Jakobs mumbled.

"Please! Pleeeease!" the young woman begged.

Sancho figured they brought her in sedated during the night shift and she woke up strapped to her bed, not knowing where she was or what was happening. He looked at her chart, noted her name, and patted her hand. "Chloe, look at me. You're going to be okay."

"He wants me dead. He tried once. He'll try again!"

Sancho squeezed her hand. "You're safe here."

"No, no, no, he knows I know! He can't let me live!"

"Who can't?" The voice came from behind Sancho, and it was so deep, comforting, and commanding, it immediately calmed the girl. The accent was British and Chloe stopped struggling to stare.

Sancho knew who it was without having to turn around. "Hey James, no worries, man, I got this."

"She clearly believes someone intends to do her harm."

"She's just confused, dude."

Sancho watched as James Flynn entered the room and approached Chloe's bed. Tall and strikingly handsome, he wore a navy blue, single-breasted, slim cut suit with a light blue shirt and a gray silk tie. It fit him tightly, which only emphasized his wide shoulders and powerful arms. Unlike Sancho, he didn't have a mark on his face. "What's your name, dear?"

"Chloe."

"What a lovely name." Flynn pulled out a pocket square and dabbed her tears. "If I remember correctly, it's from the Greek and harkens back to Demeter. The Goddess of fertility."

"*Dude.*"

"We need to get these restraints off her, Sancho."

Chloe looked at Flynn with big brown eyes brimming with tears, her voice a whisper. "Someone's trying to kill me, doctor."

"James ain't no doctor," Sancho said.

"Who are you then?"

"A friend." Flynn unbuckled one of the straps.

Sancho grabbed his wrist. "You can't be doing that, man."

"We can't very well expect her to protect herself if she's trussed up like a turkey."

Sancho watched with a worried look as Flynn unfastened each restraint. "Durkin won't be happy, dude."

"Is that who strapped her down like this? Nurse Durkin?"

"It was indeed." Durkin's harsh, flat, emotionless voice filled Sancho with fear as he turned to see her standing in the doorway.

The head nurse at City of Roses was as tall as Flynn but considerably wider, tipping the scales at over two hundred pounds. She sported an immense bosom barely restrained by her starchy, white nurse's uniform. Her hair, tied back in a tight red bun, sat atop a wide, meaty face. She directed two icy blue eyes at Sancho and Flynn.

"Mr. Perez, you know the rules. You can't let patients like Mr. Flynn run roughshod over them."

Chloe looked at Flynn with surprise. "Patient?"

"I'm sorry, Nurse Durkin," Sancho said. "But I didn't want to upset her more than she already was."

"Patients need discipline. Boundaries. Without them they feel out of control."

O'Malley and Barker loomed behind Durkin. The two burly orderlies traded smiles as they leered at Chloe's naked legs. Sancho tugged her hospital gown down as Flynn worked on opening her last restraint.

The two goons stepped into the room and pulled Flynn away from the bed. Flynn's jaw grew taught with anger. Sancho got between them and put his hands lightly on Flynn's chest. "Dude, just stay cool."

O'Malley grabbed Chloe by her right wrist and wrenched it back into the restraint. She slapped him with her left hand, leaving a red mark and enraging the big man. Barker caught her arm before she could slap O'Malley again. As she fought to free herself, Barker twisted her arm until she winced and cried out.

"Whoa, whoa, not so rough!" Sancho tried to intervene. Barker elbowed him in the gut, backing him up.

Durkin looked on as Chloe kicked and struggled. "Get those restraints back on her!"

O'Malley bent her arm back and Chloe cried out, "No! No! *No! Let me go!*"

Flynn put his hand on O'Malley's shoulder. "Enough! You're hurting her."

O'Malley tried the same elbow-in-the-gut move he used on Sancho, but Flynn turned just in time and used the bigger man's momentum to pull him back, sweeping O'Malley's feet out from under him. Down he went, his head bouncing off the floor.

Barker released Chloe's wrist to go after Flynn. He was wider, but Flynn stood taller and moved faster. He sidestepped the attack, tripping him. Barker fell and his fat head collided with O'Malley's. Both collapsed in a heap.

Nurse Durkin looked perturbed as Flynn attended to Chloe. "Are you all right?"

Chloe nodded through tears as an angry O'Malley used the hospital table to pull himself up.

Flynn casually kicked it out from under him and O'Malley fell back down, clunking heads with Barker again.

Sancho saw the syringe in Durkin's hand an instant before she injected Flynn in his right shoulder. Flynn tried to jerk away, but it was too late. He glared at her, his eyes flashing with fury. "Nurse Durkin, what did you do?"

"I gave you something to relax you."

O'Malley and Barker scrambled up, their faces red with rage and embarrassment.

Sancho took Flynn by the arm and tried to usher him out of there. "Let's get you back to your room, brother."

"I got this." O'Malley growled, grabbing Flynn by his other arm.

A tug of war ensued before Durkin finally took charge. "Let him go, O'Malley. Get those restraints back on Miss Jablonski." She then aimed her chilly eyes at Sancho. "Perez, take Mr. Flynn back to his room."

Flynn tried to turn around, but he wavered unsteadily as the sedative and antipsychotic cocktail did its thing. "Come on, James. Let's get you to bed before you take a header."

"I was just simply… I was trying… I only wanted…"

"I know, brother. I got you."

Durkin injected Chloe with her own B52 cocktail. Being much smaller, the drugs took immediate effect. She sank back into the bed as Barker and O'Malley tightened the restraints. Her big brown eyes locked on Flynn as Sancho ushered him out.

"He's not a doctor?" Chloe mumbled, her eyes beginning to droop. "What is he?"

"He's out of his goddamn mind," O'Malley said.

CHAPTER THREE

In 1429, the three kingdoms of Okinawa came together as one. The Kingdom of Ryuku. When King Shō Shin came to power in 1477, he banned the practice of martial arts. The ban continued even after Japan invaded the island in 1609. Rebels secretly practiced the ancient arts and this led to the development of kubudo, a practice that uses common household and farming implements as weaponry. They combined Chinese martial arts with their own existing arts to create what came to be known as Okinawan Karate.

Flynn awoke to the sound of someone belting the title song of Rogers and Hammerstein's *Oklahoma*. One of the older agents, a Miss Doris Frawley, claimed to have placed fourth in 1948's Miss Arkansas pageant. She often started the day with a show tune.

Flynn started the day in a very different way. He slept in a pair of sea island cotton boxer shorts and, upon waking, dropped to the floor to pump out forty press-ups. He would do them excruciatingly slowly. Until his muscles screamed. Turning onto his back, he'd do countless straight leg lifts until he couldn't do another. Rising to his feet, he performed twenty standing toe touches, twenty jumping jacks, and then handstand press-ups, upside down against the wall. From his inverted position, he saw Doris Frawley smiling at him from the doorway.

"You're looking very handsome today, Mr. Flynn."

"And you look lovely as always, Miss Frawley."

The nonagenarian grinned and shuffled off down the hallway, belting out "Oh, What A Beautiful Morning."

Flynn glanced at his roommate, still asleep in his bed. Q headed Q Branch and created all the Secret Service's state-of-the-art gadgetry. Elderly and eccentric, he always slept like a rock. Not even Doris and her exuberant singing could awaken him. Flynn opened his armoire and selected a black karate gi. He slid on the *zubon* and then the *uwagi* and tied it shut in the traditional fashion with a black *obi*.

• • •

Sancho still lived at home with his mamá, his abuela, and his tata. However early Sancho woke up, his tata was always awake before him, bustling around the kitchen, making breakfast, and getting ready for work. At five foot two, he was five inches shorter than Sancho, but broader and stockier, with a round rock-hard stomach and huge powerful hands. He worked construction and could build anything. Tough as he was, he wasn't the toughest person Sancho knew. That would be James Flynn. Though his abuela came in a close second.

Sancho drove to City of Roses Psychiatric Institute with a belly full of machaca and eggs. His Aston Martin DB 9 Volante turned a lot of heads. Few orderlies could afford such a high-end luxury sports car. In fact, none of the doctors at City of Roses owned anything comparable. Flynn gifted it to Sancho after their first adventure together. He nearly sold it numerous times and recently decided to see what he could get for it. The gas, insurance and maintenance costs were killing him, and it made him uncomfortable to drive such a fancy car. He could bank the money and buy himself a Camry. It was the smart thing to do, but he really enjoyed the looks on people's faces when they saw him behind the wheel.

He found a spot next to some doctor's gleaming Bimmer and headed inside to start his day. After punching in, Sancho made James Flynn's room his first stop. No Flynn. Next, he checked on Chloe. She wasn't in her room either. He bumped into a nurse on the way out, a slender sloe-eyed beauty originally from Jamaica.

"Hey, Wanda, have you seen Chloe?"

"I think she's with Dr. Nickelson."

"She was really upset yesterday."

"She's doing better, but she's still pretty paranoid. Thinks some Hollywood producer wants to murder her," Wanda said.

"No shit?"

"Poor thing OD'd on Demerol and almost died."

"They bring her in on a 5150?"

Wanda nodded. "Yep."

"She looks young."

"She's a baby."

Wanda continued on. Sancho checked the TV room and the activity room and finally found Flynn in the inner hospital courtyard. The outdoor area had raised planters with all kinds of shrubs, flowers, and other greenery, as well as tables for nurses and patients who wanted to take their lunch outside. Exercise classes were often held on the well-manicured lawn, but at the moment only James Flynn took advantage of the fresh air and sunshine.

Flynn often exercised there, and Sancho watched him perform a complicated-looking karate kata. He executed impressive jump kicks and punches, elbow strikes and spin kicks, knife hands and hammer fists. Sancho knew the moves, not because he practiced, but because he loved watching kung fu movies.

Flynn was built like Jean-Claude Van Damme and moved like Bruce Lee. The dude had skills, and Sancho wasn't the only one who noticed. Nurses often took their lunch outside when Flynn practiced. He always worked up a sweat and would often take off his top, revealing a torso packed with muscle and a six-pack that would put Hugh Jackman to shame. Yeah, the nurses knew he was delusional, but he was also movie star handsome and charming as hell.

Flynn finished his kata in "ready position", eyes closed, as he held his breath for a count of two before letting it out. He opened his eyes and winked at the nurses watching him, enjoying their fluttery embarrassment and blushes. He spotted Sancho sitting on a cement bench and smiled.

Sancho waved him over. "How you doing this morning, brother?"

Flynn crossed to him, mopping his face with a hand towel. "I feel good. Fit. What about you, my friend?"

"I'm better every day."

Flynn surveyed his damaged face. "Sorry about the other night."

"No worries, dude. How'd *you* sleep last night?"

"Like a block of cement."

"Durkin dosed you pretty good."

"Yes, I'm a little upset with her and her lackeys. Young Chloe was obviously in distress. I assume our enemies held and tortured her. Was she released as part of a prisoner swap?"

"Man, she's here because she's not in her right mind."

"Of course she isn't. Not after what she's been through."

"It was nice of you to help her, dude, but look at me. You really need to stay out of Durkin's way."

"Does Durkin believe that Chloe's been brainwashed and turned against us? I understand the need to debrief her, but that's no reason to treat her like a traitor."

Sancho worked hard not to roll his eyes. "All I know is you need to keep away from her."

"Durkin?"

"Chloe."

"You have a kind soul, Sancho. I applaud your empathy. Often compassion is seen as a weakness in our line of work. But we have to remember what we're fighting for. We can't become the monster to fight the monster."

CHAPTER FOUR

Flynn needed a mission. He couldn't remember the last time he'd been operational. He was built for war. For taking the fight to the enemy. Too much inaction dulled the senses. Boredom sapped his energy and blunted his battle readiness. He worked hard to stay in condition, so when the call came he'd be ready. After all, he was a Double-0. The sharp tip of the spear. Those at the top needed to unleash him. Nothing made him feel more alive than risking life and limb. Danger made life more vivid, food and drink more delicious, the touch of a woman more exquisite.

His lack of recent action allowed the Corsican to get the better of him. Why the killer let him live was a mystery. It's possible Flynn wasn't his ultimate quarry. Perhaps Flynn's pre-emptive attack derailed his plan to take out another target. Could it have been Chloe?

Flynn knew in his bones that Chloe was in danger. Yes, the torture she suffered created post-traumatic stress and sometimes that could result in paranoia, but that didn't mean she wasn't at risk. He needed to debrief her. As an expert interrogator, he knew he could discover the truth.

After changing out of his gi and showering, Flynn put on a black polo shirt, taupe chinos, and gray suede chukka boots. He found Chloe in the lounge area with a few other agents and operatives enjoying some much-needed R&R—reading and playing cards and watching the telly. She must have finished her debriefing with the powers that be because she looked exhausted. Apparently, they decided she was no longer a threat to herself or others as they'd removed the restraints.

She sat on a couch next to another agent. Ty was Black, young, rotund, energetic, and volatile. He had a teenager's intensity. Flynn appreciated his passion.

"Fact is Tupac ain't dead. Homeboy faked the whole thing. Look at the evidence. Suge Knight paid three million for a private cremation and the bastard who did it disappeared. Poof. Gone. Tupac only had a hundred grand in the bank when he supposedly died. Didn't own no property. How's that possible, right? Homie made millions."

"Ty?"

"Hey James."

"Mind if I have a word with Miss Jablonski."

"Who?"

"Chloe."

"*Who?*"

"The young lady you're talking to."

"What's her name?"

"Chloe."

"We're kind of in the middle of a conversation, brother. Talking about Tupac. Brother faked his own death."

"You can pick it back up later. I just need a few minutes with her. It won't take long."

Ty glared at Flynn and held the stare before finally acquiescing. "Fine. Gotta take a leak anyway." He lurched to his feet, hiked up his baggy shorts, and made his way out.

Flynn sat on the couch next to Chloe and studied her for a moment. Her eyes were half-lidded, her pupils huge and unfocused. Her chin drifted to her chest, her head bobbing as she went in and out of consciousness. No wonder they didn't bother to strap her back in. They had her in chemical restraints.

Flynn put his hand on her knee. "Chloe? Can you hear me?"

She moved as if underwater, slowly turning her head, fighting the sedation as she looked at Flynn. "They drugged me with something."

"Try to focus. Look at me."

She struggled to push away the fog. "They...they don't believe me."

"Don't believe what? That you're in danger?"

Tears filled her eyes. "They think I tried to kill myself."

"Tell me what happened."

Her voice was slurred, her tongue thick. "It wasn't me. It was him."

"Who?"

"Goldhammer."

"Sounds German. Who does he work for?"

"He's a big producer."

"Of what?"

"Movies," she mumbled.

"Ah, brilliant cover."

"He wants me dead." She trembled and started to cry.

Flynn squeezed her hand. "Breathe. Relax. It's okay. You're safe now."

"Don't think so."

"No one can touch you here."

"He can. He can buy anyone. Go anywhere. He's Goldhammer."

"With that kind of reach it sounds like he might have ties to SMERSH."

"Who?"

"SMERSH. It's a portmanteau of Smert Shpionam. Death to Spies. Coined by Stalin himself in 1942."

"I don't understand."

"You say he masquerades as a movie producer?"

She nodded. "He's won like three Academy Awards."

"Which allows him to travel anywhere and meet anyone. Were you sent to seduce him?"

She shook her head. "What? No! What are you talking about?"

"Goldhammer. How did you meet him?"

"At a party. I was working for a caterer."

"That was your cover?"

"My job. He asked if I was an actress and I said, yeah, and he said he was producing a movie and asked me if I wanted to audition."

"And you said yes?"

She nodded and started to shake and cry again. Flynn held her hand and tried to comfort her. "It's okay. You did the right thing."

She fought the sedation to find the right words. "I don't think I did. He wanted me to audition for him in his hotel room. I knew that wasn't right. I knew he was up to something, trying to get me alone in his hotel room. I thought I could handle him. I thought this could be my shot. My big chance."

"To get what you were after?"

"Yeah, but I think he drugged my drink. And he's so big. I couldn't fight him." Her voice cracked. "I couldn't fight him."

"But you obviously escaped."

"Hours later. I snuck out while he was sleeping. The next morning, I told my brother what happened and he wanted to go to the police. I said no way."

"Because you didn't want to blow your cover?"

"Because I knew they wouldn't believe me, but he called them anyway."

"And what did the police do?"

"They told me I needed proof that it wasn't consensual. They said without that there was nothing they could do. That it was my word against his."

"I assume that didn't sit well with your brother."

"No." Chloe shook her head. "The next day, Tyler went to Goldhammer's office and caught him outside his building. Screamed at him. Called him a pervert. Said he'd go to the press."

"And after that?"

"Tyler wouldn't let it go. Starting posting on social media. He even tweeted we had evidence. That I recorded the whole thing on my iPhone."

"Did you?"

"No."

"So what did *you* do?"

"I didn't do anything. I just wanted to put it behind me. Forget it ever happened. So I went back to work."

"With the caterer?"

Chloe nodded. "That's where I met Avi. At a party in Beverly Hills. He said he was a cinematographer. He was so charming and I was feeling so shitty, it was nice to have someone like that pay attention to me. Two nights later, I met him for drinks at the Chateau Marmont. But I think he roofied me because I woke up in the emergency room and I don't even remember how I got there. They said a maid found me in one of the rooms. Said I OD'd on Demerol. But I don't use that shit. I don't touch it."

"And you think this Avi tried to kill you?"

"I do." Her voice cracked. She started to cry again.

"That night when you were in Goldhammer's apartment. What were you looking for?"

"What do you mean?"

"Before you snuck out. Were you searching for codes for an offshore account in the Caymans? A microdot with the schematic of some sort of high-tech weapons system?"

"What are you talking about?"

"What are *you* talking about?"

A shadow fell across Flynn. He looked up to the imposing presence of Nurse Durkin. "Mr. Flynn, don't you have an appointment with Dr. Nickelson?"

"I thought that was at two?"

"It's two fifteen."

"It's funny how time gets away from me sometimes."

"Yes, and now it's time for you to get away from Miss Jablonski." Durkin hovered, staring down at him over her impressive and immovable bosom. "On your feet, Mr. Flynn."

Flynn stood and met Nurse Durkin eye to eye. "Nurse Durkin, perhaps you'd be kind enough to grace me with your given name. We've known each other for quite some time now and I feel we needn't be so formal. You could call me James and I could call you—"

She clapped her hands together twice to shut him up. "Dr. Nickelson is ready for you, Mr. Flynn. Let's not waste his time."

Flynn offered Chloe a rakish grin before making his way from the room.

ABOUT THE AUTHOR

Haris Orkin is a playwright, screenwriter, game writer, and novelist. His play, *Dada* was produced at The American Stage and the La Jolla Playhouse. *Sex, Impotence, and International Terrorism* was chosen as a critic's choice by the L.A. Weekly and sold as a film script to MGM/UA. *Save the Dog* was produced as a Disney Sunday Night movie. His original screenplay, *A Saintly Switch,* was directed by Peter Bogdanovich and starred David Alan Grier and Viveca Fox.

He is a WGA Award and BAFTA Award nominated game writer and narrative designer known for *Command and Conquer: Red Alert 3, Call of Juarez: Gunslinger, Tom Clancy's The Division, Mafia 3,* and *Dying Light,* which to date has sold over 7.5 million copies.

Haris has contributed chapters to two books put out by the International Game Developers Association; *Writing for Video Game Genres* and *Professional Techniques for Video Game Writing.*

www.harisorkin.com
https://www.facebook.com/AuthorHarisOrkin

NOTE FROM THE AUTHOR

I was a shy, skinny, bookish, bespectacled, and insecure twelve old living in the suburbs of Chicago when I first realized what I wanted to be when I grew up. I wanted to be Alexander Mundy in *It Takes a Thief*. I wanted to be Illya Kuryakin in *The Man from Uncle*. I wanted to be part of the Mission Impossible team. I wanted to be Jim West, Derek Flint, and Matt Helm. I wanted to be James Bond.

Those men had no fear. They knew karate and could scuba dive and rock climb and skydive and ski and shoot the eye out of a flea at fifty yards. They were confident in any situation and were comfortable in their own skin. I think that was the biggest wish fulfillment fantasy of all for an awkward pre-teen struggling through puberty and that's what inspired James Flynn and his adventures.

At twelve I was terrified of girls. I was always picked last in gym class. I lived a life of perpetual embarrassment. In hindsight, that's probably how most twelve-year-olds feel, but at the time, I didn't know that. So I started lifting weights. I became a gymnast. I boxed. I studied karate. I became a rock climber and learned to ski and scuba dive. I even studied in London for a year and traveled the world.

But I never did become an international super spy. Instead, I became a screenwriter and game writer, creating wish fulfillment fantasies for other nerdy twelve-year-olds. Thank you for indulging in my fantasies. I hope you enjoyed the journey. I do believe Mr. Flynn is just getting started.

Please connect with me on Twitter and Facebook and feel free to ask me anything. This is a two-way conversation.

~Haris Orkin

We hope you enjoyed reading this title from:

BLACK ROSE
writing™

www.blackrosewriting.com

Subscribe to our mailing list – *The Rosevine* – and receive **FREE** books, daily
deals, and stay current with news about upcoming
releases and our hottest authors.
Scan the QR code below to sign up.

Already a subscriber? Please accept a sincere thank you for being a fan of
Black Rose Writing authors.

View other Black Rose Writing titles at
www.blackrosewriting.com/books and use promo code
PRINT to receive a **20% discount** when purchasing.

Printed in Great Britain
by Amazon

84914304R00203